MW00613398

THE MOTHERSHIP

ALSO BY STEPHEN RENNEBERG

The Mothersea

The Antaran Codex

In Earth's Service

The Kremlin Phoenix

The Siren Project

THE MOTHERSHIP

Stephen Renneberg

This novel is a work of fiction. Names and characters are the product of the author's imagination, and any resemblance to actual persons, living or dead, is coincidental.

Copyright © Stephen Renneberg 2013

Stephen Renneberg asserts the moral right to be identified as the author of this work

Author website
http://www.stephenrenneberg.com

ISBN: 978-0-9874347-3-9

All rights reserved. No part of this publication may be reproduced, stored in a retrieval system, or transmitted, in any form, or by any means, electronic, mechanical, photocopying, recording, or otherwise, without the prior written permission of the copyright owner.

Illustration © Tom Edwards
TomEdwardsDesign.com

DEDICATION

For Elenor with love.

DRAMATIS PERSONAE

The Alien

Kaleezsha(Alashra-Warm)Nemza'ri

The Contact Team

Major Robert Beckman
Master Sergeant Henry Hooper
Sergeant Curtis 'Timer' Morie
Sergeant Orlando 'Cougar' Sanchez
Corporal Frank Tucker
Corporal Ramone 'Steamer' Massey
Captain Teresa 'Xeno' Bertolini
Lieutenant Jimmy 'Nuke' Nolan
Lieutenant Kim 'Vamp' Gerrity
Lieutenant Michael 'Virus' Kirovsky
Roland Markus
Dr. Ian McInness

The Inhabitants

Laura Mackay
Dan Mackay
Bandaka Wirrapingu
Djapilawuy Wirrapingu
Mapuruma
Wanyubi
Liyankindirr
Pete 'Slab' Wilson
Bill Kenny
Wal Roberts
Paul 'Cracker' Flanagan

PROLOGUE

Nemza'ri awoke from a cold, dreamless sleep.

She didn't remember her transport cell's rise in temperature or the tingling sensation accompanying the fading of the stasis field. All she felt was an irrational fear of confined spaces and an instinctive need to thrash wildly about inside her tiny space. She wanted to break free and escape into a tranquil blue sea, but her muscles wouldn't respond. As her mind cleared, she relaxed, remembering where she was and that she would soon be released. It was always that way after revival; confusion, followed by fear and panic, then calm.

A tiny needle pricked the base of her skull, injecting nanomachines into her neck. The microscopic machines surged through her circulatory system, dispersing an antidote to the cellular suppressant she'd taken before the flight. Soon, the outer aquatic membrane covering her bulbous amphibian eyes slid back as she regained control of her vision.

Nemza'ri saw three quarters of the cell at a glance, focusing on its dull metal sides and the transparent surface above her face as she oriented herself. Her field of vision was wide for a predator, due to her eyes being set to the side of a streamlined, elongated head. It was an evolutionary signpost to eons past, before technology, when her species had been both hunter and hunted in a dangerous environment.

Knowing she didn't have long to prepare, she concentrated on breathing and practicing muscle tensing routines that helped return dormant tissue to life. The window above her face revealed her sleep cell was already gliding through narrow metal canyons honeycombed with millions of similar octagonal capsules, each one capable of supporting its sleeping occupant for years, even if the ship lost all power. The cells were a safety precaution for mass transit, not a means of enduring long journeys, as travel times were relatively short irrespective of distance. Scattered through the maze of symmetrical chasms were rows of tiny lights, their feeble illumination barely piercing the darkness. Occasionally, she saw the blue glow of a maintenance drone floating above, but no sign of any other cells being activated. She realized this was a midflight technical call, not their final destination. It meant she'd have very little time to recover before going back under and would be aching for days after her next revival.

When her transport cell floated into a docking port, the transparent surface overhead dilated, then acceleration fields lifted her onto the platform above. A one-piece green jumpsuit floated in front of her, marked with her clan status and technical rating. While under way, because she was crew, she outranked even the Beldams, the female ruling elite, although in terms of the ship's hierarchy she was a low grade technician, only qualified to maintain the inertial accelerators used for in-flight attitude control. She'd long ago given up all hope of ever working on the superluminal drive. A brief stint in the knowledge tanks had proven to her and her superiors that the required math for more advanced work was beyond her understanding. In human terms, her intellect towered above the most brilliant scientists ever born on Earth, yet compared to her own kind, she was of only meager ability.

While she pulled on her jumpsuit, her cerebral implants relayed instructions informing her that a power fluctuation had developed in one of the hull's maneuvering thrusters. It was a simple fault requiring a component swap, but as it was related to ship safety, it had to be supervised by a qualified technician. Midflight revivals for mundane maintenance tasks always went to the most junior engineers which, in this case, was her.

Nemza'ri stepped onto the gravity lift, pinging it with her biological sonar. Her sonic lobe was located beneath a smooth bulge protruding from her forehead, enabling her to sense objects many kilometers away underwater. It also served as an efficient means of communicating with the ship's sonic receptors, negating the need for cumbersome control panels.

The grav lift swept her toward the outer hull, where a maintenance drone waited with the replacement component. She pinged the far wall, sensing the subtle variation in metal density that marked the access port's location. A narrow tunnel appeared in the wall, just wide enough for her and the maintenance drone to use in single file. She followed it in and began crawling toward the emitter housing lying just beneath the ship's outer skin. Thousands of such emitters were placed around the ship's hull, giving the great ship astonishing acceleration at low velocity and precise positioning at the center of the spatial bubble during superluminal flight.

When Nemza'ri was halfway through the outer hull, a warning siren sounded. She hesitated, certain the Command Nexus, the ship's guiding intelligence, would never have allowed her into the hull if there was any possibility of danger. The siren could only mean the Command Nexus itself had been surprised, which should have been impossible.

She wondered if she should retreat back into the interior, then the tiny crawlway closed around her as the ship's armor expanded, sealing off every weak point in the massive hull. The maintenance drone was crushed to the thickness of an atom a meter from her face, while behind her, the way back into the ship's interior vanished. The tunnel shrank in around her until the sides were just centimeters from her body. Hull sensors, detecting

Nemza'ri's presence, ensured a protective bubble formed around her while the Command Nexus prepared to deal with the unexpected emergency. If she'd been a senior officer, she might have ordered the ship to open the access tunnel, but at her lowly rank there was no possibility of overriding command protocols.

Trapped in the dark, she fought her dislike of confined spaces by resuming her muscle tensing exercises, preparing for her return to the transport cell. She knew the Command Nexus would solve the problem and release her as soon as it was safe to do so. Minutes passed and the crawlway did not reappear. She broke protocol and signaled a midlevel command system directly via one of her cerebral implants, but was surprisingly ignored. As a minimum, she should have been reprimanded for breaking communications discipline. Even the low tier maintenance system she was authorized to access told her only that all nonessential activities were temporarily suspended, but not why.

The mighty ship shuddered, slamming her body against the hull wall, leaving her floating weightless in her tiny prison. In nearly two centuries aboard ship, it was the first motion she'd ever felt, the first time she'd experienced free fall and it filled her with dread. It could only mean the internal acceleration fields had failed. Without protection from the crushing effects of inertia, any tactical acceleration by the ship would instantly crush her to death.

The Command Nexus would try to protect the lives of everyone aboard, but it wouldn't hesitate to sacrifice her to save the ship. When that fatal acceleration did not come, she realized the ship was adrift in space, leaving her entombed in a tiny, suffocating bubble. Without power, the hull's quantum geometry could not be altered to reform the access tunnel and the ship's sensors would not know she was alive, ensuring rescue parties would be unable to find her.

With only the atmosphere in her tiny bubble to sustain her, Nemza'ri directed her autonomic implants to lower her metabolic rate, reducing her air consumption to the absolute minimum. She couldn't self hibernate without drugs, but she could sleep on the fringes of coma, giving the maintenance drones time to carry out repairs and discover her presence in the outer hull. As she dropped into a deep sleep, her last thought directed her implants not to wake her again until the air's oxygen content increased.

She would either die in her sleep or awake to fresh air.

CHAPTER 1

The Humvee passed through a checkpoint in the middle of the night, manned by armed guards who checked the IDs of the driver and his solitary passenger, ensuring both were on an approved access list. Once cleared, heavy gates were opened and the army vehicle drove across the base through snow flurries to a large brick building with dark windows. The driver stopped without a word, then Major Robert Beckman hurried to the entrance. He was tall and athletic, with fair hair and a relaxed bearing that disguised his single minded nature. Beckman swiped a card reader to open the door, then stepped inside and placed his eye over a retinal scanner for the guards at the entrance.

"You're cleared to access Operations, sir," one guard said after checking his datapad for Beckman's pre-approvals. "All other doors are locked to you."

"I know the drill," Beckman said, then hurried along the corridor, wondering what it was this time. As head of Area 51's Contact Team, he was used to being roused at any hour, although it usually involved being bundled onto an aircraft for rapid deployment, not being summoned to the Operations Room.

After a short walk through the building, where he never once passed out of sight of ceiling mounted surveillance cameras, he swiped his card to enter the Operations Room. It was two stories high, with three large screens dominating one wall. Glassed-in offices occupied by military personnel looked down on several rows of computer terminals arrayed in front of the big screens. The operators were a mix of air force officers and white-shirted civilians, all with their eyes glued to their respective monitors. The Operations Chief, a civilian in his early forties, paced the room behind the second row of terminals with eyes that flitted nervously from screen to screen, taking in everything at once.

General Lawrence Hickson, the program director, stood with several other senior officers watching proceedings. When he saw Beckman arrive, he walked over and said in a low voice, "You're just in time."

Beckman glanced at the satellite plot on the screen curiously. "For what?"

"We're not sure," Hickson said grimly.

On the central wall screen was a map of the southern hemisphere spanning the Indian Ocean. A curved trajectory was plotted from Mozambique in East Africa to Sumatra in Western Indonesia. Astride the trajectory curve was a small satellite icon, just east of Madagascar, inscribed with the label 'USA-525'. The two other screens listed satellite telemetry that was updating in real time.

"Four minutes until the bird clears the horizon," the National Reconnaissance Office team leader responsible for satellite deployment reported from the front row.

"How are we tracking?" the Operations Chief asked.

One by one, the operators provided summaries of the information they were receiving.

"Pine Gap is negative."

"Diego Garcia has a good feed."

"Guam's got nothing."

"The USS Blue Ridge has telemetry, but no pictures."

"The Joint Space Ops Center at Vandenberg says the orbit is good," the NRO officer announced. "Radar is off, passive IR and optical sensors are on, feed is good. The camera is at full off angle, maximum field of view. We'll zoom as soon as we have a target."

The flashing green icon of the NRO spy satellite drifted past the tiny dot of Rodriguez Island in the western Indian

Ocean, then began to crawl north east toward Sumatra.

A phone rang and was promptly snatched up by an operator in the second row. "Uh huh, uh huh," the operator said as he scribbled notes. When he hung up, he peeled off his wire-thin headset and turned to the Operations Chief. "We just lost Global Hawk Six over the Timor Sea," he said referring to an unmanned aerial vehicle. "She never got a look."

"That's the fourth UAV we've lost in six hours," General Hickson whispered into Beckman's ear. "That's not mechanical failure. They're being shot down."

Beckman said nothing as he wondered who would be targeting their reconnaissance drones in that part of the world.

"Two minutes to first look," the NRO officer said.

An officer in the second row turned with an urgent look on his face as he listened intently to his earpiece, then he said to the Operations Chief, "Australian air traffic control report JAL flight 5144, Melbourne to Tokyo, has disappeared off their screens."

"How many people?" the Operations Chief asked.

"It was a 747, at least three or four hundred."

"Damn," an Air Force general standing toward the back muttered.

"The Australian Government has grounded all civil aviation north of the Tropic of Capricorn," the officer in the second row added. "All incoming flights have been turned back. They've declared a terrorist emergency."

Beckman gave General Hickson a curious look.

"It's a cover story," he explained. "The Aussies have lost an AWACS, two reconnaissance planes and a helo full of SAS trying to get in there."

Beckman hid his surprise. He'd joined the program from special forces and wondered if he knew any of the SAS troopers on the downed chopper. The small special forces community was tight knit and the chances were he'd served with some of them, somewhere.

On the trajectory plot, the green icon approached the Cocos Islands in the eastern Indian Ocean. "OK, here we go," the Operations Chief said. "Give me visual on one, IR on three."

The left side wall screen filled with the image of an immense tropical forest seen through wispy white clouds. The wild vista raced left to right as the satellite in low earth orbit sped toward the horizon. Its flight path, running far to the west of the target area, would carry it above the horizon for just seven seconds, before ducking and running. The screen on the right side, displaying the infrared feed, revealed yellow tropical heat shimmers in the foreground and a searing red bloom on the horizon.

"Man, that thing's hot," the IR specialist exclaimed.

"Our bird will breach the horizon in five … four … three–" The NRO operator stopped as the readout on his screen vanished. "I've lost telemetry."

The images on screens one and three were replaced by white noise, while the satellite icon on the central screen began flashing red.

"I've got nothing," a civilian technician called from the front row.

"Give me status reports," the Operations Chief demanded.

"System telemetry, negative."

"Visual and IR feeds, both negative."

"USS Blue Ridge is negative."

"Diego Garcia has lost it."

"Pine Gap had it for a few seconds, but they've got nothing now."

"Guam, negative. They never made contact."

The Operations Chief focused on the NRO civilian in the front row, who listened intently to his headset, speaking inaudibly several times. Finally, he turned and shook his head. "Vandenberg's got nothing. Chantilly confirm, all our stations have lost it. It's gone."

"I'm calling it," the Operations Chief declared, looking

at his watch. "Four fifteen AM, central time, contact lost with USA-525, presumed destroyed by hostile action. Log it."

"And that's how you scratch a two billion dollar satellite!" an operator in the second row declared.

Beckman leaned toward General Hickson and whispered, "What's going on, General?"

"It's the real deal, Bob. It came down hard and it's big."

"How big?"

"According to seismic readings, at least two million metric tons."

Beckman whistled softly, his mind racing at the implications.

"It entered the atmosphere at over one hundred and fifty times the speed of sound, decelerating all the way down," Hickson said. "We're assuming there are survivors, because it's shooting down everything we send up to look at it. So far, we have zero penetration."

"I see."

"Only us and the Aussies know anything about it. No idea how long that will last. Every satellite in sight of ground zero is gone. It's a total no fly zone, so you'll have to go in on foot. So far, they've only blinded us. They haven't attacked any population centers or strategic targets, so it doesn't fit any of the aggressor scenarios. Washington believes it's a forced landing, not an invasion. We're proceeding on the assumption that they're buying time to make repairs."

"Are we going to grab the ship, General?"

Hickson looked doubtful. "Washington wants it, but it can clearly defend itself so recovery may not be an option. Your job is to get in there and assess threats and opportunities."

"If they're shooting down aircraft and satellites, they're not going to let us get close on foot."

"I know, but they're your orders."

"Understood," Beckman said soberly, realizing Hickson

might be sending his team on a suicide mission.

"And one more thing," the General added in a tone that told Beckman he wouldn't like what was coming. "Washington's assigned two civilians to your team."

"Do they have any training?"

"One doesn't. He's a scientist. I don't know who the other guy is."

"Nursemaiding civilians will slow us down, sir. It could endanger the mission."

Hickson nodded. "I know, but this is from the top, Bob. Nothing I can do about it. You're in charge, but these two guys somehow managed to buy a ticket."

"Since you put it like that …"

Hickson gave him an uncertain look. "Hell, the damn thing will probably be gone before you even get there."

"They usually are," Beckman replied.

"You leave in an hour. You can sleep on the plane."

* * * *

Bandaka Wirrapingu sniffed the air, wrinkling his nose at the unfamiliar, acrid fumes drifting through the forest. He rested his spear on the ground as he peered warily through the trees toward the charred crash site fifty meters away. The Yolngu hunter had been searching for it since he'd seen a column of black smoke rising into the sky earlier that day. The smoke had been too black and oily for a campfire, too thin for a bushfire. Bandaka guessed the source of the fire was on the eastern slope of Mount Fleming just north of the Walker River. It had burned itself out hours ago, but the unnatural caustic odor remained like an invisible spirit haunting the land.

The only sign of life was a wedge tailed eagle circling high above on wings whose span was greater than the tallest man. Bandaka had always admired the great eagle, the largest hunter in the sky, whose presence reassured him that great spirits watched over the land.

Gathering his courage, he crept silently through white limbed gum trees toward the burnt out clearing. When he came upon a light gray tail plane marked with a forward pointing half arrowhead, he realized the smell choking the area was the remains of jet fuel that had exploded on impact. Lying on scorched earth in the center of the clearing was the blackened remains of a slender fuselage emblazoned with a red kangaroo on a white background inside a blue circle. Bandaka had seen Royal Australian Air Force fighters before, knew they flew over the land to the west and the sea to the north, but this was the first time one had ever crashed in the forest.

The jet had shattered on impact, scattering debris through the trees and igniting a series of spot fires. A battered, torpedo-shaped photo reconnaissance pod lay against a boulder with its glass covering plate shattered. Bandaka didn't recognize the camera pod or suspect the leaders of the western world were desperate to retrieve its contents. Instead, he crept past a piece of landing gear to the fire blackened cockpit. Inside were the charred remains of the pilot, still strapped in his seat wearing his helmet and a partially melted oxygen mask. Even though Bandaka lived in the forest, isolated from modern civilization, he knew fighter pilots ejected from aircraft before they crashed. He wondered why this pilot had ridden his plane into the ground, never realizing the flyer had tried desperately to eject, but had been unable to do so when every system on his aircraft had inexplicably failed.

Bandaka felt sadness for the dead man and made a sign to his wandering spirit. There was little else he could do. He looked curiously over the wreckage strewn through the trees, wondering where the rescuers were. They should have been there by now in their helicopters. The fact they weren't, unsettled him. He'd seen the great falling star, an evil omen whose terrible meaning his tribe knew well. Now this warplane had crashed, its pilot killed and no one had come.

It was very strange.

The Yolngu people had lived harmoniously in the forest for tens of thousands of years. They belonged to this ancient and sacred land, the domain of great and wise spirits, but now where there'd once been food and protection, there was a strangeness, perhaps even danger.

Bandaka decided to seek old Wanyubi's guidance. Perhaps the old man with his dreaming vision would know what was happening. He paid his final respects to the dead pilot, then headed into the forest toward his camp half a day's hike away. He thought of the signs, the falling star, the dead pilot, the circling eagle, the rescuers who failed to come and the eerie silence smothering the forest. They were ill omens, as clear to him as the spoken word. They told him to hide, to melt away into the forest where the spirits could protect him.

Bandaka had learned long ago to always obey the spirits.

* * * *

Laura Mackay gently placed the sleeping rainbow lorikeet in a cage and locked the small wire door. The injured bird had been brought in from the surrounding forest by some aboriginal children, even though Laura ran a zoological research station, not a veterinary clinic. At the insistence of the children, she'd splinted and bandaged its leg as best she could.

With her final task for the day complete, she headed back between cages filled with a dazzling array of deadly and colorful creatures. It always struck her as paradoxical that the driest continent on earth should have one of the world's most diverse ecologies. Unlike the Amazon or the Congo, the vast tropical wilderness of Arnhem Land found itself within the borders of a developed nation, an accident of history that ensured its survival. The eastern half had been an aboriginal reserve since 1931, while Kakadu

National Park protected the great tropical wetlands to the west, ensuring the region's wildlife escaped the catastrophes striking down tropical forests on other continents.

It was why, when she'd been offered the opportunity to run the East Arnhem Land Research Station, she'd jumped at the chance, even though her family thought she was out of her mind. The remote station possessed modern technology, thanks to a small research grant, although setting foot outside the compound was like stepping back a million years in time.

And that was why she loved it.

Her cramped office filled with filing cabinets, books and wildlife photographs felt more like home now than the moderately privileged life she'd left behind. When she slipped into the squeaky chair behind her cluttered desk, her husband entered with a cold glass of orange juice, which he put in front of her with a cracked leather smile.

"Time you told those kids to stop bringing you every half dead creature they find," he said. Dan Mackay was almost ten years her senior with a sinewy physique and a weathered face. He'd spent his entire life in the north, working mostly as a stockman, although now he led wildlife safaris for city types eager for a wilderness experience. When he wasn't babysitting tourists, he kept the machinery running, built new enclosures and was the bedrock of her secluded existence.

"That wouldn't stop them," she said with a tired smile as she took a sip.

"You should get some sleep," Dan said.

"I will, once I finish my report to the university," she replied with a weary sigh.

"How's the bird?"

"She'll recover." Laura yawned, dragging her fingers through her close-cropped red hair. She'd long ago given up the pretence of maintaining a hairstyle. Out here, she kept her hair short, her nails trimmed and had all but forgotten what makeup was.

"Any word on those assistants you asked for?"

"Yeah. A guy doing a PhD thesis is coming up for six weeks in September. He's doing some interesting work on the *myiagra inquieta.*" Laura caught Dan's blank look and translated. "Restless Flycatcher."

"Right," Dan said, nodding. "A bird."

She'd tried undergraduates on vacation leave, but they'd proven more interested in their own mating habits than those of the animals and she'd sent them home. The few qualified scientists who'd come for no pay would stay just long enough to research a paper, then return to the air conditioned comfort and steady pay of the big southern universities.

He began gently massaging her shoulders, causing her to close her eyes, luxuriating under his strong hands. "Looks like that meteorite started quite a fire," he said absently.

"Meteorite?" Laura said confused, then remembered what he'd told her at dinner. "Oh, the shooting star you saw this morning?"

"It was no shooting star. It was as big as a bloody mountain." The massive fireball had streaked low across the northern sky, blindingly bright even through the tall trees encircling the station.

She smiled, patting his hand, knowing his tendency to exaggerate to make a story more interesting. "Sure it was."

"No, seriously. Didn't you feel the earthquake?"

"There was a slight tremor," she conceded, remembering a vibration that had momentarily rattled the windows.

"For a few seconds, I thought it was a dinosaur killer!"

"It appeared bigger than it was because it was close."

Dan shook his head obstinately. "Nah. It was a long way off. And it was huge. It threw a lot of stuff into the air over by the Goyder."

"How can you tell?" she asked with a flicker of interest, aware the river was a long way to the west, far out of sight of the station.

"Sky's bright over that way. Must be bushfires burning where it came down."

Laura straightened, alarmed. It was the dry season when the forest was at its most vulnerable. "Which way's the wind blowing?"

"There's a bit of an easterly, but I don't think it'll reach us."

"Have you reported it?"

"Nah. Darwin's five hundred kilometers away. What are they going to do?" Dan knew as far as the Territory Government was concerned they might as well have been on another planet.

"They can get the air cranes up from the south." Laura said as she tossed her white lab coat onto a chair and hurried outside. To her right was their wooden two-story house with its wide veranda and leaky tin roof, the garage where they parked their four-wheel-drive and a machine shed that housed the generator and was topped by a satellite dish. On the other side was the aviary, a nylon net thrown over several large trees and home to nearly a hundred brightly colored birds. Between the aviary and the machine shed stood two smaller buildings, the marsupial sanctuary and the reptile house.

Laura stepped into the middle of the yard, looking anxiously toward the west. A great column of dust rose high into the night sky and spread into the upper atmosphere where it masked the normally vibrant stars. The dust cloud glowed dull orange, lit by fires and radiant heat from the impact site below. She searched the sky in vain for clouds, knowing it would be months before the rains came.

Dan followed her outside, watching the sky beside her. "See? It's got to be over near the Goyder."

"I'll call Darwin. They have to know."

"They won't do anything unless Kakadu's threatened."

Laura ran into the house, picked up the telephone,

scanning the list of emergency numbers beside it. If there was one thing she was afraid of, it was bushfires. If one came their way, there'd be no place to run, nowhere to hide. She found the Northern Territory Fire and Rescue Service number, but there was no dial tone. The line was dead.

"Not again," she whispered angrily, slamming the phone down.

She was about to hurry back outside when a thought struck her. She switched on the TV and was greeted by hissing white noise.

"Oh crap," Laura said, realizing it wasn't just the phone that was down, then she went outside, her sense of urgency replaced by helplessness. "The dish is acting up again."

Without the dish, they were cut off from the outside world. To get it repaired meant following an overgrown dirt track thirty kilometers to the nearest satellite telephone, then waiting weeks for a technician to come out from Darwin.

"It was working yesterday," Dan said, fascinated by the towering orange column of dust rising above the horizon.

"We only had the dish replaced last year," she said, not realizing the satellite it was aimed at no longer existed.

He put his arm comfortingly around her shoulders. "It'll burn itself out. It's not as bright as it was a few hours ago."

"I hope you're right."

"We'll see what it's like in the morning. If it's still bad, we'll drive down the track and make a call."

"OK," she said, watching the ominously orange sky, wondering if Dan could possibly have been right. *Was it really as big as a mountain?*

* * * *

The barking of Dan's dog roused Laura from sleep. She lay with her eyes closed, hoping it would shut up, but it kept at it. She turned to see if Dan was awake only to find his side of the bed empty. The clock on the bedside table told her it was a few minutes past four, which made her silently curse the dog for stealing her last hour of sleep before feeding time. The dog continued barking in a highly agitated manner, making her wonder what had spooked him.

A croc? She thought, snapping awake. Was that why Dan had gotten up?

The rest of the animals were strangely quiet, particularly the birds. If a crocodile was loose near the pens, they'd all be squawking. She heard Dan's heavy footsteps down the hall, then the crack of his shotgun being opened and the click of shells being fed into the chamber.

"Is it a croc?" she called, sitting up.

"Maybe," Dan replied. "Stay in the house." The screen door banged as he went outside, then she heard him calling the dog. "What is it, Blue? What you got, boy?"

Laura climbed out of bed and hurried to the window overlooking the front track. It was quiet and dark. Whatever the dog was barking at was at the back of the house. She pulled her overalls on over her pajamas, laced up her boots and ran downstairs. When she reached the kitchen, she peered through the window. Dan had not bothered to put the outside lights on, but she could see him standing in front of the garage, holding his shotgun with both hands, not aiming at anything.

She sighed in relief. *At least it's not in the pens!*

The research station was more than five kilometers from the river, but if the wind was right, the scent of her animals could carry that far. Crocodiles might come inland during the wet season when the ground was soaked and the streams were bursting their banks, but it was rare for one to travel far from water this time of year.

Dan was looking up and Blue was barking nervously at something above them, which meant it wasn't a crocodile. A shiver of fear ran down her spine as she wondered if the fire they'd seen to the west was approaching. She flicked on the switch for the outside lights, but the frosted glass in the back door remained a rectangle of darkness.

"Great," she muttered, then yelled, "Danny, is the generator on?"

When no reply came she tried the hall light, but it was out too. Laura knew he checked the generator daily, but it had been old when she bought it and its resistance to the tropics was failing. Laura hurried down the hall to the storage cupboard and retrieved a large waterproof flashlight. She switched it on, then the crack of shattering wood filled the night as if a truck had ploughed through the house. The thunder of Dan's shotgun sounded as she turned toward the back door and saw a brilliant white light fill the backyard. His shotgun boomed again as Blue's barking turned to frightened yelping, which was suddenly cut off in a squeal of pain.

"Dan? Are you alright?" she called uncertainly.

The brilliant white light cast a sharp beam through the window that glided across the floor as the source moved toward the house. Metallic rattling in the kitchen broke the eerie stillness, then the house shuddered. She approached the kitchen doorway as the sink, oven and fridge began vibrating rapidly as if fighting to break free of their restraints. The wail of tortured metal filled the house as the corrugated iron roof peeled off, then the bench top shattered as the sink and oven shot up through the ceiling as if fired from a cannon. They crashed through the floor above, showering plaster and splinters over the kitchen, then vanished skyward. Luminous white beams poured down through the holes they'd made, forcing her to shield her eyes as she glimpsed a metal surface gliding above the house.

Laura stepped back into the hall in shock, then the water pipes groaned and twisted up, spraying water as they tore free and flew toward the light. A moment later, the microwave followed as cutlery exploded from the drawers like a shotgun blast, peppering the ceiling with dozens of holes.

The flashlight began pulling her hand upwards as it tried to fly toward the ceiling. She pulled on it with both hands, but it was held in a vice like grip by an unseen force that lifted her feet off the floor. When she was half a meter in the air, she let go and the flashlight smashed through the ceiling as the fridge rocketed up, opening the way for another column of light to spear down into the kitchen.

The house now filled with the squeal of nails being wrenched from floor boards and wooden frames, then hundreds of hammer blows reverberated through the house as the nails flashed skyward like a hail of bullets. Laura threw herself against the wall to avoid being speared by them, then felt the wall vibrating behind her. She stumbled away as electrical wiring whipped out of the walls, slashing long lines through the plaster and lashing the ceiling as it flew up through the roof. She used her hands to shield her head as plaster and wood chips rained down, then she fell into a corner in terror as the white light winked off and the house fell silent.

Laura blinked as her eyes adjusted to the darkness and, shaking with fear, saw the walls were teetering. Realizing the house was about to collapse, she jumped to her feet and ran. The back door stood crookedly in her path, its metal hinges and lock missing, so she charged it shoulder first, knocking it aside and stumbling across the veranda into the yard.

She sensed rather than saw a dark mass overhead blocking out the night sky. It glided silently above her, then as the walls of her house folded like cards, the craft vanished. Laura watched aghast as her home crumbled, then realized she was surrounded by ruin. The garage and machine shed had collapsed and the land cruiser, generator and satellite dish were gone. All that remained of the metal fuel tank was a pool of burning gasoline beneath the wreckage of the machine shed. Laura knew she should try to put out the fire, but the firefighting equipment was also missing. Her only hope was that the fire breaks surrounding the compound would contain the flames.

As she climbed to her feet, the laboratory split apart and fell to the ground. Like the house, its corrugated iron roof had been torn off. Laura took a few steps toward it, afraid for the birds and animals in her makeshift hospital, then she saw tiny bodies shredded by flying metal cages. Several small animals and birds had somehow survived and were picking their way through the debris intent on fleeing to the safety of the forest. On the far side of the yard, the marsupial sanctuary and reptile house were also destroyed. Even the old metal water tank was gone. Only the aviary, made of nylon fiber netting, had survived.

"Dan? Where are you?" she called with rising alarm. "Can you hear me, honey?" The silence was chilling as she realized her husband and the dog had both disappeared.

The clatter of shifting wood snapped her attention to the remnants of the marsupial sanctuary. "Danny, is that you?" she called as tears began to trickle down her cheeks.

She saw several small animals frantically crawling and hopping to freedom. They were fleeing for their lives as a slow, dark form moved through the shadows, effortlessly pushing aside broken beams.

The crocs are out! she realized in shock, coming to her senses. Feeding time was only an hour away and they would be hungry.

The reptile house held several smaller crocs under four meters and a big one over seven. She knew the small crocs, twice the size of a man, could easily kill her, let alone the big brute which could crush a horse with a single bite. As she peered apprehensively into the shadows, a terrified squeal sounded from the remains of the marsupial sanctuary. Several broken planks were hurled clear, whipped by a long powerful tail during the frenzy of an attack. When silence returned, she heard the crunching of breaking bones as the big croc devoured its hapless prey. Laura felt a pang of sorrow for the smaller animals, but her need to survive told her they were buying her time. With the kangaroos on the run, she was acutely aware that she was now the single largest piece of meat in the area – and the most helpless.

It was something the crocs would soon figure out. She didn't understand what had happened, but she knew not a single piece of metal remained anywhere in the station. She guessed there were no guns, knives or axes left, nothing she could use to defend herself with. Now that the strange light had vanished, the fearful screeches of the birds began, drawing her attention to the aviary and its intact netting – her only possible refuge.

Laura sprinted to the net, running alongside it until she reached the entrance flap. Her fingers fumbled with the nylon zipper as she heard the soft pad of footsteps behind her. She slid the zipper halfway down, then dived in and rolled away from the entrance. Behind her, a long scaled shape surged out of the darkness and charged into the netting. The crocodile's snout came within an arm's length of her feet before the netting snagged tight, holding it at bay. She saw a flash of teeth as the croc snapped its mighty jaws, swinging its head from side to side, trying to force its way through. It was one of the smaller animals, but more than able to rip her to pieces. The croc pressed for a moment against the netting, then turned away in frustration and sullenly crept off into the shadows. Laura waited until its tail was pointing toward her, then she darted forward and zipped the half open entrance flap closed.

Knowing the crocs could force their way under the net, she stepped through the inner flap into the aviary proper and ran to a rope ladder hanging from one of the tallest trees. With her heart beating fearfully, she started climbing toward the safety of the observation platform in the canopy. When she reached the lookout, she discovered the nails holding it together had been ripped out and its floor boards had fallen. Only the camouflage tarpaulin remained, strung over nylon ropes. She pulled herself up onto a branch, using the tarpaulin for support as she watched a long reptilian form prowling outside the net, searching for a way in.

Laura wiped the tears from her cheeks as she looked to the west where the horizon glowed a burnt orange. It was unlike any bushfire she'd ever seen. Unaware it was the glow of a great metal hull cooling after its fiery entry into the atmosphere, she wondered if it was connected to the destruction of her station and Dan's disappearance. Her eyes became mesmerized by that distant radiance, by its rich color and ebbing intensity.

It was a hypnotic spell that lasted until dawn.

CHAPTER 2

Several hours before sunrise, a US Air Force C-17 transport skimmed the tranquil waters of the Gulf of Carpentaria. To avoid detection, all electromagnetic emissions had been switched off when the aircraft was five hundred kilometers out, forcing the pilot to fly manually all the way in to the Gove Peninsula. The flight crew considered night flying at low altitude without radar to be unnecessarily dangerous, yet they followed their orders to the letter, never knowing the reason why.

The C-17 crossed the coast south of the tiny town of Nhulunbuy, then flew over the tree tops to Gove Airport, a sealed runway surrounded by red earth and lush green forest with a small terminal building at its center. As soon as the jet transport rolled to a halt, the aircraft's tail ramp lowered, then Beckman and his team hurried off carrying packs and weapons.

A four-wheel-drive Australian Army truck drove up and collected them, then instead of heading toward the gravel track running southeast to the crash site over two hundred and fifty kilometers away, the truck turned north toward Gove Harbor. Since the impact, every vehicle that ventured down the Central Arnhem Road had vanished, leaving Beckman in no doubt that the long dirt track was no longer under human control.

The army truck carried the contact team to a small wharf at the tip of the Gove Peninsula where a sleek gray Royal Australian Navy patrol boat waited. Once aboard, the boat headed out into Melville Bay, swung around the northeast cape and began a long, high-speed run into the Gulf. With the satellites out of action, there was no satnav to steer by, so the crew navigated the old fashioned way, with charts, compass and dead reckoning. As with the C-17, they maintained a complete electromagnetic blackout, testing the crew's ability to navigate in darkness at high speed.

While the patrol boat raced down the coast toward Blue Mud Bay, the team ate breakfast, then assembled on the stern to complete their final checks. Beckman stood with his back to the wind, absently studying the two civilian additions to his ten-man team.

The first was Roland Markus, a dark haired, fit looking CIA officer who would provide his own assessment to the Director of National Intelligence. DNI would in turn advise the President and the National Security Council, which might create confusion if Markus' assessment was different to the advice Beckman would send to the Secretary of Defense. Such confusion could paralyze decision making at a critical moment. Judging by the way Markus carried his MP5 submachine gun, he could look after himself, but Beckman wondered if he'd follow orders.

The other civilian was Dr Ian McInness, a rather skinny scientist in his late twenties from the Area 51 technical team at Groom Lake. Beckman had seen him on base a few times, knew he was part of the massive alien technology reverse engineering effort under way there, but not his specific role. All of the recovered alien weapons and equipment they used had been analyzed by that program before being passed to the contact team to even their chances should they encounter hostile aliens.

Dr. McInness didn't carry a gun and was probably incapable of using one if he did. His pack was so jammed full of scientific equipment, he could barely lift it, which made Beckman suspect he wasn't carrying near enough food and water for an extended patrol in tropical heat. The scientist sat on one of the two inflatable boats lashed to the stern, meticulously painting sunscreen across his nose.

When he finished, he carefully placed the tube in his pack and pulled on his wide-brimmed sun hat. The moment he took his hand off the hat, it blew into the sea, then he watched helplessly as it was left rapidly behind in the boat's wake.

Beckman groaned silently to himself, then caught Master Sergeant Henry Hooper's eye. Hooper was the force protection squad leader, shorter and heavier than Beckman, with a gravel voice and years of hard experience. They'd both served in Delta and had come across to the Contact and Recovery Program together. They exchanged disparaging looks, anticipating the burden Dr. McInness would place on the team. Beckman knew no one would miss Markus, he was one of those ruthless expendable types every country had lurking in the shadows, but if the scientist died there'd be hell to pay.

Sitting near Hooper, Frank Tucker and Steamer Massey watched the scientist scornfully. Steamer, the giant African American who carried the predator missile launcher, leaned close to Tucker and whispered, "Bet you fifty, he dies first."

Tucker sat with his back against his pack slowly scraping his knife across a whetstone. Even though he carried both the deadly LSAT light machine gun and Thor, the largest of the 'specials' – their euphemism for the recovered alien weapons – he'd never lost his fascination with the fat-bladed Bowie knife. The former SEAL looked up, thought about it a moment, then shook his head slowly. "Sucker bet."

"I'll give you odds," Steamer said shrewdly, daring Tucker to take him on. Steamer could have played pro-ball for Detroit if he hadn't joined the Navy to see the world. He first met Tucker at Coronado, during phase one training. At first, they competed, trying to find out who was tougher. In the end, they called it a draw and had been a team ever since.

Tucker stopped sharpening his knife. "What odds?"

"Two to one."

"Four."

"I'm not your mamma. I'll give you three."

"Deal." They knocked clenched fists together to seal the bet. "Now I'll have to keep his wimpy ass alive until someone else goes down."

Steamer chuckled, "Babysitter!"

A navy lieutenant came down the ladder from the bridge and saluted Beckman. "We're entering the Walker River estuary, sir," he said, indicating the river mouth ahead. "It's close to high tide, so we'll be able to get in over the mud flats, then we'll head upriver as far as we can. The skipper requests you prepare for disembarkation now, as he may have to put you ashore at short notice."

Beckman acknowledged the salute, "Thanks, Lieutenant."

"We'll take you in as close as possible, but you may get your feet wet. We'll have sharpshooters on the bridge and along the railings, just in case."

"Let's hope there's no attack," Beckman said, wondering how much the lieutenant knew.

"Don't worry, we've had plenty of practice."

"You have?" he asked, surprised.

"They're sneaky bastards, but we're pretty good at spotting them."

"Spotting what?" Beckman asked, certain he was missing something.

"Crocodiles. The rivers are lousy with them."

"Really?" Beckman glanced uncertainly at the approaching shoreline.

"Oh yeah. They're a protected species, so they breed like bloody rabbits. But don't worry, we're authorized to shoot them if they go after you." The lieutenant grinned. "Can't let you blokes get eaten. It wouldn't look good for the navy."

Beckman looked bemused. "Wouldn't want to make the navy look bad."

“Just get ashore as fast as you can and head away from the river. Watch the banks. They hide in the mud, under the mangroves. Can’t see the bastards until they move, or you step on one.”

“Thanks for the warning.”

Beckman walked over to Hooper as the lieutenant returned to the bridge. “Get ready to go ashore.” The sergeant opened his mouth about to bark an order when Beckman leaned close and said in a low voice. “And make sure they keep an eye open for crocodiles.”

“What?”

Beckman shrugged.

“Right,” Hooper said, then paced between the troops. “Listen up! I hope you ladies have enjoyed this luxurious pleasure cruise, because now we’re going ashore for a little stroll in the park. There’ll be plenty of trees where we’re going, so you’ll have lots of shade.” He smiled, then sniffed deeply and slapped his chest delightedly. “Ah! And more fresh air than you’ve ever breathed before. So, let’s show these pretty little navy boys what a real military unit looks like. When we get off this ocean liner, get off fast. Keep your eyes open, your weapons ready and only fire if fired upon. You got that?” Hooper stopped and looked down at Lieutenant Jonny ‘Nuke’ Nolan, the youngest member of the team and the payload specialist.

Nuke lay snoring with his helmet covering his face to block out the sun. Beckman had recruited him straight out of MIT, based on his test scores and aptitudes. He was a physics major with an IQ that looked like a zip code and if he survived his tour with the contact team, he might well become the world’s top alien weapons expert. Until then, he was just another mission specialist Hooper had to keep alive long enough to get the job done.

The sergeant lifted Nuke’s helmet a little, peered under it and asked in a sweet voice, “Am I disturbing you, Lieutenant? Would you like a pillow?”

Nuke yawned and removed speakers squawking rap

music into his ears. "Hey, thanks Sarge. And could you get them to slow this tub down? The engines are giving me a headache."

"On your feet, *sir*!" Hooper yelled.

Nuke sat up, dropping his helmet, which rolled across the deck. Nuke's officer rank, like the other mission specialists, was mostly due to his education and pay grade, not his military standing. Beckman had made it clear from the start, when in the field Hooper was second in command, while in combat the force protection squad members called the shots. It was not the traditional chain of command, but it was designed to keep everyone alive.

Lieutenant Kim 'Vamp' Gerrity, the team's tracking specialist, caught Nuke's helmet before it tumbled over the side. She was tall and muscular, with flashing blue eyes and a tongue sharper than a bayonet. She'd started off as an air force radar specialist, found a way to detect stealth aircraft, leading Beckman to recruit her to operate the team's only alien tracking special.

With a wry grin, she tossed the helmet back to Hooper, who planted it firmly on Nuke's head as he clambered to his feet. "You lose it, Lieutenant, you go over the side after it. Got it?"

"Sure, Sarge," Nuke said, miffed.

Vamp pulled her pack on and adjusted the straps as she watched Dr. McInness trying unsuccessfully to tie off a bulging pocket on his pack, then said to Xeno in a low voice, "Do you think he's as helpless as he looks?"

Captain Teresa 'Xeno' Bertolini was the team's xenologist and medic. She had dark hair, dark eyes and a sharp mind and had been with the contact program almost as long as Beckman. She followed Vamp's gaze and smiled. "Oh yeah. They shouldn't have let him out of the lab."

Vamp tilted her head sideways, giving the scientist an appraising look. "He's kind of cute in a lost puppy, nerdy sort of way."

"He'll get eaten alive out here."

"He might, if he's lucky," Vamp said mischievously.

Xeno looked surprised at her friend's unexpected tastes. She nodded toward Markus, who sat by himself checking his weapon. "I thought he'd be more your style."

Vamp gave the intelligence officer a dismissive look. "He's too cold for me. I like them with a heartbeat and a brain."

Roland Markus, sensing he was being watched, aimed his weapon toward the coast as if checking the sights. He used the movement as an excuse to turn his back to the others, then ensuring his body shielded his hands, he lowered the weapon and eased a slender rectangular device out of his vest pocket. The front of the device contained an LCD screen above a keypad, while inside was a transmitter and scrambler alongside a telescoping aerial. Keeping the device concealed, Markus pressed the transmit button on the front panel, sending an encrypted high speed burst signal.

The transmission lasted barely a tenth of a second. To any casual listener, it would have sounded like a flicker of static. To the Australian Signals Directorate team waiting a hundred kilometers to the south at Numbulwar, it was music to their ears. The tiny settlement had the only road in the region accessible to the big ASD semi-trailer, which had come up from the south to listen for any signals emitted from the impact zone. To the aboriginal inhabitants, the big eighteen-wheeler, bristling with aerials and guarded by a dozen soldiers, was a curiosity the like of which they'd never seen before.

The mobile listening post passed the recognition signal via landline to the ultra secret ASD intelligence gathering station at Shoal Bay, Darwin. From there, confirmation that ASD was in contact with Markus was relayed via transpacific cable to the US National Security Agency, their sister organization in Fort Meade, Maryland, who passed the information on to the CIA. At the same time, a remote transmitter forty kilometers from the ASD mobile listening post sent a response.

Sitting on the patrol boat, Roland Markus watched a line of text appear on the LCD screen:

Acknowledged at 0748.
Signal Strength 93%.

Markus breathed a sigh of relief, then slid the burst transceiver back into his pocket. Casually, he glanced at the troops, reassuring himself that they hadn't noticed his call-in. Because of the risk of detection, he would not use the device again unless he had something to report.

The patrol boat motored over the submerged mud flats at the mouth of the estuary and into the grip of choking heat and humidity. Lush green mangroves closed in on either side as they cruised up river and a thousand pungent odors bombarded their senses. Hundreds of birds called in a cacophony of strange voices, from high pitched warbles to menacing shrieks while the monotonous thrum of insects hung as heavily in the air as the humidity. Giant dragonflies with wingspans larger than a man's hand skimmed the murky green water and darted into the deep shadows beneath the mangroves.

Why would they land here? Beckman wondered as the beat of the engines faded and the patrol boat nosed toward the oily black mud lining the river bank.

The lieutenant hurried down the steps from the bridge deck. "There's a rock bar up ahead, blocking the river. This is as far as we can go."

"This'll do fine," Beckman said as the patrol boat slid onto submerged mud.

Sailors ran a gangplank out that splashed into ankle-deep water, then Beckman led his team past the bridge house to the bow. Half a dozen sailors with assault rifles took up positions along the railings and on the bridge deck, watching the shore intently.

Beckman took a step toward the gangplank, but the navy lieutenant barred his way. "Wait!"

From the bridge deck, a sailor yelled out, "Over on the right, about six meters."

"Scare it off," the lieutenant ordered.

Beckman stared in the direction indicated by the lookout, seeing only mud and mangrove roots until a sailor fired three shots that struck the mud with a series of hollow thuds. The river bank came alive in a blur of reptilian fury as a five-meter, mud-coated crocodile raced into the water with an ungainly twisting gait, then vanished into the murky depths. The troops behind Beckman gasped. Not one of them had seen it, even though they'd been staring straight at it.

"Son of a bitch!" Sergeant Curtis 'Timer' Morie exclaimed. The former ranger and graduate of the US Army Engineer School at Fort Leonard Wood leaned over the side, peering into the water in search of the crocodile. "Did you see that thing?"

"That's a freaking big lizard!" Nuke declared anxiously.

One of the sailors laughed. "Mate, they get a lot bigger than that!"

"Is it safe to go ashore now?" Beckman asked.

"Nope, but you've got your orders," the lieutenant said with an amused grin. He turned to the sailors along the sides. "See any more?" No one responded, so the lieutenant moved aside. "Good luck, Major."

Beckman walked down the gangplank, splashed once in the water and jumped up onto the bank, pulling himself up through mangrove roots. The rest of the team followed, straining under the weight of their packs. Only Dr. McInness stumbled, who was saved from falling into the water by Tucker.

Hooper whispered to Beckman, "For a guy with no weapon and no ammo, he's carrying a lot of gear."

"He'll be flat on his face in two hours," Beckman said, "then we'll strip him."

The patrol boat's crew retrieved the gangplank, then the boat's engines revved, pulling the bow free of the mud.

"Make sure you cut across country," the lieutenant yelled from the bow. "The river banks will be crawling with crocs, especially at night."

"Then you've only got the bloody snakes and spiders to worry about," one of the sailors yelled, triggering fits of laughter from the rest of the crew who thought marooning a bunch of hapless Americans in the middle of nowhere was a great joke.

"Why do I feel like a greenhorn?" Hooper said under his breath as he watched the patrol boat back away.

"Because out here," Beckman replied, "you are."

The laughing sailors gave them a hearty wave for good luck as the high tech patrol boat turned and headed back down the river. The thrum of its big engines quickly faded as it disappeared around a bend, leaving them with the feeling that they were now truly alone.

Beckman turned to the team and spoke in a loud voice. "OK people, this is a recon mission. We're here to gather intel not start a war, so let's keep it nice and quiet. We've got eighty clicks of this stuff ahead of us," he said indicating the prehistoric forest around them, "so pace yourselves." He motioned to his radio and the wire mike wrapping around his cheek. "Assume hostiles are listening and have the tech to track us, so stay off the radios unless absolutely necessary. They're rigged for minimum power and very short range, but even so, no chatter. Cougar's on point, Timer's coverman, Tucker and Steamer have the flanks and Hooper's got rear security. " He pointed at Dr. McInness and Roland Markus. "You two, stay with the mission specialists in the middle at all times. Virus, give me a heads up if they fall behind."

Lieutenant Michael 'Virus' Kirovsky, the communications specialist, pointed at the civilians with two fingers, then at himself with one, ensuring they understood the order. Virus carried the team's long range radio and a recovered special able to detect alien non-radio wave communications. As such, his place was always in the center of the patrol, alongside Nuke, where Beckman could reach him quickly.

Markus gave Timer a curt nod while Dr. McInness adjusted his glasses and fished through his pack, searching for something.

"Dr. McInness?" Beckman said patiently. "Do you understand what I said?"

The young scientist looked up, "Ah yes, Major, I did, thank you. I'm to follow … him," he said, pointing at Nuke. Timer pointed to himself again, then Dr. McInness nodded and pointed at Timer. "Right, you."

"If you hear anyone say contact," Beckman said, "I want to see your face in the dirt."

Dr. McInness gave him an accommodating nod. "I'm sure we won't be fighting anyone."

"Are you?" Beckman asked skeptically.

Dr. McInness returned his attention to his pack. "No advanced civilization is going to attack the Earth. What would be the point? They don't need our resources, they have the entire galaxy for that. And even if our atmosphere wasn't poisonous to them, our microbes certainly would be. You see, Major, I'm quite sure this is not an invasion."

"So why are they shooting down our planes and satellites?" Nuke demanded.

"Sounds hostile to me," Timer said.

Dr. McInness shook his head. "They're just telling us to stay away."

"Why?" Beckman asked with genuine curiosity.

"They're buying time to make repairs or for a rescue ship to arrive. The seismic readings indicate this must be a forced landing. Trust me, Major, they don't want to be here." He sighed with evident disappointment. "We'll be lucky to even see it."

"Suppose it can't fly?" Xeno asked.

"Then they'll evacuate the crew and destroy the ship.

There'll be nothing left for us."

"You may be right," Beckman said, "but if the shooting starts, I want you on the deck. Clear?"

Dr. McInness nodded absently, "Certainly Major, if it makes you feel better." He finally found what he'd been searching for – a can of insect repellent – which he proceeded to spray all over himself, much to the amusement of the troops.

Steamer whispered smoothly to Tucker, "Fifty bucks! Looking good."

"You should have given me four to one," Tucker growled, triggering a broad smile on his friend's face.

Hooper wrinkled his nose at the sweet smelling insecticide. "With that bug bait on, those aliens will smell us coming."

Dr. McInness stuffed the spray can into his pack and turned to Hooper. "They'd have to breathe our atmosphere to do that, sergeant, which is highly unlikely."

Hooper stared at the scientist, not knowing what to make of him, then exchanged perplexed looks with Beckman, who motioned to Cougar to take point.

Sergeant Orlando 'Cougar' Sanchez was a former US Marine Corps scout sniper, a man of few words with ice water in his veins and eyes like an eagle. He'd been an instructor at Kaneohe Bay sniper school and was a veteran of multiple combat tours where he'd become a legend within the secretive sniper community. He nodded to Beckman, then without a word, jogged into the forest, quickly climbing the small rise away from the river.

"Move out," Beckman said, then the rest of the team took up their positions behind him as Hooper moved to the rear.

"Hold it!" the sergeant yelled, peering back through the trees toward the river. "Smoke!" He pointed to a thick black cloud billowing into the sky beyond the mangroves.

Beckman hurried to Hooper's side. "It's coming from the coast."

Markus raised his binoculars, studying the acrid plume. "Looks like a diesel fire. It's got to be the patrol boat."

Beckman saw Dr. McInness watching the column of smoke uncertainly. "Still think there's no threat, Doctor?"

"There must be a rational explanation for it," the scientist said, shifting uncomfortably.

"There is," Steamer said, "them peaceful aliens of yours just blasted that boat into a million pieces."

"We don't know that," Dr. McInness said. "It could be a fuel problem or an engine fire. There's no reason for them to attack that boat. How would they even know it was there?"

"Should we hike to the coast, Major?" Timer asked. "See if we can help?"

"No," Markus said flatly. "We can't afford the time."

Beckman glanced irritably at Markus. A lifetime in the military demanded he help the crew, but the mission ruled out any such luxury. "We can't help them," he said reluctantly, hating himself for saying it.

"Want me to try to raise them on the short wave, sir?" Virus asked, certain the column of smoke was outside the range of their tactical radios.

"No," Beckman said. "That would reveal our position."

Solemnly, they climbed the hill and headed into an immense steaming landscape that had changed little in sixty million years, while Roland Markus wondered if his powerful burst transmission, which had lasted only a fraction of a second, had gotten the patrol boat crew killed. If so, using it again might call down the same fate upon Beckman's contact team. It would be a heavy price, but one he wouldn't hesitate to pay to complete his mission.

A few paces ahead, Beckman was plagued by ominous thoughts, wondering how the patrol boat had been destroyed and why.

* * * *

Pete 'Slab' Wilson sweated heavily in the oppressive heat as he reached into the ice filled insulation bag inside his backpack and retrieved a beer. The tall ex-AFL footballer meticulously resealed the thermal bag, then held the cold can to his forehead to cool down before tearing off the ring pull and taking a long, relieving swig.

Bill Kenny, a bearded pub owner from Darwin, watched his friend apprehensively. "Jeez mate, you're knocking them back fast!"

Slab slowly exhaled with relief. "They're the only things keeping me going." He wiped his forehead, rejuvenated by the cool amber liquid.

Wal Roberts, a wiry shearer from Geraldton, chimed in, "When they're all gone, don't come begging for mine."

"I'm saving mine," Jack 'Cracker' Flanagan, a Pilbara miner with a dark tan and a penchant for explosives declared. "We won't get back to camp for hours."

"Hours?" Slab said miserably, removing his battered Akubra hat and brushing his hand wearily through his hair. "We should have stayed on the river."

When he agreed to come on the hunting trip, he'd assumed they'd be cruising the rivers in Bill's half cabin fishing boat, drinking beer and getting some free time away from the wives, not bush bashing in scorching heat. Three days ago, they'd driven Bill's four-by-four down the Central Arnhem Road, towing his boat on a trailer along the treacherous gravel track. After several hundred kilometers, they'd turned south onto an even worse track west of Bath Range and put the boat into the water at the Ngilipitji Community. From there, they'd motored up the Walker River for a day before making camp and, to Slab's disgust, hiking inland in search of Asian water buffalo, an introduced species that had to be culled to preserve the wilderness.

"Mate," Bill said, dismayed at Slab's lack of enthusiasm, "do you know how hard it was to get a license to hunt in here?"

“I can’t believe we paid money for this,” Slab growled, irritated they hadn’t yet seen a single buffalo.

“Well,” Wal said with a mischievous smirk, “If we don’t find any buffalo, we can shoot Slab and nick his beer. He’s as big as a buffalo and he smells like one too!”

“I say we shoot him now,” Cracker said with mock seriousness, “before he drinks them all.”

“If you bastards don’t shut up, I’ll polish off mine now and help you with yours later,” he said with a wicked grin, then emptied the can, crushed it with one hand and stuffed it back in his pack to dispose of once they got back to civilization.

Wal opened his mouth to taunt Slab again when the bushes to their left rustled loudly. Bill had his rifle up first, sighting toward the sound, while the others unslung their guns.

“Is it a buffalo?” Cracker whispered.

“Probably another bloody kangaroo,” Slab said as thick green plants were pushed aside by an unseen creature moving through the undergrowth. They listened hopefully for heavy hoof falls and snorting breaths, but heard only the rustling of leaves.

“If it’s a buffalo,” Slab said, realizing they should have seen the animal’s broad shoulders above the foliage, “it’s a pygmy.”

“That way,” Bill whispered, motioning them forward when there was no sign of the creature being aware of their presence.

“It’s getting away,” Wal whispered as they crept through the trees.

“No it isn’t,” Slab growled, then picked up a large rock and took aim at the swaying underbrush.

“What are you doing?” Bill demanded.

“We can’t shoot until we know what it is,” Slab said, then hurled the rock into the bushes. To their surprise, it landed with a dull metallic thud.

“That’s not a buffalo,” Cracker said, then a long black

oval shape floated up out of the bushes and turned toward them.

It had a glowing white strip running the length of its underside and four tubular, jointed arms protruding from its sides, giving it a spider-like appearance. At the end of its arms were slender knife-shaped probes, each slightly different in length and thickness. Rising from the machine's spine was a thin cylinder topped by a glassy black, slowly rotating disk housing a sensor package.

The surveyor floated over the bushes, scanning them as it approached. Its primary interest was geology and metallurgy, although it could gather information outside its specialty when the need arose. Its initial spectral analysis told it the four bipedal life forms carried steel objects, indicating they had access to basic industrial technology, although it failed to recognize the rifles were primitive weapons.

"What the hell is it?" Slab said, then the surveyor suddenly accelerated toward him with its two leading arms aiming their knife-like probes at his chest.

His three mates fired almost together, then the surveyor exploded, sending black metal fragments in all directions and a knife-like arm spearing into the tree beside Slab's face. He stared wide eyed at it, never having fired a shot.

"We sure blew the crap out of that!" Cracker exclaimed proudly, always fond of loud explosions.

Bill recovered a metal fragment and turned it over in his hand curiously. "Ever seen anything like this before?"

Cracker took the piece and tested its weight. "It's light! I thought for a sec it was a balloon."

"At least we got to shoot something," Wal said happily.

"Speak for yourself," Slab snapped. "You bastards didn't give me a chance."

"We should report it," Bill said. "Whatever it is, it shouldn't be here."

"Looks expensive," Cracker said uncertainly. "Whoever owns it might try to stick us for the cost."

"The bloody thing nearly poked my eye out," Slab growled, "No way I'm paying for it."

"Whatever it was, it's scrap metal now," Bill said, retrieving the metal souvenir from Cracker and slipping it into his backpack.

Slab produced his mobile phone and handed it to Bill. "Here, take my photo!" He stood beside the remains of the machine with his boot triumphantly on its metal hull like a big game hunter beside his prey.

Bill hesitated. "But … you didn't even shoot."

"No one will know," Slab said with a larcenous grin.

Cracker and Wal rushed forward to be included, then Bill snapped their photo. "That's evidence that could be used against you."

"Screw that," Slab said, as he took the camera back and reviewed the photo. "Not bad."

Bill glanced at the destroyed machine, a miserable reward for a long hike. "I don't know about you blokes, but I think we should head back to camp and get the barbie going."

"Now you're talking," Slab said, reaching into his pack for another cold beer.

* * * *

Beckman scanned the tree tops, searching in vain for the source of the strange warbling that echoed through the forest. The kookaburra's brown and white feathers made it almost invisible in the shadows of the canopy, while its call reminded him of crazed laughter.

Laughing at us? Beckman wondered as he began to appreciate how the soaking heat and monotonous insect buzz were going to tax both body and mind.

Nuke slapped the back of his neck and cursed. "Man! These bugs are eating me alive."

"They're females," Vamp explained with mock sympathy, "looking for fresh meat."

"Way to go, man," Timer said. "You're finally getting attention from the opposite sex."

Behind them, they heard a grunt as Dr. McInness tripped and fell face-first into a broad-leafed plant. His pack rattled with metal devices, then its weight dragged him sideways onto the ground. He struggled vainly to rise, pinned by his pack's weight.

Beckman turned toward the scientist, watching him flounder helplessly. "Pack getting heavy?"

Dr. McInness struggled to a sitting position, his face purple and his clothes soaked with sweat. He retrieved his canteen and gulped down its contents, then held it upside down confirming it was empty. "I need more water."

"I'll call room service. Oh wait, we're in the middle of the jungle! There is no room service." Beckman snapped, thinking, *goddamn civilians!*

"What do you expect in this heat?" the scientist demanded weakly.

"I expect you to ration your water, like the rest of us."

"I'll share my water with him, Major," Vamp said sympathetically.

"Me too," Xeno added halfheartedly.

Beckman suppressed his irritation, knowing he couldn't let him die of dehydration. "Just this once. We'll purify stream water tonight. Ration him until then." He turned back to Dr. McInness. "Now lighten your pack! Throw out everything but your food."

"I can't ... I need my equipment ... for the ship," he said wearily.

"You'll never make the ship with that weight."

"And we'll learn nothing without it."

"You'll learn nothing if you're dead," Roland Markus said contemptuously.

Beckman glanced at the CIA officer who seemed unaffected by the heat, a tribute to his good physical condition. He wore expensive light green hiking clothes, a broad brimmed hat and carried a small pack stocked with minimal food and ammunition so he could move fast should the need arise. His equipment was limited to a prismatic compass hanging from his belt and a small laminated map he kept in his breast pocket while he kept his MP5 submachine gun clipped to a chest harness. Beckman suspected Markus could easily have hiked to the ship by himself and might even have preferred to go solo if given the choice.

Dr. McInness gave Markus an indignant look. "You don't understand. We may not get another chance like this for a thousand years. This is important … for the whole human race."

"Major," Steamer said hesitantly, "I don't know nothing about science and shit like that, but I'll carry something for him."

The scientist looked up at the massive soldier with surprise. Steamer was already weighed down with predator missiles and one of the largest specials. "Thank you."

Tucker turned his head away and whispered to his large friend, "Are you out of your freaking mind?"

"You heard him, man," Steamer replied in an equally low voice, "It's once in a thousand years."

"You trying to lose the bet? Keeping him alive?"

"Nah man, it's what we're here for."

Tucker's eyes narrowed suspiciously. "Bullshit. You're going soft."

"That hurts, man, that really hurts," Steamer said with mock pain, then leaned closer and whispered. "And he's got to stay with us, if I'm going to win that bet."

Tucker gave Steamer a knowing look, then Timer raised his hand. "I'll take something."

"Me too," Virus added.

Nuke winced, testing the weight of his pack. "Not me, I've got enough stuff to carry."

Markus looked alarmed. "Major, your people are already carrying heavy loads. The extra weight will slow us down."

Beckman hid the fact that Markus' constant uninvited advice was starting to annoy him. "One item each. No more. If anyone falls behind, you dump it. Clear?"

There were nods from the soldiers, while Markus shook his head in disgust.

Dr. McInness slipped out of his pack, then gratefully began handing out equipment. When he'd halved his load, Hooper shrugged and reached for the scientist's Geiger counter.

"I'd like to keep that with me," Dr. McInness said, planning to test for radiation hourly as they approached the site. He handed the master sergeant an optical spectrometer instead.

Seeing Hooper stow the instrument in his pack, Tucker relented and relieved the scientist of a small, but heavy battery pack.

Beckman took the last item, finding Dr. McInness' pack had deflated to three quarters its original size. "Are we done?"

Dr. McInness smiled, his face now having cooled from purple to bright red. "Yes, thank you, Major." The scientist looked at the soldiers who were resealing their packs, paying him little attention. "Thank you. All of you."

Vamp helped him to his feet, then they headed west again.

* * * *

I'm dead without water, Laura thought from her refuge high among the tree tops.

She well knew the risks of dying a deranged dehydrated death under the brutal tropical sun now climbing high into the sky. That knowledge and her growing thirst drove her to action. She climbed down the rope ladder, pausing while still well above the ground to search for reptilian outlines in the underbrush. It had been hours since she'd seen any movement, but that meant nothing. Crocodiles were masters of camouflage with limitless patience.

Spying no danger, Laura continued on down to the base of the tree where she hid among the ferns carpeting the aviary floor. Minutes passed without her detecting the blink of a predatory eye or the rhythmic swelling of reptilian breathing. Overhead, the aviary birds called calmly to their cousins beyond the net, having recovered from the terror of the previous night. Assuming the birds no longer sensed danger, she crept toward the net's inner flap, pausing to look for any sign of the deadly predators lurking in the ruined buildings outside. Finding none, she unzipped the aviary's inner and outer flaps, leaving both open in the hope the birds would find their way out, avoiding starvation.

Laura sprinted to the remains of the house, then clambered onto the shattered beams pockmarked with empty nail holes. When she thought she was above the resting place of the kitchen, she pushed broken planks aside and climbed down between the collapsed walls, startling two kangaroo rats scavenging through the remains of the pantry. The tiny creatures hopped away, then she searched the crumpled storage space, finding all tinned food was gone. Packets of sugar, salt and flour had burst open and were now being carried off by an army of black ants while packets of biscuits and dried fruit remained safely sealed. Fortunately, one of the four liter plastic water containers had survived the destruction of the house. With relief, she drank slowly, careful not to spill a drop.

Her thirst quenched, she dragged the water container out and placed it alongside the ruined veranda, knowing she'd have to make it last. The water purification tablets had been stored in the four-wheel-drive for emergencies, and were certainly gone, leaving her no way to make drinkable water. If she couldn't find help in a few days, she'd be forced to drink unpurified river water, even though it would make her sick.

Laura gathered up the sealed packet foods from the

pantry, then searched for medicine to offset the diarrhea and vomiting untreated river water would cause. After scouring the wreckage unsuccessfully for the medicine cabinet, she clambered to where the remains of her bedroom now were. Squeezing down between fallen walls to where her wardrobe lay on its side, she retrieved khaki shorts and shirt, a broad-brimmed hat, sun cream and a small nylon backpack.

She was about to climb out when a piece of wood slid onto the ground on the far side of the fallen house. Laura turned toward the sound, wondering if it was just wreckage settling or if one of the crocs had found her. She waited, too afraid to move, then hearing nothing more, began to relax. Deciding it was safe, she caught a support beam above her head and started to pull herself up when the clatter of timber being pushed aside broke the silence. She froze, now certain something was rummaging through the debris at the edge of the house.

Can it smell me? she wondered, knowing crocodiles avoided moving on land during the heat of the day unless they were hungry and food was close.

Laura released her grip on the timber beam and eased herself back into the shadows, away from the sunlight pouring down from above. She turned toward the noise, peering through gaps in the wreckage, but saw nothing, then a wooden plank slid behind her barely two meters away. She suppressed a gasp, then spotted a dark shape moving silently over the debris.

How did it get up there without me hearing it? she wondered, surprised by its closeness.

Through the peepholes, she saw a metallic, shiny surface gliding above the wreckage rather than walking upon it. Laura swallowed, fighting fear as she hid in the shadows watching the ovoidal machine's slender arms poking the debris with knife-like probes. The surveyor stopped at the opening above her, revealing a glowing strip running along its underside as one of its frontal arms pushed pieces of wood and plaster aside. Several planks slid away, causing bright sunlight to shoot down into the area to her left, illuminating a tiny kangaroo rat. Startled, the little marsupial tried to hop into the shadows, but one of the surveyor's frontal arms speared down and impaled the tiny animal, which squealed in terror.

Laura's eyes widened in fright as she forced herself to remain motionless, hardly daring to breathe. Her heart beat furiously as a small panel opened in the surveyor's side and the arm deposited the tiny creature inside. The dark machine then moved on over the ruins and across the lawn. The sensor disk on top glistened in the sunlight like black glass as it studied the remains of the research station, periodically driving one of its knife-like probes into the ground, chemically analyzing the soil.

Gradually, Laura's fear subsided as the surveyor moved away. She began observing it with the mind of a scientist, realizing it was a piece of technology unlike any she'd ever seen. By the way it studied its surroundings, gathered data and collected samples, she suspected if it found her, she'd be treated like any other specimen. As the surveyor glided over the lab, she wondered if that's what had happened to Dan.

When it floated above where the animal cages had been, one of its arms stabbed into the wreckage, then retracted with a mass of color skewered on its knife probe. Laura winced when saw the white bandage covering one of the bird's legs, recognizing the lorikeet she'd operated on yesterday. The surveyor deposited the bird in another specimen compartment, then continued on toward the aviary.

It's going for my birds!

One of the surveyor's probes sliced effortlessly through the net, depositing a sample in one of its internal containers and quickly discovering the net was a proto-synthetic construct. The machine then turned on its length about to enter the aviary when seven meters of reptilian ferocity surged out of the underbrush. Massive jaws filled with large yellow teeth clamped down on the surveyor, crushing its hull and triggering electrical flashes from within. One of its arms was pinned by the giant reptile's enormous jaws while its other three arms speared the creature's head and shoulders, slicing through thick bone and muscle like butter. The crocodile's dying impulse was to shake its head, smashing the surveyor into the ground. The black ovoid exploded, blowing the crocodile's jaws apart and creating a mangled pile of bloodied flesh and melted components.

Laura watched, horrified. Even though she feared the big croc, she'd also cared for and studied it for almost a year. To see it destroyed in such a way shocked her.

She climbed up out of the wrecked house, dumped the clothes and backpack beside her supplies, then approached the crocodile's headless body. It lay next to the shattered black hulled surveyor which continued to spark and flash. The specimen compartments were partly visible, each filled with rock and soil samples, or small creatures encased in a translucent gel-like preservative.

Shrapnel from the explosion had created tears in the aviary net through which birds were fleeing, while the end of a probe arm lay on the ground nearby. She picked it up, testing its weight, finding the edge dull and the point sharp enough to make it an effective stabbing weapon.

"Better than nothing," she muttered, unaware that her new weapon was a solid state sensor capable of detecting many more elements than were currently listed on the periodic table.

With her new weapon, she returned to her supplies, quickly changed into her hiking gear and loaded the food and water into her backpack. She took one last look at her ruined home, a place where she and Dan had made a happy life, then forced herself to focus on survival, for Dan's sake as much as her own. If she was to grieve, there would be time for that later.

She wondered where to go. Gan Gan outstation was the closest aboriginal community, but she'd have to cross the Koolatong and Maidjunga Rivers to get there. Only a fool would try that as they were both swarming with saltwater crocodiles. That left either the southeast track through the Laurie Creek Wetlands to the Marrkalawa Community or the old trail to the Ngilipitji Landing Ground. The Wetlands were full of hungry crocodiles and deadly snakes, while the Landing Ground meant a tough hike over Bath Range to an air strip that might not see a plane for weeks. She decided she'd rather wait alone at the airstrip than risk the dangers of the wetlands.

"Ngilipitji it is," she said to herself, unaware that no planes were flying for hundreds of kilometers in any direction.

Laura wiped sunscreen on her face, then set off for the northwest track.

* * * *

Markus fell in beside Xeno as the team trekked through the forest. "I have a question for you," he said.

"You're not my type," she replied, having no desire to engage in conversation with him. His calculating stare made her feel like she was under a microscope while his manner indicated he was used to getting his own way. Neither were qualities she admired.

"That wasn't my question," he said without embarrassment. She wasn't his type either. Even though she carried an M16 like she knew how to use it and a small silver weapon of inhuman design with a grip too small for her hand, she was too bookish and analytical for him.

"Then we have nothing to talk about, because everything I know is classified."

"This may surprise you, Teresa, but I have the second highest security clearance here, higher than you."

"How wonderful for you." She gave him a bored look.

"Who's number one."

Markus nodded to Dr. McInness plodding through the trees a short distance ahead. "The egghead."

"Makes sense," she said. "What's your question?"

"What do you think they sound like?"

"Which ones?"

"The Bug-Eyes. I know you were there when they dissected one a few years ago." It'd been frozen a long time, but was still intact. "And you have access to the old autopsy tapes, from the forties. I assumed, considering your specialty, you have a theory."

She hid her surprise. Even Beckman didn't know she'd been part of the bioanalysis program. "If I did, it would only apply to Zetas. They're the only cadavers we've ever recovered."

"I think you mean, they're the only cadavers you've seen," he said meaningfully.

She gave him a curious look, but didn't take the bait.

"I'll trade you," he said. "Tell me your theory and I'll see what I can do about expanding your access." He pulled a freeze dried ration pack from his pocket, tore it open and began eating as they walked.

"High pitched," she said.

"Is that it?"

"What did you expect, Pavarotti?"

"Are we talking dog whistles?" Markus asked.

"Not exactly, but they'd need machines to communicate with us. And our voice box can't replicate their vocalizations."

"So you're a linguist, but you can't speak Bug-Eye?"

She gave him a reproachful look. "Technically, I'm a xenologist, not a linguist. Sorry, but I don't speak any of the Zeta languages."

Markus knew she had a PhD in mathematics and a masters in biology, an odd combination that made her a unique talent. "Your file says you're an alien language expert."

"You should work on your comprehension," she said, pleased he could make such mistakes. "I've studied storage devices recovered from crashed UFOs, helped decode languages as distinct from each other as English, Chinese and Swahili. That doesn't mean I speak any of them. What I do is more like cryptography than translation. I look for patterns and relationships which is best done mathematically. Only then can you move into actual translation."

"Except you're toting a gun, a strange job for a mathematician."

"Someone's got to read the labels. That's my job. Zeta Label Reader."

"Why don't you call them Grays?"

"I'm an American, not a white," she said simply. "I'm identified by geography, not race. The little guys come from Zeta Reticuli –

"Yes, a binary star thirty-nine light years from Earth. I've heard of it."

"– so I refer to them by their astronomical origin."

"Why not call them Reticulans?"

"It's a mouthful."

"It makes more sense than using the sixth letter of the Greek alphabet."

"Zeta has a nice ring to it and it's better than referring to them by their pigmentation."

"Sounds like you're trying to be respectful, even though those bug-eyed midgets have been peeking through our bedroom windows for tens of thousands of years."

"Composite eyes," she corrected. "And they're small insecto-humanoids, not midgets."

"That's political correctness, if ever I've heard it!" Markus exclaimed as he watched Dr. McInness stumble and almost fall.

"I'm trained to overcome my prejudices," Xeno said as Vamp caught Dr. McInness, helping him keep his feet with a reassuring smile. *Oh my God*, Xeno thought incredulously, *she really does think he's cute!*

"Really?" Markus said. "I rely on my prejudices to maintain a healthy suspicion."

"How primeval of you."

"What about Swedish?"

"Swedish? I like that." The tall humanoids had been nicknamed Swedes for their white hair and pale skin, even though they had little in common with *Homo sapiens*. "According to contactee reports, their language is supposed to sound like a series of rapid clicks, but the details are sketchy."

"Because there have been no Swedish crashes."

"Their technology is supposedly superior to the Zetas."

"Making it more reliable," Markus said, "and filling our skies with Unidentified Flying Volvos."

She allowed herself a smile. "So who do you think owns that ship up ahead? Zetas, Swedes or someone else?"

Markus looked thoughtful. "Insufficient information, but I wouldn't be surprised if you can't read the labels."

"OK by me. I'd like to identify a new language. That's why I'm hoping it's an unknown species."

I'm not, Markus thought. The Local Powers had left humanity alone for two hundred thousand years. His greatest fear was that a newcomer might not be so considerate.

Xeno didn't notice Markus had fallen into a brooding silence. "So are you going to do the spook thing and steal their technology?"

"In a heartbeat," he replied glibly, "but that's secondary."

"What's primary?"

"Figuring out why they're here. When it comes to UFOs, most people only see the bright lights and the bug … excuse me, composite … eyes. They miss the important stuff."

"Which is?"

"The relationships between civilizations." He looked at

the troops around him hiking through the forest. It occurred to him, it wasn't so long ago that man had lived in such forests, barely differentiated from animals. "There's scientific curiosity behind their study of us and a bit of political self interest."

"Political?" She furrowed her brow. "You think aliens want to rig our elections?"

"No, they don't care how we govern ourselves. There are no good or bad political systems in space. Political structures will be as diverse as the civilizations that create them, based on the psychology of each species. What I'm talking about, Teresa, is more like international relations. We're not dealing with cute cuddly little ETs who want to lavish love and affection on us, nor are we likely to face crazed invaders from outer space who want to incinerate our cities for no good reason. One is sentimental nonsense, the other is paranoid fear. The reality is much less dramatic. They're neither friendly nor hostile, but they will have one thing in common with us."

"They'll watch cable TV and eat take out?"

"They'll have *interests* and they'll act in their own best interest. If they didn't, they wouldn't have made it as far as they have. It's great power politics. Unfortunately for mankind, we're not now, and never will be a great power."

"Never is a long time, Mr. Markus," Xeno said soberly.

"How do you catch up a million years? If we advance a million years, so do they. We're like a primitive tribe of Neanderthals compared to Western Civilization."

"Tough break for the Neanderthals."

"Not so tough. The Local Powers clearly have no desire to rule Earth or they would already. They just keep an eye on us, so they know what we're doing."

"So in your great power scenario, where does this ship fit in?"

The intelligence officer looked worried. "It doesn't. In fact, if the Local Powers were still in control, it should never have landed. It breaks the pattern set over hundreds of thousands of years of peaceful isolation."

"So you think it's an attack?"

"Not without proof," Markus replied cautiously. "Launching an attack on us could be disastrous for them."

Xeno furrowed her brow. "Now I'm confused. If they're superpowers and we're Neanderthals, how can attacking us be a disaster for them?"

"Because it's a multipolar political system out there. Lots of civilizations at different levels of advancement, all looking after their own interests. A hostile power would drive peaceful civilizations to ally against it, which will eventually result in the hostile civilization being crushed by weight of numbers and superior technology."

"Like Nazi Germany."

"Exactly. There are no Nazi Germanys in space, none living anyway."

"But would attacking Earth create such an alliance? We don't know anyone, we have no friends."

"We don't know them, but they've spent millennia getting to know us. Thousands of civilizations must know we exist and have us catalogued in their libraries. We're an oddity, savage by their standards, but with as much right to exist on our homeworld as anyone else. Attacking us would attract great powers who might consider their interests are next or who might simply feel a moral responsibility to protect helpless primitives like us. In a multipolar system, it doesn't make sense for anyone to attack us."

"So why are you here?"

"In case I'm wrong."

* * * *

"Vehicle ahead," Cougar's voice sounded calmly from their earpieces as he peered through his sniper scope. "It's on the ground, metallic silver in color, no visible dismounts."

Twenty meters back, the contact team quietly slipped

behind cover, except Dr. McInness who remained standing, eager to see what Cougar had found. Beckman dragged the scientist down into the underbrush. "Stay here, stay quiet and keep your head down."

"We should approach without weapons, try to make peaceful contact."

"I'll give them every opportunity," Beckman promised.

Vamp produced a baseball sized metal sphere with a flat upper surface. They called it the crystal ball and experiments had proven it to be amazingly accurate at detecting refined metals out to three clicks. She touched the special's activation surface, scaled the range to minimum and watched its flat 'display' as pinpoints of light appeared close to a large dot representing the contact team's equipment and the location of the alien craft.

"It's a hundred and forty meters north west of here," she said. "Nothing else in the area. No movement."

Beckman hurried forward crouching, followed by Xeno in case she was needed to translate. Unbidden, Markus crept after them for a closer look. On the flanks, Tucker and Steamer took up positions where they could provide heavy weapons fire support while Nuke and Virus joined Hooper at the rear. If the contact team were wiped out, they would try to escape and report back, or at least give Virus time for a radio message if they were cut off.

When Beckman reached Cougar's position, the sniper was lying prone, still watching the craft through his rifle's telescopic sight. He pointed with one hand toward the craft barely visible through the trees.

"It's just sitting there," he whispered. "It's got a smooth skin, no joins, no markings. Looks like one piece–" He stopped abruptly then slowly swept his rifle left and right, searching. "It disappeared."

Beckman had been watching it through the trees. It seemed to have simply vanished before his eyes. "Vamp, we've lost visual," Beckman said over the radio. "It might be invisible. Give me a contact bearing."

Vamp scaled the crystal ball's range to maximum. "I've got nothing."

Dr. McInness stood and walked forward, waving his hand to attract Beckman's attention, oblivious to any danger. "Major, it's not invisible, it's gone."

"Get down," Beckman ordered, "The area's not clear."

"Yes it is," he insisted, waving his arms in the air, offering himself as a target. "See?"

Cougar focused on the area where the craft had been, finding no sign of the blurring effects of a stealth field. "He might be right."

Beckman noticed Markus scanning the area ahead with compact field glasses. The CIA officer lowered his small binoculars and nodded his agreement to Beckman. The craft was gone.

Beckman relaxed even though he was irritated Markus had also disobeyed his orders. *Can't trust either of them*, he thought, then said over the radio, "Stand down."

While Cougar went forward to scout the landing area, Beckman waited for Dr. McInness to approach, then said, "What do you not understand about staying under cover until the area is clear?"

"It was clear," Dr. McInness said.

"You could have given away our position," Beckman said coldly. "You weren't sent on this mission to get killed for being a fool, Doctor, or worse, get us killed!"

"I have no intention of getting killed, Major, but it was obvious what happened."

"Was it?"

"It detected our approach and took off."

"I was watching the whole time. It didn't fly away, it disappeared."

"It took off much faster than you could see with the naked eye. If we had a high-speed camera filming it, then played it back in slow motion, you'd see it launch. It didn't disappear, it was just very high acceleration. Trust me, Major, their craft obey the laws of physics just like ours do, only in a very advanced way."

"It could have activated a stealth field."

"We'd already seen them." Dr. McInness motioned toward Beckman's troops. "And your men are heavily armed. That's why they left."

"And if they hadn't, you might be dead now – and us with you."

Before Dr. McInness could reply, Cougar's voice sounded over the radio. "Major, I've got something."

Beckman hurried to the clearing where Roland Markus was already prowling around, examining the ground. Dr. McInness and Xeno followed while the rest of the team came up more slowly through the trees. Cougar stood amidst flattened underbrush crushed into a clockwise pattern. While the plants had been pushed into the ground, their fibers were undamaged, showing they hadn't been compressed by a physical object.

"This effect's consistent with field propulsion technology," Dr. McInness said as he paced over the ground.

Markus knelt and examined a twenty centimeter square indentation in the red soil. "It was about a thousand tons, twenty-five to thirty meters across."

Beckman gave him a curious look. "You can tell that just from the footprint?"

"We've done a lot of analysis on landing sites," Markus said. "There are three of these landing strut indentations. We'd need to study their exact depth and the soil composition to work out an accurate figure."

Cougar waited patiently at the center of the clearing. "There's a hole here, sir, a deep one." He motioned to a smoothly bored circular shaft ten centimeters across. Its sides were fused, although there was no evidence of heat having been applied.

Markus approached the borehole, produced a pencil flashlight and shone it into the shaft, finding the light faded before touching bottom. "I haven't seen this before."

Dr. McInness peered into the hole. "They could be taking soil samples or conducting a geological survey."

Beckman produced a flare, glanced at his watch, then dropped it in. The flare plunged into the deep darkness, bouncing off the sides as it fell, quickly reducing to a pinpoint.

Cougar unclipped the telescope from his rifle and focused on the flare. "I can't tell if it's hit bottom or not, sir." He continued watching, then shook his head. "I've lost it."

Beckman glanced at his watch. "The flare's still burning, so it's still falling."

"I need to take some readings," Dr. McInness said, carefully probing the fused soil around the borehole entrance. "It won't take more than half a day."

"Not today," Beckman said, motioning for Cougar to take point. The sniper turned and jogged off into the trees.

"Major, this site could have significant scientific value," Dr. McInness protested.

"More value than a crashed mothership?" Beckman asked.

The scientist opened his mouth to speak, then shrugged and climbed to his feet. "If they're collecting soil samples, that proves it's a scientific expedition."

"Or they're looking for a place to drop a planet-busting bomb," Markus said dryly.

"Major," Cougar's voice sounded in Beckman's earpiece. "There's a track west of your position."

Beckman acknowledged Cougar's report, then led the team through the forest to the track he'd had found. It was little more than a strip of hard packed red earth riven with trenches cut by wet season rains and overhung by trees that gave cover from the sky.

"It's heading in the right direction," Beckman said in a low voice to Hooper.

"The main road is closed for a reason," the sergeant said, rubbing an old scar on his face thoughtfully.

"There must hundreds of tracks like this out here. They can't be watching them all."

"Can't they?" Hooper said skeptically, then turned to the team members now filtering out of the forest. "Alright ladies, form columns either side of the road!"

"Who you calling a lady, Sarge?" Vamp called out mischievously.

Hooper grinned. "Excuse me! Ladies and women of ill repute. Form up!" He strode down the center of the track. "Now that we've got this beautiful highway at our disposal, we're going to pick up the pace."

Muted groans filled the air as they formed into two dispersed columns.

Hooper removed his helmet and let the sun beat down on his shaved head for a moment. "Ah! Feel that sunshine." He took a deep breath, making a show of enjoying the fresh air, then turned to the team with a knowing glint in his eyes. "Double time people. Move out!"

In short order, they were marching forward with purpose while Markus fell back, pausing at a bend in the track. When the team had marched out of sight, he pulled out his burst transceiver and typed a short message. He knew there was a chance the transmission would be detected, but he judged the intel important enough to warrant the risk. He hit transmit, then remembering the fate of the patrol boat, didn't wait for acknowledgement. He pocketed the device and jogged after the troops.

Far to the south, the ASD listening post at Numbulwar detected the encrypted burst signal and immediately relayed it via Shoal Bay to Fort Meade.

Survivors confirmed.
Small craft sighted.
Type unknown.
Intent unknown.

CHAPTER 3

Warm, moist air and the unknown fragrance of eucalyptus roused Nemza'ri from sleep. Her olfactory implant told her the atmosphere was an oxygen nitrogen mix with unusually high concentrations of carbon. It had been almost eight million years since her species had used carbon based fuels, so it never occurred to her that she was breathing the atmosphere of a world dependant on combusting hydrocarbons for energy.

When she opened her eyes, she discovered the crawlway to the outer hull was fully open. The sunlight coming down the tunnel was less orange and the sky bluer than on her homeworld, although the air was just as thick. Nemza'ri knew the Command Nexus would only be ventilating the ship if it had determined the atmosphere was breathable while her respiratory monitors told her it contained ample oxygen. She had little concern for alien microbes, which her bio-implants and genetically engineered immune system would quickly destroy, although she made a mental note to get an immunity booster in case this world harbored superpathogens.

The atmosphere's warmth indicated this was not their intended destination world and surprisingly, her implants had received no data stream identifying where they had landed. She was tempted to crawl to the hull to look out over the landing site, but her duty was to help with the repair work. She knew once the ship was secure, there would be time to investigate the world outside, so after a final glance at the blue sky, she crawled back through the hull to the inner passageway.

She stood on wobbly legs, surprised how weak she was even though the gravity was comparable to her homeworld's. She'd expected to see a med drone waiting with food and water, ready to subject her to a full bioscan. Instead the corridor was empty, lit only by a single flickering emergency light.

The Command Nexus had to know she was suffering from starvation and dehydration, yet it had done nothing to assist her other than allow her back into the ship. She tried reestablishing her mind link, but while the implant was fully functional, the ship wide crewnet failed to acknowledge her.

Assuming the Command Nexus had higher priorities than her, Nemza'ri staggered to the nearest grav lift and pinged it with her biosonar. She intended to go straight to her quarters to clean up and devour a protein pack or three before reporting for duty, but strangely, the sonic sensor did not respond. She tried activating it manually, but the control surface was unresponsive.

Almost too weak to stand, she triggered her autonomic implant's survival mode, flooding her body with a hormone many times stronger than adrenalin, giving her a temporary boost in strength. Her implants warned that her body would begin degrading if she subjected it to further artificial stimulation, but she simply overrode the alerts, certain she had to find her way out of the damaged section alone.

Nemza'ri summoned the ship's schematic from a memory implant, cautiously aware that with the data connect down, the diagram had not been updated for any damage suffered by the ship. She located the closest transit artery, confident emergency power would be routed to the cargo lifts so damage control drones could move heavy equipment through the ship. Her plan was to catch a ride to an aid center where she could get help and reestablish her link with the ship.

With more hope than strength, Nemza'ri pushed off the wall, inhaled the alien air and forced her feeble legs to work. It was a big ship and she had a long way to go.

CHAPTER 4

Cougar knelt beside a tree, peering through his rifle's telescopic sight at the wrecked zoological station. "I count six buildings, all destroyed. Two are burnt to the ground," he said over his tactical radio. "Looks deserted."

Further back in the forest, Vamp scaled the crystal ball's setting from short to long range, confirming the only refined metal the alien sensor detected belonged to the contact team. She gave Beckman a puzzled look. "I'm not reading the station at all, only us."

He nodded, then thumbed his radio. "Hold here," he said then moved up to Cougar's position and studied the area with his binoculars. It was late afternoon and shadows from the surrounding trees had almost spanned the ruined compound. "There's supposed to be a man and a woman living here."

Cougar swept the area with his telescopic sight and shook his head. "Don't see any bodies."

Finding no sign of life, Beckman radioed the rest of the team. "Tucker and Steamer, go left. Virus and Nuke go right. Xeno, you and Timer scout the far side of the perimeter. It looks deserted, but stay sharp."

Beckman stood and walked out of the trees toward the wrecked house. His senses were soon assaulted by the stench of death, then he saw a swarm of flies buzzing around a mangled crocodile carcass lying alongside the wrecked surveyor. "McInness, got something here for you."

The scientist hurried out of the forest, while Markus

followed more slowly and began studying each pile of wreckage in turn.

"What's that smell?" Dr. McInness asked as he reached Beckman.

"What smell?" Beckman said, pretending not to notice.

The scientist held a handkerchief over his mouth, then approached the surveyor, spraying the flies with insect repellant – to no effect. He retrieved the Geiger counter from his pack and checked the wreckage, obtaining only a faint ticking.

"Nothing but background radiation," he said as Beckman watched from a distance, then he returned the Geiger counter to his pack and peered into the surveyor's torn outer casing. A series of solid metal cubes ran through the center of the machine surrounded by specimen compartments. One had been punctured by a crocodile tooth and showed signs of having exploded. It had torn free of its mount, so Dr. McInness removed it for closer study.

"It could be its power supply," he said, then examined the dull metal strip beneath the machine.

"Do you recognize the technology?" Beckman asked.

"No, but we need to get it back to Groom for analysis."

"We'll pick it up on the way out."

Dr. McInness pointed to the exposed compartments with their gel encased specimens. "It was collecting samples, more evidence they're scientists, not invaders."

"Depends what they're collecting samples for," Markus said suspiciously.

"In case you hadn't noticed," Beckman said to the scientist, "this place looks like a bomb hit it. Not very friendly."

Dr. McInness glanced uncomfortably at the wrecked buildings. "The tremor from the ship's impact could have caused this."

"These buildings have survived tropical cyclones," Markus said. "A little shaking wouldn't have knocked them down."

Hooper completed a circuit of the compound, then reported to Beckman. “No bodies, no vehicles, no sign of a fight. They could have driven out, but that fire smells like gasoline. They’d have needed that fuel to get out of here.”

Beckman studied the charred remains of the garage and the machine shed. “If it was deliberate, why burn only two buildings? Why burn any of them?”

Hooper shrugged uncertainly.

“Search ten meters beyond the tree line,” Beckman said, “in case there are bodies out there.”

Hooper gave a curt nod and headed off to organize a search while Markus wandered toward the collapsed laboratory, studying the debris intently.

“What’s wrong with this picture?” he asked.

Beckman glanced at the collapsed building and shrugged. “Apart from the fact it’s been smashed to pieces?”

Markus picked up a wooden beam and pointed to holes in it. “The nails are gone.” He dropped the beam and motioned to the remains of the building. “They’re all gone.”

Beckman blinked, surprised he’d missed it. Now everywhere he looked, he saw empty nail holes. “You’re right.”

Markus motioned to the other buildings. “There’s no metal anywhere.” He turned to the burnt out remains of the garage, piecing the clues together. “They didn’t drive out.”

“That’s why Vamp couldn’t get a reading,” Beckman said, remembering the crystal ball detected only refined metals. He turned to Dr. McInness. “Any idea what could have done this?”

“A very powerful electromagnetic force,” the scientist replied. “These buildings would have contained computers, communications, other samples of our technology. They could have taken it all for study, just like I’m taking this,” he said, holding up the damaged cube.

“It’s an extreme way to collect samples,” Beckman said

doubtfully.

"It would have appeared to be a treasure trove of our civilization's artifacts," Dr. McInness persisted, "especially if it was abandoned."

"Or they took the people here as specimens," Markus said.

"Unfortunately, if they're very far ahead of us, they may not consider us an intelligent species," Dr. McInness said. "That would affect the kind of rights they'd allow us."

"If they're so smart," Beckman said, "how come a big lizard ate their toy?"

"It's a scientific instrument, not a weapon. It wasn't designed to–"

"Major!" Vamp's voice sounded urgently in their earpieces, her eyes riveted to the crystal ball. "Incoming! Very fast, from the west."

He thumbed his mike. "Is it airborne?"

"Can't tell. It's almost on top of us."

Beckman flicked his M16's safety off as a silver metallic flash leapt over the trees and landed in front of the remains of the marsupial house. It was a machine composed of four sections threaded by a central spine. A glassy black sensor disk was mounted on top of the spine providing three hundred and sixty degree vision across the EM spectrum, while the three lower sections were made of highly reflective metal. The two thin cylindrical sections below the sensor disk were each fitted with a pair of long multi-jointed arms equipped with spherical hands and four flexible digits. Each cylinder could rotate independently around the spine, giving the arms complete freedom of movement. Below the arms, the spine terminated in a downward pointing, conical hip attached to a pair of slender legs with feet equipped with three claw-like toes. The machine's skeletal appearance gave the impression of thin fragility, yet it moved with athletic grace and astonishing speed. When it hit the ground, its legs bent to absorb the shock, then it raced forward so fast it became a silver blur.

Beckman's rifle was pointed straight at the robotic seeker. For a fraction of a second, he knew he could make the shot, but Dr. McInness' insistence that these aliens were scientists, not invaders, made him hesitate.

"Hold your fire unless it attacks!" he bellowed, wondering whether a bullet could even catch the super fast machine.

The seeker charged straight toward Beckman who switched his weapon to full auto, but kept his finger off the trigger. He braced, expecting it to knock him down, but at the last moment, it swerved to the right and came to an instant stop beside the destroyed surveyor. One of its multi-jointed metal arms scooped up the wrecked drone, then sprayed a milky white 'fluid' over it from the palm of its hand. The substance ran over the surveyor as if it were alive, quickly enveloping it.

Dr. McInness watched intently, suspecting the substance was programmable. "It's spraying nanotechnology, molecular machines."

The seeker dashed forward again, gathering up other surveyor pieces and sliding them into the nanomembrane. When the seeker scooped up the last of the wreckage, it raced back to the dead crocodile. In a single fluid motion, its free hand ripped away a slice of the reptile's flesh and added it to the nanosack it carried in one hand.

"It's taking a sample of what destroyed the other machine," Dr. McInness said.

The seeker sprinted past Beckman, so close he felt the press of air as it passed, charging at Dr. McInness who stumbled back in surprise, tripped and fell. It snatched the metal cube from the scientist's hand without touching him, added it to the nanosack, then dashed away at high speed, leaping into the air just before it reached the marsupial house and vanishing over the tree tops.

"What the hell was that?" Nuke said.

"That skinny mother can run!" Virus exclaimed,

From beside the ruins of Laura's house, Tucker switched his machine gun's safety on. He glanced at Steamer a few meters away with his M16 ready. "I had it! I could have taken it any time."

Steamer grinned, "Man, you always say that."

"You know it's true."

Vamp watched the marker representing the seeker slide across the crystal ball's display surface and pass out of range. "It's gone," she said, doing a quick calculation. "It was travelling at least four hundred kilometers an hour."

Dr. McInness climbed to his feet, his cheeks flushed with embarrassment as he dusted himself off. "Sorry," he said meekly. "Its speed surprised me. I thought it was–"

"Forget it," Beckman cut in. "You were right. It wasn't an attack, just a cleanup."

Xeno's voice sounded in Beckman's earpiece. She and Virus had worked their way around to the northwest side of the compound, just inside the tree line. "Someone walked out of here, Major, heading west."

Beckman clicked his mike, "How long ago?"

"The tracks are fresh, maybe a few hours old."

Dr. McInness looked relieved. "They didn't take human specimens after all."

Markus thumbed his mike. "How many tracks?"

"One set," Vamp replied.

"One specimen, one survivor," Markus corrected.

"We'll follow the tracks while they head west," Beckman said, hoping to catch whoever was ahead of them. "I want to know what happened here."

Markus looked at the western sky apprehensively, then met Beckman's eyes. "They know we're here now. They'll be waiting for us."

"I know."

"So what's going to happen when we get close to their ship?" the CIA officer asked.

Beckman rested his hand on his recovered weapon. "They'll underestimate us."

* * * *

The contact team camped at the foot of a rocky escarpment when the light failed. They ate cold rations and cleaned weapons by the light of the moon, finding night brought no respite from the heat and humidity.

Afterwards, Virus listened to the signals detected by his recovered communicator. He wore headphones connected to a tiny crescent shaped device too small for the human ear. The engineers at Groom Lake had mounted the alien device in a rectangular housing which sent its output to his headphones and provided a means of operating its tiny control surface.

No one knew what medium it used, only that it wasn't electromagnetic. Its existence suggested that only specialist research units observing Earth were equipped with radio receivers, which reduced the risk of the team's tactical radios being detected. Groom Lake scientists suspected the communicator picked up the wearer's brain waves directly, converting them into audible messages and negating the need for a microphone. If true, it was calibrated to non-human brains, which accounted for the inability of researchers to transmit messages with the device. Signals from extraterrestrial vehicles watching the Groom Lake facility were regularly detected by it, some had even been partially translated, but mostly the intercepts were useful for measuring the volume of alien chatter and little else.

"Anything?" Beckman asked as he and Xeno approached.

"Maybe," Virus said uncertainly. "I'm getting two short, high pitched sounds, then long periods of silence. It could be static. It's not like the usual intercepts."

He passed Beckman the headphones who pressed one can against his ear and listened until he heard it, then handed the headphones to Xeno. "Are there always two bursts?"

"Yeah. The first is longer and varies in length, the second is always short, same length. I've been listening every few hours since we landed. The traffic's increasing."

Xeno listened to several transmissions, then said, "It's not a language. There isn't enough information to form meaningful sentences."

"May I?" Markus asked, extending a hand.

Xeno gave Beckman a questioning look, who nodded, then she passed the communicator to the CIA officer who listened to several sequences before handing the headphones back. "Sounds like encrypted data bursts. The first signal is the message, the second is the confirmation."

Dr. McInness sat on his pack nearby, staring at his notebook computer. Without looking up, he said, "I realize it's the job of soldiers and spies to be suspicious, but there are other explanations. It's probably nothing more than telemetry from scientific instruments; soil analyses, weather reports, pictures of gum trees and kangaroos. Maybe they're warning their sample collecting machines not to get eaten by giant lizards."

"How do you explain the increase in traffic?" Beckman asked.

"It takes time to deploy data collectors." He looked up from his computer. "Twice we've been close to their equipment, once at the borehole and once at the research station. Both times they fled to avoid contact with us. If they were hostile, don't you think they'd have attacked by now?"

"They have attacked," Markus said. "They destroyed the patrol boat, shot down our aircraft and destroyed our satellites."

"Sounds hostile to me," Beckman said.

"Not if they saw them as threats and were defending themselves."

Unconvinced, Beckman turned to Virus. "Have you tried decrypting it?"

"I was going to run it through my computer tonight,

once I'd recorded enough to work with," he said, indicating the notebook sitting on his pack.

"Keep recording. Even if you can't crack it, the eggheads at Groom might make something out of it."

Steamer clambered to his feet and pointed to the western sky. "Yo, what's that?"

A sphere of brilliant red light floated low in the sky, so bright, no detail of the craft itself was visible. It glided silently to the north for a few seconds, then descended into the forest.

"Looked like it was on fire," Timer declared. "It might have crashed."

Dr. McInness stood up, holding his computer under his arm. "It wasn't on fire, it was a photoelectric effect caused by its propulsion field."

"Say what?" Steamer said, giving the scientist a confused look.

"It's basic physics," Dr. McInness explained. "Einstein worked out the formulas for it over a hundred years ago. Their vehicles emit fields which ionize and excite the air particles around them. That generates a plasma which gives off photons, which is the light we saw. The stronger the field, the higher the photon energy, the more the color of the light shifts toward the blue end of the spectrum."

"It was red, not blue," Tucker said.

"It was hovering. That's a low power maneuver, so the color was down at the red end of the spectrum. For high power maneuvers like take offs, the photon energy would be much greater. That's when the light shifts to blue or white. It's a bit like a jet engine getting louder the faster it goes because of its increasing impact on the air."

"So it made a controlled landing?" Beckman asked.

"No doubt about it," Dr. McInness replied.

Beckman turned to Cougar. "Distance?"

The sniper gauged the range in the darkness, then said, "Four hundred meters."

"Close enough." Beckman nodded to Hooper, who had

already pulled his pack on in anticipation of the next order.

"All right people, mount up," Hooper said in a firm, even voice. "You know the drill, fast and quiet."

Cougar jogged off into the forest, pulling his pack on as he went. In the campsite, the team loaded their packs and were ready to move in seconds. Beckman started after Cougar as the others fanned out either side of him while Markus stayed a short distance behind where he could observe without getting in the way.

Dr. McInness blinked, still holding his computer in one hand, surprised at how quickly they had moved out. "Wait!" he yelled, hurriedly stuffing his gear into his pack, then following before he'd sealed the flap, his metal cases jangling discordantly inside. He tripped and spilled the pack's contents, then on his knees, hurriedly pushed his instruments back in looking after the disappearing soldiers.

Beckman glanced back at the scientist, then Hooper said, "Want me to shoot him?"

"No, just keep him out of trouble," he replied, then continued on through the trees as Dr. McInness got to his feet and came hurrying after them, his equipment clinking noisily in his pack.

Vamp glanced back at Dr. McInness with an amused smile, then produced the crystal ball and scrolled out its range until the target appeared on screen. "I've got multiple contacts. Looks like dismounts."

"It's a sightseeing party," Nuke said lightly.

Behind them, Hooper waited for the scientist to catch up, then raised a finger to his lips. "Shh!"

"You didn't wait for me," Dr. McInness protested.

"You weren't ready," Hooper said. "Now, slow and quiet."

"Right, slow and quiet," the scientist said, "like a commando!"

"Or in your case, a librarian."

Dr. McInness wrapped his arms around his backpack, trying to silence the rattling as he followed Beckman under

Hooper's close supervision.

"I've got a visual," Cougar's voice sounded in their ears as he focused his sniper scope on the craft from the cover of a clump of ferns.

It was octagonal, five meters high and more than twenty across, with a smoothly curved upper hull dotted with circular windows. The red spherical light that had sheathed the vehicle while it was airborne was gone. Now, a narrow beam of brilliant yellow light blasted down from beneath the vehicle into the ground. Steam boiled up from the borehole, billowing around the craft as compressed black droplets rose through the center of the beam into the vehicle.

First Beckman, then Markus, reached Cougar's position from where they observed the craft.

"If they have the same scanning technology Vamp does," the CIA officer said, "they know we're here."

"Maybe they're ready to talk," Beckman said as a solitary clink sounded behind him, signaling Dr. McInness and Hooper had caught up.

"Stay here," Beckman said.

Dr. McInness looked alarmed. "Major, as the representative of the scientific community, I should accompany you–"

"Not until we know what we're dealing with," Beckman said, nodding toward the master sergeant close behind him. "Sergeant Hooper will ensure you obey my orders."

Dr. McInness glanced uncomfortably at the grizzled veteran, whose stony expression left him in no doubt the major's orders would be followed.

Beckman shrugged off his pack and crept toward the craft. He discovered it was darker on top, with green and yellow running lights spaced at the octagonal corners, while the glow from beneath its underside cast long, sharp shadows across the ground.

He thumbed his mike. "Vamp, are you still tracking dismounts outside the vehicle?"

"Affirmative, I've got multiple contacts."

Cradling his rifle, he paused at a thicket of ferns to view the vehicle from close range. It appeared to be a single piece of metal from top to bottom with no welds or seams, a trait typical of the molecular bonding found on all recovered craft at Area 51. It was one of the reasons why the reverse engineering teams had so much difficulty disassembling them.

He decided to approach openly and was about to stand when a hand clamped firmly on his arm. Startled, he rolled onto his side, tearing free of the grip and bringing his rifle around to face his attacker. A dirt-smeared elfin face crowned by short red hair stared back at him over the barrel of his M16. Laura Mackay raised a forefinger to her lips, advising silence, then nodded toward a stand of trees to her left.

Beckman followed her gaze to where the glassy black sensor disk of a seeker protruded above the underbrush. The slender, quad-armed machine was crouched and motionless as if listening, then Beckman heard movement through the undergrowth. Suddenly, the seeker darted forward with tremendous speed, followed immediately by terrified animal shrieks.

Ten meters back, Steamer swung his rifle toward the sound, whispering, "What the hell was that?"

Tucker pulled on his night vision goggles and saw a dark shape through the trees. "I see it," he said in a hushed tone as the agonized shrieks continued to drift through the forest.

"What's it look like, Tuck?" Nuke asked, his eyes flitting apprehensively into the dark.

"Oh man," Tucker said ominously. "It's horrible!"

"What is?" Nuke demanded in a nervous whisper.

"Its fangs are huge!"

"Fangs?" Nuke repeated fearfully. "Aliens don't have fangs? … Do they?"

"And its claws, man, they're like bayonets."

Nuke went white. “Bayonets?”

“Uh-oh! It’s coming this way! It’s coming for you, Lieutenant!”

Nuke stared into the trees ahead, gripping his rifle, anticipating an alien horror charging at him out of the darkness. “Where? I can’t see it? Where is it?”

Tucker peeled off his night vision glasses and burst into silent, throbbing laughter.

“Screw you, man,” Nuke whispered as his fear turned to embarrassment.

Steamer shook his head, grinning. “Tucker, you’re a sorry son of a bitch.”

“I know, that’s why you love me!”

The animal screams were cut off as the thud of a heavy carcass hitting the ground thundered out of the darkness. The seeker slashed at flesh, then stood holding a red mass dripping with blood which it immediately sealed inside a nanomembrane.

Beckman glanced at Laura, who had a look of revulsion on her face. “What is it?” he whispered.

“A buffalo heart,” she replied.

The seeker dashed to the craft with blurring speed. A circular section of the hull irised open, allowing it to streak inside without pausing, then the opening sealed shut behind it.

“Were you here when it landed?” Beckman asked.

“I was close,” she said, nodding to the left.

“Major,” Vamp’s voice sounded urgently in his earpiece. “There’s a contact moving toward you.”

Beckman assumed she meant Laura, not realizing the zoologist carried no metal, making her invisible to Vamp’s crystal ball. Dry leaves crunched behind him, then he spun around, bringing his M16 up as a metallic hand caught the rifle barrel and snatched the gun out of his hands. The seeker lifted the weapon, turning it for its sensor disk to examine, then extended a thin metallic finger to the trigger and pressed experimentally. The M16 released a three shot burst, although the seeker's grip on the weapon's barrel was so strong, there was no sign of recoil.

With growing understanding, it repositioned the weapon so there was line of sight from its sensor disk along the barrel. Holding the weapon with its lower pair of arms, it fired a burst at a tree a dozen meters away. The seeker turned, ramping up its optical sensor for enhanced night vision and targeted a tree two hundred meters away. It fired another three shot burst with perfect accuracy, severing a branch Beckman could barely see.

Damn! Beckman thought astonished, *Great shot!*

The seeker now selected a branch more than a kilometer away and fired. Beckman didn't see the bullets miss their target, although the seeker did, giving it an understanding of the weapon's limited accuracy. It turned to Beckman and aimed at his head, curious to assess what damage the weapon could inflict upon the primitive biped who'd carried it. Before it could fire, one of Cougar's depleted uranium slugs crashed into its lower torso. It staggered and turned toward the sniper's position as a second bullet shattered its glassy black sensor disk. The seeker's arms spasmed, buckling the rifle's barrel as it stumbled blindly backwards, then Cougar's third shot smashed its upper chest, triggering an electric flash. The alien machine froze, then toppled back, stubbornly holding onto the rifle's twisted barrel as it hit the ground.

The brilliant light beneath the alien craft winked out, immersing the forest in darkness, then the surrounding air glowed a dull red as its propulsion field activated. The woodland became bathed in a ruby glow that turned orange as the craft powered up.

"Movement!" Vamp yelled. "Multiple contacts, all around us!"

Beckman heard the underbrush being swept aside as machines raced through the forest. Small dark surveyors sped past the troops hiding among the trees so fast they barely saw them. In the growing light generated by the craft's power up, shiny skinned seekers raced out of the darkness toward the vehicle, some carrying nanosacks full of samples.

Beckman drew his special – a blunt nosed 'midget' – and aimed at a seeker coming straight for them. Before he could fire, it scooped up its crippled sibling without slowing and swept past. Openings appeared in the alien vehicle's hull wherever a machine arrived, as if any surface could become an entry point. In a matter of seconds, all of the machines had retreated inside and its hull had sealed seamlessly shut, then the octagonal craft vanished.

For a moment Beckman was too astonished to think clearly, then he remembered Dr. McInness' explanation of hyper acceleration. He looked straight up in time to glimpse a brilliant blue white light high in the sky as it streaked away to the west.

"Clear," Beckman called into his radio as he climbed to his feet, then helped Laura up. "I take it you're from the research station?"

"Yes. My name's Laura Mackay. Who you are?"

"Robert Beckman, US Army."

"A little late, aren't you?"

"Late?" Beckman said puzzled.

"Something crashed here two days ago, destroyed my home and kidnapped my husband. I'd call that late."

Before Beckman could reply, she strode off into the clearing made by the vehicle as Dr. McInness stormed toward him with flushed cheeks and popping eyes.

"Are you out of your mind?" the scientist demanded.

Beckman gave him a puzzled look. "What?"

"Your people fired on them. Now they think we're hostile."

"It was going to shoot me in the head, Doctor," Beckman said emphatically.

"You shouldn't have gone in there with any weapons. This should never have been a military operation. I warned them. This is no job for trigger happy Rambo's!"

Beckman ignored the scientist and followed Laura into the clearing. The vegetation under foot had been crushed in the same circular pattern as at the previous landing site and another borehole had been drilled at its center. Laura crossed to where the water buffalo lay dead beside a gum tree. Beckman followed, noting neat circular holes had been cut through its chest and skull where its heart and brain had been removed.

"This is weird," she murmured. "There's no blood around either wound. The incision was sealed as soon as it was made."

Markus emerged from the trees, while further out, the shadowy forms of the rest of the team could be seen filtering toward the landing sight.

"How many of you are there?" Laura asked

"Twelve," Beckman replied, "including two civilians."

"Is that all?"

"We're a reconnaissance unit."

She stood up and motioned suspiciously at the small silver special at his hip. "What's that?"

"An experimental weapon. Top secret."

Markus cut in. "Why don't you tell us what's going on here, ma'am?"

Laura hesitated, breathing deeply as she fought to control her emotions. "I don't know. They took my husband … destroyed everything. I don't know what they want," she said, then described the encounter at her research station the previous night.

While she told her story, Dr. McInness examined the buffalo's wounds. When she finished, he said, "The technology sealing the borehole wall and this incision are the same. Both were fused without heat."

"So?" Beckman asked.

"It means they can transfer energy at quantum levels without thermal effects. It's a whole new approach to quantum mechanics. To use such advanced science in such mundane ways – for digging holes and cutting up animals –

means they've that technology a long time."

"We know something else, Doc," Cougar said. They all turned toward the sniper, curiously. "We know we can kill them."

"Yo Coug! You da man!" Timer yelled appreciatively, high fiving him.

"You shot an unarmed machine in the back!" Laura said.

"It was armed," Nuke said, "It had an M16 with a forty millimeter grenade launcher!"

"She's right," Beckman said soberly. "They weren't looking for a fight."

"Weren't they?" Markus said skeptically. "It took your weapon without you getting a shot away."

Beckman suppressed his irritation at the comment, while the troops sobered. They knew normally, the only way Beckman would ever surrender his weapon was if he were dead.

"So you're going to the Goyder?" Laura asked.

Beckman nodded. "That's the plan."

"Will you rescue my husband?"

Beckman hesitated. "I can't promise that."

Her eyes clouded. "Do you think he's dead?"

Better for him if he were, Beckman thought, dreading the prospect of being treated like a specimen. "I don't know."

"Where are you headed?" Markus asked.

"There's a landing strip the other side of Bath Range. I was hoping someone would land there before I ran out of supplies."

"There's no aircraft flying for a thousand kilometers in any direction," Beckman said.

Laura looked confused. "Why?"

"Because," Markus answered, "they shoot down every damn thing we send up."

Dr. McInness rounded on Markus abruptly. "We don't know that. Their technology may be causing electrical failures in our aircraft. There's bound to be a logical explanation for it."

"There is," Virus said, "their air defenses kick ass!"

"So, I have no hope of rescue?" Laura asked.

"None," Beckman replied.

Laura looked thoughtful, "Then I guess I'll have to go with you."

"That's impossible."

"Would you rather I die out here by myself?" She glanced at the members of his group, realizing none were local people. "I take it none of you know this country?"

"None of us knew Arnhem Land even existed forty-eight hours ago," Beckman said.

"I've been to the Goyder three times in the last two years," she said. "I know the local people and there's no one who knows this land like the aborigines. They've lived here for sixty thousand years and they don't trust outsiders, which means you'll never see them." She folded her arms. "Unless I'm with you."

"Native guides would give us an advantage," Hooper said meaningfully.

God help me, another civilian! Beckman thought, knowing Hooper was right. In any event, he'd already decided he couldn't leave her out here alone, unarmed and short of supplies.

"She can't stealth," Markus said. "And she's not cleared for our technology."

"She's already seen the specials," Beckman said, then turned to Laura. "If you're coming with us, you'll have to keep up. We can't slow down for you."

"I've hiked from one end of Arnhem Land to the other," she said sharply, "in monsoons and in hundred degree heat. You'll be lucky to keep up with me."

Muted laughter rippled around the clearing.

Beckman suppressed a smile at her bravado. "All right. Stick with Xeno. Do what she says."

"That's me," Xeno said, giving Laura a welcoming

smile. “You can call me Teresa if you like.”

Beckman turned to Hooper. “Let’s move. I want to put distance between us and this clearing.”

* * * *

Bandaka reached camp as the moon climbed high into the night sky. Liyakindirr, his closest friend, sat in front of the fire playing his *yirdaki*, known in the south as a *didgeridoo*. The instrument was only ever played by men and was as important to Yolngu culture as their ancient songs and ritual dances. The Yolngu had inhabited northeast Arnhem Land since the time of the *Wangarr*, the powerful ancestral beings who had divided the lands among the clans and delivered to each their tribal laws and dialects. It was an ageless union little understood by the *balanda*, the non aboriginal peoples who had spread through the lands of the south.

Djapilawuy, Bandaka’s wife, poked a stick into the burning embers, testing the progress of the kangaroo roasting beneath the campfire, while Mapuruma, his young daughter, sat beside her eagerly awaiting the feast.

“Where is the old one?” Bandaka asked as he approached.

Djapilawuy nodded to a large boulder. “In his place,” she said, sensing her husband’s unease. “Does the falling star still trouble you?”

“It fell close,” Bandaka replied with dread. In his culture, to see a falling star meant death approached. The closer the star, the nearer would be the person who died.

Liyakindirr ceased playing, letting the haunting sounds of night replace the thrum of his *yirdaki*. “Then we should go away from here,” he said. “Tell the white men.”

“They know,” Bandaka said solemnly. “One of their planes crashed.” Bandaka pointed his spear at Mount Fleming. “Over there.”

“The smoke we saw?” Djapilawuy asked.

Bandaka nodded. "The pilot was dead." They'd all seen fighters screaming across the skies before and knew they came from Tindal Air Base far to the south west.

"Could that be the death prophesized by the falling star?" she asked.

Bandaka shook his head ominously. "He was not close to us."

Liyakindirr nodded grimly, knowing his friend was correct.

Djapilawuy glanced at their daughter, fearing for her safety. "The old man dreams," she said, motioning to the darkness beneath a large rock at the edge of camp. "He fears the sign."

Bandaka walked past the fire, followed by Liyakindirr, toward the old man's dreaming place. They found Wanyubi sitting against the rock, staring into the darkness with meditative stillness. He was wrinkled by time and wore a hide loin cloth, although he had long ago ceased to carry a spear. They squatted respectfully beside him, waiting to be acknowledged, listening to the crackle of the stringybark in the fire.

"A strangeness in the land disturbs the spirits of our ancestors," Wanyubi said from his dreaming state, his words barely above a whisper.

"What is this strangeness?" Bandaka asked in a hushed tone.

"Even the great spirits do not know," he said, raising his eyes to the night sky. "It should not be so."

Bandaka felt his stomach knot. He was a simple hunter. He didn't understand the ways of the spirits, but he knew Wanyubi did. He found the old man's confusion disturbing. *How could the spirits not know?* "Where are the white men, Wanyubi? Why haven't they come?"

"Soldiers come from the morning sun."

"Should we find them?"

Wanyubi shook his head slowly. "They cannot protect us. They do not understand the danger." The old man's face filled with sadness. "They cannot escape their fate."

"What should we do?" Liyakindirr asked with a twinge of fear.

"Hide." Wanyubi's eyes scanned the shadows of the forest. Slowly his face turned to the trees beyond the campfire. "Evil comes."

Bandaka followed the old man's gaze, then turned urgently back to Wanyubi with a look of fear. "It's coming here? Now?"

Wanyubi nodded to the young hunter. "It hunts us."

Bandaka jumped up and ran back to the fire, calling in a low, urgent voice, "*Go marrtjina! Go marrtjina*!" 'Come here! Come here!'

Mapuruma stood and stared at her father, confused.

Bandaka pointed with his spear to the south. "Run and hide! That way!"

The urgency in his voice sent Djapilawuy darting for the trees with Mapuruma in tow. Liyakindirr grabbed his weapons and the *yirdaki* and jogged after them, while Wanyubi slipped quietly away into the night. None gave a second thought to abandoning their camp, which they could easily replace.

Bandaka sprinted through the forest until he was far beyond the glow of the campfire, then he hid, determined to understand what the spirits could not. He watched the camp, illuminated by the flickering fire light and listened to the forest. When nothing unusual appeared, he began to wonder if the old man had made a mistake, then he saw a faint glow gliding between the trees in the distance. It grew steadily in brightness as it approached, although Bandaka heard no footsteps. The silence of the night was soon shattered by the cracking of branches as the approaching form smashed aside low hanging limbs like twigs. When the glow neared the camp, Bandaka saw there was not a single light, but a pair of half-orbs spinning beneath a dark central mass.

Bandaka suppressed a gasp as the machine moved into

the fire light. It was jet black in color, taller than a man and shaped like a spinning top. Two small spheres rapidly orbited the sharp bottom end, their lower halves glowing brilliant white. Most confusing of all was the absence of a physical connection between its body and the spheres which made the machine float silently in the air as if by magic. Above the rapidly rotating spheres were four snaking arms extending from the upper curve of the spinning top, each ending in three double-jointed digits. A column rose above the arms, passing through a glassy black metal sensor disk to a flattened sphere. Extending horizontally from the sphere was a short tubular shape which Bandaka's refined survival instincts warned was a weapon.

The machine halted beside the fire, then thousands of points of blue light shone from the edge of its sensor disk, scanning its surroundings. One of the snaking arms speared into the campfire, sending embers and burning pieces of wood flying. It lifted the half cooked kangaroo out of the fire, holding it up for its sensor disk to analyze. When it had finished, it flicked the half burned carcass away. No blood or flesh remained on its arm, which was composed of a frictionless alloy no particle could adhere to without molecular bonding.

A chill of fear ran down Bandaka's spine when he saw the ease with which the floating machine had discarded the heavy kangaroo carcass. That fear drove him to begin crawling down the slope, wanting to get away from the floating beast, careful to keep rock outcrops and trees between himself and the camp.

Earlier in the day, the robotic tracker had examined the crash site where the jet fighter had come down. It had detected Bandaka's footprints, a single hair follicle and several microscopic skin fragments. From those few clues, it had mapped his DNA and constructed an anatomically perfect, three dimensional representation of his body. What it had failed to do was match his species with any of the tens of thousands it had on record. The tracker had determined from the limited size of Bandaka's brain that it was following a creature on the threshold between animal instinct and sentient intelligence. It was clearly of the same species as the pilot of the crashed aircraft, a flimsy vehicle that relied on air pressure rather than propulsion fields to remain airborne. The tracker had sent its findings to the Command Nexus, which concluded the air pressure vehicle and the low level primate piloting it were part of a feeble deception which required investigation.

The tracker, directed to capture Bandaka, amplified the sensitivity of its sensor disk receptors, magnifying star and moon light until the depths of the forest became visible, while scaling down those receptors affected by the campfire's glow. It was the campfire, standing between him and the tracker, that blinded it to his presence.

All around the campsite, the tracker sensed motion and heat from swarms of insects and many small and large creatures. It knew it was mapping an environment teeming with movement, a world that belonged to the very rarest category of habitable worlds, one super abundant with life. That abundance made it difficult for the tracker to separate out the biometric clutter generated by the surrounding biosphere's myriad life forms. It was rapidly cataloguing millions of species, from the most innocuous microbe to the mammalian bipeds it now hunted, but much remained to be done before the Command Nexus would be satisfied.

The tracker's long snaking arms collected more DNA samples from the campsite, leaving no trace undiscovered. It used the genetic information to build profiles of Bandaka's group, quickly discovering that five primates had gathered around the fire shortly before its arrival. From their tracks and DNA residue, it determined they'd moved off to the south. Using their genetic structure, it calculated their individual physical speeds and the time it needed to capture them. The tracker scanned their escape route with its thermal sensor, but boulders that had soaked up hot sun all day now radiated enough heat to mask the primate's distant thermal signatures. The signal clutter was amplified by the slithering, hopping and flying of thousands of creatures between it and the fleeing humans. It tried filtering out the interference, but it was only a tracker, not a planetary exploration drone. It was designed for tactical reconnaissance, not to survey new worlds, which it was only doing now out of necessity.

The tracker decided to flush out any primates hiding nearby. The barrel of its energy cannon swiveled toward the south and fired a series of low intensity blasts, striking tree trunks in a fifty meter arc. Each shot drove back the darkness with a brilliant orange flash, then as the energy pulses cut through the trees, the rending crash of branches falling to the ground filled the night.

Bandaka lay flat on his stomach, shielding his head with his hands as burning trees crashed down around him. He suppressed the urge to run, certain he'd be killed the moment he showed himself. He remembered an old lesson he'd been taught long ago, a lesson he'd drilled into his daughter until it was second nature to her.

Courage hides, fear runs.

Up the slope, the tracker watched patiently as terrified birds took to the air, startled creatures hopped for their lives and snakes slithered away into the darkness, but none of the primitive bipeds showed themselves. The tracker concluded the creatures were out of range, then as it was about to start after them, it received a new mission from the Command Nexus. It immediately turned east, heading toward its new target.

From his hiding place, Bandaka watched the glow of the tracker's antigravity pods move away into the forest. He knew the black monster was connected to the crashed plane and to the soldiers who were coming up the valley. He remembered old Wanyubi's warning that the soldiers didn't understand the danger they faced. Of that, Bandaka was sure, as sixty thousand years of tradition screamed a warning.

Evil spirits had entered the land.

* * * *

Bill Kenny flipped the steaks on the portable barbeque, then took a swig of beer. His three mates idly watched the sizzling meat with growing hunger as they lounged in camp chairs in front of their tents. Slab sat with his feet up on an ice filled cooler, while Wal angled a small satellite dish in different directions searching for a signal.

"Give it a rest, mate," Cracker said. "It's buggered."

"Nah, this thing's as tough as nails," Wal said, not realizing the satellite he was looking for no longer existed.

"Batteries could be flat," Cracker suggested.

"I checked them before we left. I should be picking up something."

Cracker leaned back, staring up at a sky filled with many more stars than could ever be seen from a big city. "We could be the last men on Earth out here."

The battery powered mozzie zapper popped again, signaling the sudden end of another mosquito.

Cracker glanced at the glowing blue light beside Slab with disgust. "What the hell did you bring that for? We're supposed to be roughing it."

Slab yawned, eyeing the electrified insect trap with satisfaction. "I hate bugs," he said, knowing the camp lights would summon every insect in sight. "They eat me alive."

"Why do you think we brought you?" Wal asked. "You're the bug bait, so nothing lands on us."

Slab sleepily stretched muscles sore from a day of hiking. "You're just jealous of my tasty blood," he said, yawning.

"It's not the taste that attracts them," Cracker said with an exaggerated wince, "it's the smell."

"I'll remember that when the crocs come up here tonight

and eat you," Slab said, glancing toward the river. They'd camped some way inland from where they'd tied up Bill's fishing boat to avoid the risk of attracting the giant reptiles. Even so, they kept their guns close. "Just keep your screaming down, I need my beauty sleep."

Cracker pulled a stick of dynamite from his pocket and waved it at the big ex-footballer. "Any croc comes near me and I'll blow its bloody head off."

Wal's eyes bulged. "You're not keeping that stuff in our tent!"

The old miner laughed, holding the dynamite with practiced familiarity. "Don't worry, Wal, it's been at least two years since I blew anyone up – by accident."

"I told you not to bring that stuff," Bill said dismayed.

"You'll thank me if we go hungry," Cracker said. "A few of these in the river and we'll have fish for a month."

"A few?" Bill said surprised. "How many did you bring?"

"A dozen sticks." Cracker waved away his friend's concerns. "It's perfectly safe." He pulled a small timer out of his pocket. "Needs a detonator to go off."

"You can't set them off out here, mate," Bill said. "The aborigines will go nuts!"

"What they don't know won't hurt them."

"There's nothing out here they don't know about. We've got a permit to shoot buffalo, not blow the bloody river up."

Cracker relented. "OK, no fishing, but if a croc comes up here, I'm sticking this in its gob, permit or not."

Wal made one last attempt to find a channel, then put the satellite receiver down, defeated. "I wanted to see if there was any news about that machine we shot today."

Bill looked dubious. "If someone's poking around out here without permission, it sure as hell won't be on the radio."

"I bet it was looking for uranium," Slab said, looking at the ground through droopy eyes, almost asleep. "Doing it sneaky, so the aborigines … don't know ... what's going on."

Cracker looked doubtful. "Nah, mining companies don't take a crap out here without approval from the locals. It was something else."

"It was digging for something," Wal said as Slab's head lolled forward and he fell into a drunken stupor.

They fell silent, gauging how deep was his sleep, then Bill whispered, "Do you think he's going to want his steak?"

"We'll split it," Wal said, "and tell him he ate it. He's so drunk, he won't have a clue."

Cracker nodded and went to take a drink, but as the can reached his lips, it was suddenly ripped out of his hand. "What the hell?"

Bill's eyes widened incredulously as Wal jumped to his feet and backed away, then Cracker followed their gaze to where a large black tracker floated at the edge of their camp site. It glided toward the fire light, towering over Cracker and prickling his skin with an invisible electromagnetic force. Cracker stumbled out of his chair and turned to face the machine as one of its four semi-snaking arms held the yellow beer can up to its sensor disk. It turned the can slowly, detecting lettering that belonged to a previously unknown language. It tested the strength of the can by squeezing it with its metal fingers, crushing it easily. Amber liquid shot out through bursting seams and poured onto the ground, then the tracker flicked the can away.

"What is it?" Bill asked.

"Stuffed if I know," Cracker said as they backed away, giving it room.

The tracker floated silently into the camp on rotating antigravity pods. An invisible force knocked Cracker's chair sideways while Slab remained in a drunken coma, oblivious to the tracker's presence. Thousands of laser-thin blue beams flicked out from its glassy black sensor disk, scanning and analyzing the campsite while the men shielded their eyes with their hands.

Bill nodded to the metal box behind the tracker where the hunting rifles were stored. "Get the guns, Wal!"

Wal glanced at the locker, then at the alien machine, fearful of attracting its attention. "You get the guns."

"You're closest."

Wal cursed silently, then edged around the tracker, shielding his eyes from the bright blue scanning beams. When he reached the gun locker, one of the tracker's arms speared into it, punching through its metal side like paper. Its three fingers spread apart like a grapple, then it whipped the locker away. A second metal arm punctured the gun locker's other side, then both arms held it up for its sensor disk to scan. A third arm deftly released the catches, opened the lid and retrieved Bill's hunting rifle.

"Got any other bright ideas?" Wal muttered as he backed away.

The tracker took only seconds to conclude it was a primitive kinetic weapon that fired chemically propelled projectiles, then it turned the locker upside down. It scanned each rifle as they fell to the ground, then tossed the locker and Bill's gun away. Its sensor beams winked out, then having detected thermal irregularities in the box beneath Slab's feet, one of its arms speared the cooler and ripped it away. Slab's feet fell to the ground, but too drunk to wake, he snorted and continued sleeping.

"I knew that bastard could sleep through a train wreck when he was drunk!" Cracker declared.

"Stuff him," Wal growled desperately. "That bloody thing's got our beers!"

The tracker tore open the cooler lid and scanned the cans floating inside, wondering why these primitive bipeds stored metal cylinders containing liquid of negligible nutritional value in a near freezing environment. Unable to resolve the mystery, it dropped the cooler, spilling its contents onto the ground as it turned its attention to the barbecue.

The tracker floated across the camp, past a blissfully sleeping Slab, to the three legged gas cooker. Spectroscopic analysis told it the flames were the result of combusting a carbon based gas which released toxic byproducts into the atmosphere. One of its semi-snaking arms picked up the barbecue and raised it for closer inspection. The burnt animal flesh and blackened onions sizzling on the hotplate told it the bipeds were omnivores, then it squeezed the gas cylinder experimentally, testing its tensile strength. The cylinder buckled and exploded, sending a wall of fire against an invisible shield enveloping the tracker, but doing no damage to its metal arms and torso.

"Let's get out of here," Wal said, starting for the trees.

The tracker's single cannon rotated and fired a single low power shot into the ground at Wal's feet, forcing him to freeze.

Cracker slid his hands unobtrusively into his pockets. "How smart do you reckon that thing is?" he asked.

"Pretty bloody stupid," Wal snapped, raising his hands in surrender. "It wrecked the cooler."

Cracker removed his hands from his pockets holding a detonator and a stick of dynamite, then slowly brought them together.

"You mad bastard," Wal said when he saw what he was doing, "you'll get us all killed!"

Cracker wound the timer without looking at it. He'd been setting timers for twenty years and knew them by touch. "Fifteen seconds ought to do it."

"Do what?" Bill demanded, edging away.

"I think it's too bloody curious for its own good."

"If the gas didn't hurt it, what makes you think dynamite will?" Bill asked.

Cracker ignored him, waving the dynamite in the air. "Here boy!" He whistled, like he was calling a dog. The tracker drifted toward him, then one of its arms shot out to grab the dynamite, but Cracker pulled the explosive away just in time. He turned his back to the machine and held the dynamite close to his chest.

"It'll spear you," Wal warned.

The alien machine moved closer to Cracker, intrigued by his strange actions. One of its arms grabbed the miner's ankle and lifted him off the ground, holding him upside down. Cracker realized it could have snapped his leg like a twig, but he kept the dynamite pressed close to his chest and activated the timer. It turned his body to see what he was hiding, then another of its arms caught his left wrist and pulled it clear of his chest, leaving only his right hand holding the explosive.

It's taking too long, Cracker realized as he counted down.

Suspended by two of the tracker's arms, it brought him in close. A prickling force pressed against his face as his body slammed into its shield, finding it resistant to sudden movements but malleable to gentle pressure.

Its arms are sticking through, Cracker realized.

The tracker's third arm shot toward his free hand, but he lunged forward, pushing the dynamite into the invisible bubble. At first, it felt like he'd struck a solid wall, then as he lost momentum, the repulsive force designed to stop high velocity impacts weakened and his hand slid through the field. When the dynamite was inside the bubble, he let it go and pulled his hand out. To his surprise, the explosive floated weightlessly in front of his face on the other side of the shield so close that he saw the small red digital timer count down to zero.

Damn! He thought as he realized he was going to take the explosion full in the face. *Never thought I'd blow myself up!*

The dynamite exploded an arm's length from Cracker's face. The bright flash blinded him momentarily as the blast struck the inside of the shield bubble and was channeled back at the alien machine. It shuddered as its antigravity pods sparkled with energy and winked out, then began skating around inside the shield bubble, out of control. The tracker fell to the ground, then the bubble collapsed, freeing a cloud of gas left from the explosion and letting the two antigravity pods shoot off into the trees like cannon balls.

Cracker fell awkwardly, then rolled clear as the heavy machine toppled toward him. He narrowly avoided being crushed, then scrambled to his feet, finding his ankle weak but not broken.

Realizing the machine was dead, Wal gave Cracker an appreciative look. "Good one, mate."

"You could have been killed," Bill said soberly.

"What was I supposed to do? It buggered the cooler," Cracker said with a crooked grin. "And you know how much I hate warm beer!"

Slab snorted, half opening his eyes with a horrified look. "Did someone say warm beer?"

* * * *

The contact team camped beneath a rough sandstone cliff, inside a pass that cut across Bath Range from east to west. The rugged trail had been used by aborigines for thousands of years and was littered with ancient rock paintings and long extinct campfires. Paperbark trees grew from every cranny in the rocky escarpment, while the shrill calls of kites and the squeals of their prey occasionally pierced the night.

Finding sleep elusive, Beckman climbed to a rock ledge where he could see the valley to the west. Several times he saw balls of light streak across the sky at many times the speed of sound. They were red, orange, blue and brilliant white, reminding him again of Dr. McInness' explanation of how color related to their energy levels.

"What do you think they're doing?" Laura asked from the shadows, startling him. She sat with her back against a rock, hidden in the darkness.

"I don't know," he said, surprised he hadn't seen her.

She lifted her eyes to the sky. "I wonder where they come from?"

"That star, second from the left," Beckman said, then shook his head. "Just kidding."

Laura smiled briefly, then sank back into her thoughts. After a while, she said, "The aborigines see the night sky differently to us. We see constellations in the stars. We join the dots. They see animals and spirits in the blackness between the stars." She pointed to a dark part of the sky. "That's a kangaroo. Can you see it, hidden in the darkness?"

Beckman couldn't see anything resembling a kangaroo.

"And over there, that's a wombat, and right above us is an emu," she said, indicating the different shapes. She saw the confusion on his face, adding, "I can't see it either, but it's real to them. Maybe they're right, and we're wrong."

"It's different," Beckman agreed, realizing the aboriginal view was as alien to him as if they'd come from another world.

They sat contemplating the patterns in the heavens and watching glowing alien craft streaking across the western horizon, then Laura asked, "Do you think my husband is alive?"

"I couldn't say."

"What are they doing to him?" There was a fragile quaver in her voice. "I've heard stories, but I've never believed them."

He remembered the contact reports he'd read, the top secret assessments that circulated in rarefied circles, none of which he could discuss with her. Even though he couldn't see her face, he felt her eyes boring into him, anxiously awaiting an answer. "I'm told advanced civilizations wouldn't use medieval torture techniques to gather information."

"Do you believe it?"

Maybe. "Absolutely. I'm sure he's in no pain."

"Will they release him?"

"Most do," Beckman said cautiously. "It depends on whether they respect our individual rights or not. The problem is, they're calling the shots, not us."

"But he's a human being," she said, "they can't treat him like …?"

"One of the animals you were studying?"

The comparison chilled her. "We're not animals."

"If they're a million years ahead of us, they won't consider us equals."

"But we're civilized."

"If you were floating up there looking down on Earth, what would you think of us? We've got wars, poverty, illiteracy, malnutrition, terrorism and hatreds based on race, religion and politics. We must look like murderous barbarians to them."

"That sounds almost philosophical."

"I've been trained to understand their point of view. We just have to hope they know what they're doing."

"What are they doing?"

"I'm not sure about this particular ship, but some of them have been watching us a long time, studying us, preparing for contact. We assume they've had a lot of practice meeting new civilizations and they know the timetable."

"What timetable?"

"However long it takes us to figure out how to get out there."

"When will that be?"

"Not in my lifetime. It's a very long way off." He gave her a reassuring look. "They've been visiting us for tens of thousands of years. If they wanted to hurt us, they'd have done it long ago, when we were less able to defend ourselves. The fact they haven't tells us they're not conquerors."

"Including what came down in the Goyder?"

"That's what we're here to find out."

Laura gazed toward the western horizon, relieved the glow of the previous night had gone. She thought it meant the fires had died down, unaware it was the result of the great hull's ability to rapidly shed heat. "So what does it take, to do what you do? To hunt these things?"

"I don't hunt them. I investigate, recover evidence, make friendly contact if possible." *Assess threats*. "Some of us are special forces trained, others are technical specialists."

"Have you ever made friendly contact?"

"No, they don't want to talk to us, not yet anyway. Been close a few times."

"I guess you must have some interesting dinner conversations."

Beckman smiled sourly. "Not really. My father is a retired two star. He was proud of me when I graduated from the Point and made it into Delta. Now he thinks I'm a desk jockey going nowhere fast. And I have to let him keep on thinking that."

"That must be tough."

"It comes with the territory … and I wouldn't want to do anything else," he said without a trace of disappointment, checking his watch. "You might want to get some sleep. We've got a long march tomorrow."

"I am tired," Laura stood up. "Goodnight, Major." She started to climb down the rocks, then hesitated. "I am grateful you came along," she said, then clambered down.

He watched her until she was safely back in camp, then looked to the west. Far across the valley a brilliant white light raced above the trees like a shooting star and vanished, filling him with foreboding.

What are you doing here? he wondered.

* * * *

Dan Mackay drifted through a disembodied dream state. Occasionally his mind cleared long enough to sense a relentless throbbing deep in his head and an unseen pressure holding him in place.

He remembered Blue had been barking and a brilliant beam had shone down on him and the dog. He'd fired his gun only to have it torn from his hands and sucked skyward, then he and Blue were floating above the yard as a dazzling light rushed toward them. After the light, there was a black emptiness and strange dreams.

In a rare moment of clarity, Dan realized he was a prisoner. The thought triggered a bolt of fear that sent adrenalin surging through his body, reviving him. He found he could squint through his eyes, enough to see a cone of brilliant white light flooding down over him. The glow of a surgical field encased his body, holding him immobile, while silver threads penetrated his skin in a dozen places, probing his organs and collecting microcellular samples used to map his biology.

A veil of darkness surrounded the light, where half seen spherical shapes with long, slender metallic arms moved, seemingly unaware of his fight for consciousness. Occasionally, thin robotic arms reached out to him from the darkness, touching him in ways he didn't understand, then he saw a silver thread had pierced his forehead. It reached to the very center of his brain, recording and decoding every pathway, every thought. Terror overcame him as he realized it was the cause of his terrible pain. He tried to scream, but could only muster an anguished moan.

One of the spherical shapes drifted out of the darkness toward him, unsure why the specimen was conscious. It took only a moment to discover the creature's body was flooded with a hormone that had increased its heart rate and contracted its blood vessels. Before the specimen could injure itself, its neurological system was disconnected from its brain and bioelectric impulses were administered to neutralize the hormone's effect.

In a heartbeat, Dan fell back into the dark depths of an induced coma.

CHAPTER 5

Beckman decided to break camp before dawn and cross the rocky ridge known as Bath Range while the light was still weak. By mid morning, they had descended into the cover of a sprawling forest laced with streams that fed water lily covered billabongs surrounded by bamboo-like pandanus palms. When the sun neared its zenith, they emerged into a cleared corridor recently carved through the wilderness. The ground had been crushed flat into a smooth surface where fallen rocks, trees and plants had all melted together into a gently curving road.

Beckman found the surface spongy to the touch and discovered a silver thread running through the center. The metallic streak was as wide as his boot and his hairs stood on end as he approached it, indicating it was generating an electromagnetic field. Slender silver poles, each mounting a cross arm supporting a pair of diamond shaped objects, stood every few hundred meters along the metallic strip.

Timer pulled his helmet off and scratched his head. "Why are they building roads?"

"They don't like walking," Nuke quipped.

Laura looked north and south along the corridor, horrified. "It took millions of years for this forest to grow and they've destroyed it in a day."

Hooper poked the road with the barrel of his M16. "Looks way too permanent for my liking."

"The Romans conquered the known world by building roads," Markus said warily.

"They have hypersonic vehicles," Dr. McInness said.

"They don't need roads."

"I agree," Beckman said. "It's not a road. So what is it?"

"A sensor?" Vamp suggested, producing the crystal ball. It showed the road curved gently away to the south, while it came to an abrupt end two clicks north at a slowly moving contact marker. "The end is that way," she said pointing. "There's something up there.

"If they're still building it, it's not active," Dr. McInness said as he examined the metallic thread, rubbing the excited hairs on his arm. "This is an energy conduit. It must power those towers."

Beckman turned to Hooper. "We'll follow the road north, find out what's building it. Stay in cover."

Hooper nodded. "Back to the trees people. This ain't no sightseeing trip."

They followed the road from the safety of the trees until they reached the crest of a hill where they heard tree trunks snapping and boulders shattering, although not the roar of earth moving equipment. From the tree line, Beckman, Markus and Dr. McInness watched a beetle-shaped machine silently inch down the far slope, crushing all in its path. The crack of splintering tree trunks ceased as the beetle halted, then a circle dilated in the machine's seamless rear and a pole fitted with a cross arm slid out on a metal cradle. The cradle rotated the pole to the vertical, then the base of the pole glowed brilliant red and slid into the ground, sending black smoke billowing into the air from the entry point. Once the pole was firmly embedded, the smoke cleared and the cradle retracted into the machine. The circular door resealed then the cracking of tree trunks began anew as the beetle started grinding through the forest again.

"How far are we are from the landing site?" Dr. McInness asked.

"Twenty-five clicks," Beckman replied, noting the curve of the corridor reached around the crash site.

"Those towers could be weapons," Markus said.

"We don't know what that technology is," the scientist said, trying to allay their fears. "It's big enough to be an interstellar communicator, so they can call for help."

"There's only one way to know for sure," Beckman said. When they gave him curious looks, he added, "I want to be in position to board that thing when it plants the next pole."

* * * *

The snapping of tree trunks thundered like gunshots through the forest as the road builder approached their position. An invisible force effortlessly crushed boulders beneath it and knocked down trees, then quantum blended their substances into the road as it laid the energy conduit. High on the beetle's steeply sloping hull was a single horizontal slit window which provided glimpses of interior walls, but showed no sign of occupants.

"Any time now," Beckman said, hoping they'd calculated the distance from the last pole correctly.

Xeno and Virus readied themselves beside Beckman, while the rest of the team formed a loose skirmish line behind them. Even though Dr. McInness had insisted on boarding the vehicle, Beckman had refused to allow him to go for the scientist's own protection. Surprisingly, Markus had shown no interest in going along. He was satisfied to sit with his back to a tree and observe from a distance. Beckman already knew the CIA officer was more than capable of looking after himself and wondered if he'd slip away into the forest if they got into trouble and continue on alone.

When the road builder had almost reached them, Dr. McInness suddenly cried out and scrambled back in fright, losing his glasses and pack. Tucker calmly whipped out his Bowie knife and plunged the carbon steel blade into a slender form slithering on the ground. He twisted the knife to the sound of crunching bone, then lifted the blade, revealing a cream colored head. He raised the blade high, showing the others the two meter long, thin bodied, copper-brown snake.

Dr. McInness relaxed, then with an embarrassed look, recovered his glasses as muted chuckles rippled up the line.

"It's a taipan," Laura explained.

"Skinny runt," Tucker said, unimpressed.

She gave Dr. McInness a sober look. "It's the deadliest snake on Earth, fifty times more toxic than a cobra."

Dr. McInness adjusted his glasses nervously. "I see."

Tucker looked at the snake with renewed respect. "Is it good eating?"

"Not if you swallow the poison sac," Laura said.

Nuke chuckled. "Deadliest snake on the planet and he wants to eat it!"

Tucker scowled at Nuke, then flicked the dead snake at him.

"Hey!" Nuke said as he swatted it away, afraid of being scratched by its fangs. "Get the hell away, man!" He scrambled back from the snake's lifeless body as subdued laughter sounded around them. "That's not funny!"

"Not as funny as if it'd bitten your ass," Steamer said, sitting with his back against his pack while Tucker's granite face cracked a smile.

"Shut the hell up!" Hooper hissed angrily.

Beckman's eyes returned to the beetle-like machine, now floating silently a short distance from their position. It was as high as a two-story building and as long as an eighteen-wheeler.

"Let's go," he said, then jogged to the rear of the machine with Xeno and Virus close behind. Their body hair prickled as they neared the field beneath the road builder, then a rear section of its hull dilated and a cradle slid out supporting a silver pole.

Virus and Xeno linked hands, giving Beckman a step up into the circular entry. He found himself in a long compartment running the length of the vehicle, lined with racks containing silver metal poles and cross arms. The cradle was held by an armature that extended from a rectangular machine that had a pair of robotic arms for assembling the poles and cross arms. Satisfied he was alone, he pulled Xeno and Virus up into the vehicle, then gave Hooper a thumbs-up.

The cradle rotated to the vertical and began deploying the pole, then Beckman led them to the end of the compartment.

"No markings anywhere," Xeno said.

"And no control panels," Virus added, noting the lack of visible doors or hatches leading to other sections of the vehicle.

Beckman was reminded of a lesson drummed into him at Groom Lake: Stone age man wouldn't know how to use everyday items, because such things were inconceivable to them and in the face of truly advanced technology, he might fare no better than a cave man.

Would I recognize their doors? he wondered as the cradle finished deploying the pole and retracted, then the rear hatch irised shut filling the compartment with soft yellow-orange light and air that irritated their eyes.

"There's got to be a way through," he said, running his hand across the metal wall at the end of the compartment, then turning to find himself facing the slit windows he'd seen from outside. He'd felt no sensation of movement as he'd been transported from the lower to the upper level. "Neat trick."

He stepped out of the transport alcove, finding his head scraping the ceiling, then approached two low seats and a pair of black panels in front of the slit window. The panels sloped gently toward the chairs and were made of a featureless glass-like material with no controls or data displays. Other seats stood on opposite sides of the control room facing wall mounted screens filled with tiny swirling symbols that Beckman found strangely disorienting.

He looked away from a wall screen, blinking to clear his

head, then leaned toward the slit windows. They provided a clear view of the skinny white gum trees outside, which the road builder was again knocking down, although without the slightest vibration registering inside.

Xeno appeared in the alcove with an astonished look. "I was staring straight at you, then you were gone." She stepped out of the alcove, touching the ceiling. "This is low."

"Yeah, they're shorter than us," Beckman said, then Virus arrived a moment later.

"Nice ride," he said. "My first teleporter."

"Elevator," Beckman corrected, certain they'd travelled straight up one level.

Xeno glanced at the four vacant seats. "Where's the crew?"

"It's either automated or remotely controlled," Beckman said.

Xeno watched one of the wall screens flowing with curling shapes, then moved from left to right, seeing how the symbols shifted relative to each other. "These displays are three dimensional."

Beckman avoided looking at the screen that had her attention. "They make me dizzy."

She winced, feeling it herself. "Me too."

"Have you seen those characters before?"

"They're not familiar." Xeno retrieved her computer and a digital camera from the satchel she carried, plugged them together and began recording the wall screen. The computer analyzed the pictures, comparing the symbols to its language database, then she smiled. "Not one match. It's a totally new language."

"I was afraid of that," Beckman said soberly. A new language meant a new species, one that might have a different attitude toward less advanced civilizations.

Xeno's computer began plotting recurring patterns in a way that surprised her. "The information isn't just in the symbols, it's also in the spatial relationships between them and the way the shapes change. It's a spatial language, using more dimensions to transmit information than we do."

"It gives me a headache," Virus said, looking away.

"They have a more refined spatial ability than we do," Xeno said thoughtfully. "Or their thinking is more multidimensional than ours. Even if we knew what it meant, we'd need a computer to read it."

"I'm sure the lab rats will be studying that recording for years." Beckman said as he sat in one of the cockpit seats, finding it surprisingly wide. "Someone's got a huge butt."

Xeno aimed her camera at Beckman's seat. "Their physiology's certainly different to the few species we do know."

"Just don't ask me to sit next to one on a plane," he said, standing.

"Wow!" Virus exclaimed from the other command seat. He was staring into the panel in front which was now alive with disorienting, multicolored, three dimensional shapes similar to what the wall screens displayed.

"What happened?" Beckman asked as Xeno aimed her camera at the display.

"I touched it and it just came on. It must have a proximity sensor, but that's not the freakiest thing." He tapped the display with his bayonet, causing it to ring hollowly. "Totally solid. Right?" He slid the bayonet into its scabbard, then lowered his fingertips into the display as if he was dipping them in water. "Wrong."

"Its quantum structure changes," Xeno said, astonished, "on contact with living tissue."

"Have we seen anything like this before?" Beckman asked.

Xeno shook her head. "Not that I know of."

Beckman's expression darkened. "It's more advanced than the Roswell wreck."

"Hell yeah," Virus said. "I can feel it … connecting to my fingers."

Beckman put his hand on Virus' shoulder. "That's enough."

"Major, we're not going to learn how this stuff works by watching pretty lights on the wall."

Reluctantly, Beckman released his shoulder. "OK, but take it slow."

"Yes sir," Virus said, sliding his hand into the display toward a glowing yellow helix. "It's got hold of my hand." His eyes widened in surprise. "It's in my head!" He took a deep breath as images flooded into his mind. "Oh man, there's way more here than what you see on the panel." His fingers swept through the helix, changing the swirling patterns, then the vehicle shuddered, the first sense of movement they'd felt since climbing aboard. Virus immediately withdrew his hand and the helix returned to its previous setting. "It's a power control! I know what it wants me to do. It's like sculpting. I control it by molding its shape and visualizing a new form to change many settings at once."

"Is it dangerous?" Beckman asked.

"It doesn't seem to be."

"What did you mean, it's in your head?" Xeno asked, keeping her camera focused on him.

"It's teaching me, not with words, more like impressions." He searched for a way to explain it. "It's communicating with me through my nervous system … direct to my brain." He slid his hand back into the control interface. "I'll get the hang of it. I just need a little practice."

"OK," Beckman said, "just don't run over our people outside."

"I'll be doing burnouts in no time," Virus said as he tried shaping the helix again.

Beckman turned to the other console, passing his hand experimentally over it, testing for a proximity sensor. It flashed on, depicting a topographical map of the region a hundred kilometers across.

"Finally, something I recognize," he said, impressed by the navigation station's detail. Overlaying the map were four glowing yellow markers, each trailing a circular arc marked by equally spaced red dots. The four arcs formed an incomplete circle with the Goyder River crash site at its center. Beckman guessed the most easterly yellow point represented the vehicle they rode in and the red dots were the poles.

"They're creating a perimeter," he said as Xeno photographed the map. "Looks about fifty kilometers across."

"Whatever they're building," she said, "it's almost complete."

"Ugh!" Virus groaned as he passed out and his head flopped into the display console, sinking up to his ears.

The vehicle lurched suddenly, almost knocking Beckman off his feet, then he caught Virus by the shoulder and pulled him back into the chair. Virus' head rolled sideways, eyes flickering beneath closed lids, breathing shallowly. His hands fell away from the display, allowing the vehicle to return to autopilot.

Xeno put her camera down and pressed her fingers to Virus' throat. "He's alive, but his pulse is erratic."

"Let's get him out of here," Beckman said, angry with himself for letting Virus experiment with the alien technology. He lifted him out of the seat and carried him to the transport alcove, then in the blink of an eye, they were in the pole compartment followed a moment later by Xeno.

Beckman set Virus down and gently slapped his face, trying to rouse him. "Virus, can you hear me?" When he didn't respond, he thumbed his mike, "Hooper, Virus is down. We'll need help getting out."

"Roger that," Hooper replied through a hiss of static.

"Have Timer standing by with two demolition charges," Beckman added.

"Understood."

Xeno gave him a curious look. "You're going to destroy

this vehicle?"

"No, just buy some insurance."

The rear door irised open as the central machine's robotic arms attached a pole to a cross-arm. Once joined, the cradle slid outside, then Beckman dragged Virus to the hatch and passed him down to Hooper who was waiting outside with Timer and Cougar. Once Virus was clear, Xeno climbed out, then Beckman pulled Timer up into the vehicle.

"Put charges and radio detonators on two of the cross arms."

"You got it," Timer replied, reaching into his satchel for an explosive.

Outside, Hooper carried Virus into the trees while Xeno retrieved her medical kit and began checking his vitals. Beckman watched the pole slide into the ground behind the road builder then glanced at Timer who was taking forever to attach the explosive.

"What's the hold up?"

Timer shook his head in frustration. "I can't attach the C4. These things are totally nonmagnetic, nonstick. I'll have to tie them on!"

He cut a length of wire from a reel in his satchel, wrapped it around the cross arm and tied it to the explosive. Just as he finished rigging the first charge, the cradle slid into the compartment.

Wary of being trapped, Beckman said, "One will have to do." He motioned for Timer to get out, then they jumped as the hatch began irising shut, rolling easily on the spongy alien surface.

"Should I blow it now?"

"No," Beckman said, climbing to his feet. "Set up a radio relay as we go, so we can blow it from twenty-five clicks away, if we need to."

Timer looked concerned. "That'll take most of my radio detonators."

"OK," Beckman said as they hurried to where Xeno was

attending to Virus, watched anxiously by the rest of the team. The communications specialist's skin was pale, his body trembled and his eyes fluttered as if he was dreaming intensely, but she could do nothing to rouse him.

"He's in shock," she said. "There are no physical injuries, but we need to get him to a hospital."

"There's no evac." Beckman said, certain no aircraft could fly this close to the crash site. He turned to Tucker. "Rig a stretcher. We'll carry him."

Tucker produced his Bowie knife and went in search of stretcher poles while the shotgun cracking of trees beneath the road builder faded into the distance.

* * * *

While the team prepared to hike out with Virus on a stretcher, Markus slipped away to the edge of the alien road. He checked no one was following him, then pulled the tiny transceiver from his pocket and typed a brief message.

Ground vehicle constructing perimeter.
Purpose unknown.

He attached a series of photographs he'd taken with the transceiver's built in camera during Beckman's boarding attempt, aware sending photographs would increase transmission times, but convinced the intel was worth the risk. When finished, he extended the transmitter's antenna.

"What are you doing?" Laura asked.

Markus turned slowly toward her, shielding the transceiver with his body as he wondered how she'd gotten so close without him hearing her approach. "Just looking around."

"What's that in your hand?"

Markus hid his irritation. "Spy stuff," he said, ceasing to hide the transceiver. "I could tell you what it is, but then I'd have to kill you." He smiled and tapped the send button. "I'm going to have to ask you not to mention this to the others."

"Why should I agree to that?"

"Do you want to see your husband again?"

She stiffened. "Of course."

"Then you need to trust me," he said as the ASD team's acknowledgement appeared on the radio's small screen.

"You mean trust you, not them?" she asked, nodding toward the soldiers.

"I don't want to destroy what's up ahead."

"And they do?"

"Not yet, but the military destroy what they don't understand. On the other hand, anything I don't understand is potentially … useful."

"To Uncle Sam?" she asked cynically.

He shrugged, conceding his intention. "Your husband's chances of survival are better if we capture, rather than destroy that ship. If you tell Beckman about this," he said holding up the transceiver, "He'll take it, then I can't help you."

She hesitated uncertainly. "You know my price."

Markus nodded. "I'll do everything in my power to see your husband is returned to you unharmed." He looked her up and down thoughtfully. "How well do you know this terrain?"

"Well enough."

"Could you lead me out of here, if I had to get out alone?"

"Where do you want to go?"

"South."

"There's nothing that way for a thousand kilometers."

"We wouldn't have to go far." He lifted his transceiver. "I can call in a ride once we reach … Num-war Road," he said, stumbling uncertainly over the name.

"Numbulwar Road," she corrected. "It's not much of a road, but I can find it. The question is, why should I? How does that help my husband?"

"Leave that to me."

She adjusted her backpack straps absently. "All right Mr. Markus, your little secret's safe with me – for now."

His face showed a hint of relief. "You better get back, before they miss you."

Laura hesitated, giving him a curious look.

"I'll be along in a minute."

Laura turned and picked her way back through the trees. Before she reached the others, an incoming message appeared on the his radio's LCD screen:

Vehicle origin unknown.
Alien orbital activity nil.
Recovery remains viable.

Markus pocketed the transceiver and started back toward the soldiers, deep in thought. The assessment team at Langley had been unable to match the alien vehicle's design to any of the civilizations in regular contact with Earth and deep space tracking stations worldwide had not detected any alien craft arriving in orbit to render assistance. It suggested the downed ship was far from home and its location may not be known to those who built it. Markus could barely contain his excitement as he realized the magnitude of the opportunity almost within reach.

This could be the holy grail!

* * * *

In the early afternoon, after a long hike through the steaming forest, the contact team felt a strange prickling force in the air. Their hairs stood on end and their radios hissed with static. It grew rapidly in strength, silencing the birds and ending the interminable thrum of the insects. It was as if a switch had been thrown, casting a deathly silence over the forest.

Nuke scanned the tree tops apprehensively. Not watching where he was going, he bumped into Steamer and a spark of electricity arced between them.

"Ow!" Nuke declared, rubbing his arm. "You zapped me!"

Tucker winked at Steamer, then hovered a finger at the back of Nuke's neck, beneath his helmet, watching as a tiny electric flash flickered between them.

Nuke spun around slapping at his neck like it was a mosquito bite. "What's wrong with you, man?"

Tucker chuckled as Beckman turned to Dr. McInness. "Any ideas?"

The scientist studied the clear blue sky overhead uncertainly. "It's an enormous build up of static electricity, but I have no idea what's causing it."

Markus ran his hand over the hairs on his arm, fascinated by how rigidly they stood to attention. A few paces back, Laura tried smoothing her short red hair, finding it sprang back once her hand had passed.

"This gives new meaning to having a bad hair day," she said, then a shattering thunder clap rumbled over the land and in an instant, the static charge vanished.

Tucker aimed his finger at the back of Nuke's neck again, disappointed when nothing happened. "It's gone."

Nuke saw what Tucker was doing and backed away, gesturing with his middle finger.

"No, it isn't," Laura said, pointing up through the trees at the eastern sky.

They turned as one to see a translucent curtain rise into the air from one end of the horizon to the other, blurring the sky as it climbed. Slowly it arched over their heads, angling toward a point high above them, turning the azure sky into a shimmering blue-white blur. The curtain became dome shaped as it rose, forming a central hole in the sky which rapidly shrank to nothing. When the hole vanished, a white flash burst from the apex and rolled down the sides in a single stabilizing wave. The harsh tropical sunlight was gone, replaced by a gentle milky light that cast soft shadows across the forest floor.

"It's coming from the alien road," Beckman said, realizing the circular perimeter was complete.

"What is it?" Laura asked.

With the entire team hanging on his every word, except for Roland Markus who'd already drawn his own conclusion, he said, "It's not a crash landing, it's a bridgehead."

CHAPTER 6

Nemza'ri finished her third protein pack, feeling her strength slowly return. She'd found the tasteless, colorless nutrient in the emergency rations of an escape pod. The tiny lifeboat was undamaged, but its power supply had inexplicably failed, forcing her to manually crank open its hatch. It never occurred to her that in those first desperate hours, the Command Nexus had drained the power reserves of more than three thousand escape pods to stay alive. The gamble had bought enough time to repair one of the secondary power plants, providing a trickle of energy sufficient to revive basic systems and restore limited maneuvering.

Her hunger satisfied, she studied the pod's command terminal, finding there was insufficient energy to activate it. The terminal could give her access to command layers her implants could not, so hoping to find a way to power it, she summoned the tiny craft's technical specs from a memory implant. The escape pod was little more than a life support system with sub light propulsion, although there was a basic repair kit on the lower level.

She climbed down through a crawl space in complete darkness, searching for the kit with her biosonar. The cramped metal walls reflected her pings, blurring her sonic vision, but with the help of the tech specs, she found the kit and carried it up to the habitation level. It contained no spare energy cells, but it did hold a pair of cylindrical power transceivers. In the scramble to evacuate ship, some pods would be overcrowded while others would be almost empty. The transceivers compensated for this by allowing a swarm of escape pods to share power while under way.

She placed the first transceiver close to one of the escape pod's energy conduits and the second next to the nearest emergency light in the corridor outside. The paired transceivers automatically transferred energy from the emergency light to the tiny lifeboat, bringing the pod's control terminal to life. Nemza'ri plunged one of her hands into the terminal, instantly registering a link with it through the synapses of her central nervous system. The synaptic link allowed the implants in her brain to meld perfectly with the terminal, making her part of the escape pod, and through its docking link, part of the ship.

With a wave of relief, she sent her crew designation to the pod management system and requested assistance. The Command Nexus and its myriad sub foci could hold billions of conversations with organic and artificial intelligences simultaneously without taxing its powers, yet no response came. She tried a crew only emergency channel and was immediately told her that because she lacked command rank, she was not authorized to communicate directly with the Command Nexus. It was the wrong response, which was impossible because the ship never made such mistakes.

She tried the emergency channel again, wondering if she'd made an error. This time the response was sharper, informing her that because she'd ignored the first directive, her crew status had been suspended pending a fitness evaluation and she was ordered to report immediately to Urban 4432 for a full biodiagnostic.

Nemza'ri stood alone in the shadows of the escape pod, stunned. Now she knew something was definitely wrong with the ship's guiding intelligence. Urban 4432 was an orbital city thousands of light years away. She wondered how the Command Nexus could possibly give such a patently illogical order?

Triggering another memory implant, she searched

through millions of Command Nexus protocols for an explanation, but there was none. A simple thought appeared in her mind, a thought that filled her with dread and a sense of hopelessness, yet it was the only possible explanation. For a moment, she refused to believe it, but her lightning fast mind working in perfect harmony with her cerebral implants eliminated every other possibility. Nemza'ri knew it was the worst disaster imaginable.

The ship had lost its mind!

CHAPTER 7

Bill steered his half cabin fishing boat past bleached rocks jutting from the mangroves. The big V6 outboard was at full throttle, planing the boat high and fast across the murky green water and sending its wash rolling onto the muddy banks. Onboard, the four men watched the strange shimmering curtain towering before them in silence, more confused than afraid.

The fishing boat rounded a gentle bend, bringing the base of the translucent wall of energy into view. It sliced across the water like a dam, causing the river to break its banks and inundate the surrounding forest, while beyond its oscillating energy waves, the forest and sky appeared as a shifting green and blue mirage.

Bill throttled back until the engine was idling, letting the boat drift fifty meters from where the curtain blocked the river.

"I bet whoever put that there didn't have a permit!" Wal declared indignantly.

Bill pointed to a dirty brown smear beyond the energy curtain. "That's the bloody river bed. It's bone dry!"

Slab's eyes followed the curtain up to its apex, struggling to gain perspective against its monotonous blur. The small black dot of an eagle circled slowly to the southwest hundreds of meters in the air, yet far below the soaring dome top. "It must be ten kilometers high."

"More than that, I reckon. Twenty or thirty k's, at least," Cracker guessed as he pulled a battered pair of binoculars from a locker and scanned the base of the curtain from north to south. "It looks like someone's bulldozed a bloody road through there and there's a light pole over near the trees."

"Let's take a look," Bill said, easing the throttle forward.

They motored slowly toward the southern bank where the curtain emerged from the river, hearing a faint hum of vibrating air particles as they approached. Bill throttled back near the submerged mangroves where they could see the alien road running down into the river. A metal pole stood on the shore inside the energy curtain supporting a pair of diamond shaped objects that glowed like the sun. Wal picked up his hunting rifle, squinting against the dazzling light, and squeezed off a well aimed shot that sparked harmlessly against the shimmering energy wall.

"It's going to take more than a pea shooter to bring that thing down," Slab declared.

Cracker produced a stick of dynamite from his private stash. "Get me closer."

"That pop stick won't even scratch it," Slab said.

Cracker looked defiant. "You want to be stuck here forever?"

Slab fell into a brooding silence as Bill steered the boat to where the road met the flooding river. Cracker pushed in a fuse, set the timer and prepared to hurl it at the curtain when Slab stood up.

"Give it here," he said, sticking out his huge paw.

Cracker hesitated, then handed it to the hulking ex-footballer. Slab locked one hand around the railing for support, then hurled the dynamite at the bank. It landed at the foot of the pole just in front of the curtain and well beyond the water.

"I've still got it," Slab declared with a self satisfied smile.

"Lucky throw," Wal said mischievously. "Wind caught it."

"Piss off, Wal," Slab said, knowing there wasn't the hint

of a breeze, then the dynamite exploded. The blast rippled briefly up the side of the curtain shielding the pole before quickly dissipating.

"Crap!" Slab said disappointed. Resigned to his fate, he removed a beer from the boat's electric powered cooler and prepared to drown his sorrows. "Guess we're stuck."

"The whole forest is going to be knee-deep in water in a few hours," Bill said.

Cracker studied the flooding shoreline apprehensively. "We need to get to higher ground while there's still time."

"Not more bloody hiking!" Slab moaned.

"We can't stay here," Cracker said. "This place will be lousy with crocs in no time."

Slab scanned the rising water irritably, knowing he was right.

"There's a high plateau up river," Bill said as he pushed the throttle forward and headed the boat away from the energy curtain.

"Then what?" Slab growled. "Sit there 'til the beer runs out?"

"It's not that bad, mate," Wal said brightly. "We've got bread, we've got onions, we've got lots of crocodiles. We can make croc burgers!"

Slab gave him an irritated look. "Shut up, Wal."

* * * *

Cougar dropped to one knee and scanned the forest ahead through his sniper scope. "There's nothing out there."

"I'm telling you," Vamp's voice sounded emphatically in his earpiece, "I've got multiple contacts, dead ahead."

Cougar performed another slow sweep with his rifle, examining every shadow. "I don't see anything. They must be invisible."

"Hold position," Beckman ordered over the radio, then motioned for Laura to follow and together they crept through the underbrush to Cougar's position. Beckman handed her his binoculars and said, “You know this country. Tell me if you see anything that shouldn’t be there.”

She gave him a doubtful look, then examined the shapes and shadows lying across their path. After a while, she shook her head. “I don’t see anything, sorry.”

“Movement!” Vamp’s voice sounded urgently in their earpieces. “Two contacts, heading right at you. Fast!”

Cougar and Beckman raised their weapons, searching vainly for targets.

“Where?” Beckman demanded.

“They’re right in front of you,” Vamp declared anxiously.

Beckman held his M16 at eye height, finding nothing, then a glint from above caught Laura’s eye. She looked up to see two shiny metal seekers falling feet first through the trees toward them.

“They’re above us!” she yelled.

The silver seekers landed either side of them. One sprayed Cougar’s face and chest with nanomembrane which immediately flowed around his head. He dropped his rifle and clawed desperately at the milky white substance as it tried to cover his mouth, cutting off his air supply.

The second seeker sprayed Laura, sending nanomachines swarming around her torso, pinning her arms to her sides as Beckman brought his pistol up. Before he could fire, the first seeker kicked the gun out of his hand with dazzling speed, then sprayed him, pinning his left arm and cocooning his legs down to the knees.

Seeing Cougar was suffocating, Beckman pulled the knife from his boot scabbard with his free hand and yelled, “Cougar, freeze!”

The sniper went rigid, then Beckman stabbed the knife into the nanomembrane trying to flow over his open mouth. Cougar gasped as he got a breath of air, then the membrane started to close again. The sniper wedged his fingers in the hole, clawing at the substance to prevent it sealing over his mouth.

Beckman turned and lunged at the nearest seeker with his knife, but it swatted the blade away, then its thin metallic fingers clamped on his ankle and hoisted him into the air, holding him at arm's length as he flailed helplessly upside down. The second seeker wrapped an arm around Laura's chest and lifted her off the ground, oblivious to her wild kicking attempts to break free. Twenty meters away, the rest of the team realized what was happening and took aim at the two machines.

"Shoot if you have a clear shot!" Hooper yelled, unable to get an unobstructed angle himself.

The two seekers bent knees and launched themselves into the tree tops with their two captives. Hanging upside down, Beckman's stomach churned as the ground fell away at a dizzying angle, while the Hooper and the others watched helplessly from below, unable to fire for fear of hitting them. The seekers caught a tree trunk and pushed off with their feet, propelling themselves sideways through the canopy toward the ground, well away from the team.

"Careful, guys," Vamp yelled over the radio as her eyes darted from the two fleeing seekers to the crystal ball. "The other contacts are still ahead."

When the seekers landed, Beckman's helmet struck the ground hard, dazing him, while Laura's captor held her high enough that her feet never touched down. Beckman blinked stars from his eyes and tried to grab his captor's metal legs while it prepared to leap again, then a thud sounded as the seeker shuddered from an impact.

Beckman thought it must have been a bullet striking the machine, then realized the team was out of range. He looked up to discover a blackened, slender pole protruding from the robot's upper torso as it regained its balance and scanned the forest, finding nothing. A second long projectile hit the machine from the other side, smashing through its thin, unarmored hip. It turned toward the new threat, momentarily detecting a shadow within a shadow, then nothing. Beckman glanced at the seeker holding Laura as another long projectile punched through its lower torso, then he realized what they were.

Spears!

The lower arm section of Laura's seeker sparked around the spear's entry point, then the machine spasmed and fell sideways, its spine severed. A compartment opened in its hip section and a cylindrical data pod popped up a meter above the fallen seeker. The tiny device spun slowly on its axis, recording the scene via dozens of miniscule black sensors pockmarking its surface. A rhythmic beat drew Beckman's attention as a spinning object sliced through the air above the forest floor and crashed into the data pod, hurling it into a tree.

Beckman searched for the source of the attack, but the forest was deserted. His seeker spasmed, dropping him on his shoulder as it fell to its knees, ejecting its own data pod before collapsing onto the ground. The little data recorder shot off into the forest, skimming the thick green foliage with increasing speed, intent on escaping to report the incident.

Bandaka stood up and crashed his nulla nulla into the cylindrical device as it sped past. The hardwood club crushed one side of the device, shorting it out and slamming it into the ground. He gave a yell in a language unrecognizable to Beckman as Liyakindirr appeared from his hiding place and gave his own whoop of triumph. Bandaka shouldered his fire hardened club and strode forward, watching Beckman and Laura struggling against their nanomembrane restraints.

"Nice club," Beckman said, eyeing the primitive weapon. "Glad you know how to use it."

Bandaka grinned a broad piano teeth smile, starkly white against his jet black skin as Hooper ran up. The master sergeant watched astonished as Liyakindirr planted a foot on one of the machines and wrenched his spear free.

"Low tech, but effective," Beckman said as he realized

Vamp's crystal ball had detected the men by the hunting knives they wore at their hips.

"Yeah," Hooper agreed as he tried cutting through the nanomembrane enveloping Beckman's torso. As soon as his blade passed through the milky white substance, it immediately flowed back together. "I can't cut this stuff," Hooper growled in frustration, then sheathed his knife. He took Beckman's arm across his shoulders and pulled him to his feet while Laura stood awkwardly, able to walk unassisted.

Bandaka recovered his spears from the seeker's torso, setting off a new series of short circuits while Liyakindirr retrieved his boomerang. They exchanged a few words in Yolngu, then Bandaka fell in behind Beckman, while Liyakindirr jogged off into the bush.

"Where's your friend going?" Laura asked.

"To get the others," Bandaka replied. His wife and daughter hid among the trees to the southwest, although they'd not seen Wanyubi since they'd fled their camp and were growing anxious for his safety.

Beckman studied the hunter as they headed back to Cougar's position. He was tall and lean, far more slender in build than an African, and his skin was dark as midnight. He wore the barest of loin cloths, and while Beckman sweated constantly, Bandaka was unaffected by the heat and humidity. He was as well adapted to his environment as any man had ever been.

"Thanks for the help," Beckman said.

Bandaka's gleaming white smile returned, revealing an infectious friendliness that took Beckman by surprise. "We lucky. The runners are thin, they got no guns."

"Have you seen other machines with guns?"

"Yeah, bigger than them two. It shot at us, but we hid." Bandaka sobered. "Can't fight that one."

Beckman and Hooper exchanged concerned looks, then Bandaka tilted his head sideways, studying Laura. "You the animal doctor, from over near Marrkalawa people?"

Laura nodded. "Yes. Have we met?"

"I am Bandaka. Saw you once. My daughter take you bird to heal."

"What's her name?"

"Mapuruma."

Laura tried to remember a young girl by that name, but couldn't place her.

Beckman studied the hunter's weapons. "How'd your spears penetrate those machines?"

Bandaka raised one of his spears for Beckman to see, indicating the blackened point. "Stone tip, wood very hard." In the same hand, he held up a paddle-like object about a meter long. "Use spear thrower." He dropped his club, then attached his spear to a notch at the end of the paddle and demonstrated how he used it.

"It's like a lever," Laura explained. "They can throw a spear two to three times further with it than by hand. It's called a Woomera. The missile test range down south is named after it."

Hooper studied the primitive weapon with growing understanding. "With the stone tip and the thrower, those spears pack a punch."

"Wood very hard," Bandaka said, showing how he could not flex it. "Fire make it harder."

"It's not steel," Laura explained, "but it is one of the hardest woods on earth."

"And those robots have thin skin," Beckman said, realizing they were fast, vulnerable scouts, built for speed not strength. What worried him was the other machine Bandaka had seen, the one they'd run from. He remembered what he'd said, *Can't fight that one*.

Bandaka scooped up his club and started walking again. The hunter considered telling Beckman about Wanyubi's warning, but they came upon Cougar before he could speak. The sniper was propped against a tree, his head and shoulders wrapped in nanomembrane penetrated by a breathing tube Xeno had inserted into his mouth to give him air. She now worked desperately to prevent the milky white substance from enveloping the breathing tube while the rest of the team had formed a defensive circle around them, watching for another attack.

"There's no way to cut this stuff," Xeno said in a brittle voice, worried she was fighting a losing battle.

Dr. McInness knelt beside Cougar and pulled at the nanomembrane experimentally, watching how it fought to envelop the sniper's face. "This behavior isn't chemical. It's programmed, perhaps at the moment it was sprayed." Dr. McInness touched the membrane with his forefinger. "It doesn't run up my hand, because it's not programmed to do that."

"So how do we get it off?" Beckman demanded impatiently.

"There must be a trigger, an instruction that turns it off."

Laura struggled against her bonds, finding she could move slightly, but if she pushed too far, the nanomembrane tightened its grip, constricting her movements. "If they're machines, can't we cut their power?"

Dr. McInness brightened. "They might be too small to have their own power supply, so … they must draw power from the environment."

"Like plants?" Laura asked. "They use photosynthesis."

"I was thinking of something more on the quantum level," Dr. McInness said absently, then realized he was over thinking the problem. His eyes widened and he exclaimed, "We need a blanket!"

Xeno retrieved a Mylar first aid sheet from her medical kit. "Will this do?"

"Let's see. Wrap it around him, tightly."

She did as she was told, completely covering Cougar's head and shoulders and holding the edges down to block out the light. Suddenly Cougar threw off the blanket and jumped to his feet, spitting the tube out of his mouth. Sliding down his shirt was a dull, metallic ooze that formed into globules and fell onto the ground creating small viscous pools at his feet.

"You were right," Dr. McInness said. "Blocking out the light cut its power supply and wiped its memory." He dived into his pack and produced a small, plastic sample box. "Hold still," he commanded as he scraped ooze into it from Cougar's shirt.

Xeno shook the remaining memory wiped nanomachines from the blanket, then wrapped Laura in it. A few seconds later, Laura pushed the blanket away.

"That stuff's disgusting," she declared, shaking globules from her clothes.

Xeno shook the blanket clean again. "Your turn, Major."

"Wait!" Dr. McInness said, placing a hand on Xeno's arm. "Major, do you mind if I conduct an experiment?"

Beckman scowled. "You're kidding?"

"One minute," Dr. McInness pleaded, "That's all."

Markus, who'd been watching proceedings curiously, added, "It could be useful intelligence."

Beckman sighed. "Make it quick."

The scientist scooped up a large blob of memory wiped metallic ooze from the ground and splashed it onto the nanomembrane imprisoning Beckman. As soon the mercury colored ooze touched the white membrane, it changed color, blending into the active nanomachines and expanding across Beckman's leg and chest.

"Hey! What are you doing?" Beckman demanded angrily.

Dr. McInness looked delighted. "Did you see that? The programmed part passed instructions to the memory wiped part."

"Get this alien crap off me, now!" Beckman ordered.

Xeno and Hooper wrapped the blanket tightly around him, then the pressure on his legs and arm vanished as the ooze slid away. While he shook it off, Liyakindirr appeared, followed by Djapilawuy and little Mapuruma. Ambling up behind them was old Wanyubi.

Bandaka smiled with relief at the sight of the tribal

elder, although the seriousness on the old man's face was unmistakable. Bandaka introduced them, then Wanyubi asked Beckman, "You boss man?"

"I am."

Wanyubi appraised him with the same doubt hardened drill sergeants had shown him when he was a first year cadet at West Point. "Go back, while you can,"

"I can't do that."

"The spirits have gone," the old man said, motioning at the shimmering energy dome overhead. "The sky is lost."

"We're going to the Goyder River," Laura said.

Wanyubi turned his attention to her. "You *balanda* women who study animals."

She nodded, remembering *balanda* was a corruption of the word Hollander, the word the Yolngu used to refer to all Europeans. It was an ancient reference to the time when the Dutch had ruled the East Indies to the north of Australia, now modern day Indonesia.

Wanyubi looked grave. "There is only death there."

"My husband's there."

Wanyubi nodded solemnly, sensing her pain.

"We could use your help," she said.

"We go to the coast," Wanyubi replied.

"You can't," Dr. McInness said, pointing at the energy dome overhead. "The way is blocked by that."

Wanyubi studied the sky and nodded, realizing it was true.

"We have weapons and training," Beckman said, "but we'd have a better chance with your help."

Wanyubi glanced at their weapons, unimpressed. "You fix the sky?"

"We'll try," Beckman said unconvincingly.

Realizing their fate was decided, Wanyubi said, "I show you something. Come, you see."

"See what?"

The old man gave him a grave look. "Where evil spirits live."

* * * *

Bill steered the fishing boat through a narrow gorge strewn with pencil-thin waterfalls. The steep rock walls formed a stifling cauldron where the still air, searing heat and buzzing insects lulled the senses. Occasionally they glimpsed the great red sandstone massif of Parsons Range in the distance, a stark splash of color beneath the translucent energy dome vaulting the heavens, then the ochre colored cliffs would close in, revealing ancient aboriginal paintings secreted beneath rocky overhangs.

As they motored up river, they searched for a landing spot, but with more than fifty crocodiles every kilometer, nowhere was safe. At the beginning of the twentieth century, creatures up to nine meters long with jaws large enough for a man to stand in had ruled these waters, then Europeans had hunted them almost to extinction. Now they were protected and were growing in size and number, ensuring it was only a matter of time before monsters once again ruled the remote northern rivers.

Eventually the gorge walls gave way to a shelving slope beneath a tree covered plateau. Bill nosed the fishing boat into the bank not far from a rocky waterfall that blocked further navigation. When the boat bumped ashore, Wal leapt off the bow and tied a line to a stunted tree, then they unloaded the camping gear and food, leaving the beer in the boat's cooler until their camp was established.

"There's a pair of eyes over there," Cracker said, nodding to a stretch of river bank hidden beneath a tangle of pandanus palms.

"Where?" Wal asked apprehensively.

"He won't bother us," Bill said, instinctively feeling for the old revolver strapped to his hip, then they carried their gear up the slope to the plateau and followed a stream inland until they found a suitable campsite.

"Whose stupid idea was it to camp up here?" Slab

growled as he flopped down beside the stream, splashing handfuls of water over his head.

"At least there are no crocs up here," Wal said brightly.

"Yeah, because crocs aren't stupid," Slab snapped.

"You could keep them company down by the river," Cracker suggested.

"Not bloody likely."

They pitched their tents, then returned to the boat for the beer and a fishing net to store the cans in the river to keep them cool, now that the ice was gone. Bill pocketed the net, then passed two cardboard boxes full of beer from the boat's freezer to Slab. He balanced one on each shoulder, about to jump off the boat, when he noticed a broad shadow gliding across the beach. He looked up to see a large rectangular craft floating silently above them. Rows of blue lights ran along its side, while a flat oval device filled the middle third of its underbelly.

"That's not from around here," Slab said, directing his companions' attention to the craft.

When it was directly overhead, the oval hatch vanished revealing two circular nozzle-like machines separated by a glowing red square. They felt the heat of a blast furnace radiate from the red square, then a pair of brilliant white beams shot down from the nozzles and locked onto the boat. The aluminum fishing boat shuddered, then the remaining beer cartons floated up out of the open cooler. One of the cartons Slab held was torn from his grip, forcing him to wrap both arms around the other. The cartons floated up inside the beams, then when they touched the red square there was a flash of light, liquefying the aluminum cans into droplets that were sucked into the craft while the beer was vaporizing in a puff of steam.

Bill felt a sharp pain in his jaw as his old metal fillings fought to tear themselves free of his teeth. Instinctively, he clamped his jaw firmly shut, then lost his footing as the boat lifted clear of the water. His revolver flew from its holster and spun up toward the harvesting vehicle, while loose change was pulled from his pockets and followed the pistol skywards.

"Jump!" Cracker yelled, backing away as the boat started to rise with increasing speed.

Bill leapt over the gunwale into knee-deep water, then remembering the half full fuel tank, began splashing toward the rocky beach, yelling, "Run!"

The others scrambled up the rocks while Slab continued to wrestle for control of his last precious carton of beer. It rose slowly into the air, lifting him off his feet as the fishing boat tilted stern up, pulled by its heavy engine toward its destruction. The line Wal had tied to a tree went taut, anchoring the boat in the air, then Slab let go and fell into the shallows.

The line parted, freeing the fishing boat to float up to the glowing contact furnace. When it touched the red square, the boat flashed into a cloud of molten droplets and its fuel exploded. When the flames cleared, the metal droplets had been sucked from the air, leaving no trace of Bill's fishing boat.

Slab picked himself up with mounting rage, half covered in mud, swearing furiously as the harvester glided silently away toward the west.

"Now we're really screwed," Bill said.

"No joke!" Slab said angrily as he stomped up the bank. "No bloody boat and no bloody beer!"

"It's like the Bermuda Triangle," Wal whispered, staring at the now empty sky.

Slab gave him an incredulous look. "There's nothing out here but crocodiles, aborigines and us," he said, wiping thick black mud from his trousers. "They'd have to be the dumbest bloody aliens in outer frigging space to land here!"

Bill started up the rocky slope. "We should see if the camp's still there."

If it was, they'd still have guns, food and fresh water, enough to survive. With unspoken agreement, they scrambled up the jagged slope.

"This is the crappiest holiday I've ever been on," Slab complained as they followed the stream to their camp. "We should have gone to Cable Beach and got smashed."

"No mate, then the wives would have come," Bill said.

When they reached their camp, they found it was untouched.

"It's all here," Wal declared happily. "We're OK."

"You bloody Pollyanna." Slab gave Wal's shoulder a back hander. "We're hundreds of kilometers from anywhere. Aliens have nicked our boat, swiped our beer and left us stranded in the middle of a million bloody crocodiles. How the hell is that OK?"

"Well, it could be worse," Wal replied.

"How?" Slab demanded.

Wal pondered the question, then replied seriously, "They could have slept with our wives."

They exchanged intrigued looks, imagining their wives being ravished by aliens, then Cracker said dryly, "If aliens saw my wife, they'd invade another planet."

"If we're back late," Bill said, "my wife will make them wish they had!"

They erupted into laughter, dropping down into the shade of the trees, then slowly felt the thirst of a Top End afternoon take hold.

"If only those bloody aliens hadn't knocked off our beer," Slab lamented miserably. "They must be cruel bastards."

CHAPTER 8

Wanyubi led the contact team west along a tree-lined ridge toward the Walker River. Occasionally, they spotted mineral harvesters in the sky, but none came close. When they neared the river, they saw a dense column of steam rising in the distance, then as the ridge angled north, they reached a vantage point atop cliffs overlooking the river.

Wanyubi knelt beside a scrawny paperbark tree and pointed to an imposing white cylindrical structure standing on a narrow strip of land between the far river bank and the sandstone cliffs beyond. The tower was at least a hundred meters high, crowned by a shallow domed roof halfway up and encircled by a series of brilliant, glowing red rings. Shimmering waves of heat radiated from the rings, partially obscuring thin horizontal vents positioned below the domed roof. Super heated steam billowed from the vents and boiled skyward, forming a white column that dissipated at high altitude.

Spaced evenly around the central structure were five, small domed buildings, each topped by a diamond-shaped object that projected a brilliant white beam at the main building's rings. All six structures were spotlessly clean and the ground they stood upon had been graded perfectly level with laser-like precision.

"Looks like a power station," Markus said, recalling images of steam rising from curved white cooling towers.

"They're long past thermal power," Dr. McInness said, unconvinced. "It's more likely to be an industrial facility of some kind."

Beckman studied it through his binoculars. "They sure built it fast."

"It's got to be prefab," Dr. McInness said. "Probably self erecting. We're planning to do something similar on Mars."

"Not the same," Markus corrected. "Mars is uninhabited."

"This is nuts," Beckman said, lowering his binoculars. "They've been watching us for thousands of years, making sure we know as little as possible about them. Why screw it up now?"

"Different club," Markus said cryptically.

Beckman nodded. "That's got to be it."

"What club?" Laura asked.

"Like the UN," Beckman said, "only not as screwed up."

"The Local Powers clearly have agreed to keep us ignorant of their existence," Markus explained, "so we don't live in perpetual fear or do something stupid like worship them as Gods."

Beckman lowered his binoculars. "Except whoever built that thing doesn't give a damn if we know they're here or not."

"They're not playing by the rules," Markus agreed. "This is way outside the norm."

"Shitty deal for us."

"There is still one peaceful possibility," Dr. McInness said. "If their ship is badly damaged, they may be unable to hide their presence, so they're using that energy dome," he said pointing skyward, "to keep us out while they make repairs."

Markus snorted dismissively. "That's a lot of ifs, Doctor, too many for my book."

"Not if that facility is manufacturing what they need to get their ship back into space," he insisted. "And if it's self erecting, it might also be self disassembling."

"That would only be true," Beckman said thoughtfully,

"if they couldn't call for spare parts or for rescue, which means …"

"They're trapped," Markus said, sensing opportunity, "a very long way from home."

Bandaka pointed to the sky to the north. "Look!"

A harvester flew in over the structure and came to a hover at the northern end. A dark hole appeared in the ground, then a stream of material poured into it from the vehicle's cargo hold. When it had unloaded, the harvester flew off to the northeast and the hole in the ground vanished.

"I'll be damned," Beckman said, "they're dump trucks."

"Which makes that structure industrial," Dr. McInness said confidently. "I'd really like to get a look inside, Major."

"Once we know what they're building in there," Markus said, "we can assess what kind of shape their ship is in."

"I agree," Beckman said slowly.

"I'm coming," Dr. McInness said emphatically. Before Beckman could protest, he added, "You may not like it, Major, but it's my job. I know more about alien technology than all of you combined – and you'll have to shoot me to stop me going."

Beckman sighed. "I guess I can't shoot you." He turned to Bandaka. "Is there a way across the river?"

Bandaka nodded. "Not far."

"Show me."

* * * *

Bandaka guided them to rocky shallows that dammed the river like a natural weir. It was hidden from the alien installation by a sandstone spur that ran almost to the water's edge, allowing them to cross unseen.

Once across the river, they hiked up a tree covered ridge separating them from the industrial complex. When they neared the ridge top, a harvester swept in low over the tree tops on its way to delivering its cargo, showing no sign of detecting them. They waited until it had flown out of sight, then continued on to a rock ledge with an unobstructed view of the alien structures.

When all eyes were on the facility, Beckman said, "See any defenses?"

There was a muted round of negatives from the team, then Hooper said what they were all thinking. "It's got to be guarded."

Markus carefully swept the facility with his binoculars, then pointed to the river side where a series of animal carcasses lay rotting in the heat. "Something killed those animals."

Beckman focused his binoculars on the dead animals, all of which had suffered horrific burns, then he searched in vain for the cause. "I don't see any weapons."

Bandaka's keen eyes studied the bodies, then he said, "I will find them."

"How?" Beckman asked.

The native hunter held up his spear and thrower. "With these."

* * * *

Bandaka and Liyakindirr had been gone for more than an hour when an emu trotted to the edge of the forest. The tall flightless bird hesitated, then a rhythmic beating of spears on woomeras sent it charging at a full sprint onto the artificial surface. It loped toward one of the small domed buildings at fifty kilometers an hour, but was quickly frightened by the glare of the energy beams and the heat radiating from the tower's glowing rings. Spooked, it changed direction, trotting toward the river then was suddenly engulfed in a ball of flame. When the smoke cleared, the flightless bird had been reduced to a smoldering mound of flesh.

Tucker whistled appreciatively.

"Goddamn!" Steamer muttered.

"Kentucky Fried Emu," Nuke declared.

"Anyone see where that shot came from?" Beckman asked.

Vamp, the only member of the team not watching through binoculars, looked up from her crystal ball. "No movement."

"I got zip," Hooper said.

Nuke, who was filling in for Virus on communications, listened to the recovered communicator. "There were no signals. I don't think it's remotely controlled."

"There was no flash, no light," Dr. McInness said, "so it's not a plasma or laser based weapon. They could be using high intensity microwaves. That would require a lot of power, so if those small buildings are power plants…"

"Right." Beckman said. "Break into teams, one team per building."

Hooper organized the spotters, then a skinny rust colored dog dashed out of the trees, avoiding the unfamiliar structures. A yell from the forest sent the skittish wild dog trotting across the clearing between the southern power plant and the central tower. The wily old scavenger skirted the nearest building, sniffing the ground, then broke into a sprint and was immediately incinerated, triggering gasps and impressed whistles from the spotters.

"Something glowed on the building closest to the river," Xeno said, "two thirds of the way up."

They all focused their binoculars on the eastern tower.

"Got it," Hooper declared. "There's a recess with a turret. It's white like the tower."

Beckman examined the location with his binoculars, finding the emplacement was equipped with a short, translucent tube-like weapon. "I see it."

"Thor might take it out," Hooper suggested, referring to Tucker's plasma cannon.

Beckman shook his head uncertainly. "It's stationary." The big special was adept at auto-selecting moving targets, but would struggle to identify an immobile gun emplacement. "Even if you could hit it manually, we've got to assume it's got counter battery capability," Beckman said, remembering another alien weapon he and Hooper had encountered in the Andes years ago, one that could locate the source of any attack and instantly destroy it. He wasn't going to risk that again.

"It might not matter," Dr. McInness said cautiously. His binoculars were focused on one of the towers to the west.

Beckman pointed to the gun emplacement to the east. "It's over there."

"I know," Dr. McInness said without reorienting his binoculars. "But it's the only one. The other emplacements are empty."

"What?" Beckman said, furrowing his brow and quickly checking the other towers as gasps of astonishment rippled down the line.

"What the hell is wrong with them?" Timer asked, amazed.

"There's a huge blind spot on the west side!" Beckman said incredulously, realizing it was why the two animals had been able to run across the facility before being killed.

"The weapon's covering the entrance to the main building," Xeno said, spotting a small recessed door at the foot of the central tower.

"It's a trap," Hooper warned.

Tucker nodded. "Those sons of bug-eyed bitches are just itching to fry us."

"Maybe they haven't had time to finish their defenses," Markus suggested.

"If it's a scientific expedition," Dr. McInness said, "They might not have many weapons."

"Either way," Beckman said, "We go in after sunset."

* * * *

The moon appeared as a blurred orb through the energy dome as Beckman's squad waited in the thermal weapon's blind spot, west of the alien facility. The glare of the five energy transmission beams bathed the area in harsh white light, denying Beckman the cover of darkness he'd hoped for. At the edge of the forest, Hooper signaled the force protection squad was in position to provide covering fire, then Beckman led his squad out of the trees.

He'd decided to ignore the power plants to save time, much to Dr. McInness' dismay, and head for the central tower. As they approached the massive structure, the roar of steam blasting from the vents assaulted their ears while the heat radiating from the thermal rings clawed at their skin and cast a dull red hue over their clothes. When they reached the foot of the tower, they found the white wall to be seamless and spotlessly clean.

Xeno shielded her face from the ferocious heat with her arm. "We'll fry if we stay here!"

They'd already scouted the tower from a distance and knew the only entrance was on the other side, guarded by the thermal weapon. It left them no choice but to blast their way in. Beckman drew his special, a smooth-skinned, silver weapon with a child-sized hand grip and a sighting mechanism intended for compound eyes. It fired a concentrated plasma charge that sliced through carbon steel like butter and had an intelligent targeting system that pushed against his hand to move the weapon to the perfect firing position.

He felt the tower's white skin with his free hand, searching for a weak spot, finding the metal surprisingly cool under the searing heat of the rings. Finding no irregularities, he stepped back and fired a single exploratory burst into the wall. The midget flashed, then a tiny hole surrounded by hairline fractures appeared in the wall.

"It's brittle," Dr. McInness said surprised. "It looks and feels like metal, but I think it's a ceramic composite."

"It'll take forever to cut through it with pinholes," Beckman said, holstering the special and drawing his 9mm Beretta. "Let's see how brittle it is."

He fired several shots into the wall in a vertical line, finding the big, slow moving slugs caused much longer fracture lines than the midget's hypervelocity particles. He nodded to Timer, who stepped forward and slammed his rifle butt into the web of cracks, multiplying the fracture lines, but the wall held.

"One shaped charge ought to do it." Timer said.

"Make it fast," Beckman ordered.

While the others moved away, Timer placed a shaped charge in the middle of the fracture lines and activated the timer. "Fire in the hole," he yelled as he ran clear.

The air shook as the explosive punched a meter-wide opening in the wall, then Beckman stepped through with his Beretta drawn before the smoke had cleared. He found himself in a corridor running parallel to the outer wall and lit by soft orange tinted light glowing from rectangular wall panels. He sniffed the air, finding it filled with the same strange odor he'd encountered inside the road builder.

Timer scowled after his first few breaths, "What's that disgusting smell?"

Dr. McInness wiped his eyes with a handkerchief as the alien air began to irritate his eyes. "It's an oxygen nitrogen atmosphere, but with traces of ammonia, sulfur and methane." He inhaled more deeply, adding. "It's breathable."

Beckman scowled. "It didn't smell this bad in the beetle."

"The road builder kept opening its rear hatch, letting in our air," Xeno said.

Beckman started down the passageway, finding once again there were no recognizable doors or controls, unaware he lacked the auditory ability to detect the sonic interfaces.

"Major," Xeno called from behind. Beckman turned to

see she was standing beside a slight recess in the wall he'd missed in the feeble light. "This remind you of anything?"

"Yeah," he said, then stepped into the recess, a twin of the elevator they'd encountered inside the road builder. A moment later, he found himself standing in a large circular room with a domed ceiling. Display screens were spaced evenly around the walls above black control panels with overly wide chairs. Embedded in the center of the floor was a large circular window glowing with light. He leveled his pistol and stepped from the elevator, finding the control room at the top of the tower was empty.

"Hiding again," he muttered to himself. "Sneaky little critters."

Dr. McInness appeared in the spot Beckman had just vacated, his face glowing with excitement. "Fascinating!"

"Virus thought it was a teleporter."

"It's a very fast elevator equipped to neutralize inertial effects. I expected something like this on a ship, but using acceleration fields in an elevator is just showing off."

"Maybe they just hate elevator music," Beckman said as he approached the circular floor window. It was composed of curved segments separated by thin metal frames. Several of the segments were cracked, while one section was filled with a metal panel that had been cut to fit the space. Beneath the window was a yawning abyss, revealing the tower was an enormous hollow cylinder. "Wow!" he said stepping back, fighting vertigo momentarily before taking a deeper look.

A circular black machine floated in the center of the chamber, halfway to the ground. Five glowing transmission beams fed it energy from the power plants outside, while a series of thin red guide beams stretched from the machine to the wall, keeping it precisely in place. The skin of the machine was laced with conduits that snaked over it like veins while antigravity panels glowed bright blue beneath it, balancing it in the air. Below the machine, swirling brown clouds boiled furiously, prevented from rising by an invisible barrier while large intakes sucked the clouds from the chamber. Illuminating it all was a brilliant white beam blasting down from the machine into the billowing cloud.

As the other team members arrived, they spread out around the circular window curiously, except for Markus who took one look then moved to the wall mounted screens. Dr. McInness paced out across the floor window with an increasingly puzzled look.

"I don't know what the hell it is, either," Beckman said.

"It's a drill," Markus said, his attention riveted to a screen depicting the central tower in profile with horizontal lines dividing the Earth's strata beneath it. Markus indicated a vertical line stretching from the tower down into the Earth. "It's drilling a very deep shaft."

Beckman approached Markus, studying the screen. "How deep?"

"If I'm reading this right, they're nearly through the crust."

"Man, if they dumped a bomb down there," Timer said, "They could smoke the whole freaking planet."

"They could do that from orbit," Dr. McInness said dismissively as he joined them in front of the display. "This is what the boreholes were for. They were looking for a location where Earth's crust was thinnest."

"Why do they want to drill through the crust?" Beckman asked.

"To reach the mantle, maybe even the core. If they're looking for minerals, the planet's core is a giant spinning iron ball, the largest mineral deposit on Earth."

"That's a lot minerals to repair one damaged ship," Beckman said, wiping his watering eyes stinging from the irritating atmosphere. He turned to the others. "Go over this place with a fine-tooth comb. Look for anything: hair follicles, scales, creepy green skin. I want to know what we're dealing with and what they're after. And be careful of those control panels, I don't want any more stretcher cases."

They dispersed to examine the control room while Beckman returned to the circular floor window. There was something about it that bothered him, but he couldn't quite decide what. He touched the window, finding it cool even though the heat on the other side must have been incredible.

"There's something outside admiring your handiwork," Markus said, motioning at a display showing a real time image of the hole Timer had blown through the outer wall.

"It's probably an automated repair unit," Dr. McInness suggested.

Beckman activated his radio. "Hooper, is there anything near our entry point?"

Hooper took a moment to reply. "There's a red, golf ball sized object floating outside the entrance. Cougar's got it sighted."

"Don't shoot," Beckman radioed, certain that destroying the probe would warn whoever was watching the transmission that hostiles had entered the facility. "Just keep an eye on it."

"Major," Xeno called from a control panel on the far side of the window.

Beckman walked over to her, avoiding the window, then she indicated the side of the control panel. The lower half was charred black and the metal had buckled. The floor by contrast was clean and smooth.

"It was damaged, before they installed it," she said. "There's another damaged panel over there."

He ran his hand over the metal which had obviously been exposed to intense heat. He stood and studied the window again, thinking, *That's what's wrong with it.* The cracks in the transparent panels and the metal sheet that had been cut to fill one segment indicated the window had been damaged. He stepped toward it, realizing one of the five energy emitters was circular, while the others were elliptical.

"This thing's jury-rigged," he said.

"I knew it!" Dr. McInness declared with obvious relief. "It is a forced landing."

"Or sloppy maintenance," Markus said.

"This is a fantastic first contact opportunity," the scientist said. "We have to help them."

"They don't want our help, Doctor," Beckman said.

Markus realized the control room showed other signs of patchwork repairs. "So we have a beached whale trapped on the ground and no one to help it," he said. "It's a gold mine, waiting to be exploited."

Dr. McInness eyes narrowed in alarm. "You can't be serious! We can't even figure out the artifacts we've got. What would we do with a mothership for God's sake?"

"Get every scientist on the planet to take it apart," Markus replied. "Advance our technology a hundred thousand years in a single century."

"You don't know what you're talking about. Even if we could figure out their science, we couldn't use it. Our industrial base is far too primitive. The Romans could never have produced a microchip, even if they knew what it was. It's impossible!"

"Are you sure?" Markus persisted. "Suppose there's a computer on board that explains how their technology works? How to build industries to make motherships? What then? All we have to do is translate their language and we've got it all."

"Tempting as that sounds," Beckman said, "stealing their technology isn't our mission,"

It's not your mission, Markus thought.

The scientist turned to Beckman. "Major, now that we know this is not an attack, we should make sure Washington understands there's no threat here, then we offer our assistance."

"That's a terrible idea," Markus said. "The last thing we should do is help them."

"They're in distress," Dr. McInness said. "If we assist them now, show them they can trust us, we could make a friend."

"Or it's a colony ship," Beckman said, "and they can't reach their destination so they've decided to set up house here."

"That's ridiculous," the scientist declared. "Earth is already inhabited."

"So were the Americas and Australia before Europeans arrived," Beckman said. "Now who's running things?"

"Call for reinforcements," Markus said. "Grab the ship. It's the smart thing to do."

"I'm not starting a war until I know who I'm fighting. And I'm not risking the short wave until I'm sure what message to send." Beckman raised his hand for silence as Dr. McInness began to protest. "You may be right, Doctor, and if you are, we'll send your message, but I'm not convinced we know enough to offer them help." He glanced at Markus. "Or to make enemies of them. Not yet."

"Found something," Timer announced from beside a featureless wall. When they turned to him, he said, "Now you see me." He took a step and vanished only to reappear a moment later.

"Where does it go to?" Beckman asked.

"A subway station."

Beckman approached the elevator panel. "We'll check it out while the others finish up here," he said, then stepped onto the floor plate.

In a blink, he was standing in a rectangular chamber hewn from the bedrock next to a row of squat machines. Orange-tinted light panels embedded in the smooth rock wall illuminated a line of transport capsules that stood facing a pair of circular tunnels. The capsules were the size of small trucks, with open hatches revealing empty cargo bays running the length of each.

Beckman drew his Beretta as he stepped cautiously into the underground chamber. A panel slid open on one of the machines to his left and a metallic cube sixty centimeters across floated out. The floor illuminated beneath the cube as it glided across the chamber, reminding Beckman of a conveyor belt without the belt. A light flashed on the far wall at the cube's height, stopping its horizontal movement, then another flickered on the left wall pushing it toward the first capsule in line. Beckman followed the cube, watching the floor glow beneath it as it drifted toward the cargo capsule. A yellow beam inside the capsule caught the metal block and placed it on a stack of identical cubes.

Markus, Dr. McInness and Timer emerged from the elevator's alcove as Beckman holstered his pistol and lifted one of the cubes.

"Heavy?" Dr. McInness asked as he approached.

"Oh yeah," Beckman said, dropping the metal block back in place.

The scientist touched the cubes curiously. "It's a mine and a smelter. The drill vaporizes everything it touches, they extract minerals from the gases and vent the waste as superheated steam. Fast and efficient."

Beckman gazed thoughtfully at the empty transport capsules and the row of refining machines along the wall. "So what's wrong this picture?"

Dr. McInness looked puzzled, but Markus said, "The scale."

Beckman nodded. "This thing is built for mass production." He frowned. "I'm sorry, Doctor, but are they trying to repair a ship or build a new one?"

"Or a fleet of them?" Markus added.

"We know their ship is huge," Dr. McInness said. "Our seismic readings told us that. What we don't know is how badly damaged it is. They might need a lot of material to repair it."

"There's obviously no chance of a rescue," Markus said meaningfully. "No chance anyone will help them if we go after the ship."

Beckman watched the row of refining machines, waiting for the next ingot to appear, but none did. "So what's taking so long? It's made one ingot since we got here."

"They haven't reached the mantle yet," Dr. McInness said. "Once they do, production will increase. If they reach the core, it would increase again."

Beckman nodded. "And where the hell are the guards? Why only one lousy gun to protect all of this, if they need it so badly to repair their ship?"

Their earpieces hissed with Hooper's voice, his signal breaking up from the interference of the surrounding rock. "Air veh … incoming … a transport."

"Acknowledged. Xeno, you get that?"

"Yes sir," she replied from the control room above.

Beckman turned toward the elevator when Hooper's voice sounded again. "It's unload– … looks … dirt."

They heard the rattle of the harvester's cargo rumbling down a chute nearby, then a cube emerged from one of the refining machines and floated across into the first transport. The capsule's hatch closed, then it floated off the ground and shot into a tunnel at high speed. Behind it, the other capsules floated forward in unison, each advancing one place in the line.

Beckman looked into the tunnel after the departed cargo capsule, now invisible in the darkness, thinking, *They just got another full load of metal.* His instincts told him he should have destroyed the capsule, preventing them resupplying until he knew what they were up to. *Too late now!*

Hooper's voice sounded again. "… dump truck's mov … north eas …"

"Understood," Beckman acknowledged as an empty transport capsule burst out of the second tunnel at high speed, came to an instant stop and joined the end of the line.

"We could use that tunnel as a short cut to the ship," Timer suggested.

Beckman shook his head. "It'd be too easy to get trapped in there."

"That was a fast turnaround," Markus observed, certain

the newly arrived transport capsule was the same vehicle that had departed with a full hold.

"We need to slow them down," Beckman said. "Timer, can you collapse the roof onto the drill?"

"What!" Dr. McInness exploded.

"If it's anything like the wall we blew in," Timer said, "no problem."

"Have you lost your mind?" Dr. McInness demanded.

"Put a few charges down here too," Beckman said, "just in case we fail to take out the drill."

Timer moved off to set explosives on every third machine.

"Destroying this installation will be an act of war. It's madness!"

Beckman turned to the scientist, suppressing his irritation. "I'm not letting them have these minerals until I know what they're using them for – and they say please."

"You'll ruin any chance we have of establishing friendly relations with them."

"If they want friendly relations with us, Doctor, they can damn well ask for them."

Dr. McInness turned to Markus. "You can't let him do this. It's insane."

Markus' face was stone. "I agree with him."

"You could be getting us into a war we have no hope of winning, of even surviving!"

"They've got a weakness," Beckman said, "and I'm not about to let them fix it until I know what they're up to. Now, do you need to be helped into the elevator, Doctor?"

The scientist glowered at him, then stormed to the gravity lift.

When he vanished, Markus said, "He's right about one thing, blowing this place up is a risk."

"I know, but if they're hostile, destroying it won't change anything and if they're friendly, they'll accept an apology."

"You could have told him that."

"I don't have to explain my orders."

"It could be for nothing," Markus said, "if they can repair it as fast as they built it."

"That depends on how many drills they've got," Beckman said, doubting there could be many.

Markus stepped onto the elevator and vanished while Beckman waited for Timer to finish, then they took the lift back to the control room.

"Time's up, people," Beckman said as he stepped off the subway elevator.

Dr. McInness watched with rising anger as Timer set shaped charges around the floor window and at the base of the domed ceiling, then placed a satchel charge in the center of the window.

When Timer finished, he turned to Beckman. "All charges are on the same circuit," he said, holding up his radio detonator. "When I hit this, the floor and ceiling will blow together, dropping the satchel with a three second delay onto the drill head. The machines in the subway are rigged to blow when the main charges trigger up here."

Beckman nodded approvingly. "Good, let's move."

Xeno and Markus disappeared onto the elevator. Beckman was about to follow when Vamp yelled out behind him. He turned to see her staring at the empty subway lift.

"Ian just went back down," she said.

"We don't have time for this," Beckman snapped. "Go get him. Knock him out if you have to. We'll wait for you at the entry point. Timer, go with her. Check he hasn't damaged your charges."

Timer and Vamp went down to the cargo terminal while Beckman took the other lift to the ground, wondering what the scientist thought he would achieve. He should have known Beckman would never let him interfere with his orders.

Eggheads! he thought as he reached ground level.

* * * *

Dr. McInness pulled a C4 charge away from a smelting machine as Timer and Vamp stepped from the elevator into the underground chamber. When he heard their approaching footsteps, he turned to them. "I'm not going to let you do this."

Timer held out his hand for the explosive. "Give it to me, Doc."

"This is madness," the scientist declared as he pulled out the detonator pin. "We can't afford to make enemies of these people."

"We don't want to hurt you, Ian," Vamp said as she circled around to his left, distracting him as Timer darted forward and punched him in the stomach. Dr. McInness doubled over, gasping for air as Vamp relieved him of the explosive and guided him to his knees.

"Breathe," she said sympathetically, tossing the C4 to Timer who began reattaching the explosives.

* * * *

"Air vehicle inbound," Hooper reported as Beckman jogged along the passageway to where Markus and Xeno stood by the hole, inhaling fresh air and wiping their watering eyes.

"Acknowledged. We'll extract when it's clear," Beckman radioed as he took a deep breath of fresh air and blinked irritants from his eyes.

"Good, huh?" Xeno said.

Beckman nodded appreciatively as Hooper's voice sounded again, "It's not a dump truck. It's heading for the top of the tower."

From his vantage point among the trees, Hooper watched a small rectangular transport circle the tower and slow to a hover. It turned its tail toward the billowing column of steam as its rear cargo door dilated and two slender seekers leapt through the steam onto the roof.

"It's dropped two runners on top of the tower," Hooper reported.

Beckman thumbed his mike. "Timer, have you got McInness?"

"Yes, sir," Timer's voice crackled back. "I'm resetting the charges now."

Beckman's mind raced, certain the two seekers on top of the tower were heading for the control room where they'd disarm Timer's explosives. "Hold your position, the control room is compromised."

"Affirmative," Timer replied.

"How are they getting out?" Xeno asked.

Beckman shook his head grimly, wondering how far below ground the subway terminal was? Five meters? Fifty kilometers? Could they survive the blast down there?

"The vehicle is landing on the east side," Hooper reported, "under the gun emplacement."

Where it's protected, Beckman realized, certain the seekers weren't a maintenance team sent to repair their entry hole. "Can we extract without being seen?"

"Negative. The golf ball is covering the entrance."

"What about the runners on the roof?"

Hooper scanned the column of steam masking the top of the tower with his binoculars. "I've got zero visibility. Enemy position unknown."

Enemy! Beckman thought, appreciating how fast Hooper had classified the seekers. "Cougar, take out the golf ball."

"Roger that." Moments later, they heard a metallic clang as his depleted uranium bullet shattered the alien sensor, then Cougar's clinical voice announced, "Target destroyed."

"The runners on the roof could be waiting for us to step outside." Markus warned.

"No, they'll protect the drill," Beckman said, wondering if the transport was carrying a combat force to cut off their escape

"You've got to do it," Markus said, guessing his dilemma.

"Do what?" Xeno asked, puzzled.

Beckman avoided her eyes, hating himself for the order he had to give.

"Do what, Major?" she demanded anxiously.

"If you wait, they'll disarm the explosives!" Markus warned.

A shocked look appeared on her face as she realized what they were thinking. "Our people are still in there!"

"I don't have a choice," Beckman snapped, then thumbed his mike. "Timer, we can't get you out. Hostiles are heading for the control room. Blow the charges in thirty seconds."

There was a moment's silence as Timer processed the order, then the combat engineer's voice sounded calmly over the radio. "Roger that, detonate in three zero seconds."

"They'll be killed!" Xeno declared angrily.

Beckman ignored her. "Head straight for the tree line. Go!"

Xeno hesitated, then seeing he'd made his decision, she clambered through the hole in the wall and ran for the trees. Markus followed, then Beckman, who looked up at the tower as he ran, searching for incoming fire, but there was none, confirming his assessment. They seekers were going for the control room.

* * * *

"Don't … do it!" Dr. McInness wheezed.

Vamp dragged the scientist his feet. "Run or die!"

"We can reason … with them," he said, resisting her.

"Not today," she said, lifting him onto her shoulder and starting for the subway tunnel.

When Timer saw where Vamp was headed, he yelled, "We'll be trapped in there."

"That's better than being killed out here," she yelled

without looking back.

"Oh crap," Timer muttered, realizing she was right.

He unclipped a grenade from his belt, pulled the pin and rolled it onto the elevator plate. It instantly vanished, carried by the gravity lift to the control room, buying them a few more seconds, then he turned and sprinted for the subway tunnel, pulling the aerial out on the remote detonator as he ran.

* * * *

When they were halfway to the tree line, Beckman spotted Steamer kneeling at the edge of the forest with a Predator missile on his shoulder, while the rest of Hooper's squad lay camouflaged nearby with their heavy weapons at the ready.

"Contact! South side," Hooper's voice sounded with professional coolness.

Beckman glanced over his shoulder as a large black machine twice the height of a man rounded the tower. The battloid floated off the ground on two glowing sleds that supported a thick armored torso, cylindrical in shape and encircled by two rings, each mounting eight flexible arms. The shorter, lower arms held silver disks while the longer, snaking upper arms were tipped with slender pyramidal weapons. Mounted atop the torso was a sensor disk sandwiched between slabs of plate armor, leaving only a horizontal slit exposed at the disk's edge.

The warning drummed into Beckman by the Groom Lake brains trust flashed through his mind: assume non-terrestrial ground forces have superior firepower, absolute precision and are impervious to your weapons. Under no circumstance engage them in the open.

This is as open as it gets, he thought bitterly, thumbing his mike. "Fire!"

Steamer had the hulking black battloid already targeted. He pressed the trigger, feeling the launcher buck as the small missile ejected on low thrust, then the rocket motor kicked over to full burn, sending the Predator streaking out of the trees. He kept the launcher's targeting reticle fixed on the battloid as the missile skimmed the ground, passing under a transmission beam between a power plant and the tower.

The battloid brought one of its disk arms up to face the missile as it exploded. The blast struck an invisible counter force radiating from the shield disk and was deflected harmlessly away as electric blue lines of energy rippled over its surface. The shield arms arranged the disks equally around the battloid, providing three hundred and sixty degree protection. After the missile detonation, the shield ring rotated, moving the shield that had taken the hit to the rear where it could regenerate in safety while the weapon arms rose like cobras to fire over the shields.

"Down!" Beckman yelled.

They threw themselves onto the smooth, spongy surface as rapid fire energy bursts erupted from the weapon's tips, rending the air with a series of hypersonic shrieks, then the energy burst began to arc down to where they lay.

* * * *

Laura watched in horror from the ridge top. "Do something!"

Nuke shook his head slowly, his face white with anguish. "I can't. I have my orders."

"What orders? To hide?"

Nuke glanced at his backpack which he had to protect with his life. If he had to choose between helping the team and saving his pack, he was under strict instructions to abandon the team. "Yes. Hide."

"Screw your orders," Laura snapped as she tore open the nearest backpack and began frantically pulling its contents out.

Nuke stood up. "What are you doing?"

"They're going to be slaughtered down there."

He stepped toward her. "We can't give away our position."

Laura spotted a squat silver pistol in the pack. Thinking it was a alien special, she grabbed it and darted out of his reach, running toward a rock ledge overlooking the mining facility.

Nuke caught her arm as she tried to aim, yelling, "That's a flare gun. It's useless."

Laura slammed her elbow into his chest, knocking him back. "It's better than nothing," she said and fired horizontally. A smoke trail shot out from the ridge top, then the flare exploded into a miniature star above the battloid.

"Now you've done it!" Nuke declared.

* * * *

The battloid's thermal sensors detected an intense heat source floating overhead. It matched no known weapon signature, but its programming automatically elevated the intense thermal contact to the top of its target list. It positioned three shield emitters above its armored sensor disk to meet the aerial threat and angled all eight energy cannons skyward. The pulse streams struck the flare simultaneously, igniting its magnesium fuel. The battloid's tactical intelligence interpreted the explosion and extreme heat as an increasing threat, compelling it to keep its weapons focused on the expanding fireball above.

"Use specials," Beckman yelled when he saw the battloid was distracted. He knew if a Predator missile couldn't punch through its shields, their other conventional weapons would be useless.

Tucker had already switched to Thor, the team's only plasma cannon, the most powerful infantry weapon ever used by man, but painfully slow to recharge. He touched the firing surface, sending a brilliant orange pulse streaking across open ground. It struck one of the battloid's shield with a dazzling flash, sending electric blue ripples flickering across the disk's surface as the shield teetered on the brink of collapse.

Before it could take another hit, the shield ring rotated again, moving the weakened shield emitter away to recharge. Hooper immediately fired Conan, the second largest special, striking an energy cannon as it peeked above the shield wall. The explosion showered the battloid with flaming hot metal and left the weapon arm swaying like a headless snake, while the other weapon arms ducked down behind the safety of the shield wall.

Beckman glanced back at the central tower, wondering why it hadn't exploded. Had the seekers disarmed the explosives and killed Timer?

"Concentrate all fire on the nearest shield," Hooper barked over the radio.

At least one of us is thinking straight, Beckman thought, once again thankful for the master sergeant's coolness in combat.

Bursts of glowing orange light erupted from the trees as Hooper and Steamer concentrated their Conan plasma rifles on the same shield. It sparked and collapsed, forcing the battloid to rotate the shield emitter away before it was destroyed.

An overloaded emitter slid past Xeno, presenting her with a gap in the combat drone's defenses. She let loose with her little Tom Thumb special, firing tiny orange spurts through the opening, striking its torso, but failing to penetrate its armor. Markus saw the opening too and fired a well aimed burst from his MP5, raking the naked emitter disk with nine millimeter slugs. The shield emitter exploded, then was rotated away as the battloid placed a fresh shield between them.

Beckman thumbed his mike. "Timer, blow the charges!" He listened for acknowledgement, but none came.

The flare overhead flickered and died, then three of the battloid's weapons peeked above the shields and fired at

Hooper's position. The surrounding forest exploded in flames, then its weapons ducked down behind its shields before they could be targeted.

"It can't shoot through its own shields," Beckman yelled to Xeno as he opened up with his midget. "Aim for its weapons."

Together, they fired at the top of the shield wall, forcing the battloid to keep its weapons down behind cover, then a weapon arm dropped to the ground and fired beneath its overlapping shields. Beckman rolled sideways as a searing blast flashed by, blistering his skin, then Xeno fired at the low angle cannon, forcing the battloid to snap its shields together as another weapon arm went high.

It's analyzing our tactics, reacting to our moves, Beckman realized, leaping away again as the raised energy weapon fired.

The clank of a machine gun sounded as a line of tracer shot out from the forest, raking the battloid's elevated weapon, forcing one cannon to duck behind the shields as another popped up and fired at the trees. The tracer fell silent as Tucker darted away into the darkness and the forest exploded in flames behind him. Somehow the former SEAL had escaped the inferno that had consumed Hooper's position and was drawing the battloid's fire to give them a chance.

Markus jumped to his feet, sprinted a short distance toward the trees, then went to ground again, holding his fire, waiting for a clear shot at the next weapon to expose itself.

He's a cool one, Beckman thought, admiring Markus' patience in the heat of battle, waiting like a sniper for a kill shot even with chaos breaking all around him. *No, not a sniper,* Beckman realized as he watched Markus sighting, *an assassin.*

Another stream of tracer erupted from the trees, then the battloid slid a weapon arm between its shields at waist height and fired, turning Tucker's new position into a firestorm. Beckman couldn't see if Tucker had escaped as a second weapon rose up and fired continuously into the forest, felling trees amidst a spreading sea of flame.

Markus sighted precisely on the joint connecting the cannon to the arm and fired a single controlled burst. The bullets severed the unarmored joint, sending the weapon spinning uselessly away. Before the severed cannon hit the ground, he was on his feet again, running to a new firing position.

Another weapon arm shot up, aiming at Markus, but before it could fire, Xeno hurled a grenade at the battloid. The elevated cannon spun toward the grenade and fired, catching it in mid air. Instead of exploding, the thick orange cloud of a smoke grenade appeared.

The battloid's sensors immediately detected the orange cloud glowing in the glare of the energy transmission beams. The strange spectral readings resembled a corrosive nanoweapon particularly effective against armor, causing the battloid to elevate the orange smoke to the top of its target priority list. It began backing away as it fired three weapons at the cloud in a desperate attempt to avoid being consumed by a metal eating nanoswarm.

It's confused, Beckman realized, unaware that the battloid was not programmed to fight a force that relied on something as primitive as smoke for signaling.

Xeno and Beckman fired at the cannon's arm joints, while Tucker opened up again with his machine gun, firing from a new position deep in the forest. When the battloid weapons ducked for cover, Beckman glanced back at the tower, knowing they were out of tricks and wondering why it hadn't blown?

* * * *

Timer was almost to the subway entrance when he heard metallic footsteps on the fused rock floor as a seeker stepped from the elevator alcove. He could see the dim outlines of Vamp and Dr. McInness ahead in the tunnel, running into the darkness. Timer estimated the distance, certain they'd survive the blast.

He'd hoped to be inside the tunnel when he triggered the explosives, but he knew the runners were too fast. He heard the clatter of metallic footsteps racing toward him, then silence as the seeker leapt into the air to close the distance.

"Fire in the hole" he yelled without looking back, then he dived toward the tunnel entrance, pressing the remote's detonation button while still airborne.

Behind him, the airborne seeker raised an arm, preparing to drive its metallic claw fist through his chest, then the Earth shook and everything went black.

* * * *

One seeker had remained in the control room to identify the purpose of the off-white material placed around the floor and ceiling. It didn't recognize the substance as an explosive, because no advanced civilization used chemicals for such purposes. It was only when it investigated the package in the center of the floor window that it realized the material relied on combustion, rather than particle annihilation, to generate a limited shockwave. Before it could compute the likely energy release, the C4 detonated.

The window shattered beneath its metal feet, releasing a wave of searing heat from the drill chamber which detonated the C4 in its hands, blowing off both its lower arms and ripping open its multilayered torso. The seeker fell into the drill chamber amid collapsing roof and window fragments, then crashed onto the drill head, cracking its sensor disk.

It struggled to stand on crippled legs as falling debris rained down around it, smashing the laser positioning sensors that kept the massive drill head aligned with the transmission beams. The impact of the collapsing roof knocked the drill out of position, letting the energy beams scour deep gashes in the drill's hull. The glowing blue gravity plates holding the drill head aloft flickered and winked out, then the excavation beam blinked off, instantly reducing the temperature by thousands of degrees and plunging the massive bore hole into darkness.

The seeker leapt off the doomed drill head toward the floor above, but a large section of falling roof slammed onto it, driving it down into the black steaming cloud toward the bowels of the Earth. Starved of power, the drill fell, allowing all five transmission beams to intersect in the center of the chamber.

Feedback instantly flashed along the beams to the power plants outside, overloading the delicately balanced magnetic fields that contained reactions hotter than any metal could withstand.

A moment later, the five power plants exploded as one.

* * * *

The flash was blinding as shockwaves were channeled through the power plant's transmission conduits at the tower, missing Beckman, Xeno and Markus, but catching the battloid side on. Its already weakened shield emitters shorted out as the robot warrior was driven sideways. Its arms flailed to prevent it being pushed off its antigravity sleds, then a section of power plant wall travelling faster than a bullet slammed into it like a supersonic sword. The battloid cart wheeled past Beckman, coming to rest on its side with its armored torso peeled open like tin foil.

Beckman's ears rang as he blinked spots from his eyes, then as his vision returned, he saw a dirty brown cloud boiling skyward from the tower's shattered roof like an erupting volcano. The battloid lay pinned on its side, its shield arms pushing against the ground while its weapon arms began cutting into the wall segment embedded in its back.

"It's still alive," Xeno said, horrified.

"It's not alive," Beckman growled through gritted teeth. "It's a goddamn machine!"

The battloid finished cutting a slab of wall from its back. When the severed segment crashed away, its shield arms began pushing the ground in an effort to right itself. Still too weighed down to move, the battloid's weapon arms cut holes in the wall section still embedded in its torso. Its weaponless arms threaded the holes and pulled the remaining section free with a metallic groan, revealing a gaping wound sparking with electricity. It dropped the metal slab, then all sixteen of its arms began pushing on the ground.

"No you don't!" Beckman declared angrily, jumping to his feet and running toward the crippled monster.

The battloid swung a shield arm at him, but he rolled under the blow and back to his feet without slowing. Holstering his special, he grabbed a grenade and leapt onto its torso, pulling the pin and hurling the explosive into the machine's open wound.

A weapon arm struck him in the chest, swatting him away like a fly. He hit the ground hard, stunned as another weapon arm snaked above him, rising like a viper about to strike, then the grenade exploded inside its torso. The weapon arm swayed dizzily, then collapsed at his feet while the other arms went limp and the massive battloid crashed to the ground.

Beckman stood slowly, wheezing from the battloid's last blow. "Now it's dead!"

He stared at the shattered tower and the five wrecked power plants burning furiously down to their foundations. The extent of the devastation surprised him, as he'd intended only to disable the mine, not obliterate it. With the mineral extraction system destroyed, the tower was no longer releasing pure steam into the air, but an acrid cloud of vaporized minerals pouring from the deepest mineshaft ever sunk into the Earth.

They won't fix that in hurry! he thought, then thumbed

his mike. “Timer, Vamp, acknowledge.” He waited a few seconds, wondering if they could possibly have survived the blast below ground, then repeated his call, but no response came.

“Steamer’s dead,” Hooper radioed weakly.

Beckman was shocked the man mountain was gone, then he realized a third of his team were dead. He started for the tree line, spotting Hooper’s profile against the fires. The sergeant was limping with one arm hanging by his side. Nearby, Tucker emerged from the shadows carrying his empty machine gun in one hand and Thor in the other.

“Steamer took one full in the face,” Tucker said bitterly. “He never had a chance.” His eyes were glazed and his jaw clenched as he fought to contain his grief and rage at the loss of his best friend.

Hooper pushed through waist-high ferns, then rested his good shoulder against a tree. The right side of his face was blackened and the skin on his right arm was badly blistered. He still held Conan, although his carbine was missing. The right side of his uniform had been burned away, exposing a partially melted Kevlar plate. He pulled the plate out, examined its twisted shape then dropped the now useless armor on the ground.

Hooper motioned to the fire burning furiously at the edge of the tree line. “Steamer’s over there, or he was. There’s nothing left.”

Beckman nodded solemnly, taking it in with a heavy heart.

Markus ran his eyes over the survivors, then studied the ruined buildings burning in the clearing. “Sergeant,” he said, “you saw one of their vehicles land on the other side, right?”

“Yeah, behind the tower.”

Markus turned to Beckman. “We need to move. There could be more of those things on the way and we’re in no shape for another fight.”

“Timer, Vamp, do you read, over!” Beckman signaled

again, but still there was no response.

"They're gone," Markus said.

Beckman scowled, knowing even if Timer and Vamp were alive, trapped below ground, he couldn't help them. It wasn't Markus being right that irritated him, it was that he took their loss so easily. Silently, he cursed Dr. McInness for being a fool and costing him the lives of two of his team. It was why he hadn't wanted civilians along in the first place.

Hooper wiped his ash smeared face. "If they hadn't blown that place, we'd all be dead."

"Yeah, that mother owned us," Tucker said, his eyes locked on the burning trees where Steamer's ashes smoldered. His grief had already hardened into a hatred that demanded revenge.

Xeno sat on the ground, head down, her face white with shock. "We are so screwed. No way we can stop machines like that."

"Hey!" Hooper barked angrily, summoning up what little strength he had left. "It's dead. You're not. Remember that."

The rebuke surprised her. She saw the determination in his eyes and realized she really wasn't a soldier. She was a scientist in khaki not meant for violence like this.

"You did good out there," Beckman said, sensing her uncertainty. "Popping that smoke grenade was smart. I wouldn't have thought of it." She looked surprised. "The only way we're going to beat those things is with brains, not firepower. We need you."

She took a deep breath, gathering her strength and nodded. "You can count on me, sir."

"I know I can."

"We can't stay here," Markus said, scanning the sky for more transports.

Beckman studied Hooper's burns warily. "Can you make it?"

"Yeah," the sergeant said weakly, standing straight.

"Let's move," Beckman said, starting up the ridge to where the others waited.

Soon, a dirty brown rain began to fall as water trapped deep in the Earth's crust since the planet's creation rose as steam and cooled. By the time they reached the others, the rain had become a deluge, extinguishing the fires and soaking the land in primordial waters.

* * * *

Timer opened his eyes to impenetrable blackness, unable to move, cocooned inside smooth, cold rock. A hissing sound shattered the silence as a flare ignited beyond his head revealing how the subway tunnel had folded over him like a blanket. The molecular bonding that knitted the wall together had refused to tear, both protecting and enveloping him.

"I can hear breathing," Dr. McInness said uncertainly.

Timer heard hurried footsteps, then Vamp's hands locked around his shoulders and dragged him free. "You alive?"

He stretched slowly, discovering his body was a patchwork of aching muscles, but no broken bones. "Yeah, but you'll have to carry me."

"In your dreams," she said, then thumbed her mike. "Major, do you read me?" Long seconds of silence passed. "Beckman, this is Vamp, acknowledge."

"They can't hear you," Dr. McInness said. "There's too much rock blocking the signal."

"Yeah," she said, examining how the smooth tunnel roof pressed flat against the floor, pinching off the entrance. Unlike a simple cave-in, the subway's elastic walls had not broken, but had sagged under the weight of millions of tons of rock now separating them from the surface.

In the sharp light of the flare, a twitching movement caught her eye. She unslung her M16 and aimed it at long silver fingers clawing at the tunnel floor close to where

Timer had lain. Her eyes followed a tubular arm, past a sensor disk to where the ceiling crushed it against the floor.

"They don't quit, do they?" Timer said.

"Neither do we," she said and fired a burst into its sensor disk, then its fingers spasmed and ceased moving. "Got any more C4?"

"No, only a couple of grenades." The rest of his explosives were in his pack on the ridge with Nuke, while his rifle was buried back in the tunnel entrance. All he had left was his special, still in its holster.

"Ammo's the problem," Vamp said, knowing they carried emergency rations and water for twenty-four hours.

"Ammo?" Timer laughed, abruptly stopping when his bruised ribs complained. "What are we going to shoot down here?" The flare sputtered and went out, returning the tunnel to absolute blackness. After a moment, Timer asked apprehensively, "Got another?"

"One more. I'll save it."

"For what?"

She pulled him to his feet by his Kevlar vest and turned him toward a pin prick of light in the distance. "That."

"No way," he said, thinking the longer he focused on the light, the further away it seemed.

"Start walking."

"So we're just going to stroll in there and say, 'Yo, aliens! What's happening?'"

"Got a better idea?"

"We just blew their shit to hell!" Timer exclaimed.

"We'll say sorry."

"Sorry might work," Dr. McInness said.

She released Timer and started toward the distant point of light.

"Man, this is really going to suck." Timer muttered as their footsteps moved away. He sighed, and started limping after them. "Hey, wait up!"

CHAPTER 9

Nemza'ri had known from her first breath since landing that the great ship had been holed. The warm, humid air flooding every corridor was breathable, even if tainted by a strangely intoxicating fragrance she did not recognize, for she'd never smelled eucalyptus. Her olfactory implants told her the fragrance was biological and harmless, although its presence warned of the extent of the damage. Nemza'ri wondered why the ship's automated repair drones had not already sealed the breach and repressurized the hull. Had the damage been too great or had the Command Nexus, with its inexplicable loss of judgment, simply failed to coordinate the repairs effectively?

Whatever the explanation, she knew her first duty was to the safety of the ship. Using the life pod's command terminal, she'd located the nearest damage control center eighteen decks away. The grav lifts were inoperable, forcing her to make a series of dangerous climbs through unlit transit shafts and navigate a maze of darkened corridors using only her biosonar. It was a journey made more difficult because the acoustic identifiers in the walls and the ship's position locater system were dead.

When Nemza'ri reached the damage control center, she found the acoustic beacon above the access hatch was active, giving her hope the center's organic power supply was still working. She pinged the bulky hatch and was relieved to see it dilate, then entered a large rectangular chamber lit by the glow of two large wall screens. To her surprise, she found all of the center's bulky heavy lift suits were still in their racks rather than out leading the repair work. In an emergency, they would normally be in constant use. The fact they were sitting idly in a damage control station filled her with unease.

She approached the screens, finding one hissing with static, overlaid with symbols indicating the command net – the complex mix of communications and sensors monitoring the life of the massive vessel – had failed. The other screen displayed damage reports from all over the ship, reports that had not been updated for many days. As she skimmed them, one caught her attention, filling her with horror.

The stasis sleep system had suffered a catastrophic malfunction!

She pinged the screen to display all reports from the sleep chamber, but found no recent updates. It was enough to tell her the command net had failed when the sleep chamber had called for help. She wondered if the Command Nexus' inability to save the ship's inhabitants had caused a reality-rationality break in its awareness. Such failures were rare, but not unknown.

Nemza'ri felt an urge to rush to the nearest heavy lift suit and race to the heart of the ship, but her training held her back. She pinged the screen, recalling all damage reports and was shocked to discover there were over a hundred and seventeen thousand of them! Her implants scanned them all in a matter of minutes, updating her memories with information related to critical systems and ignoring the rest. When she'd finished, the scale of the cataclysm was fully apparent to her.

Her review complete, she climbed into a heavy lift suit with a sense of hopelessness and waited for it to seal around her. It connected to her implants via her nervous system, becoming an extension of her body, allowing her to hold an eggshell without cracking it or bend neutronium bulkheads like melted plastic. A wide oval section of the helmet in front of her face became transparent as the suit began feeding a visual overlay directly into her mind, then she activated the suit's exterior lights and headed to the sleep chamber.

Nemza'ri forced herself to proceed calmly, even though she was driven by a desperate desire to rescue as many as she could. The damage reports had left her in no doubt as to the magnitude of the disaster and the unlikely possibility of finding survivors. The knowledge filled her with a terrible dread as she finally grasped her fate.

She was alone.

CHAPTER 10

Bandaka led the team up the rugged eastern slope of Parson's Range in darkness and rain, following an ancient track used by his people for tens of thousands of years. When they reached the plateau, they could see the five glowing calderas down by the river, all that remained of the destroyed power plants. There was no sign of alien activity, even though Beckman had expected at least a reconnaissance mission if not a punitive strike to punish those responsible for the destruction.

"Where are they?" Xeno asked.

Nuke pointed to the smoking ruin below. "Those wimp ass aliens got the message, there are serious bad asses on this planet!"

"Maybe," Beckman said unconvinced. Determined to get well away from the mantle mine, he had Bandaka guide them deeper into the forest until Hooper could go no further. When he finally called a halt, Xeno tended the sergeant's burns as best she could and threaded an intravenous drip for Virus who remained unconscious on his makeshift stretcher.

Beckman approached Nuke who was fiddling with Virus' communications gear. "Anything?"

"The short wave is dead."

"Are they jamming us?"

"No, there's just nothing out there." Nuke glanced up at the starless sky. "I'm betting that dome blocks radio waves." He held up the recovered communicator. "On the other hand, this thing is going nuts. The traffic is increasing by the hour."

"Talking about us, no doubt," Beckman said.

Nuke shrugged. "Whatever they're saying, there's a lot more of them saying it than a day ago, and they don't care who's listening."

"Keep me posted," Beckman said, then returned to his backpack to eat a dehydrated ration pack, while nearby the others were engaged in muted conversation.

Laura said, "I used to think all this UFO stuff was some kind of mass psychosis."

"That's how we like it," Markus said wryly. "Only crackpots see UFOs and while there's no evidence, that's how it'll stay."

"And you discredit what evidence there is," Xeno added as she returned to her pack.

"We don't have to do much," Markus explained. "They don't want to be seen. If they did, we couldn't stop it. One landing on the White House lawn would take care of that."

"There are photos," Laura said. "I just never believed them."

"Of blurry, out of focus blobs," Markus said. "You can thank automatic cameras for that. They can't handle the extremes of light and dark, especially at night. They'll always over expose a brilliant light against the night sky. Saves us a lot of work."

"It helps that the light's not coming from the ship's hull, but from the air around it," Xeno said. When she saw Laura's confused look, she added, "Their ships are surrounded by propulsion fields that ionize the atmosphere. That's why they glow at night."

Markus suppressed a yawn. "We say UFOs don't exist because there are so many cameras out there and no good photographs. Simple, yet believable."

"You make it sound like a game," Laura said.

"It's no game," Markus replied soberly. "The truth is we made a big mistake."

Laura looked confused. "We did?"

"We dropped the big one much sooner than we should have. It got the attention of the Local Powers." Markus nodded toward the night sky where the real great powers were. "They'll let us have our wars, but nuclear weapons is pushing the envelope. Before 1945, there weren't many UFOs here. Earth was a back water. Once we started nuking cities, sightings went through the roof. It took a couple of years for them to get set up. I'm talking bases, people, equipment. They've got logistics to manage, just like us. By 1947, they were here in strength and have stayed ever since."

"If I were them," Beckman said, "I'd be watching us too."

"Are they frightened of us?" Laura asked.

Markus shook his head. "Suspicious, contemptuous maybe, but not afraid. They're monitoring us so they know how close we are to getting out there, where we could really make a nuisance of ourselves."

"We're too warlike," Xeno said.

"They don't trust us," Beckman added.

"But we haven't had a major war in decades," Laura said, "a world war I mean."

"You don't remember World War Two," Markus said, "but it's not your memory that counts. It's theirs. A thousand years ago our life span was thirty-five years. Now it's eighty or ninety. In a thousand years, it'll be over a hundred and fifty. The more advanced you get, the longer you live, and we've got good intel that alien life spans are measured in centuries. They remember our world wars, dozens of small wars, tens of millions of people killed, our cities fire bombed and nuked. That's their personal experience of us today. Not what they've read in history books. What they saw. You know what that means?"

"Yeah," Beckman said, "the sky is full of old people in spaceships."

"It means," Markus said, "we need a thousand years of peace, without war, genocide or nukes before we're no longer dealing with beings who've seen our barbarism first-hand. We may forgive and forget, but everyone watching us remembers."

"You paint an ugly picture of us, Mr. Markus," Laura said.

"I'm just trying to see us from the other side."

"We are what we are," Beckman said. "If they don't like it, they can kiss my hairy butt and go back to Alpha Centauri or wherever the hell they come from. If we want to nuke ourselves into the stone age, that's our business."

"It's that kind of attitude that's got us under the microscope," Markus said.

"Suppose we scrapped our nuclear weapons," Laura said, "and had a thousand years of peace, what then?"

"Depends where our technology is at," Markus replied. "You don't see the US rushing to establish diplomatic relations with remote South American tribes living on roots and dirt, do you? What would be the point?"

"Depends if they had oil," Beckman said dryly.

"We don't have the kind of oil they're interested in," Markus said. "Open contact with alien civilizations will be the most difficult experience the human race will ever have. We think we're the center of the universe, top of the food chain, but we're not. We're trained to think once we get interstellar travel, we'll be out there playing a leading role, uniting the galaxy or some such nonsense. Our big psychological challenge will be dealing with the fact that we'll never be center stage. That role was cast millions of years ago."

"We'll get a bit part," Beckman said, "if we're lucky."

"We'll be more advanced then," Laura said.

"So will they," Markus said. "No matter how far we advance, they'll still be ahead us, maybe advancing at a faster rate than us, widening the gap. We'll never catch up. We should be thinking about how we can craft a small peaceful place for ourselves, where we'll be accepted, where we can go where no *Homo sapiens* have gone before, unarmed and wary of treading on anyone's toes. Leave the phasers and photon torpedoes at home, because they'll just make people out there mad at us and will be useless anyway."

"People like you want us to roll over and play dead," Tucker said as he scraped his knife on a whetstone. "Not me. I'm nobody's doormat, no matter how advanced they are."

"That's because you haven't accepted our place in the universe," Markus said.

"Why not educate the world now?" Laura asked. "Get people ready for it."

"No need," Markus said. "We're a long way from open contact."

"We need to learn to get along with each other," Xeno said, "before we have any hope of getting along with thousands of alien civilizations, all more advanced than us."

"Try telling that to the zealots," Beckman said, then turned to Laura. "Groom Philosophy 101. Once aliens exist, God will have a few questions to answer. Like, is man made in the image of God, or is ET?"

"That's easy," Laura said. "Woman is made in the image of God and man is there to take out the garbage."

Markus smiled. "The tough question for the zealots will be, does ET have a soul?"

"Surely scientific civilizations are well past spiritualism?" Laura said.

"You're an atheist?"

"I believe in what I can put under a microscope. I'm prepared to believe in God, if he'll give me a blood sample."

"Would you be surprised to know," Markus asked, "that we have reports of extraterrestrials indicating they have spiritual beliefs?"

"I would. Maybe they're not as far ahead of us as you think."

"One day," Markus said, "we'll have to face the possibility that man is just one of millions of species that have a spiritual nature. If we have a soul, ET does too. You see, we're not just interested in their technology, we're also trying to figure out how they tick. That's why we have philosophers on the payroll as well as physicists."

"So where does that leave religion?" Laura asked.

"If you believe Christ is our planet's World Savior," Markus said, "then it stands to reason every inhabited planet has its own World Savior, who will teach them what they need to know. Those teachings may not work for us, but they'll work for them. The moral of the story is there are no nukes or missionaries in outer space. Which is why they haven't landed here to teach us their religions or conquer us. And that's why if we ever get out there, we can't expect to convert other species to our beliefs."

Beckman glanced at his watch, surprised to discover dawn was barely four hours away. "It's late and we've got a long trek tomorrow. Better get some rest."

While the others stretched out to sleep, Laura's mind continued to tick over for a long time, wondering just how far behind Earth's neighbors mankind really was. She fell asleep thinking she wouldn't like the answer.

* * * *

The drop ship approached Tindal Air Force Base at mach eight, undetected by the base's air traffic control radars and missile batteries. The multiple radar signals were absorbed by the craft's perfectly non-reflective hull, which was optimized to avoid detection systems far more advanced than radar.

The drop ship raced above the eucalypts as it completed its tactical analysis. Crude chemical explosives were stored in multiple locations, but it was the concentration of enriched Uranium-235 that had drawn it to the area. While nuclear explosions lacked the focused destructive power of quantum weapons, they nevertheless posed a threat that could not be ignored. Near the fissile material, the drop ship identified more than two hundred aircraft that relied on air flowing over curved wings to generate lift, rather than the far more effective propulsion field technology it used. Unable to determine their role, it assumed the flimsy craft were decoys camouflaging a genuine threat, supporting the Command Nexus' overall assessment that the inhabitants were conducting deception operations with primitive technology.

The drop ship passed over the perimeter fence at 4.13 AM, decelerating in a fraction of a second to a complete stop. A hundred meters away, a four-man Royal Australian Air Force air field defense squad looked up in amazement. The craft's approach velocity had been so high, and its deceleration so rapid, it seemed as if a brilliant ball of white light had simply appeared out of nowhere inside the south east perimeter fence.

The squad leader fumbled frantically with his radio. "Foxtrot Four to Tower. There's something in the air, inside the fence!"

"It's probably the moon," a bored control tower officer replied.

"It's not the bloody moon!" the corporal yelled back as his three companions covered the object with their rifles.

"What does it look like?"

"A ball of light," the corporal replied, unaware the glowing spherical field hid the drop ship's rectangular shape. "It's about twenty meters across."

The air traffic controller sighed skeptically. "Mate, there's nothing on radar."

"Screw the radar. Look out the bloody window!"

Fifty meters from the defense squad, the operators of a rapier missile battery struggled unsuccessfully to get a radar lock. On the far side of the runway, an American patriot battery couldn't get a lock either, so they fired by line of sight, hoping for in-flight acquisition. The missile got halfway to the target before its rocket motor inexplicably cut out and it nosed into the ground and exploded.

The control tower finally spotted the ball of light in the distance, then sirens began wailing across the base as startled Australian and American crews raced to their Super Hornets, Lightning IIs and Raptors dispersed through hardstands east of the runway. Each hardstand was covered by a curved metal roof and flanked by revetments to shield the parked aircraft from bomb blasts. Not far from the aircraft shelters, army crews ran to Tiger and Apache attack helicopters. Gradually, turbines began to whine and rotors began to turn, but it was all too slow.

The drop ship's rear hull dilated and a heavily armored battloid floated out, unseen inside the ball of light. As soon as it cleared the transport's hull, it dropped through the glowing propulsion field to the ground. The spherical light above the battloid seemed to vanish as the drop ship accelerated away, only to instantly reappear half a kilometer further along the runway. A second battloid emerged, then the ball of light disappeared again as the drop ship climbed to geosynchronous orbit where, safely beyond the reach of ground based weapons, it fed orbital intelligence to the two armored robots.

The Mark II battloids, with improved shields and weapons, floated toward the dispersed aircraft and the men trying to get them aloft, while the drop ship jammed the base's communications and scanned a circular zone ten kilometers across. Over the next few billionths of a second, the two machines on the ground and the drop ship high above confirmed priorities, allocated responsibilities and agreed tactics, then they opened fire.

The first battloid blasted the patriot battery, turning it into a blazing inferno. On its flank, the RAAF air field defense squad opened up with their assault rifles. Their bullets flashed uselessly against the machine's shield wall, alerting it to the presence of their feeble kinetic weapons.

The battloid knew a Mark I had been destroyed hours before and such weapons had played a part. It immediately reordered its targeting priorities to ensure all kinetic weapons would be rapidly eliminated, then the four soldiers and the rapier missile battery vanished in a wall of fire.

The black battloid then advanced as its energy cannons incinerated fighter jets in their hardstands and detonated the bombs slung beneath their wings. Flaming shrapnel from the explosions cut flight and ground crews to pieces and flew high into the air before raining destruction upon nearby aircraft and buildings.

Across the runway, an Apache climbed into the air and raked the second battloid with its thirty millimeter chain gun. The battloid's shields flashed, then one of its weapon arms popped up above its shield wall and fired. The gunship exploded and crashed onto the concrete apron, its spinning rotors carving a bloody swath of destruction through nearby ground crew and choppers alike. The battloid blasted the other helicopters with all of its weapons simultaneously, igniting fuel tanks and rockets and scattering dead and burning bodies.

With the aircraft reduced to blazing hulks, the battloids approached the buildings housing the base's equipment and weapon stockpiles. Air field defense personnel fired small arms, rifles and machine guns, while glowing energy streams laced the air, cutting them down. A squad of US Marines managed to launch a shoulder fired javelin missile, but the battloid shot the missile out of the air, then the marines vanished in a sea of flame. The two massive armored combat drones swept on through the fires, gliding over charred corpses, destroying bunkers and incinerating buildings, determined to leave nothing standing.

A US air force general carrying a briefcase chained to his wrist and a colonel holding a small tool set ran to an isolated building surrounded by army trenches and razor wire. The building stood alone, beyond the end of the runway, far away from the operational areas of the base. The soldiers guarding it knew the officers by sight, but still took a moment to glance at their IDs. Once past the checkpoint, the officers ran inside to where thirty nuclear-tipped missiles sat on carriages ready for transport to strike aircraft that no longer existed. The weapons had been brought in at tree top level from the south the day before, after having undergone rapid deployment from their storage facility in the US.

The colonel unscrewed a panel on the first missile, while the general keyed open the security locks on his briefcase. There'd been no Presidential order, no agreement of governments, but they had standing instructions not to allow these weapons to fall into enemy hands. The general pulled out a red folder, glanced at the serial number on the side of the missile and looked up its arming code.

The thunder of explosions and the chatter of automatic fire grew louder as the battloids approached and regular and special forces fought vainly against an enemy they could not match.

"Got it," the colonel said, as he pulled the panel clear. He was sweating as much from fear as from the rising heat, but he was determined to carry out this last order.

The shock waves from nearby explosions shook the building, then a searing energy beam tore through the metal walls. The general winced at the heat, but didn't waste time looking up. Instead, he read out the arming code in a clear and methodical voice while the colonel typed in the long alpha numeric series. When the colonel finished, a red light activated forming the word ARMED.

"Set the timer to zero seconds," the general said.

The colonel carried out the order. "Done."

"Let's see how these sons of bitches like fifty kilotons," the general said, knowing he was about to die.

Together, they reached for the fire button, their last act. Before their fingers touched the control, a scorching energy stream swept through the dormant nuclear weapons, incinerating them both. Radioactive material from thirty exposed cores scattered across the floor as the roof collapsed and the building was engulfed in a fire storm so hot, steel burned like paper.

Seven minutes after the drop ship had appeared, the two battloids ceased firing. The base and its aircraft had been destroyed and its small arsenal of nuclear weapons neutralized.

There were no survivors.

* * * *

The point of light marking the tunnel exit seemed as far away as ever. The tunnel was clear of obstructions, but their progress was slow because they had to feel their way through the darkness. Vamp and Dr. McInness walked together while Timer lagged behind, checking his radio every few minutes, hoping to find an alternative to heading into certain captivity.

"You're wasting power," Vamp complained.

"Either the batteries are dead or we are," Timer said.

"We'll have some explaining to do," Dr. McInness said, "but they won't boil us in oil."

"They'll chop us up like bugs," Timer declared pessimistically.

"They already know how the human organism functions, probably better than we do. And anyone advanced enough to get here should have highly evolved legal and ethical standards. Torture will certainly be unacceptable to them."

They walked on in silence, then Vamp asked, "How do you think they got here?"

"Wormholes?" Timer suggested.

"I very much doubt it," Dr. McInness said. "They're not practical or stable."

"They got here somehow," Vamp said.

"If I had to guess, I'd say the clue lies in inflation."

Timer blinked. "You want to increase the price of space travel?"

Dr. McInness chuckled. "Not that kind of inflation. I'm talking about what happened to the universe immediately after the big bang. It expanded very rapidly, much faster than the speed of light. It shows two points can move apart at superluminal velocity by stretching spacetime itself. That's the key."

"How would that work for a ship?" Vamp asked.

"An inflationary drive would have the ship remain stationary inside a bubble of local flat space. The ship itself doesn't move, so the crew wouldn't experience acceleration and there'd be no relativistic mass effects, no time dilation, no problems trying to go faster than the speed of light. Spacetime would contract in front of the flat space bubble and expand behind it. The bubble surfs on an expanding wave of spacetime, potentially travelling many times the speed of light, even though the ship itself isn't moving."

"Space surfing," Timer said thoughtfully.

"Einstein's equations support this model, but we'd need to generate huge quantities of energy and have a good supply of exotic matter to make it work, neither of which we have, plus we'd have to figure out how to generate the flat space bubble itself."

"These guys up ahead must have figured it out," Vamp said. "Maybe they can explain it to you, then you can explain it to us."

They couldn't see the scientist's face in the dark, but it beamed with hope. She'd hit upon his deepest desire.

* * * *

"Emergency action message incoming," Chief of the Boat Joe Paxton declared as the printer kicked to life.

Captain Bourke, commander of the nuclear powered cruise missile submarine *USS Michigan*, watched the coded message print out. He stood in the sub's nerve center, surrounded by crewmen seated at their consoles, aware something strange was happening topside. The *Michigan* had been on alert ever since they'd been ordered to make a high speed run across the Java Sea, through the Sunda Strait into the seas north of Australia. There'd been no explanation, yet the urgency and secrecy of the directive had been clear. The boat was now at its highest state of readiness, although the skipper was still unsure if this was a drill or something more serious.

When Paxton retrieved the EAM from the printer, the skipper glanced at Commander Thompson. Keeping his voice relaxed to mask his tension, he said. "Break out the code book, XO."

"Aye sir," the boat's executive officer said, turning to the stainless steel safe containing the boat's most secret documents.

While the XO retrieved the launch codes, two officers translated the EAM into plain English. When they'd finished, they presented themselves to the captain. Lieutenant Biddle, the communications officer, and Ensign Caldwell both fell into the rigid formal speak of the decoding procedure.

"Message seven, sir," Lieutenant Biddle reported in a clipped Bostonian accent.

"Report message seven," the XO said from the captain's side.

"Report message seven, aye sir," Biddle replied crisply. "Captain, message seven is valid and requires authentication using code ID golf, lima, delta, oscar, tango."

Captain Bourke leaned forward to study the EAM verification code a moment, then nodded. In practiced unison, all four officers read aloud the nine word verification code, checking each word with the greatest of care.

When they finished, Lieutenant Biddle said, "Captain,

the message authenticates."

Ensign Caldwell added, "I concur, sir, the message authenticates."

Commander Thompson nodded, "Captain, I concur, the message authenticates."

A cold chill ran down the skipper's back as he declared, "The message is authentic. Action directed?"

"Captain," Lieutenant Biddle began. "Message seven directs Michigan to launch a Tomahawk nuclear missile at the site specified in the message. The launch window opens at zero five hundred local time and closes at zero five fifteen." The lieutenant then read off the latitude and longitude of the target site.

"Very well," Captain Bourke said, "obtain the captain's key from the captain's key safe."

"Obtain the captain's key from the captain's key safe, aye sir," Lieutenant Biddle replied with rigid formality.

The skipper picked up the intercom microphone, and announced to the ship, "Now hear this, this is the captain speaking. Authorized entry into the captain's key safe has been granted. Disregard all captain's key safe alarms." The entire procedure had taken only minutes to perform, as carefully choreographed as the finest ballet. Now properly completed, it had unlocked the use of tactical nuclear weapons.

While the two junior officers went to retrieve the captain's key, the skipper and the XO pored over a map of the region, carefully plotting the coordinates with a grease pencil.

"It's just jungle," the XO whispered, confused.

Captain Bourke furrowed his brow. "The Australian Government must have agreed to this." But why would they? There was absolutely no reason to fire a nuclear weapon at empty wilderness. It made no sense.

"Should we seek confirmation?" the XO whispered.

There was a nagging doubt in the captain's mind, yet all his years in the service told him he had to proceed. He shook his head slowly. "The message is authentic. We launch as ordered." Bourke knew his only duty with such an order was to execute it immediately, without hesitation.

The click of footsteps on the metal deck signaled the return of the two junior officers holding the chord attached to the captain's key. Once again, Lieutenant Biddle recited his part of the procedure, exactly as he'd been trained to do.

"Captain sir, entry into the captain's key safe is complete. We have obtained the captain's key."

"I concur, sir," Ensign Caldwell added in accordance with procedure.

"Very well," Captain Bourke said, then the two junior officers deposited the key into his hand. "I accept custody of the captain's key."

Once the captain had possession of his key, Commander Thompson said, "Captain, I recommend battle stations missile."

"Very well," Bourke said, "Officer of the Deck, man battle stations missile."

The Officer of the Deck repeated the order over the intercom, "Man battle stations missile."

A series of commands rang out through the boat as the *USS Michigan* shifted to a war footing.

Master Chief Paxton announced, "Con, Chief of the Boat, prepare to hover at normal launch depth."

The captain checked the coordinates one last time. "The target is verified as correct," he said. *But how can it be?* He wondered, then pushed the thought from his mind and focused on the chain of command, his duty and his trust in the code authentication procedure.

"The target is verified as correct, aye sir," the weapons officer replied, then retrieved the missile control key from a nearby safe and handed it to the officer seated at the missile launch console.

The *Michigan* carried the high yield, one hundred and fifty kiloton version of the sub launched Tomahawk land attack missile. She'd fired conventionally armed Tomahawks against littoral targets before, but never a nuke. In the midst of his anxiety, Captain Bourke was struck by the thought that this was the first time in history a submarine would launch a nuclear weapon in anger.

Finally, the weapons officer confirmed the missile was ready for launch, then read out the firing solution. "Bearing one seven four degrees, range to target, seven hundred and twelve nautical miles."

The captain swallowed, then took the intercom. "Weapons con, the firing window is open, you have permission to fire." He said a silent prayer, then turned his key.

"The firing window is open, you have permission to fire, aye sir," came the precise response as the weapons officer turned his key.

The Tomahawk was expelled from the sub in a bubble of highly compressed air that carried it to the surface. When it burst out of the sea, onboard sensors detected the missile start to fall back toward the water, then its rocket motors burned to life. Moments later, it was streaking over the calm blue Timor Sea at high subsonic velocity.

"One away," the weapons officer announced as he watched the telemetry, satisfied it had been a perfect launch.

Over the intercom, the captain announced, "Weapons con, permission to fire is removed."

"Aye sir," the weapon's officer replied. "Permission to fire is removed."

"Secure from battle stations missile," Captain Bourke said. His hands were sweating, his heart beating, although the crew would never have guessed. In his mind, one question burned.

What the hell am I attacking?

* * * *

Laura woke to the sound of rustling backpacks, hushed whispers and sleepy yawns. It was still dark except for the glimmer of dawn on the eastern horizon. She sat up to discover the aborigines had returned, having slept a safe distance from the camp in case the soldiers were attacked during the night.

Xeno tossed Laura a ration pack. "Here, try some dehydrated, calorie dense boot leather for breakfast."

"Thanks," Laura said, then tentatively tore open the ration pack.

Suddenly, the western horizon flashed from darkness to brilliant white filling the forest with a harsh light. The dome became instantly visible as vibrating waveforms rippled across its surface near the horizon and reached two thirds of the way up its side before petering out. Beyond the energy wall, a glowing mushroom cloud rose into the sky, slowly fading from sight as the dome melted back into the darkness.

"Arma-freaking-geddon!" Tucker declared.

"That's torn it," Cougar said.

"Oh shit," Nuke muttered as a thought struck him, then he snatched up the headphones and anxiously listened to the alien communicator.

Markus wiped sleep from his eyes, unable to look away. "It detonated outside the dome."

"That was a nuke?" Laura asked incredulously.

Beckman stared at the sky. "I'd say it was a hundred, maybe a hundred fifty kilotons."

"Had to be a Tomahawk," Markus said, "judging by the low angle detonation."

"We must be in serious trouble to go nuclear so fast." Beckman said.

"Why'd the aliens let it detonate?" Markus wondered. "Even flying nape-of-the-earth, they could have taken it out before it hit the shield."

Beckman glanced up at the still intact dome. "They either didn't see it coming or they're showing us how tough they are."

Tucker grunted in disgust. "So much for dropping the big one."

"I can still hear their chatter," Nuke said relieved, looking up. "I don't know how, but the EMP didn't fry our gear." He put the communicator down and opened his backpack, being careful to use his body to shield its contents from Laura.

Xeno checked her notebook computer and video camera. "Same here. My electronics are good."

Markus whistled. "So the shield lets in light, but can stop an EMP in its tracks. Impressive."

"Stop a what?" Laura asked.

"An electromagnetic pulse, a blast of radiation from the explosion that's death to electronics," Nuke said absently, his attention focused on the contents of his pack.

Beckman watched Nuke anxiously. "What's the payload status?"

Nuke looked, relieved. "All good."

Beckman relaxed as a grim expression appeared on his face. "Then it's up to us."

Laura sensed a change in attitude of those around her, from despair to resolve. She leaned sideways, glimpsing the contents of Nuke's pack. She saw a keypad and digital display sitting on a silver metal housing containing a glistening black ovoid snugly wrapped in black foam. Glowing in green lettering on the display panel were the words "Diagnostic Mode" and below it a list of tests all marked with "100%". When Nuke saw her staring at the device, he pulled the pack's flap over the top of it.

"What is that?" she demanded. When no one answered, she turned to Beckman. "Major?"

"It's a weapon," Beckman replied.

"What kind of weapon?" she asked suspiciously.

The soldiers exchanged knowing looks, avoiding Laura's gaze.

"It's a nuke?" she asked, shocked.

"No," Beckman said in a way that didn't reassure her.

She glanced at the recovered communicator visible inside Virus' pack, noting how it was cradled inside a housing built for it by Area 51 engineers. It resembled on a smaller scale the housing in Nuke's pack. She turned back to Beckman, wide eyed. "Oh my God, it's one of their weapons! Isn't it?"

Beckman nodded. "They could be a million years ahead of us. This evens the odds."

"What is it?"

"An antimatter torpedo," he replied. "We pulled six of them out of a wreck in nineteen forty seven."

Nuke stood, shouldering his pack. "The antimatter inflates spherically at the speed of light, annihilating everything it touches."

"Everything?" she repeated uncertainly.

"Dirt, rock, air," Beckman said. "Alien motherships. Phht! Everything out to three clicks, gone in the blink of an eye."

"Adios muchachos," Tucker said grimly.

"How can you be sure it'll work?" she asked.

"There's a crater on the dark side of the moon," Beckman said. "It's a perfect circle six kilometers across. It'll work."

"The moon!" Laura said incredulously.

"We couldn't risk detonating it on Earth," Beckman said. "Not until we knew what it was."

"How could you blow up the moon without anyone knowing about it?"

"There was a NASA probe called Mars Polar Lander," Beckman explained. "It supposedly crashed on Mars because a bunch of eggheads couldn't get their math right. Truth is, it didn't go to Mars. It made a perfect landing on the dark side of the moon, then we blew it up."

"This is not the dark side of the moon!"

"It might as well be," Markus said.

"The outside world tried to nuke them and failed,"

Beckman said, "making that warhead our only hope."

Laura swallowed apprehensively. "How much will be destroyed?"

"Everything within the blast sphere," Nuke said. "The crater will be six kilometers across, three deep."

Laura tried to imagine a crater that size where the Goyder River currently flowed. In time, it would become the world's deepest freshwater lake. The idea repulsed her. She glanced at Markus, who said nothing.

He knew! she realized. That's what he meant about the military destroying what they didn't understand. She turned to Wanyubi, sitting cross legged, listening to every word. "What do you say? This is your land."

Wanyubi looked up toward the shield dome obscuring the stars. "I cannot see the spirits in the sky. It is not meant to be this way."

"There's no radiation from the weapon," Beckman assured her. "No after effects. It's clean."

"That's not comforting," Laura snapped. "A nuke has already gone off. What about its radiation?"

"The President had to authorize the use of nuclear weapons. He's telling us to use the torpedo as surely as if he'd handed me the order himself. Your government must have agreed, because they know there's nothing they can do to fix this. Not now."

"This forest is millions of years old," she said desperately. "You'll destroy it."

"It'll recover," Beckman said. "It may take a hundred years or a thousand, but if we don't knock out that ship, we may not be around to see it."

Laura wanted to scream, but knew it would change nothing. Everything her life had stood for to that moment was being torn apart.

Bandaka approached her. "We belong to the land. If the land survives, we survive."

"Our children will go on," Djapilawuy said, glancing at

her daughter. "They will see the forest again."

"I'll take that as a yes," Beckman said, turning toward Wanyubi who nodded solemnly.

"Where will you set it off?" Laura asked.

"We're going to shove it up their ass," Tucker declared malevolently.

"Yeah!" Nuke exclaimed. "Biggest freaking enema in history!"

"We have to get close enough for the ship to be inside the blast sphere," Beckman said. "We'll know more once we have eyes on the target."

"What about my husband? He's on that ship."

"This was never a rescue mission," Beckman said apologetically.

She glanced at Markus, who refused to meet her eyes. "That's it then," she said.

On the far side of the camp, a weak moan sounded. Virus rolled sideways, holding a hand to his pounding head. He opened his eyes, blinking weakly, then spoke incomprehensible words in a voice straining to reach a high pitch beyond his physical capabilities. Everyone stared at him in astonishment.

His words were of a language unknown to Man.

* * * *

"Sonar contact, bearing one seven five degrees, speed..." the sonar operator stopped mid sentence, struggling to grasp what his instruments were telling him.

Captain Bourke turned to the operator curiously. "Speed?"

The sonarman gave the *Michigan's* captain a confused look. "Over two thousand knots, sir, submerged."

"That's impossible!" Commander Thompson snapped as he hurried to the sonar operator's console.

"Heading?" the captain asked.

"Straight for us."

"Battle stations," the captain ordered. "Launch countermeasures."

The XO leaned toward the sonar screen as a marker raced across it toward the *Michigan*. "There must be something wrong with your instruments."

The sonar operator ran his eyes over the controls. "No, sir."

Captain Bourke stepped toward the sonar display, then the operator handed him his headset. Bourke pressed one of the cans to his ear, but instead of the familiar beat of high speed propellers cavitating through the water, he heard the whisper of water particles being pushed aside by an acceleration field that ensured the speeding object never came in direct contact with the water.

"It's not a torpedo," the captain said as he watched the contact close on them. "Hard a port, seventy degrees."

Before the massive submarine began to turn a silver ellipsoid struck the *Michigan* amidships, plunged into its nuclear reactor and detonated. For a moment, the dark depths of the ocean burned with the radiance of a star, then the sea water collapsed into the empty airless void that had formed where SSGN 727 had been. There was no wreckage, no surge of bubbles or debris, no hope of escape.

The *USS Michigan* had been annihilated at a molecular level.

* * * *

Markus borrowed Tucker's entrenching tool as the team prepared to move out, indicating he was going to attend to his morning needs in the absence of a proper latrine and ensuring he would not be followed. He caught Laura's eye, indicating he wanted to talk, then once out of sight of the troops, he drew his transceiver and quickly typed:

Request:
1. Rationale for use of nuclear weapons.
2. Confirmation of mission priorities.
Urgent. Beckman planning to deliver payload.

He knew Nuke had been receiving nothing on the radio and the dome's ability to filter out a nuclear blast's EMP made him doubt anyone would receive his signal, but he had to try. The ASD listening post was barely a hundred kilometers away and their equipment was extremely sensitive, so he hoped they would pick up some trace of his message.

"Are you going to let them do it?" Laura demanded.

"I haven't decided," he said, making no attempt to hide his burst transceiver.

"Getting anything?" she asked, nodding to his small radio.

"Not yet. I may have to make a judgment call." He gave her a questioning look. "Can I count on you?"

Laura looked surprised. "Me? What do you want me to do?"

"I'll let you know … Well?"

"You can, if you stop them destroying that ship with my husband inside," she said, realizing Markus might be Dan's only hope.

"Good." The CIA officer drove the entrenching tool into the ground, levering up a spade full of dirt. He glanced at Laura. "That's all."

She felt mildly irritated at being dismissed, as if she was in his employ. Without a word, she turned and headed back to camp. When Markus finished digging a shallow hole, he checked the transceiver.

Its LCD screen remained blank.

CHAPTER 11

The heavy lift suit flashed a priority alert into Nemza'ri's cerebral implants. She ignored it, focusing instead on lowering the damaged sleep cell onto the med lab floor. It was the third functioning transport unit she'd found with the suit's biosensor, giving her hope there were more survivors.

The occupants of the three cells had suffered terrible burns and would require extensive nanoregeneration before they would regain consciousness. Considering the heat the octagonal cells had been exposed to, it was a miracle any had survived. The sleep cells were scarred black and splattered with droplets of molten metal, but incredibly, their biostasis fields had not collapsed although their emergency power modules were almost fully depleted.

She released the cell then summoned six spherical, multi-armed med drones to transfer the charred occupant to a regrowth chamber. Once stabilized, millions of nanomachines swarmed around the blackened body, replacing hundreds of damaged implants, amputating ruined limbs and cloning replacement parts to rebuild the patient's bioform. It was a slow and dangerous process he might survive if he were lucky.

DNA analysis identified him as a mid level ground unit commander, not scheduled for revival until planetfall plus two. Technically he outranked her, although not being crew meant in matters of the ship he was no more than cargo and being male, he would always defer to her irrespective of grade. While she was glad she'd found another survivor, her inability to find a ship's officer worried her. Being the only surviving crew member meant she was in command of the ship even if the Command Nexus refused to recognize her rank. Saving passengers was her duty, but she desperately hoped to find one of her more senior sisters to take command.

Knowing she could do no more for this latest survivor, she turned her attention to that annoying alert sounding deep within her mind. She'd assumed it was yet another malfunction, but her training and discipline would not allow her to cancel the message until she'd followed the required termination protocol. To her amazement she discovered it was a genuine combat alert, a warning that the deployment shield had been struck by a low yield fusion weapon.

Nemza'ri wondered who would dare use such outlawed weapons against them. They were universally hated by all sentient species – even her own – and the consequences of building, let alone using radiological weapons were too severe to contemplate.

She requested a status update from the tactical sublayer distributing the combat alert. The response was immediate, informing her that the Command Nexus had been suppressing orbital and atmospheric defenses since landing and had mounted punitive strikes to secure the area of operations. The deployment shield was in place, although no contact had been established with Fleet for many days. General threat levels were high, reinforcement unlikely and enemy action was interdicting resource supply, retarding fabricator output.

It had not occurred to her that the ship was under attack. Now that she knew the situation, her perspective changed from a desperate need to save survivors to an unquestioning commitment to defend the ship against its unknown enemy.

Nemza'ri immediately questioned the med drones as to the status of the males. Two were viable, but required growth hormone treatment that might kill them in their weakened state. The hormone could be extracted from myrnods; aggressive, predatory creatures native to her homeworld that were stored in several locations throughout the ship. Finding those creatures – if any had even survived – required her to temporarily abandon the search for survivors, even at the cost of their lives.

It was her duty. She was crew, she was nominally in command and most importantly of all, she was female.

CHAPTER 12

Vamp led Dr. McInness and Timer toward the end of the tunnel, periodically glancing at the crystal ball's display surface. The recovered scanner indicated no contacts, yet she couldn't believe there were no guards. She pocketed the alien scanner and crept to the tunnel exit with her gun raised. A smooth floor several football fields in length stretched out before her, beneath a cavernous chamber that rose through the rock to the surface several kilometers above.

She glanced into the shadows behind her. "Wait there, Ian," she said, motioning for Timer to follow.

Timer drew his special, but remained several paces behind as she stepped out onto the fused rock floor. Her footsteps clicked hollowly on the laser smooth surface, while the emptiness towering above made her feel insignificant. The twin subway tunnels were the only features in the enormous rock walls rising around her.

"No sign of the metal cubes," she said, certain the transport capsule had unloaded there. The chamber was large enough to be a huge underground logistics and manufacturing center in one, but for now it was empty. Her eyes followed the chamber walls, up past yellow-orange light panels to a dark rectangular ceiling. She aimed her M16 at white points of light in the ceiling, studying them through her gun's telescopic sight.

"Oh my God!" she murmured.

"What is it?" Timer whispered anxiously, still reluctant to leave the tunnel mouth.

"We're under the ship! I can see open hatches."

"Really?" Dr. McInness said. He rushed out into the open and looked up, unable to contain his curiosity. "It's huge!"

Vamp unclipped her telescopic sight and passed it to him. "Is it what you expected?"

He peered through the low power lens. "It's bigger," he said delighted. "Somehow, we got our calculations wrong."

Timer stepped out looking for an exit, but finding none, said, "I knew it. We're trapped!"

Dr. McInness handed the telescopic sight back to Vamp, then wandered across the floor, staring up at the hull, frustrated he couldn't get closer. "There must be a way–"

A white beam flashed down from above and enveloped the scientist. Without any sensation of movement, he found himself shooting up through a shaft of light. Vamp and Timer fell rapidly away as glistening rock walls flashed past in a blur. A moment later, he passed through a three layered hull and was deposited on an enormous polished deck, then the transport beam winked out leaving him blinking in near darkness. A few dim yellow-orange lights flickered against a wall a hundred meters away, while impenetrable shadows obscured the other walls. Feeling alone and small in a giant's lair, he heard a distant clang of metal resonate through the great ship's superstructure.

There were four large circular openings in the deck and suspended high above each were translucent conical projectors. He approached the closest hatchway and peered down into the chamber below. Its bottom appeared to be a tiny square of light so far away he couldn't see Vamp or Timer. He felt his head spin with vertigo and stepped back, then one of the conical projectors glowed to life. A transport beam flashed down into the chamber, then Vamp appeared. The beam swept her sideways, deposited her on the deck and switched off. She leveled her M16, turning full circle.

"We're alone," Dr. McInness assured her, then a distant

metallic clang sounded. “Except for that.”

She looking up at the conical projector above the hatch. “I guess that’s how they got the ingots up here.”

“Yes, it’s a cargo handling system.”

The beam flashed again, then Timer appeared beside Vamp. “Cool ride. Now let’s get the hell out of here.” He glanced down into the cargo hatch, spat into the void and watched his spittle sail into the shadows below. “Watch that first step.”

Vamp noticed the three layers surrounding the cargo hatch. “That’s a thick hull. Looks kind of tough.”

“They’d have to deal with radiation, meteorites and who knows what else,” Dr. McInness said.

Timer fired a blast from his midget special at the inner layer, then studied the impact point. “Not a scratch. It’s got to be armor.”

Dr. McInness glanced around the cavernous deck. “It looks like an empty cargo ship to me. Considering its size, they’d need a thick hull for structural strength.”

“There’s no hatch door,” Vamp said, pacing around the circular opening.

“Could be an iris,” Dr. McInness said, “like what the road builder had.”

Timer glanced at his compass, looking for a bearing to follow, finding the needle was spinning slowly. “Hey, my compass is screwed.”

“May I?” the scientist asked. Timer gave him the compass, then he held it close to the deck, but the needle continued to spin slowly. “There’s an electromagnetic field inside the ship. I wonder if it’s the engines?”

Timer eyes widened. “You don’t think it’s going to take off, do you?”

“I hope not,” Dr. McInness said as he handed the compass back.

A high pitched, animal screech sounded from a long way off, then Timer turned, eyeing the darkness nervously. “What the hell was that?”

"Whatever it was, it didn't sound friendly," Vamp said.

"I wonder if that's their language?" Dr. McInness said.

"If it is, that's one conversation I'm not having," Timer said, firing his special blindly into the darkness, using the flash to illuminate the cargo hold.

"Stop firing that thing," Vamp said, "you're giving away our position."

"You think they don't know we're here?"

"I don't know. Just keep it together, OK," she said, then pointed at a distant wall light. "That way. Let's go." She led them at a run to the island of light, stopping at the metal wall as rapid, scratching footsteps sounded in the distance.

"It's headed this way," Timer whispered.

Vamp produced the crystal ball, but the only readings were themselves. "It's not carrying metal," she said, pocketing the alien sensor. "Let's keep moving."

They hurried along the wall, searching for a gravity lift alcove or a passageway out, moving from one flickering island of light to the next while soft, scraping footsteps followed them. Several times, they saw a dark shadow prowling beyond the light, then another high pitched screech sounded from the darkness.

"There are two them," Vamp whispered.

"And they have our scent," Timer said, listening to the scratching footsteps circling beyond the light.

"If they're trapped in here without food or water," Vamp said, "they'll be hungry."

"You do realize," Dr. McInness said, "if an alien creature ate us, the microbes in our body would kill it?"

"Yeah Doc, but if it's an animal," Timer said, "it's not going to know that."

"Hmm," the scientist said, "you might be right."

In the flickering light, a hulking, round shouldered form prowled beyond the sputtering light, sniffing their strange, alien scent. Vamp fired a single shot from her M16, glimpsing thick shoulders, four muscular legs and yellow teeth in the muzzle flash. The starving creature darted away with surprising speed, knowing it was stalking meat unlike any it had tasted.

"Damn!" Timer said. "It's big."

"Did you hit it?" Dr. McInness asked.

"Winged it maybe," she said, starting along the wall toward unbroken darkness.

"Hey!" Timer said. "We can't leave the light, not with those things out there."

"You want to stay here?" she asked sharply.

Timer glanced over his shoulder. "Yeah. Let's wait until it attacks, then smoke its ass."

"Wait how long?" she demanded. "An hour? A day? Until there's fifty of them out there?"

"Fifty?" Timer repeated uncertainly.

"Listen for footsteps. If it gets close, start shooting. I'll aim by the flash of your special," she said, then not waiting for his agreement, she started along the wall into the darkness with Dr. McInness close behind. They hadn't gone far when another heavy metallic clang vibrated through the ship, reminding them that somewhere, repairs were proceeding.

"Why don't they turn the lights on?" Timer said, peering into the darkness.

"They would if they could," Dr. McInness said. "They must be short of power."

"That's not all they're short of," Vamp said. "This place has been scrubbed clean."

"Automated systems probably keep the ship spotless," the scientist said.

Vamp stopped when she found a dark wall blocked their path. "It's a dead end."

"So we have to go back, past those things out there?" Timer asked nervously

Dr. McInness ran his hand over the obstruction, down to the floor. "It's recessed into the deck. I don't think it's a wall."

"Timer," Vamp said, "one shot."

Timer fired into the darkness, startling two large shapes that darted away, giving Dr. McInness a moment's light. "There they are!"

"It's an air tight door," the scientist said. "It runs right across the deck."

Timer heard scraping footsteps creeping toward them. "They're coming in," he said, then shouted, "Come on, here I am."

"Shh," Vamp said, listening.

Timer ignored her and yelled at the darkness. "You want a taste of this, come and get it!" He fired several shots into the darkness, seeing the creatures lope away.

"Quiet!" Vamp ordered. "Listen."

In the silence, they heard a barely audible dripping.

"Water?" Dr. McInness said surprised.

"Even the plumbing leaks on this tub," Timer said. "No wonder they crashed!"

"Let's follow the door," Vamp said, starting across the deck.

They hurried toward the sound of dripping water, then as they neared the center of the deck, a large black mass loomed before them, jutting out into the air above their heads. Before Vamp could investigate, a wild screech sounded as maddening hunger overpowered the creature's stalking instincts and it charged. She tossed her last flare at the sound of claws scrambling across the metal deck as Timer fired, filling the darkness with strobing flashes.

On its homeworld, the creature's claws would have propelled it over the soft muddy ground of its riverine hunting grounds faster than any terrestrial animal could run, but on the hard metal deck, its clawed feet slid as it hurled itself at them. Vamp had an impression of large sloping eyes, triangular teeth jutting from dark red gums and a streamlined snout with lips pulled back in a ferocious snarl. Behind the head were thick shoulders, powerful forelegs with webbed feet, each armed with a single long yellow claw, then a short body with squat hind legs and a long whipping tail.

Timer's special locked onto the target, pushed his hand to the left and unleashed a series of plasma bolts that cut through the creature's massive shoulders as if they were butter. Beside him, Vamp fired several bursts into its skull. Its forelegs folded as Timer's special sliced it in two, then it slid in a bloody pile of flesh toward them. Timer kept firing, chopping the flesh into charred pieces until the creature's lifeless carcass slammed into the massive door beside him.

"You wanted a piece of me! Now you got it," Timer declared angrily, "you freaking ugly space mutt!" He fired several more times at the dead carcass. "How do you like that, huh?"

Dr. McInness stepped forward, intending to examine the creature, but Vamp caught his shoulder. "Not this time, Ian."

"But this is a creature from another world."

She stepped toward it cautiously. "I don't care if it's the creature from the black lagoon, it just tried to eat you." She jabbed the point of her gun into the side of its jaw experimentally, triggering an autonomic response that snapped its jaw shut. "Even dead, it's dangerous."

Dr. McInness looked at the beast's teeth with renewed respect. "OK, no touching," he said, studying it in the light of the flare. "It's not a tool user. Its head is mostly bone, so low intelligence. Judging by the webbed feet and the tail, it's an amphibian, which suggests a watery homeworld."

"And there's at least one more of those things out there," Vamp said, turning to the dark mass above their heads. The flickering light of the flare revealed it was a vehicle pinned between two blast doors which had slammed shut, suspending it above the deck. The vehicle was ovoid with a streamlined hull, no visible windows or hatches and a gently sloping bubble on its upper side mounting two dome shaped gun turrets. Incredibly, the enormous doors had not crushed it.

"Looks like a tank," Vamp said.

"Or a tow truck," Dr. McInness said, unconvinced.

Timer fired his special at the vehicle, then looked for any sign of damage. There was none. He touched the impact point and shook his head. "Not even warm. Definitely a bad ass."

Vamp ducked beneath the tank and crawled between the air tight doors it had wedged apart. On the other side, a slab of metal deck had fallen from above, leaving a narrow space between it and the big doors. She edged her way forward to where a sliver of light separated the two, followed by Dr. McInness, then Timer who kept watch for the second creature. The air became humid and scented with eucalyptus and the dripping sounds became more pronounced.

When she reached the jagged edge of the fallen deck, a large condensation droplet splashed down near her boot, drawing her gaze up to a tunnel of destruction blasted through hundreds of decks above. The wrecked decks were blacked out, except for a few flickering lights and flashes from short circuiting power conduits. A pole shaped maintenance drone with a conical coolie hat and four snaking arms floated alongside a ragged deck cutting away torn metal. The rim of the drone's coolie hat glowed softly from its propulsion field while two of its arms held cutting torches that rained sparks onto the shattered decks below. Far above the maintenance drone was a tiny pinpoint of sunlight marking the shaft's exit point at the top of the ship.

Vamp was shocked by the scale of the disaster and the pitifully small repair effort. She was about to step out from behind the fallen deck for a better view when a high pitched amphibian screech sounded close by. She froze as a frenzy of shrieks erupted in reply from below. She threw Timer and Dr. McInness a warning look, commanding silence. When the bout of screeching died down, she inched forward for a better look, being careful not to reveal herself.

A wisp of fresh air washed over her face as she caught a glimpse of a yawning chasm beyond the fallen deck. Just a step away, the deck she stood on ended above a jagged hole in the triple armored hull. Sitting on the far side of the hole were five amphibian predators while many more swam in an ash-choked pool fed by the river outside. Metal shards speared into the murky water alongside a charred tree trunk wedged against the pool side.

Occasionally one creature would pass too close to another and be greeted with an angry screech of warning. If the warning was ignored, the threatened creature would surge out of the water and swipe one of its clawed forelegs at the other, forcing it to dart out of reach or fight for its life. The warning shriek would start the others screaming, then after a while, the ruckus would die down.

One of the animals surfaced with the rotting corpse of a crocodile in its mouth. It sped across the water to the fallen deck Vamp cowered behind, which angled down into the pool. When it reached the deck, it surged out of the water, then tore at the crocodile's stomach. The others immediately swarmed toward the carcass, knocking each other aside to get at the rotting meat. One of the creatures was clawed in the scramble and bleeding, was set upon by the others who were caught in the grip of a wild feeding frenzy. In moments, the rotting crocodile corpse and the bleeding creature were stripped to the bone.

Vamp crept back behind the bulkhead and whispered to her companions, "There's a hole in the ship. It's full of water and dozens of those creatures, all starving."

Timer gulped. "Can we get through?"

"There's too many to fight. They're so hungry, they're eating each other. If they saw us, we'd be dead." She pointed to the fallen bulkhead they hid behind. "They're using this deck like a ramp into the pool."

"That explains why the cargo hold is empty," Dr. McInness whispered. "Explosive decompression. The air tight doors tried to close when the hull was breached, but the … tank wedged them open."

"We'll have to go back," Vamp said.

"Are you crazy?" Timer demanded. "At least there's light out here. Who knows how many of those things are back there in the dark."

"Can't be as many as there are in the pool."

"Let me see," he said, squeezing past her for a look.

Several of the amphibians prowled along the edge of the hole while others swam in the ashen waters. He realized she was right, they couldn't fight them all. Suddenly one of the creatures standing on the lip of the pool looked up and shrieked as a red blur streaked down into the water, sending a splash high into the air. The creatures screamed furiously and dived after their hapless prey, determined to tear it to pieces.

Timer turned to them. "They're after something in the water."

The pool grew quiet as the creatures swam down after their prey, then flashes illuminated the water deep below the surface. One of the creatures surged up from the deep, was airborne long enough to breath, then dived down to renew the struggle.

One look told Vamp this was their chance. "Let's go."

"Go where?" Timer asked.

"Up there, while they're distracted," she said, then pulled herself out onto the fallen deck and began scrambling up. The deck was punctured in many places, creating holes that turned it into a natural ladder, giving foot and hand holds. Timer and Dr. McInness climbed after her as milky flashes illuminated the pool below, then as Vamp reached the deck above, she heard scratching footsteps charging toward her. She aimed her M16 at the deck above as a long jaw and yellow teeth came speeding toward her, too fast to get a shot away. The creature's jaw swallowed the barrel of her rifle, forcing the gun backwards, wedging the butt into one of the footholds, then the creature cartwheeled over her, pivoting on the rifle. It hit the deck below her with a thud, holding onto the barrel with its powerful jaws trying to tear the weapon from her hand. She fired a burst, blowing the back of its bony head off, then the creature slid down the ramp into the water, leaving a trail of dark blood behind.

Vamp quickly pulled herself up to the deck above, then lay prone and sighted on the pool with her M16 as the others clambered up. In the pool below, the white flashes stopped and a red bipedal form leapt out of the water. Vamp knew at once it was a metallic suit, not a machine, shorter than a man with an overly large helmet.

The heavy lift suit's back was angled toward them, concealing the helmet's translucent visor, while five creatures clawed vainly at its metal exterior. In its left hand, the suited figure held a white nanonet encasing two unconscious creatures while in its right, it held a silver bar which flashed each time it jabbed its attackers. The stun rod forced the myrnods back, hurling some into the water and knocking others onto the deck. When the creatures had been driven off, the heavy lift suit made a propulsion field assisted vertical jump straight up six levels to a ragged deck, then vanished into the dark interior of the ship. Behind in the pool, the remaining myrnods descended on the beast Vamp had killed and consumed it with cannibalistic fury.

"That was one of them," Dr. McInness whispered excitedly.

"Yeah. Too bad we didn't see its face," Vamp said.

"What do you think it wanted with those mutts?" Timer asked.

"Don't know," she said, nodding for them to crawl away from the edge.

When they were out of sight of the pool, they crept through the shadows to flickering emergency lights where they found another enormous cargo deck sucked clean by explosive decompression. They hurried across it until they entered a broad well lit corridor as wide as a freeway. They kept close to the wall until a broad archway appeared without warning. The arch was flush to the wall with no nearby controls and was large enough for the black 'tank' they'd seen to pass through.

"Can't see their elevators or doors," Timer said.

Dr. McInness studied the arch curiously. "There must be something different about their vision." He glanced at the orange tinted wall lights thoughtfully. "Judging by the color of their light, I'd say they evolved under a K type star. That would make their eyes more sensitive to infrared than ours."

"If we don't figure out how to spot their doors," Vamp said, "how are we going to find the exit?"

"Stick close to the walls," the scientist replied. "The doors appear to have proximity sensors." He stepped into the archway, finding no trace of a door retracting into the walls. "It's like it's part of the wall. There must be something very weird happening on a quantum level."

Timer gave him an impatient look. "What we need is something weird happening on a let's get the hell out of this rat trap level."

Vamp stepped past Dr. McInness into an enormous rectangular chamber hundreds of meters across with only a few scattered yellow-orange lights high up on the walls to soften the shadows. Filling the chamber were rows of circular silver platforms, each with matching silver disks floating above them. The larger the platform, the higher the disk floated, while beside each platform was a shallow metal saucer half its size. Most of the platforms were empty, except for a cluster near the entrance that glowed with light.

Dr. McInness started toward the platforms with unbridled enthusiasm, but Vamp caught his arm, restraining him. "Wait," she said, searching for any sign of movement.

Timer stepped through the arch and moved away to the left, studying the chamber warily. "Looks clear."

"OK." Vamp released her grip, then together they walked to the first illuminated platform. When they had moved a few meters from the arch, the wall flowed together, seamlessly swallowing the archway. Vamp took a few cautious steps back to the wall, triggering its proximity sensor to open the door again, reassuring her that they weren't trapped.

Dr. McInness moved past the active platforms, finding each contained a partially formed machine. Most were mere skeletons awaiting further equipment, while some were almost complete except for their outer bodywork. Five of the largest skeletons were battloids, sitting on sled housings that had not yet been equipped with antigravity field generators. The embryonic battloids lacked armor, weapons and shields, but the central housing, power plant and most of their internal systems were finished.

"Now that's a big mother," Timer said appreciatively, eyeing one of the battloids.

Vamp's attention shifted from the cluster of illuminated platforms to the endless rows of inactive platforms filling the chamber. There were too many to count, but she guessed there were thousands of them. She walked around an embryonic battloid, unaware of its military purpose, then studied the other platforms, realizing the largest could have accommodated the 'tank' wedged between the blast doors below.

"It's a manufacturing facility."

"So where are the spare parts, the tools?" Timer asked. He drew his knife and moved to poke the nearest skeletal battloid with it. As soon as the blade passed over the edge of the platform, a golden cloud appeared around the point. He pulled the knife back, startled. "Did you see that?"

"Did you see this?" Vamp said, catching his wrist and lifting it to inspect his knife. The end was missing.

Timer eyes bulged in amazement. "It ate my knife!"

"Imagine what it would have done to your hand."

Timer swallowed uncomfortably as the hiss of

equalizing air pressure signaled the arch had opened. Vamp grabbed Dr. McInness and dragged him down behind the platform while Timer ducked behind a skeletal battloid.

A coolie hat type repair drone floated in carrying a block of twisted metal the size of a small car. It flew toward a platform holding its skeletal twin and dropped the metal onto the smaller dish beside the platform. The repair drone turned and flew back through the arch, while a golden cloud glided from the platform to the dish. It swirled around the salvaged metal, which vanished in seconds, then the cloud returned to the platform and enveloped the skeletal maintenance drone. Internal parts seemed to form out of the air, tentacle arms grew from nothing and an outer skin appeared as the cloud's luminosity faded. Moments later, a new maintenance drone was complete.

The brim of the coolie hat atop the drone's slender body glowed to life, floating it off the platform. Fully cognizant of the mothership's desperate need, it tilted forward and glided out through the archway. On the platform where it had been created, the golden cloud swirled again, creating the beginnings of a new skeleton. When the luminosity faded to nothing, the cloud vanished, having exhausted its supply of salvaged metal.

Dr. McInness stared at the partially formed drone with delight. "You can tell yourself a thousand times, but until you experience it, you just don't understand! Not at all!" He beamed a smile at her.

Vamp looked at him sideways. *He is kind of cute for a geek, but mad as a hatter!* "Understand what, Ian?"

"Clarke was right! Advanced technology does look like magic to primitives!" He glanced around the room, then pointed to Timer. "You wanted to know where the equipment was, where the spare parts were. Well, it's right here! We're surrounded by it!"

"Yeah, we sure are," Vamp said, worried.

"It's nanotechnology, developed to an incredible level,"

the scientist said. "No, it's more than that. It's manufacturing at a molecular level. Nanomachines convert raw metal into molecules and reassemble them into whatever form they want. That's what the cloud was, trillions of nanomachines. The platform must have an acceleration field that allows them to fly. I doubt a machine that small could generate its own field. Or could it?" He shrugged and laughed. "Who knows. It's beyond me!"

"So all they need are minerals and they could make…?"

"Anything!" he said, turning to the rows of platforms. "Each platform is a factory, a million years ahead of ours."

Vamp studied the skeletal battloid on the platform nearby. "Good thing we blew their mine up," she said soberly. "Not that it slowed them down much. Now they're cannibalizing their own ship for raw materials."

"And scavenging the countryside," Timer added, remembering the research station stripped of metal.

"What choice do they have?" Dr. McInness asked. "They can't repair their ship without resources."

"With this technology, they can build another mine," she said, "as many as they need."

Dr. McInness looked at one of the larger platforms, estimating its capacity. It appeared to be large enough to construct another drill head. "You're right," he said with relief. "We haven't done them any permanent harm."

Vamp looked apprehensively at the endless rows of nanofabricators. "With enough raw materials, this place could pump out thousands of machines an hour. Tens of thousands!"

"Yes, amazing isn't it. With this technology and enough resources, we could wipe out world poverty in a week."

"Or they could build an army that could wipe us out in a day," Timer said scornfully.

The scientist looked aghast, then gazed at the sprawling facility with growing unease. The rows of platforms of all sizes led off into the distance, their productivity limited only by the raw materials available to them. In a heartbeat, he knew if their suspicions were correct, it meant only one thing.

The ship was a colossal time bomb.

* * * *

The striker was a black, elongated wedge twice as long as it was wide, with 'wingtips' that curved down thirty degrees before sloping gracefully back to a spear like tail. Small spherical turrets with needle-like weapons were mounted at each wingtip and a pair of thin glowing strips ran along its underside brightening each time it accelerated or banked. Along its leading edge was a narrow glassy black sensor strip giving it battlespace vision from horizon to orbit, although its thermal sensor – calibrated to the cool temperate environment of the mothership's original destination – was almost useless in the tropical heat.

While the striker was capable of suborbital flight, it preferred to hug the ground for cover rather than expose itself at high altitude. As a piece of airborne artillery, it was normally allocated fire support missions by the mothership, but the ship's bombardment control center had been destroyed, forcing it to autonomously locate targets of opportunity. Even though it was self aware, stealthy and mobile, the striker was an inferior perimeter guard, fulfilling that role now only because no sentry drones had survived and it would be days before replacements could be constructed. It had shot down aircraft and neutralized satellites to ensure no hostiles flew over the mothership and now it searched for the primitives who had destroyed one of the few operational battloids.

Its heat saturated thermal sensor scanned the forest from tree top height, unaware Cougar hid just below. Further back, the rest of the team watched the aerial weapons platform glide above the forest canopy, drifting left and right, scanning to the horizon. Cougar lay motionless, keeping the striker in his sights until it shrank to a distant black dot loitering above the trees.

"Clear," he said, then crept through the trees over ground covered with a sprinkling of fine ash. He stopped at a sandstone ledge protruding out over jagged cliffs and looked across the Goyder River to a wall of gray metal spanning the valley. For a moment he thought it was a fortress, then realized it was the mothership itself. It was composed of enormous armored slabs pockmarked with tiny black dots. The ship was like a city encased in metal, stretching more than twelve kilometers up the valley. Its sides towered above the ridge tops and in places had torn through the surrounding sandstone cliffs like chalk. At the top of the metal wall, the hull sloped back sharply into a ridge that ran the length of the ship. There was no gash through the valley indicating it hadn't glided in to land but had come down vertically, crushing everything beneath it. The forest covering the valley floor had been knocked flat by the impact and incinerated, while the normally ochre colored cliffs looked as if they'd been seared by a blow torch. Where the ship blocked the river, ashen water had backfilled into a small lake that was slowly drowning the charred valley.

Cougar swept his telescopic sight over the ship, finding not a single window anywhere along its length, then Beckman and Markus crept up beside him.

Beckman whistled softly when he saw the ship's size. "It's too big for one torpedo."

"It's not two million tons," Markus stated. "More like twenty."

"We'll set the warhead off inside where it can do the most damage, next to a reactor or a weapons stockpile. The timer will give us twenty-four hours to get clear." Beckman studied the stranded behemoth through his binoculars, focusing on the pockmarks that he discovered were circular holes twenty to thirty meters across. "What the hell? … It's shot to pieces." A few tiny repair drones floated like insects buzzing around an colossal corpse, nibbling at the damage with cutting torches and sending waterfalls of sparks cascading down the side of the hull.

"That didn't happen when it landed," Markus said.

Beckman wondered what could have caused such damage, certain of one thing, "It's not flying out of here anytime soon."

"It's a wreck, not a threat," Markus said, his mind racing at the possibilities.

"Thank God for that," Cougar said, lowering his sniper scope. "No invasion."

Beckman's jaw tightened. "So why'd our guys try to nuke it?"

"Did they?" Markus asked doubtfully.

"We all saw the flash."

"Suppose it was the Chinese or the Russians trying to stop us getting our hands on it."

"And risk starting a war?" Beckman shook his head. "Not likely."

"My God!" Laura exclaimed as she edged up behind them with Bandaka following a short distance behind. "Is my husband in there, Major?"

"Maybe."

"If our people did attack it, they couldn't have known what shape it's in," Markus persisted. "You can't attack without confirmation."

"I can't get confirmation," Beckman said, his mind made up. "We'll stealth in while there's still light." He was well aware the alien stealth gear they carried was tricky to use during the day, impossible at night.

"You can't, not now."

"Watch me," Beckman said, certain the nuclear attack could only have been made with Presidential authority. "We'll destroy the core of the ship, then your vultures can pick over what's left."

"That's a mistake," Markus said coldly, glancing at Laura, seeing she didn't agree either.

"It's mine to make." Beckman turned to Bandaka. "Can

you get us down there without being seen?"

The aboriginal hunter studied the blasted wasteland below, then nodded. "I know a way."

* * * *

Dan Mackay's world lacked form. He didn't know how long it had been since his capture as he no longer measured time in hours and days, but in terms of dreams.

Now the dream was a golden ellipse that morphed into a ring, then two rings. A glowing red line threaded the rings then both ends of the line curved up to meet, forming a third ring that locked the first two together.

When the geometric patterns had first appeared, they'd been simple shapes; cubes, pyramids, spheres and the like, then they'd become progressively more complex. Though he didn't realize it, the more complex shapes correlated with advanced scientific concepts, none of which he recognized. To him, they were simply perplexing shapes and colors, not the keys to the mysterious inner forces of nature.

His captors, having mapped every molecule in his body and unlocked the key to his DNA now probed the inner recesses of his mind, precisely measuring his intelligence. By determining his brain responses, they discovered their specimen was capable of understanding fundamental and obvious relationships, but found him wanting in other respects.

For Dan Mackay, the dreams continued unabated, without explanation or purpose.

* * * *

Bandaka led them along a tree covered ridge to a narrow trail leading down into the valley where they rested before descending. When everyone had stripped off their packs and began eating cold rations, Markus nodded to Laura, indicating it was time.

She leaned toward Xeno, pointing at her entrenching tool. "Could I borrow that?"

"Sure," Xeno said, handing her the collapsible spade.

Laura took the tool and headed off into the trees, following the instructions Markus had whispered to her shortly before they'd made camp. When she was out of sight, she dug a small hole and peed in it. He'd been adamant, she had to pee. When she finished, Laura fixed her clothes, took a deep breath and screamed with all her might, then held the entrenching tool up like a club and pretended to watch the trees. Behind her, heavy footsteps came running, fanning out on both sides.

Tucker was the first to reach her, aiming his M16 in the direction of her gaze. "What was it?"

"One of those four-armed things," she said as Beckman ran up. "It was watching me, while I was ..." She motioned to the wet soil at the bottom of the pit, then pointed at the forest. "It went that way."

Worried their position had been discovered, Beckman said to the team, "Sweep out a hundred meters, no further. Destroy it if you can."

Tucker led a loose skirmish line through the trees with Bandaka and his group following, searching for tracks.

"Xeno, take her back to camp," he said, then started after the troops.

As Xeno started to move off, Laura said, "Wait," then began filling in the hole, delaying her return as Markus had instructed.

In camp, Nuke and Hooper remained, watching after their comrades. Markus put his ration pack down, then keeping his eyes on them, stood and reached into his pocket for a bent rod shaped weapon. The special lacked the raw destructive power of the plasma weapons Beckman's team carried, which is why they knew nothing about it, why it had been diverted to Markus' own covert unit. The consensus was that alien scientists used the non-lethal device to subdue specimens for examination, perhaps even human specimens, although Markus suspected it might have been used by alien law enforcement.

With his hand in his pocket, he set the stunner to minimum power, then with Nuke and Hooper's attention diverted, he slid it out and shot them both in the back. On low power, they'd only be out for a few minutes and would suffer mild headaches for several hours after they came to.

Their bodies twitched as he ran to Nuke's backpack and pulled it open, revealing the antimatter warhead inside. He knew his tiny stun gun couldn't harm the heavy torpedo and that there wasn't time to disassemble the detonator, so he set the stunner to full power and fired at the delicate electronics pack created by Area 51's design team. With the weapon's electronics crippled, Markus resealed the pack, set the stunner to minimum power and buttoned it into his trouser pocket. He sat down against his own pack and fired several bursts from his submachine gun into the trees, away from where the troops were patrolling.

Beckman's voice sounded in his earpiece. "Who's firing?"

Markus let off another burst, then thumbed his mike. "We're under attack. Nuke and Hooper are down."

He fired once more, then placed his MP5 on the ground and pressed the stun gun's firing surface. The tiny recovered stunner discharged, causing his body to convulse, then he slumped sideways onto the ground, unconsciousness.

* * * *

Markus was the last to regain consciousness. Hooper and Nuke were sitting up, blinking spots from their eyes, sipping water, while the rest of the team strapped on their stealth gear. Laura sat quietly by her pack watching the CIA officer apprehensively.

"What happened?" Beckman asked as Xeno flashed a

light into Markus' eyes, checking his retinal response.

The intelligence officer took a slow breath, tried to rise, then thought better of it. He found his stunned leg completely numb. "It was a runner. It came in fast. I got a few shots off before it hit me with a flash of something."

Beckman looked around the camp, wondering why the machine had attacked. It hadn't killed the three men there and the short wave radio was useless while the dome was up. It had to be something the machine wanted … or feared? His eyes came to rest on the backpack holding the antimatter torpedo.

"Nuke," he said, "run a diagnostic."

The payload specialist eyes widened, then he tore open the backpack flap to find the control system was unresponsive. "It's dead," he muttered, then removed the electronics pack's access plate, finding blackened burn marks at key connection points where the system had shorted out. "The electronics are fried."

"What about the torpedo itself?"

"I'll have to decouple it from the housing to get to the control surface. It'll take at least an hour."

"You've got five minutes," Beckman said.

Nuke gave him an incredulous look, then sighed. "I guess I could cut it out. The electronics are useless anyway."

"Do it," Beckman said, then approached Hooper, running his eyes over the sergeant's charred and blistered wounds. Hooper sat beside Virus, nursing Conan in his lap. He still wore his big Model 500 pistol low on his left hip, but the burns had forced him to pass his pack to Laura.

"Never saw it coming," Hooper said, his face pallid.

"You're too weak to go in with us."

"I'll make it."

Beckman gave him a grim look. "You'll endanger the mission."

Hooper glanced at his blackened skin despondently. The burns had forced him to discard his shirt and it was only the heavy painkillers Xeno had dosed him with that allowed him to function at all. "It looks worse than it is."

"I want you to go back over the ridge. Take Laura with you." Beckman handed him Timer's radio transmitter. "This is the detonator for the charges we left back on the tower. I don't even know if they're still there, but if we fail, that's our only chance. You'll need line of sight from the east side of this plateau. If you get the shield down, transmit the word 'citadel', then hide because all hell will break loose."

"Citadel, got it," Hooper said, pocketing the transmitter. "How will I know if you've failed, if I have to send the message.

Beckman glanced at Nuke who had removed the torpedo from his backpack and was aggressively chopping through the electronics assembly with metal cutters. "If you get the dome down, send it."

"When do I move out?"

"As soon as you can walk." Beckman turned to Virus. "You'll go with him."

Virus shook his head weakly. He lay against his backpack, eyes closed, shutting out the light to temper the pounding in his head. "Sir, you need me."

"Not if you can't make it." *Not if they've damaged your mind.* One look told him Virus was incapable of hard marching. His skin was pale and clammy and dark shadows had formed beneath his feverish eyes.

Virus washed down two painkillers with a swig of water. "I understand their stuff … some of it anyways." He tapped his temple. "I remember … fragments about systems and symbols. They fed me instructions for … species like us."

"Like us?"

"Lesser species, conscripts. They use them to operate support machines. The console thought I was there to be trained. It drained my memories, learned to talk to me, then it shoved stuff into my head. Too much, too fast." He pressed his palms against his eyes, relieving the pressure momentarily. "I wasn't smart enough. That's why I couldn't handle it. Lesser species are … smarter than us."

"Can you use what they taught you?"

"Some of it."

"We'll have to leave you behind if you can't keep up."

"I wouldn't have it any other way."

"OK. Strap up and strip the short wave down to minimum weight for Hooper."

"Yes sir," Virus said, rousing himself.

Hooper glanced up at the dome's distortion pattern high above them. "If the explosives are still there, we'll bring it down."

"Good luck," Beckman said, not expecting to see him again, then returned to his pack to pull on his stealth gear.

It comprised two circular emitters worn front and back of the torso, held in place by an Area 51 developed vest. The emitters had been recovered last century, presumably used by alien observers who wanted to get close to humans without being seen. The power cells were classified technology, built by General Electric with enough charge to power the emitters for forty five minutes. With an open stretch of ashen wasteland to cross, they'd be sitting ducks if the power cells failed before they reached the mothership.

While Beckman strapped on his stealth vest, Tucker helped Bandaka into Steamer's kit. "When you press this," Tucker explained, "no one can see you."

Bandaka looked confused. "How can no one see me?"

"It bends light around you."

"Will the great spirits see me?" Bandaka asked apprehensively.

Tucker looked puzzled. "Great spirits?"

"Yeah, they'll see you," Beckman said, "but no one else."

Bandaka wriggled uncomfortably as the vest rasped against his bare skin, then as Tucker tightened the straps, he added, "It'll switch off by itself when it's out of power."

"How will I know it's off?"

"You'll know," Tucker said emphatically.

Markus sat up, surprised the team was preparing to use the stealth kits while Nuke was hastily hacking through the torpedo's Area 51 housing. *Surely he's not going to send the 'citadel' code!*

Beckman finished adjusting his vest, then approached Nuke. "Well?"

The payload specialist looked up grimly. "The good news is the solenoid's still working. The torpedo must have shielded it from whatever hit my pack, so I can still generate a magnetic field to detonate the torpedo. The problem is the power pack's wasted."

"Could you use Hooper's stealth pack?" Beckman asked.

Nuke shrugged. "I guess I could hot wire it, but there's no timer."

"Set it up, then show me how to detonate it manually."

Nuke arched his brow in surprise, then replied barely above a whisper. "Yes sir."

Suddenly, everyone had stopped what they were doing and were looking at Beckman. He turned to them, seeing their confusion. "I'll give you all as much time as I can to get clear," he said, then was met with stunned looks as they realized he intended to stay inside the ship, alone. One by one, they returned to their preparations in silence.

Bandaka turned to his family and friends and said his farewells, knowing the soldiers could not find their way down the cliff face without him. He lifted Mapuruma into his arms and hugged her, then set his daughter down and put his arm around Djapilawuy. He kissed his wife on the cheek and whispered something to her as the rest of his group gathered around him one last time.

Markus climbed to his feet, hobbled over to Beckman and spoke in a low voice, "This is madness."

"It's improvisation. You don't have to come. No one

will think ill of you." He adjusted his stealth kit's straps, then approached Laura. "This is as far as you go. Hooper will take you back across the ridge."

"What about my husband?"

"We'll look for him on the way in. If we find him, they'll bring him, but that ship is huge. He could be anywhere."

"If you destroy the ship, you'll kill him."

"Is one man's life more important than the entire planet?"

She opened her mouth, but said nothing. It was an impossible question she couldn't answer.

Markus watched with suppressed anger, realizing he'd failed to save his holy grail, then he began strapping on his own stealth kit, determined not to let Beckman ruin everything.

* * * *

The four buffalo hunters followed the ridge north of their camp toward where they'd seen a column of steam rising the previous night. The dirty cloud it had formed dissipated by dawn, replaced by wispy threads of smoke snaking skyward from the ruins of the power plants and the mining tower.

"Must have been a bloody big explosion," Cracker said, wishing he'd seen it.

"That's what they get for nicking our beer," Slab declared.

They started down the slope for a closer look, searching for any sign of movement. When they reached the edge of the forest, they stepped carelessly into the clearing, surprised at the spongy surface beneath their feet.

"It's Astroturf," Wal said. "Anyone got a footy?"

"Hey!" Slab barked. "We play football on grass, not plastic carpet."

A soot-like dust sprinkled with metal droplets covered

the ground. Bill picked up a tiny metal ball and turned it in his fingers before showing it to the others. "Metal rain."

They gave the nearest destroyed power plant a wide berth because of the intense heat radiating from its foundations and headed toward the wrecked central tower. Its featureless wall rose like a three story building to a jagged edge where the upper section had been blown off. Wall fragments were strewn around the tower as far as the river where a flock of birds now perched on a segment jutting out of the water like an island.

Cracker moved ahead of the others, surveying the damage until he discovered a rectangular craft parked halfway between a shattered power plant and the tower. A piece of blackened wall pinned the transport to the ground, having cracked one of the three circular windows on its side on impact.

Cracker waved to the others. "Found something."

When they caught up, Bill said, "Looks abandoned."

The transport was covered in a thin layer of soot while the metal raindrops that had landed on its roof had fused to its hull.

"Where's the pilot?" Slab asked, looking around for a body.

"He might have been inside one of those buildings when they blew," Cracker suggested.

Wal discovered the rear circular hatch was open. "It's unlocked." A larcenous look appeared on his face. "Let's nick it and get out of here."

"Who's going to fly it, Einstein?" Slab demanded. "You?"

"Hey, no plan's perfect."

They peered in through the circular hatch at an empty cargo compartment with vacant mounts on each wall for spare battloid weapons and shields.

"It's a truck," Bill said, recognizing the tactical transport's utilitarian nature.

Slab climbed inside and moved through the

compartment curiously.

"Careful mate," Cracker said warily.

"There's nothing–" he said as he reached the end of the compartment and vanished.

"Slab!" Bill yelled, jumping into the transport and running to where his mate had disappeared. He felt the wall, looking for a door, then found himself facing a control console, two chairs and a horizontal window flanked by smaller circular windows. Before Bill could speak, Slab dragged him down to the floor.

"Take it easy," Bill said, pushing Slab's big hands away.

"Shh." Slab pointed at the main window. "There's something out there."

Bill sobered as Wal appeared on the elevator pad and was promptly tackled to the ground by Slab.

"What did you see?" Bill asked, not bothering to explain to Wal why his face was jammed into the deck.

"A metal snake," Slab replied, then pushed Wal back onto the elevator plate. "Tell Cracker not to go outside." He let go, sending Wal back down before he could argue, then he crawled to one of the pilot seats and peeked through the window.

A thick black disk a meter across floated in front of the transport's snub nose. It was equipped with six tentacled arms, each possessing a set of dexterous metal fingers. The disk floated on a glowing, orange dome while three more tentacle arms rose from the top of the disk and ended in glassy black sensor eyes that swayed constantly, watching in every direction. One of the eye tentacles snaked down beneath the vehicle to examine the craft's underside, a second studied where debris had peppered the transport's side and the third floated free, observing the area surrounding the ruined mantle mine.

Slab ducked as the third eye swayed past the control room window. "It's giving this thing the once over."

Several dull metal clangs sounded from below, then an electrical hiss began.

"It's repairing it," Bill said.

Cracker appeared on the elevator plate. "What's going on? Wal's babbling some rubbish about you blokes rugby tackling him."

A tentacle eye outside turned toward Cracker, who stared back in surprise as Bill dragged him to the floor. The eye drifted toward the control room window for a better look as Bill pulled Cracker up beside Slab hiding behind the pilot seats.

"You think it saw us?" Bill asked.

Slab crawled to the wall and eased himself up, trying to catch a glimpse of the eye outside. Instinctively, the hairs on the back of his neck stood up, then he turned to see a glassy black eye staring at him through the side window. Another eye was watching from the other side.

"Oh yeah," Slab said, "it saw us."

Cracker and Bill stood slowly and stared back at the robotic eyes studying them. The lights in the control room blinked on while the two consoles in front of the pilot's seats glowed to life, displaying geometric patterns adorned with swirling characters.

"Oh-ho," Bill said apprehensively.

A loud clang reverberated through the control room as an access panel was slammed shut on the transport's belly. A faint machine hum began, then the craft floated silently off the ground. Outside, the wall fragment was pushed away by the transport's propulsion field.

"We're moving!" Cracker exclaimed, feeling no inertia as the ground outside fell away.

The battloid transport rose above the tree tops as gently as a hot air balloon, then as the forest spread out before them, it turned to the west, bringing the ragged ochre cliffs of Parson's Range into view. Without any sense of motion, the craft accelerated to twenty-five times the speed of sound.

Wal appeared on the elevator plate with an alarmed look on his face. "The back door's closed." He pushed past them to stare astonished at the green landscape sweeping beneath them in a blur. "Hey, we're flying!"

"No mate," Bill said gloomily, "we're history!"

* * * *

Bandaka led the way down into a crevice whose normally ochre walls had been coated in ash from the great fire that had raged after the landing. A third of the way down, the ragged rocks opened into a natural stairway where the stream they followed ran over a series of ledges and mini waterfalls all the way to the valley floor. Only Virus found the going difficult, even with Tucker staying close, catching him when he stumbled.

After emerging from the crevice, they followed a rocky spur that hid them from the mothership. Beyond the spur, ashen waters crept toward them as the river slowly inundated the lowlands. Floating in the water were thousands of charred trees and the rotting corpses of countless birds and animals. A few birds that had flown in from the surrounding valleys now picked their way over the watery graveyard or circled above in search of food. Amid so much death, the birds were unusually quiet, although for once they had nothing to fear as none of the crocodiles had survived the nuclear-like impact.

Bandaka avoided the water, choosing to stay close to the cliffs, stopping only when the spur ended and open ground began. When Beckman came alongside, he pointed his spear at the edge of the cliff a short distance ahead. "They see us there."

"How far to the ship?"

Bandaka looked thoughtfully at the rocky terrain, made more difficult by so many fallen trees. "You very slow." He motioned to a point in the sky where the sun would be by midday. "Sun go there before we reach other side."

Beckman realized Bandaka was estimating two hours to cross. "We must go faster. As fast as you."

The aboriginal hunter's look showed he doubted they could keep up, then Beckman raised his voice for everyone to hear. "We're stealthing from here. We've got forty five minutes. Bandaka will set the pace. Be sure to keep up or you'll get caught in the open when the power cells fail." He turned to Bandaka and pointed to his stealth gear. "When I turn this on, we won't be able to see you. You must make a sound we can follow."

Bandaka tapped his boomerang against his spear. "Like this?"

"Perfect. Pick the easiest, fastest path." He turned to the others. "Stay close together. I don't want to lose anyone going in. Virus, last chance to drop out."

Virus swallowed another painkiller and said, "I'll make it, Major."

"All right, let's do it," Beckman said, then activated Bandaka's stealth field.

The aboriginal hunter blurred before him, then when Beckman stepped back from the light bending field, Bandaka vanished completely. One by one, the rest of the team activated their stealth fields and faded from sight. When Beckman turned his on, the world transformed to an altered dimension of shifting shadows and ghostly silhouettes, created by the scintilla of light that penetrated the field and revealed the surrounding world.

"Go Bandaka," Beckman said, "as fast as you can."

The hollow click of tapping wood moved off around the rocky headland. Beckman immediately followed the sound while behind him, the rapid crunch of boots told him the others were rushing to keep up. They'd trained long and hard for stealth movement, mostly with blindfolds, but occasionally with power cells. Normally Beckman or Hooper made the guide sound, but Bandaka had a good eye for the terrain and was their best chance for a fast crossing. He followed an ancient track around the spur until they were clear of the river, then led them away from the cliffs toward the ship.

Ahead, the great bulk of the mothership loomed before them. Even in the shadowy, ethereal world of warped light, the sheer size of the dark mass ahead overwhelmed Beckman's senses. He forced himself to focus on Bandaka's tapping, but the closer they got to the mothership, the more its sheer bulk distracted him.

A shadow streaked overhead, catching Beckman's eye. It came from the east, moving too fast for him to recognize its rectangular shape in the stealth field's shadowy world. For a moment, he wondered if it was searching for them, then it was gone, passing out of sight above the mothership.

Whatever it was, it hadn't seen them.

* * * *

"Strewth!" Wal declared as the transport skimmed over a faceted metallic plain. To their left, the hull sloped gently up toward the ship's central spine half a kilometer away, while to their right, it ran almost level for more than a kilometer until it curved down out of sight.

"It's a big bastard," Bill said.

Cracker nodded. "Bloody oath."

"It's a wreck." Slab motioned to the jagged holes dotting the hull.

"I hope they have insurance," Wal said.

Slab gave Wal a harsh look, then realized the transport was decelerating rapidly. The abrupt change in velocity with no inertial effect defied their senses, yet they saw the hull passing more slowly beneath them. A large rectangular hatch with smooth, rounded edges opened ahead.

"That's where we're going," Bill said uncomfortably.

"Not me," Cracker declared as he slid a detonator into a stick of dynamite.

"You can't use that in here," Slab said.

"You got a better idea?" When Slab gave him a helpless look, Cracker said, "Get back."

He set the timer, then placed the dynamite on the

console. His fingers touched its surface long enough to cause its molecular structure to dissolve, letting the explosive sink into it. Cracker watched in surprise as the console tried to establish a bioelectric link with the dynamite, then he ran to where the others crouched at the rear of the control room.

When the dynamite exploded, the front panel directed the blast upwards, blowing out the cockpit window while the down blast was like a bullet into the transport's brain, scrambling its control systems. The vehicle's propulsion field vanished, unleashing a blast of wind through the shattered window, while the lights in the cockpit failed and the interior acceleration fields collapsed. The sense of motion violently returned as air buffeted the transport and gravity took hold. With no wings, the non-aerodynamic transport fell like a stone.

"Good one, Cracker, you bloody idiot!" Slab growled, shielding his face from the air roaring through the window.

"Hang on!" Bill said, grabbing for the base of one of the pilot's chairs.

The transport belly flopped onto the ship's upper hull, bounced into the air and careened over the open docking bay. Waiting in the bay below was a Mark I battloid, a tracker and three seekers. They saw the transport bounce over the open hatch, aware it had suddenly gone silent, then the agile seekers jumped up out of the docking port and bounded after the crippled craft.

The transport hit the hull again, bounced several times, then slid across the ship's armor, sparks flying from its underside. It narrowly missed one of the yawning wounds in the hull as the gentle downward slope angled the transport toward the side of the ship.

Cracker used one of the pilot's chairs to pull himself to his feet and look outside. "We're not going to stop in time," he yelled, pointing to where the faceted hull angled down to the charred wasteland several kilometers below.

"A metal probe up my arse would have been better than

this," Slab said as he hung on against the wild vibrations.

"We could jump," Wal suggested.

Slab glanced outside incredulously. "Great idea, Wal! You go first."

The transport began to slew sideways, losing speed as it slid obliquely toward the edge of the ship. Bill looked back through the starboard window and saw tiny silver shapes leaping after them. At the other side window, Cracker spotted a dark cavity in the hull, dead ahead. Before he could shout a warning, the transport skidded into the circular hull breach. The sound of grinding metal was instantly replaced by the whistle of air as the transport fell toward the deck below. It landed hard, knocking them off their feet, then careened through a dark hangar, skidding through wedge-shaped fighters saved from decompression by their deck clamps. The fighters exploded in flames as they were smashed aside like toys, then the transport speared nose-first through the bulkhead at the end of the hangar and stuck fast.

Wal lay piled against the control console, staring up dazed through the smashed cockpit window. "That wasn't so bad! Any landing you can walk away from, right?"

"Piss off, Wal," Slab growled.

Bill climbed shakily to his feet and looked out at the darkened storage deck the transport had nosed into. "They'll be coming for us."

Slab aimed his rifle through the broken cockpit window. "I'm ready!"

"I've got a better idea," Cracker said. "Let's bolt."

Slab hesitated, then realizing he was right, tossed his backpack through the open window and clambered over the transport's stubby nose to the deck. As he reached for his pack, a maintenance drone floated past and inspected the damaged bulkhead. Slab fired once, hitting the drone's coolie hat propulsion system, then it sparked and fell onto the deck where its telescoping arms twitched and went limp.

“They’re not so tough,” Slab said as the others slid down the transport’s nose.

“Trust you to pick a fight with a weak one!” Wal declared.

“It wasn’t weak. Look at those bloody arms. They’re like metal snakes!”

While Slab prodded the lifeless drone with his rifle, the others shouldered packs and took in their surroundings. The transport’s nose had punched through a bulkhead, wedging its body tightly in place, barring access back into the hangar. They were in a cargo hold stacked full of metal cubes, each a meter and a half square. Bill approached the nearest stack, noting the strange symbols on each.

“Serial numbers?” he said, running his hand over the cold silvery metal.

When his fingers passed over a cluster of characters, a circular panel marked with five pictograms appeared. He tapped each image in turn until the cube’s side became translucent, revealing small containers packed tightly together. Bill found his hand could pass through the translucent surface, so he pulled a container out. It was the size of half a loaf of bread and had one symbol marked on it. When he touched it, the top of the container vanished and the sides became boiling hot.

“Ow!” he cried, dropping it.

The others gathered around curiously. The container had landed on its side, spilling a pungent smelling, thick yellow liquid with small pink cubes onto the deck.

Slab sniffed, wincing. “Is that food?”

“Looks like something my missus would cook,” Wal said, “only better.”

Bill prodded one of the cubes with his fishing knife. It was spongy to the touch and released a thin pinkish fluid that might have been blood. “It’s some kind of meat.”

Cracker knelt down and dabbed his finger in the yellowish stew, then cautiously tasted it with the tip of his tongue. He made a face and spat. “Tastes like crap!”

They started moving down the corridor between the stacks of storage cubes, opening them randomly. They all held food containers filled with stew-like contents.

"If it's food, there's no variety," Cracker said. "It's all the same."

"Like McDonalds," Wal added brightly.

"They remind me of ration packs," Bill said thoughtfully, "like I had in the army."

Slab had advanced ahead of the others, finding the symbols on the storage cubes had changed subtly. He opened one and retrieved a container full of a dark cold liquid. He sniffed it, finding it odorless so he took an experimental sip. He winced at the sour taste, immediately spitting it out and tossing the drink container away in disgust.

"Jeez! How'd these bastard get here drinking crap like that!" he exclaimed.

"No wonder they nicked our beer," Wal said.

A metal shriek sounded behind them. They turned as the transport shuddered and was dragged slowly back into the hangar.

CHAPTER 13

Nemza'ri attached a fusion torch to her heavy lift suit, then sealed the pipe linking the insemination tank she'd just repaired to the amniotic storage vat. She'd salvaged parts for the complex plumbing system from seven damaged reproduction units, although she had no way to test her work. Nanofertilization was the technological equivalent of her species laying unfertilized eggs in the rivers and estuaries of her homeworld which were then externally fertilized by the males, although they hadn't used such random reproductive methods for millions of years.

A day ago, she'd known almost nothing about clonic insemination, a process using cloned genetic material for reproductive purposes. What she knew now was pure download, force fed into her cerebral implants from the ship's science base. She regretted having to purge her memory implants of the engineering knowledge she'd acquired over two centuries aboard ship, but her implants lacked the capacity to retain it and master reproductive genetics simultaneously.

Her shipboard duties and low rank had barred her from reproducing, however, with the ship now in danger she had no choice but to reverse her sterilization in order to replace those who had lost their lives in the sleep chamber. It was not something she desired or dreaded, it was simply her duty.

Nemza'ri parked the red heavy lift suit on one side of the damaged med lab, then climbed out and approached the insemination tank. Lying on operating tables nearby were the two unconscious myrnods she'd captured in the cargo hold. Tubes extended from their chests, draining the precious growth hormone that would accelerate the cloning of genetic material harvested from the male survivors and increase her spawn's growth rate. When she'd stockpiled enough of the growth hormone for reproductive purposes, med drones would administer it to the surviving males to accelerate their recovery.

She instructed the tank to drain the amniotic vat, then peeled off her one piece coverall. When the insemination tank was full, the liquid was warmed to match her body temperature, then she activated her implanted pain suppressors. Once her body had gone numb below the neck, a spherical med drone inserted a long needle into her lower back, guiding it perfectly into her reproductive sac. If not for the pain suppressors, it would have been an excruciating process, but all she felt was a slight pulling of her skin. The needle released the final component of the fertility activator, then her implants monitored the reactivation of her long dormant reproductive system while keeping the nearby med drones advised of her progress.

When she was ready, a pressure field formed in front of the tank and the access hatch dilated. Nemza'ri took a deep breath, compressing air into her quad lungs, then stepped through the field into the synthetic amniotic fluid. Control fields positioned her in the center of the tank, then a med drone passed a sphere containing the cloned male cells into the tank.

The access hatch reformed, sealing her in as control fields moved the fertilization sphere to a position in front of her hips. A cloud of nanomachines swarmed into the tank, penetrated the sphere and collected the precious cells stored there while control fields gently separated her legs. Another swarm of nanomachines entered her body in anticipation of her first ever reproductive cycle in over three hundred years of life.

Nemza'ri felt nothing but the warmth of the fluid around

her and the gentle press of control fields holding her in place. Her diagnostic implants gave her constant updates, monitoring every cellular process with precision. She knew exactly when the nanomachines extracted her newly produced eggs, when the cloned male cells were inserted into them and the moment of each fertilization. Throughout the process she received a running tally of viable eggs, knowing each would mature rapidly in the tank due to the myrnod growth hormone.

When the nanofertilization process was complete, a barely visible mist of nanomachines floated before her tending the newly fertilized eggs. The mist carried the eggs through an outlet into an adjoining gestation tank, then control fields guided Nemza'ri back to the insemination tank's entrance.

The eggs would incubate rapidly in complete safety, then the hatchlings would be provided with nutrients laced with myrnod hormones to continue their accelerated development. If there were no further doses, the hatchlings would still grow at an accelerated rate, reaching adulthood in a decade, but with constant additional doses, they would mature in a single year. After hatching, nanomachines would begin inserting implants at infancy and the downloads would begin. It was a process she could repeat indefinitely every few days and, if required, her eggs could be cloned to accelerate the process.

When she stepped from the insemination tank, her implants informed her that more than fifty thousand eggs had been successfully fertilized with zero failures. All would be hatched. All would mature. Nemza'ri was well satisfied, for the ship no longer needed an engineering technician to maintain inertial accelerators. It required personnel.

It required a breeder, which was what she had become.

CHAPTER 14

Beckman glanced at his watch, estimating the stealth kit's power cells had only minutes of life remaining, thinking, *We can still make it.*

He glanced up at the dark wall towering before them. In the shadow realm of the stealth field, the ship's circular wounds looked like the underworld lairs of the dead. Many were hundreds of meters above the valley floor, while one hull breach touched the ground ahead. Bandaka was leading them to it, moving fast across ground crystallized by heat and covered with ash, then suddenly his monotonous tapping stopped moving.

"What is it?" Beckman asked as he caught up.

"Fireflies," Bandaka's disembodied voice replied.

Beckman had been distracted by the ship's overpowering bulk while Bandaka's keen eyes had spotted points of brightness forming a perimeter around the ship. The tiny lights were the size of small marbles, large enough to generate their own propulsion fields, and they circled each other at knee height constantly changing direction, simulating insect behavior to deceive intelligent motion sensors.

"Find the biggest gap you can," Beckman said loud enough for the others to hear, already anxious about lost seconds. "We'll go through single file, time our runs to avoid the fireflies."

Bandaka studied the firefly perimeter a moment, then moved off to the right so fast the others had to jog to keep up. Beckman heard someone behind him fall, then scramble back to their feet so they wouldn't be left behind. Soon, Bandaka stopped again.

When the others caught up, he said, "We cross here."

"No more tapping," Beckman said. "Once you're through, get to the ship." The hull breach was barely two hundred meters away. "Nuke, if we get caught in the open, detonate the warhead."

"How did I know you were going to say that?" the payload specialist muttered.

"Sound off before you go through, so we don't all go at once. Bandaka, you first, then me."

"I go now," Bandaka said, then the soft patter of his footsteps faded as he loped toward the fireflies.

"I'm moving out," Beckman announced, then hurried toward a pair of lights that flew in short fast circles before darting away, momentarily creating a gap. He sprinted through the opening, then jogged for the hull breach, glancing at his watch as he ran, thinking, *this is going to be close*.

He was almost to the ship when the ghostly world flashed white and a wave of heat washed over his back. Without slowing, he glanced over his shoulder to see a pillar of flame drop a long barreled sniper rifle, then a blackened corpse crumple to the ground as bones turned to ash.

It's Cougar! Beckman realized with a sickening feeling. He hadn't seen what had fired, but he guessed a firefly had penetrated the sniper's stealth field. Forcing himself to grieve later, he thought, *they know we're here.*

Outside the perimeter, Markus saw the fireflies swarm around Cougar's ashen remains. He sprinted through the gap, hoping the fireflies would close the opening after he was through, preventing Nuke from crossing. Without the torpedo, Beckman would have to find another way to destroy the ship.

Close to the hull breach, Beckman heard a chorus of boots trampling fused ground behind him as the others raced through the gap left by the distracted fireflies. Tucker, the strongest and fittest, was the last to cross. Ahead of Beckman, a cave mouth as dark as night loomed out of the ghostly half light, its lower lip just above his head. When he got to the hull, Bandaka's slender arm appeared beside him, reaching into his stealth field. It was a strange apparition of an arm with no body, groping blindly for him from a ghostly world.

"Help me," Bandaka said.

Beckman placed the hunter's hand on his shoulder, then cupped his own hands beneath Bandaka's leathery foot and launched him up into the hull breach. A moment later, a spear tip lunged down in front of Beckman's face. He caught it and scrambled up into the opening, then turned to watch for the others.

"Three are close," Bandaka's voice whispered from the twilight to Beckman's right.

"How can you tell?"

"I see their tracks."

Beckman heard approaching footsteps, but couldn't see them in the shadow world he inhabited. He turned to examine the hull breach, finding a gradually sloping tunnel had been blasted through the triple layered hull deep into the ship's interior, melting through many decks. As he tried to make out the details, he realized the light reaching his eyes was growing in intensity.

My power cell's failing, he thought, then heard the smack of boots clambering up the hull at the end of Bandaka's spear.

"Only just made it," Markus declared. "I can see color."

Beckman looked across the blasted landscape to the escarpment, discovering hints of red and orange among the ash streaked cliffs, a sure sign his stealth field was powering down. On the approaches to the ship, the ground blurred in several places where stealth fields were losing their ability to bend light, then another distortion appeared immediately below them.

"Man, what a hike!" Nuke declared as Bandaka pulled him up, then he stepped into the tunnel and flopped exhausted onto the deck, shrugging off his heavy backpack.

Beckman saw another blur approach, then Bandaka hauled Xeno up into the ship.

"Everyone, up the ramp," Beckman said.

Markus and Xeno clambered up the tunnel's slick metal slope while Nuke carried his pack one handed after them. Beckman now searched for Tucker and Virus, soon spotting a single smear of twisted light racing toward the ship, but no sign of a second. He wondered if one of them had been killed without him realizing it, then the approaching blur betrayed a hint of dappled green. The green wraith inside the blur took on the double form of Virus with his arm across Tucker's shoulders. Virus' stealth field was no longer functioning, its power cell having failed prematurely, while Tucker's was close to collapse.

"Hurry, goddamn it," Beckman whispered, silently cursing himself for letting Virus come, then incredibly, they stopped.

Beckman bit off an urge to yell at them, to order them to run, as they turned to face the perimeter. Virus balanced his M16 on his hip, angled up forty-five degrees and fired his grenade launcher at the fireflies buzzing the perimeter. A moment later, a phosphorus grenade exploded in a cloud of white hot embers irresistibly drawing the fireflies to it.

Tucker lifted Virus over his shoulder and jogged toward the ship. Behind them, fireflies swarmed toward the phosphorus cloud while in the sky far to the south, a black speck approached at hypersonic velocity. Tucker reached the ship as his stealth field failed and hurled Virus up into the hull breach like he was tossing a sandbag. Beckman caught Virus and dragged him in as Tucker hauled himself up by Bandaka's spear.

"Go, go, go!" Beckman yelled, pushing Virus toward the tunnel.

In the sky outside, the black speck grew into the wedge-shaped striker. It fired at the burning phosphorus, turning the area into a boiling lava pool, then swooped toward the movement it detected in the hull breach.

Tucker charged up the tunnel with Virus and Bandaka, then as Beckman followed, his stealth field gave out. It was like turning on a light. In a glance, he saw the swath of destruction inside the ship clearly, the ragged decks, the twisted debris and the pools of recently molten metal.

Light flashed behind him as the striker bombarded the entrance and a wave of heat rolled up the ramp after him. Beckman charged into a shadowy compartment lit by a single flickering light and darted sideways as the blast erupted from the tunnel.

"Incoming!" he yelled as he threw his back against the bulkhead, glimpsing rows of floor to ceiling latticeworks, empty except for a handful of dark metal spacesuits that had survived the whirlwinds of explosive decompression. Another blast flashed in through the entrance and struck the ramp half way up, its flash revealing the faces of his team peering out from among the empty suit cradles, weapons ready.

Behind him, the striker swooped into the hull breach, coming to an instant stop as it assessed the situation. It nosed up, angling its wingtip cannons into the tunnel and fired two brilliant orange blasts that streaked up through four decks and exploded against a damaged bulkhead. The heat from the blasts startled Beckman with their intensity, warning him that even a near miss would be fatal.

Tucker circled around, then tossed a grenade into the tunnel. It clanged hollowly on naked metal as it bounced down the slope toward the striker which scanned it, finding it matched none of the millions of weapon profiles it had on record. It guessed the grenade was an explosive device and from its size, assumed its yield to be a thousand times more powerful than it was.

To evade the shockwave, the striker accelerated up

through the tunnel, leaving the grenade to explode harmlessly near the entrance. It shot into the suit compartment at high speed and turned sharply away from the flickering light, plotting its course by design schematics that had not been updated for ship damage. The striker careened off a collapsed bulkhead and crashed into a partially melted lattice, cracking its horizontal sensor strip and wrapping lattice strands over its leading edge, further obscuring its vision. It tried stabilizing itself as Beckman, Tucker and Xeno opened up with specials from three sides, then its shield collapsed, allowing super heated particles to slice through its lightly armored skin, triggering an internal explosion. The striker lurched sideways, crashed through an empty latticework and fell tail first onto the deck. Beckman and the others continued firing, carving the machine that had killed Cougar into pieces long after it had been neutralized.

"Cease fire!" Beckman ordered.

He stood as the others emerged from their hiding places. Only Virus remained on the deck propped against an empty suit cradle, his face white and dripping with sweat. Beckman approached him, noting his sickly complexion. "You don't look so good."

"I just need a minute, Major," Virus said weakly between sips from his canteen.

Beckman turned his attention to the surrounding compartment. There were at least twenty rows of rectangular wireframe lattices standing side by side, vaguely reminding him of a locker room.

"Major," Nuke called from beside a bulky, dark blue metallic suit a meter and a half tall wedged in a supporting lattice. It was bipedal, disproportionately wide at the chest and hips with an oversized, elongated helmet. The side facing the hull breach were scalded black while its remoteness from the tunnel of destruction had saved it from being sucked into space when the compartment had decompressed.

When Beckman approached, he saw it was cracked apart like a clamshell, with a vertical split from head to foot revealing a padded interior able to mold to its occupant's form. The inside of the helmet lacked anything resembling controls or view screens, just small silver surfaces at the top and rear which – unknown to Beckman – enabled the suit to communicate directly with the wearer's implants.

Markus tapped the metal, which rang hollowly. "Sounds like armor."

Beckman studied the mounts at each shoulder and the attachment brackets on the forearms. "Could be for tools or weapons."

"It's nothing like the suits at Groom," Xeno said, remembering the silky metallic body suits studied at the materials analysis lab. She looked inside the armored suit, gauging its size. "And it's bigger inside. They're not Zetas."

Nuke moved slowly along the lattice work, casually looking over the few other surviving suits, stopping at the last one in line. He used his hand to push the clamshell open, then a horribly burned corpse toppled out, hitting him in the chest before falling to the deck.

Nuke jumped back startled, then wiped burnt alien flesh from his clothes. "Ugh!"

The body was bipedal, three quarters the height of a man, almost fifty percent wider with an overly large head.

"Ugly son of a bitch," Tucker said.

"Unlucky more like it," Markus said. "It almost got the suit shut. It might have survived if it had."

Beckman gave Xeno an inquiring look. "Do you recognize it?"

"It's definitely a new species," she said. "How much time do I have?"

"Two minutes."

Xeno pushed a video camera into Nuke's hand, then knelt beside the body, pulling on white plastic gloves. Nuke started recording, then she said, "Specimen One."

She examined the charred flesh on one side and its swollen and blotched blue gray skin on the other. "Burns indicate exposure to extreme heat. Skin discoloration is typical of tissue damage from decompression. Both contributed to cause of death." She measured the dimensions of the head. "Skull length, forty six centimeters. I'd need to perform a craniotomy to accurately assess brain to body mass." She gave Beckman a hopeful look.

"We don't have time."

She nodded, disappointed, then turned the elongated chin to the side curiously. "Long chin, evolved to balance skull weight. That's an advanced evolutionary marker." Xeno produced a slender probe and a pencil thin flashlight from her kit, then pushed back the alien's thin lips, revealing small triangular teeth.

Tucker looked impressed. "Nasty little chompers."

"Teeth for tearing flesh indicating it's a carnivore." She ran the probe around the mouth, checking its teeth. "No sign of cavities or cracks."

"Hey!" Nuke declared, "they've got a dental plan in outer space."

Xeno shone the light on the flat nose, which was little more than two vertical slits. "These nostrils may seal shut in water." She lifted the probe to the tennis-ball-sized eyes located at the side of its head. "Eye placement indicates a wider field of vision than humans, possibly … two hundred and seventy degrees in the horizontal, more in the vertical." She slid its thin translucent eyelid back and aimed the spotlight into the eye. "The eye is covered by a retractable layer similar to what amphibians have for underwater protection." The pupil was a dark vertical slit, surrounded by a blue iris flecked with light green. "Multiple lenses in the eye, one segment is floating. It may work like a short zoom lens." She traced imaginary lines from each eye, estimating the field of vision of each. "The specimen has limited stereoscopic vision for depth perception, significantly less horizontal range than humans have."

"That means it's not a predator, right?" Nuke said. "So they're not dangerous."

"She said it was a carnivore, Lieutenant," Tucker said sharply.

"Oh," he said deflated.

"The specimen has good spatial perception," she continued, "but the narrow stereoscopic vision suggests its ancestors didn't hunt in the open. It could be an ambush predator."

"Ambush predator?" Nuke repeated uncertainly. "What's that?"

"A sneak attacker," Tucker declared.

Xeno nodded. "That's their evolutionary origin. Ambush predators wait in hiding, then surprise their prey with a fast, unexpected attack."

"You wouldn't know they were coming until your cities were burning," Beckman said.

"That could make them highly secretive, deceptive," Markus said, "maybe masters of espionage."

"Those are highly speculative interpretations," Xeno said cautiously.

"But not implausible," Beckman said, wishing for the first time that Dr. McInness was there to provide his perspective.

She leaned over the skull examining it carefully. "The specimen has no visible ears, suggesting it may be deficient in hearing," she touched the pronounced, dome-shaped bulge on its forehead, "although it has a large frontal lobe with a firm cartilaginous covering." It reminded her of something, but she couldn't remember what. She moved to the amphibian's smooth hairless arm. "Muscles are firm, but not overly hard, indicating fitness but not excessive muscle strength."

"Damn, a dental plan and a gym membership!" Nuke exclaimed. "They are advanced!"

"Are you getting this?" Xeno demanded of Nuke with a trace of irritation. "The skin is quite tough," she continued, pressing the probe against the amphibian's arm. "Body shape is uniformly streamlined, but fingers are not webbed."

"Your assessment?" Beckman asked, anxious to move on.

"It's highly advanced with some interesting adaptations. The brain development could be millions of years ahead of us, even with those teeth. We're physically stronger, but judging by cranial size, they have the IQ points."

"How does it compare to a Zeta?" Markus asked.

"Brain to body mass ratio might be comparable, unless that rear skull extension has brain mass in which case … they could have twenty percent on the Zetas."

"Finished?" Beckman asked.

She nodded, then her eyes widened with realization. "Dolphins! That's why it has no ears. It doesn't need them." She pointed to the alien's bulging forehead. "This dome could be biological sonar. It wouldn't need much stereoscopic vision, if it hunted with sonar. They might hear and see acoustically with that lobe."

"Great!" Nuke declared pessimistically. "It's a super predator!"

Beckman cast a wary look at the diminutive, partially charred corpse. "All done?"

"Yes sir," she said, retrieving the camera from Nuke and slipping it into her pack.

"Step back."

Beckman rolled the corpse sideways with his boot and fired a line of carefully aimed shots through the side of the creature's skull. Fragments of bone and a dark viscous blood splashed onto the deck from the wounds and pooled beneath its head, then he drove his knife into the bullet holes and levered the skull open. With the brain exposed, Beckman wiped his knife clean on the creature's skin tight body suit and nodded to Xeno.

She shone her flashlight into its elongated skull, pushing against the tissue with her probe. "The brain tissue extends all the way back, sir."

Beckman's jaw hardened. "Meet the new top of the food chain, people."

"Oh man, we are so screwed," Nuke said dismally.

Tucker gave Nuke a fierce look. "Anything living can be killed, Lieutenant."

Virus joined them, feeling his strength returning. Deep within his tortured mind, he remembered what the amphibians called themselves, but it was unpronounceable. Another word appeared in his mind, a word used by too many languages to count.

"They're called … Intruders." Virus winced as he fought to clarify his thoughts. "It's not what they call themselves. It's what others call them. Other civilizations."

"Why?" Beckman asked.

Virus stared at the charred corpse, the mere sight of which triggered disturbing, implanted feelings. He had an automatic response that mistreating its corpse was wrong. Even though he'd struggled to absorb the technical information he'd been force fed, he found he couldn't shake the obedience training. "They go ... where they're not wanted."

Beckman watched the mutilated corpse leak blood onto the deck with growing trepidation. "I never did like uninvited guests. Let's go."

* * * *

Vamp held onto a twisted bulkhead and leant out into a circular chasm of melted metal more than a hundred decks high. The sky was a mere pinpoint of light above while a well of darkness below echoed with the swirl of water. This time there were no shrieks from starving myrnods or the hiss of cutting torches nibbling at torn metal. The only sign of life was a tiny finch fluttering from one ragged deck to another, lost in a gigantic maze of destruction.

She pulled herself back in to where Timer and Dr.

McInness waited. "Whatever hit this thing cut through it like butter."

They'd worked their way up through immense cargo decks sucked clean by explosive decompression, along passageways as wide as six lane highways to smaller more specialized compartments. Occasionally they triggered proximity sensors that opened archways revealing armories, hangars and wrecked laboratories whose purposes they could only guess at.

A partially closed blast door framed by soft yellow-orange light lay ahead. It was held open by a four legged robot with thick metal arms and fingers clamped so tightly onto the door that they'd crushed the metal, leaving impressions of its hands in the surface. Its torso was dented in many places from glancing blows received from objects that had struck it as they were sucked into space.

"The power must have failed as the door was closing," Dr. McInness said as he started toward the robot, eager to inspect it.

Vamp caught his arm. "You don't want to mess with that, Ian."

"It's clearly deactivated."

Vamp glanced at the battered robot then released his arm. "OK, but not too close."

Dr. McInness stepped closer, finding one side was seared black and two of its legs had partially melted from the intense heat source that had drilled through the ship a short distance away.

"Judging by those arms, I'd say it's some kind of cargo handler," he said, leaning toward its thick limbs.

"It didn't want to be sucked out," Timer said.

"Yes," the scientist said slowly, deep in thought. "It must have had a sense of self preservation. Hmm, even their lowly cargo haulers have enough self awareness to save themselves from destruction."

The cargo handler's left arm rotated around its spherical elbow joint and clamped onto Dr. McInness' ankle. He groaned and fell as his bones snapped like twigs, then Vamp stepped forward and aimed her M16 at the machine's elbow joint.

"No! No!" the scientist wheezed in agony. "Ricochets."

She hesitated, then turned to Timer. "Hit the elbow with your special." She glanced down at Dr. McInness. "OK?"

"Yeah," he said through gritted teeth, "just don't shoot my leg off!"

Timer angled his special as far away from the scientist as he could, then touched the firing surface, blasting a pinhole in the elbow joint. The cargo handler's arm shuddered and released its grip, then Vamp dragged Dr. McInness clear. A moment later, the four-legged cargo handler pushed itself to a sitting position with its still functional right arm. It wobbled a moment, then climbed onto its two good legs, using its partially melted legs as crutches. Vamp let the scientist go and raked the machine's torso with her M16, but the bullets bounced off until her gun clicked empty.

"Reloading!"

Timer grabbed Dr. McInness and dragged him through an archway onto a balcony bordering a broad circular transit shaft that ran vertically up through every deck in the ship. It was lined with six pairs of silver magnetic strips that supported cargo platforms covered by translucent domes. With nowhere else to go, Timer took the scientist's right arm across his shoulder and headed for the elevator platform, yelling, "This way."

Vamp slammed a new clip into her rifle as she backed after them, saving her ammo now that she knew the cargo handler's hull was too thick to penetrate. The robot lurched after her, its left arm hanging uselessly from its elbow while its good arm reached out, its metal claws snapped rhythmically. Vamp fired single shots at the glassy black sensor bulb on top of its torso, scoring several glancing hits that cracked the shiny surface, but didn't slow it down.

Timer carried Dr. McInness onto the cargo elevator,

lowered him to the floor, then realized the transparent walls and domed ceiling were featureless. "Where are the controls?"

"Must be remotely controlled," Dr. McInness said as he propped himself against the side of the elevator.

Vamp backed onto the platform firing single shots at the robot's sensor dome. "Go!"

"No controls," Timer said, motioning to the blank walls.

Vamp slid a grenade into the launcher mounted beneath her M16. "Fire in the hole," she yelled, then popped the grenade and jumped behind the translucent wall. The grenade exploded against the robot's torso, sending it sliding back across the deck and peppering the cargo platform's dome with shrapnel, leaving dozens of white impact points. The cargo handler lay motionless a moment, then pushed itself up onto its legs and started lurching toward them again.

"Is that a forklift or a tank?" she muttered, dropping her M16 and drawing her tiny silver special. The 'Tom Thumb' was the smallest and least powerful of all the recovered weapons, but it packed more focused firepower than her M16. She touched the firing surface, triggering a stream of super heated plasma that punched through the cargo handler, then it exploded, scattering arms and legs in all directions.

"So much for self-preservation," Vamp said as she holstered her special.

An alarm warbled several times, then a high pitched voice spoke in an incomprehensible language. The elevator's door materialized, locking them inside as the under powered cargo platform began sliding slowly upwards.

Vamp sighed. "I guess we got their attention."

* * * *

The groan of grinding metal filled the storage compartment as the transport was dragged back through the bulkhead, then three seekers sped through the ragged opening like silver streaks. They came to a sudden stop and scanned the empty aisles before them, finding several supply containers had been opened but no sign of the four humans. The seekers separated and began searching the aisles as their metal feet clanked loudly on the deck plating.

Bill hid in a cross aisle in the middle of the chamber, listening to the metal footsteps march toward him. Wal and Cracker were together two rows across, while Slab hid in the row behind. Bill gave Cracker a questioning look: *what should we do?*

Cracker shrugged, then Wal slid his rifle's safety off, causing the faintest click.

The three seekers stopped, each registering the sound and instantly exchanging data to triangulate Wal's position. He'd barely removed his thumb from the safety when two of the machines sped forward. They appeared either side of him and Cracker, snatched the guns from their hands and shot electric charges into their spinal cords. Paralyzed, they collapsed onto the floor, their muscles twitching from nerve shock.

Two rows away, Bill raised his rifle, but the nearest seeker darted toward him with blurring speed and wrenched the gun from his hands. Before he could react, one of its arms flashed out and touched his neck, pumping electricity into his body and sending him crashing to the floor.

Slab heard the muffled sounds of his mates being overpowered, then metallic footsteps marching up and down the aisles searching for him. He pulled himself quietly up onto a stack of storage containers with barely any headroom, then brought his rifle forward ready to shoot. When the tip of his gun's barrel protruded beyond the edge of the containers, it was immediately detected by a seeker. It informed its companions of Slab's location, then leapt onto the container stack and scrambled toward him on hands and knees.

Slab turned and squeezed off a shot. His bullet struck the top of the seeker's sensor disk, splintering its vision. It veered sideways as he fired again, dodging his second shot as it circled in toward him. He fired again and again, missing each time as the seeker darted sideways faster than he could turn in the cramped space.

A second silver blur swept in behind him and tried to tear the gun from his hands, but Slab held on, his thick muscles bulging as he refused to let go. It lashed out at his spine with one of its free hands, trying to paralyze him, but he kicked out wildly, knocking it across the aisle into another stack of containers as the first seeker reached him. It sent a bolt of electricity into his spine, then fighting paralysis, he fired a shot that ricocheted off its hip. It grabbed the barrel with two hands and bent it ninety degrees, then the second seeker leapt back across the aisle and stunned him again, this time with a stronger charge.

Slab groaned, let go of the rifle and slumped helplessly onto his face. The first seeker scooped him up like a rag doll and carried him down into the aisle toward the hole in the bulkhead. He struggled to focus, glimpsing the other seekers holding his mates who were as helpless as he was.

The alien robots carried them back through the hangar, past the wrecked transport and burning fighters then leapt up onto the hull. Slab's head spun as the world wheeled crazily around him and the seekers bounded toward the ship's central spine. His face flopped close to the metal hull with each stride, but never hit, although the wild rocking motion made him nauseous, even as air blasted his face.

Near the spine of the ship, the seekers leapt into an open hatchway, diving down into a large circular cargo shaft with six pairs of silver stripes that disappeared into the darkness far below. In the same shaft, almost a hundred decks below, Vamp, Dr. McInness and Timer were trapped in a cargo platform slowly rising toward them.

The seekers caught the narrow ladders lining the shaft's inner wall with their feet, then launched themselves into the air with the agility of monkeys swinging through trees. They bounded from ladder to ladder as cargo platforms swept by at all angles and the sky shrank rapidly away.

Slab was about to be separated from his breakfast when the seekers landed on a cargo balcony, then sped through an archway into a large laboratory containing a rectangular table beneath a cluster of bright lights. Pinned to the table by a milky white nanomembrane was a sleeping man attended by two spherical med drones. He was gaunt with stubble on his chin and dark stains of weariness under his eyes.

Lining the wall was a white bench with equipment stations spaced along it. Floating med drones with delicate telescoping arms tended experiments and moved research samples from station to station. Most instruments contained the dissected remains of animals and birds, each sample carefully sorted and categorized, while others contained disassembled pieces of a shotgun that were being subjected to metallurgical and chemical tests.

The seekers dropped the four paralyzed men on the deck and passed their rifles to the med drones for analysis. Some of the drones used surgical lasers to sever their backpack straps, then deposited the packs on the bench tops for examination as tables rose out of the floor beneath the men. Nanomembrane emerged from the tables, swam over their bodies and pinned them down with gentle, vice-like grips. Once they were restrained, the seekers disappeared back down the corridor at high speed.

Slab was the first to have feeling return to his body, earlier than the med drones expected. They had already completed mapping the human genome, but were yet to analyze enough specimens to precisely compute stun charges for different body masses. They'd already identified thousands of bio-agents that could eliminate part or all of life on Earth, but the production of such organisms required extensive repairs to the genetic engineering labs. With few resources and many higher priorities the Command Nexus had been forced to temporarily exclude bio-toxin based elements from its contingency plan.

All Slab knew was that he could wiggle his toes and he itched in places he couldn't scratch. The nanomembrane restraining him felt soft, yet resisted his every movement. Nearby, Wal lay with his mouth open, staring blankly at the bright light above his table while Cracker blinked, trying to focus. Bill was outside Slab's line of sight, although a med drone was carefully laying out the contents of Bill's pack for analysis.

One of the med drones floated into view carrying a surgical laser, a white circular ball of sterilized cloth and a shiny silver machine fitted with a circular cup at one end. The cup seemed familiar to Slab, then his eyes darted across to where a knobby emu leg stood perpendicular to the bench, held by a cup the twin of the device in the drone's metallic hand.

It's going to dissect me! he thought as his eyes darted back to the spherical robot.

A rectangular surface extended out from the table in line with his left shoulder, then the nanomembrane slid away from his left arm allowing the drone to move it onto the extension. Once his arm was in place, the nanomembrane began to flow from his chest out along his arm as the med drone aimed its laser scalpel at his elbow. The tip glowed as a red beam stabbed down onto the table extension and began moving toward his arm, filling Slab with terror. Adrenalin surged through his body, forcing paralyzed muscles to life and imbuing Slab with the strength of primal fear.

He grabbed the laser scalpel, surprising the drone, which instructed the nanomembrane to flow up to his wrist. The nanomachines dragged his upper arm down, locking it to the table while his big paw refused to release the laser scalpel. He found the delicate tentacle holding the laser cutter to be coldly metallic and hard as steel, yet it was designed for fine work and lacked the strength to overpower him. He twisted the scalpel, forcing the beam away, trying to snap the tentacle.

Knowing Slab was an air breather, the med drone wrapped one of its free tentacles around his throat and began to squeeze as the nanomembrane began to claw at his fingers. Slab realized he lacked the strength to stop it prying open his fingers, then he heard an urgent, incomprehensible moan to his right. It was Cracker, too paralyzed to speak, making meaningless noises, trying to tell him something.

What? Slab wondered, unable to speak as he choked in the grip of the med drone.

Cracker moaned again, opening his mouth wider as he strained to make a word.

Speak up! Slab thought, his face turning red from suffocation.

Realizing he couldn't form a word, Cracker partly closed his mouth and hissed, casting his eyes toward the bench top.

Snake noises? Slab wondered, not understanding, wanting to tell Cracker what a bloody useless idiot he was, then realizing he wasn't hissing like a snake. He was hissing like a burning fuse.

The nanomembrane pried open Slab's little finger, but he twisted the laser cutter toward the bench, angling the beam into Bill's backpack, then sideways to Cracker's, where it burned through six sticks of dynamite. They exploded, blowing out the nearest wall and hurling wrecked med drones and debris across the lab and through the archway into the transit shaft beyond.

The nanomachines covering Slab and the others shielded them from the blast as a med drone crashed into a wall and exploded against the compartment's central power conduit, plunging the med lab into darkness. Starved of photo electric energy, trillions of nanomachines covering the men turned to a viscous ooze.

Slab blinked, adjusting his eyes to the darkness as he sensed the binding force holding him down was now a cold gooey mass dripping onto the floor. The med drone tentacle around his neck slid away as he lifted his arm, peering at the fluidic blob pooling in his hand, wondering, *What is this crap?*

* * * *

The lights in the cargo shaft winked out as the explosion in the med lab above cut the shaft's power supply. Vamp, Timer and Dr. McInness braced as their cargo platform lost touch with the wall's magnetic strip and began to fall through darkness. It picked up speed as the floor tilted down on one side, then the platform burst out into a light filled section of the shaft. With power suddenly restored, emergency measures automatically activated, jerking the platform back to the magnetic strips. Only one magnetic lock caught, spinning the platform sideways and rotating the floor to the vertical.

They slid down onto the transparent dome as emergency brakes brought the platform to a halt. Timer, on hands and knees, looked down through the dome into the shaft below. It seemed to fall away forever, triggering a wave of vertigo and a fear that the translucent wall would shatter beneath him.

"That was close," he muttered.

A tiny hammer blow sounded above them as a small metal object bounced off the top of the dome. They all looked up as a hail storm of wrecked equipment and med drone parts – blown out of the lab where Slab and his companions were held – began to pepper the top side of the translucent canopy. White impact points appeared with each strike, sending cracks multiplying across its surface into a spider's web of fractures. When the debris storm ended, the platform was left rocking precariously by its single magnetic lock. The elevator door had vanished, opened automatically by the platform's emergency escape system, although they were halfway between decks.

Vamp sensed a dark mass high above, silhouetted against the distant light of the sky, then she jumped to her feet as she realized it was falling toward them.

"Get out!" she yelled urgently.

Dr. McInness lay closest to the exit, but couldn't walk on his broken ankle. She caught the back of his jacket and dragged him to the archway. There was a small ladder near the magnetic strip, but she knew there was no time to use it.

"Timer! Help me!" she yelled.

Timer staggered toward her with a welling bruise on his forehead where he'd struck his head and grabbed the scientist's other arm.

"What are you doing?" Dr. McInness asked anxiously.

"Better you don't know," Vamp said, then they threw him through the archway onto the deck below.

They grabbed their weapons and jumped after him as another cargo platform plunged out of control into the light. They landed on the deck as it crashed into their platform, shattering both domes into thousands of shards and tearing their elevator from the magnetic strip. The two wrecked platforms then tumbled into the shaft, bouncing off each other and the walls as they hurtled toward the bottom far below.

"Ouch!" Timer said. "Next time, I'm taking the stairs."

"I wonder what caused that," Dr. McInness said as color returned to his face.

"Maybe it's the ship's way of fighting back," Vamp said, standing.

"You think it did that on purpose?" Timer asked apprehensively.

"I don't know," she said, "but let's not wait around to find out."

She helped Dr. McInness to his feet, then with his arm across her shoulder, they hobbled across the landing. An archway opened before them into a short corridor that led to a large circular room with a rounded ceiling and a single, broad chair at its center. The walls and floors were featureless and smooth, made of the same glassy black material they'd seen on control consoles and sensor surfaces.

Vamp lowered Dr. McInness into the chair so he could rest a moment. As soon as he sat down, a sphere of light appeared in front of his neck, eye height for the mothership's amphibian crew. Cautiously, he probed the light with his finger tips, finding it made his skin tingle.

"It's some kind of field."

She gave it a wary look. "Don't mess with it, Ian." She reached for his arm. "Slide out."

He waved her off. "This close to the chair, it must be a control interface."

Timer glanced warily into the corridor. "Or an alarm calling an army of pissed off tinheads to kick our butts."

Dr. McInness eased his hand into the sphere, finding the tingling sensation increased.

"Remember what happened to Virus," Vamp warned.

"Dare to learn," he said carelessly, then winced suddenly, grabbed his wrist and screamed in agony. "Argh!" Vamp rushed forward to pull his arm out, then he grinned. "Just kidding. It's actually quite pleasant. Feels a like a glove."

"Not funny!" She punched his shoulder hard.

He pushed his hand fully into the light sphere. The room vanished around them, replaced by a beautiful blue green world floating amidst a sea of stars. Wispy white clouds drifted above continents, archipelagoes and oceans, while polar caps two thirds the size of Earth's own framed the world. Sunlight lit the western hemisphere revealing vast cultivated plains and cities that swallowed every coastline, but no forests or jungles, for they had been cleared eons before. The mountain ranges, rather than being capped with snow, were tipped in metal. They had been hollowed out and filled with immense atmosphere scrubbers that replenished the world's oxygen, something its ecosystem had lost the capacity to do long ago. Between the continents, quilted oceans filled with marine farms produced the bulk of the world's food supply while submerged desalination plants supplied its fresh water.

By contrast, the eastern hemisphere was in the midst of night. Its outline was marked by the light of one unending city that wound along its coast for thousands of kilometers, forming a single band of light that vanished beyond the edge of the world. City lights charted the course of thousands of rivers, estuaries and lakes, many of them artificial, designed to provide an ideal home for billions of amphibian inhabitants.

Floating above the world were thousands of ships and structures so large they were cities in their own right. The ships ranged in size from a few hundred meters to leviathans many kilometers long resembling the mothership itself, while the great orbital cities were spheres hundreds of kilometers across. Each city followed a similar pattern, a central disk with spherical domes on either side filled with spires. The central disk provided power, atmosphere and gravity, making life virtually indistinguishable from the sprawling coastal cities below. The orbital habitats and visiting ships floated above the world in layers, each layer a higher orbit, stacked on top of each other out to the fringes of the planet's gravitational field. Flitting between the ships and the orbital cities were thousands of small cargo vessels, streaking in and out of orbit at a frenetic pace. Some were aerodynamically streamlined, others were not. In the distance, the orbiting cities became tiny specks, while many more went unseen at even greater distances.

Towering above it all, a radiant yellow-orange star shone, slightly smaller than Sol, yet a third closer to their planet than Earth was to its sun. To eyes evolved under a yellow sun, the star cast a bright orange hue over every ship and city in orbit and tinted the color of the oceans and polar caps. Beyond the watery world and its glowing star was a night sky filled with stars, far closer and more densely packed than Earth's Milky Way sky.

No one spoke for a long time, so captivated were they by the blue green globe of the Intruder Homeworld and the technological triumphs that floated above it.

Finally, Timer said, "I guess that's not Earth."

"It might be," Dr. McInness whispered, "a million years from now."

* * * *

Slab tried to stand, but found his legs were like rubber. He rolled off the examination table onto the floor, landing in a slippery puddle of nanoslime. Nearby, Wal fell onto the floor and lay there twitching while Bill dropped his legs over the side of his table and sat up, supporting himself with both hands.

"They'll be coming," a raspy voice announced from the dark. It was the voice of a man starved of food and water and wearied by constant examination. He'd been spared dissection because he was the only sentient specimen the ship had obtained. He sat up slowly, weak but glad to be free after days of confinement, then lowered himself onto his feet and gingerly made his way to where Slab was learning to crawl.

"G'day," the man said with a crooked smile, slipping an arm around the big ex-footy player and helping him to his feet. "I'm Dan."

Slab tried to speak, but his tongue wouldn't obey. He made an unintelligible slurring sound as he found he could stand with Dan's support.

Cracker spotted a familiar dark shape on the floor, eased himself off the table and walked stiff legged to where Bill's old Browning A-bolt hunting rifle lay. It was loaded, but in the darkness and wreckage of the lab, there would be little hope of finding more ammunition. With the gun in his hand

and two sticks of dynamite in his pocket, Cracker's spirits began to rise. He held the gun up for the others to see, but Bill barely noticed. His attention was on the glimmer of light coming from the elevator shaft. There was no sign of movement, but he realized Dan was right, they didn't have long.

Wal staggered to where the bench had been. Twisted metal surrounded the hole blown through the bulkhead by the dynamite. It opened into a room containing rows of transparent cylinders filled with a clear, slowly bubbling liquid. The explosion had shattered many of the containers, spilling the liquid onto the floor. Wal didn't recognize the room as a mass casualty medical facility, but he saw a faint illumination coming from a corridor at the far end – a way out.

He turned to the others and pointed. "Thaa waaay." In spite of Wal's rubbery lips, they understood.

Slab let go of Dan and, this time keeping his balance, stumbled to their escape hole. Wal crawled through first, tumbling onto the floor on the other side, finding it covered in a thin layer of viscous fluid spilled from the bubbling cylinders damaged in the explosion. He tried cursing, but the sound that came from his mouth was unintelligible, then the others clambered through, splashing him as their boots landed in the fluid. He wiped the strange substance from his face, feeling a tingling sensation as it reacted with his skin, then he stood and grinned in amazement.

"I feel bloody fantastic!" he said as the paralysis and every ache in his body disappeared.

The others looked at him curiously, feeling like old men, barely able to stand.

"It's this stuff," Wal declared enthusiastically. "Try it."

"Pih orf, Waa!" Slab growled.

Wal breathed in deeply. "I feel ten years younger."

"Yuuu loo like shii," Slab slurred.

Wal snatched the rifle from Cracker's hands and smashed the butt into one of the cylinders. It shattered, spilling a wave of clear liquid onto the floor, washing their wobbly legs out from under them and saturating them all as they splashed in it on the floor.

Slab sprung to his feet and stomped toward Wal with clenched fists as Wal shrank back grinning, "You feel better, don't you?"

Slab raised his fist about to let Wal have it, then realized he felt better than he had in years. It was as if time itself had lifted from his shoulders. He lowered his fist slowly, flexing his muscles, testing his new found strength. "Jeez, I reckon I could go four quarters at the Gee. And kick a dozen goals!"

The others stood up, stretching. Not only were the after effects of the electric shock gone, but old muscles felt young again, tired joints moved like silk. Even Dan's weathered face, dehydrated and starved, now glowed with renewed vigor.

Wal opened the water bottle by his side, gulped down the last of its contents, then held the bottle under the small waterfall flowing from the container he'd smashed.

"What are you doing now?" Slab demanded.

Wal gave him a larcenous grin. "Mate, do you know what women would pay for this stuff?"

Slab looked astonished, then exchanged thoughtful looks with the others. Moments later, they were all gathered around the broken vessel, filling their canteens with the miraculously curative liquid.

CHAPTER 15

Beckman's team picked their way through a maze of corridors, past storage compartments, manufacturing facilities, hospitals and dormitory style sleeping quarters for tens of thousands. Some were in perfect condition. Others had been utterly destroyed by the same thermal weapon that had created the hull breach they'd used to enter the mothership.

Always, Beckman pushed on toward the center of the ship, hoping to find a place where their antimatter weapon could do the most damage. After several hours, they came across a blast door the size of a four story building. It showed none of the quantum malleability of the archways that appeared unexpectedly in walls, and while it seemed thick enough to withstand a hydrogen blast, part of it had been vaporized. Stretching away at sixty degrees was a shaft of destruction reaching all the way to the outer hull, revealing a destructive power far greater than their antimatter torpedo.

"This is one seriously messed up hunk of junk," Nuke said as he ran his hand over congealed rivulets of metal.

Beckman climbed into the circular hole blasted through ten meters of door armor and walked through to an immense chamber several kilometers long. Its towering ceiling was shrouded in darkness except for a few isolated sunbeams shining down through vertical blast holes, revealing an ocean of molten metal that had cooled suddenly when exposed to the frigid vacuum of space. Frozen whirlpools marked where explosive decompression had sucked liquefied metal toward space, only to cool before it could flow out. Rising from the sea of slag were thousands of twisted rectangular frameworks hundreds of meters high, standing like skeletal tombstones amidst a silvery graveyard.

Bandaka wrinkled his nose at the pungent stench pervading the chamber. "Death walks here," he whispered and made a sign.

Beckman started forward, followed silently by the rest of the team, awed in the face of such destruction. He hadn't gone far when he spotted an octagonal capsule half submerged in frozen slag, its sides partially melted although its upper transparent surface remained intact. He peered in, finding nothing but ash and the outline of an amphibian imprinted on the inside by a brilliant flash.

"They would have died fast," he said.

"That's how I want to go," Nuke said, clicking his fingers. "Blink and I'm dead. Feel nothing."

"Be careful what you wish for, Lieutenant." Tucker said, nodding meaningfully at Nuke's pack.

The young payload specialist looked startled, having forgotten he might get his wish sooner than he liked.

They soon discovered fragments of other capsules, torn from the most remote corners of the great chamber, spared liquefaction by their distance from the forces unleashed upon it.

"There must have been thousands in here," Markus said, wondering *How can this ship be a threat to us? They're all dead!*

Beckman tried to imagine how densely packed they'd been within the towering honeycomb structures that once filled the chamber. "Not thousands. Millions."

"Maybe it was a colony ship," Xeno suggested.

"It's got a lot of armor to be the Mayflower," Tucker said doubtfully.

"It's not a colony ship," Virus said weakly as he sipped from his canteen. From the recesses of his tortured mind, he sensed the ship was designed to function in a way that suited the nature of the species who built it. He knew they thought of it as a *mother*-ship, but there was more to the meaning of that word than he understood. There was a power in the mother aspect which eluded him. It was part strategy, part technology, part biology. He shook his head slowly, frustrated the answer remained beyond his reach.

They fanned out, following paths of melted metal, moving between twisted funeral pyres like ants crawling over the corpse of a great beast. When they were almost halfway through the chamber, Beckman climbed a rise and ran his eye around the distant shadowy walls, picking out one dark hole after another. Markus stopped beside him, following his gaze.

"Notice the angles?" Beckman asked.

"Yeah. This was no accident."

"Someone was shooting at this chamber, trying to kill whoever was here," Beckman said, certain the terrible wounds suffered by the great ship all converged on this one point.

"They succeeded," Markus said, convinced everyone aboard was dead. "This ship isn't a threat, but whoever destroyed it is."

"Don't jump to conclusions," Xeno said, joining them. "We don't know the good guys from the bad guys or why this ship was destroyed."

They continued on through the chamber, finding no sign of life. When they were two thirds of the way across, Bandaka held up his spear, signaling them to listen. Everyone stopped, then they heard the distant scraping of loose metal, the first sound they'd heard not of their making. After a moment, the crash of a heavy object landing on crumpled metal rang through the chamber.

Beckman, Xeno and Markus crept to the top of a mound of wreckage where they saw a red bipedal machine standing knee deep in twisted metal. It had thick robotic arms and legs, a multi-jointed torso and, unlike the other machines they'd seen, a large elongated metal dome for a head rather than a flat sensor disk. At the end of each arm were four short, double jointed metal fingers that could move in any direction.

At a glance, Beckman knew its proportions matched the alien corpse Xeno had examined. "No survivors, huh?"

"We should capture it," Markus said, "for questioning."

"Or we could try to make friendly contact," Xeno suggested.

Markus shrugged. "I prefer my way."

The heavy lift suit stood with its back to Beckman, showing no sign its occupant was aware of being observed. It effortlessly wrenched a blackened girder free to retrieve a trapped octagonal sleep cell, then finding its occupant reduced to ash, turned and tossed it on the mound behind. For a moment, the heavy lift suit's transparent faceplate came into view allowing Beckman a glimpse of an elongated chin and the forehead bulge of a biosonar lobe.

Nemza'ri stopped as a suit sensor detected multiple heat sources nearby. The thermal readings were higher than for her own kind and in an area she'd already searched for survivors. She turned sharply, using the thermal tracks for direction, and looked straight at three native life forms observing her.

For a moment, Beckman stared into large blue green eyes with a black, vertical slit pupil. The alien's eyes blinked horizontally in surprise, then it hurled a damaged transport capsule at them, using the heavy lift suit's enormous strength to turn the sleep cell into a deadly projectile.

Beckman, Xeno and Markus leapt back as it crashed into their vantage point, then multiple clicks sounded as the team readied weapons, expecting the suited figure to come charging at them. Instead, the chamber filled with the crunching sound of heavy boots bounding across the chamber floor.

It's running, Beckman realized, jumping to his feet and scrambling back to the top of the mound in time to see the alien leap into the air. It made a propulsion field assisted jump across half a kilometer of wreckage between partially melted lattices and beams of sunlight, then vanished behind a pile of debris near the far wall. A moment later, a metallic clang echoed through the chamber as an access hatch slammed shut.

"Not very sociable, are they," Beckman said.

Xeno nodded. "At least we know who's controlling the runners."

"We should get out of here," Markus said, wary of being trapped.

Beckman jumped down from the mound. "Let's move," he yelled, then they started running between twisted honeycomb structures toward the far side of the sleep chamber.

Markus dropped back, staying close to Nuke, looking for a chance to grab the torpedo and end Beckman's plan to destroy the ship.

"Anyone see an exit?" Beckman called as he surveyed the eight blast doors along the far wall, all closed. He considered ordering them to fall back to the last hull breach when Xeno pointed to a door on the right.

"That one's open," she said, pointing to a meter high gap between the deck and the bottom door.

"Incoming! Six o'clock," Tucker yelled, raising his special.

Two spinning top shaped trackers floated down through a hull breach in the ceiling, momentarily captured in sunlight. They'd barely cleared the opening when three weaponized seekers flashed past them, free falling into the chamber. The upgraded seeker's upper arms were now equipped with energy cannons while their lower arms carried shield emitters, miniature versions of what the battloid had used.

Too many to fight, Beckman thought as they raced to the

open door, keeping formation around Nuke even as they scrambled over piles of debris.

Nuke didn't waste time looking back, but ran straight for the exit, relying on the others to cover him and listening for Beckman's order to detonate. The others fired as they ran, using a mix of specials and assault rifles, forcing the seekers to take evasive action. The large trackers landed on the chamber floor and began gliding over wreckage toward them while the much faster seekers leapt from mound to mound, firing their twin cannons each time they were airborne.

Beckman and Tucker laid down controlled, suppressing bursts while Virus fired his grenade launcher at a pile of wreckage in a seeker's path. When the seeker landed, the grenade exploded, burying it, then a tracker fired its heavier cannon at Virus as he jumped away, blowing apart the debris he'd been standing on.

Nuke reached the blast door, finding it pried open by a squat robot that had served as an emergency jack during the initial rescue operation. He crawled under the door then ran a short distance down the corridor before stopping to connect the power cell for a manual detonation.

"The package is hot," he radioed with his finger over the detonator button.

"Standby," Beckman said, turning to cover the rest of the team as Xeno scrambled under the door and took up position in front of Nuke.

Ten meters out, Virus stumbled and fell in front of Markus, who ran past him without stopping. When Markus reached the door, he dived beneath it without looking back. Once through, he came to his knees and aimed at the emergency jack, thinking if he could destroy it, Beckman would be trapped on the other side.

"Back here," Xeno called, covering the door with her rifle.

Markus glanced back, looking down the barrel of her M16, then reluctantly moved to join her. He took up position behind Nuke, where he could stop the young lieutenant carrying out an order to detonate.

Outside the blast door, Tucker stopped and aimed Thor at a seeker leaping on a low, fast trajectory to the left. The heavy alien weapon used its own acceleration field to push against his hands to achieve perfect targeting, then it fired. The armed reconnaissance robot angled its mini shields at him, but Thor's heavy plasma blast punched straight through them, cutting the slender machine in two. Thor emitted a high pitched whine as it began charging up as he turned and ran for the door. Behind him, the seeker Virus had buried with a grenade climbed out of the wreckage and leapt into the air, firing as it ran. Tucker dived away, shooting again as Bandaka helped Virus reach the door, then they crawled under together.

The third seeker rotated its cannon arms and fired at Tucker as he dived under the door with Beckman right behind him. Its cannon blasts struck the door harmlessly while Beckman pulled the pin on a grenade and placed it on the squat machine, then a pair of seeker legs landed outside the door.

"Fire in the hole!" he yelled as he scrambled after Tucker, got to his feet and ran clear.

The seeker dropped to its hands and knees and crawled under the door, firing its cannons as it scrambled after them, then the grenade exploded. The jack folded and the massive blast door crashed down, crushing the slender robot.

With weapons ready, they listened for any sign of the door being forced, but the corridor remained silent. The remaining robots, knowing their weapons could not penetrate the armor, withdrew in search of another way in.

Finally, Beckman turned to Nuke. "Stand down."

Nuke exhaled with relief and disconnected the power pack. "Package disarmed."

The tiny speakers in their ears sounded with a voice distorted by static. "Nuke, is that you?"

They all exchanged surprised looks as they recognized the voice of someone they thought dead.

"Vamp, this is Beckman. Report."

"I'm with Timer and Dr. McInness, sir. We've got the ship's schematic. Can you identify your position?

"We just came through a blast door on the north side of a compartment several kilometers long."

There was a moment's silence, then Vamp said. "We've got it. We're thirty eight levels above you and half a kilometer further north. Follow the corridor you're in, turn left at the first ramp. I'll talk you up."

"Affirmative."

"Hurry, Major. There's something up here you've got to see."

* * * *

Two more hours, Laura thought, knowing that was how long her husband had to live, how long it would take to reach the ridge overlooking the Walker River. From there, Hooper would have a clear line of sight to transmit the signal that would bring down the shield dome, allowing the mothership to be destroyed and her husband killed.

They'd been moving fast since separating from Beckman and the others. Liyakindirr had led them along a near invisible track, carrying the short wave radio for Hooper who limped steadfastly after him. The sergeant held Conan in his good hand while his blackened right arm hung lifelessly by his side. Bandaka's wife and daughter followed Hooper, ready to help him if he faltered, then Wanyubi and finally Laura brought up the rear.

The old man suddenly stopped in front of her and said something in *Yolngu Matha*. Laura didn't understand his words, but his tone was unmistakably urgent. Before she knew it, he'd vanished into the forest, along with Djapilawuy and Mapuruma.

Liyakindirr turned to Laura and Hooper. "They found

us!"

Laura looked back, searching the forest but saw nothing. By the time she turned back, Liyakindirr had disappeared into the bush, leaving the radio pack on the track where he'd been standing.

Hooper raised his special with one hand, turning slowly, watching the trees. "Hide," he wheezed through gritted teeth.

Laura drew the sidearm Xeno had given her and took cover among the trees beside the track. She waited, barely breathing, until a flash of sunlight reflecting off polished metal caught her eye. There were two of them, silver blurs racing through the trees crisscrossing each other's path in a search pattern heading straight for Hooper. The soft, machine gun patter of their footsteps and the whipping of leaves against their metal bodies as they raced through the underbrush grew louder. When they were close, she realized these seekers were different from any she'd seen before. They carried weapons and shields and their bodies were coated in thin armor.

Hooper went down on one knee and aimed Conan at the combat seekers, who were already tracking him. They recognized his weapon and immediately darted sideways at high speed, circling in opposite directions. He pressed the plasma rifle's firing surface and relaxed his arm, anticipating the push of the weapon's acceleration field as it repositioned itself for a perfect shot. Conan tried target locking the first seeker, but the robot was moving too fast for its inertial targeter. The alien weapon pushed again and again, constantly correcting and turning Hooper in a circle as the seekers spiraled in toward him. The Intruders had fought and defeated Conan's builders and knew the exact angles and velocities needed to neutralize its targeting system.

They're too fast, Hooper realized. He tried fighting the acceleration field, pushing the weapon to aim ahead of the seeker, but its automated targeting system fought against him, refusing to fire and dragging his hand back.

"Goddamn it!" he growled, unaware the Area 51 engineers had failed to discover the security lock that disabled the weapon's inertial targeter. He dropped Conan, drew his big .50 caliber pistol, sighted on the nearest seeker and fired. The seeker's small shield flashed as it deflected the heavy slug, then it veered away into the trees as it realized it was under attack from a kinetic weapon whose characteristics it did not know.

The second seeker turned sharply toward Hooper, who fired his big pistol repeatedly. The bullets hammered its shield, sending electrical force lines radiating from the impact points, then seeing he was distracted, the first runner doubled back, coming to an instant stop behind him. It aimed its cannons at his back as a wooden spear shot out of the bushes and bounced harmlessly off its armored skin. The blow knocked it off balance as it fired, sending the blasts flashing over Hooper's head, then the combat seeker's cannons spun toward the spear's origin and raked the forest with withering energy blasts.

Laura now fired from behind a tree, striking the seeker's torso and shields repeatedly, unable to penetrate, then her gun clicked empty as the robot's cannon arms spun toward her.

"Uh-oh," she whispered and dived away as it fired, cutting the tree in half, then Hooper holstered his pistol, picked up Conan and aimed at the seeker's back from point blank range.

"Out run this," he said, touching the firing surface as its cannons rotated toward him.

He felt a slight push from the alien weapon as it locked on, then it unleashed a single, massive blast that blew the robot to pieces. Further out, the second seeker circled away at high speed, instantly aware its partner had been destroyed.

Liyakindirr ran to Hooper's side. "Hurry," he said, reaching for the radio pack, but Hooper caught his arm.

The side pocket was open and two black rectangular devices had fallen out. One was Timer's radio detonator, the other had a short black aerial and a display that pulsed the same signal repeatedly. He picked up the burst transceiver, turning it over curiously. In a flash of understanding, Hooper realized it was broadcasting a radio signal into the ether.

"This is how they're tracking us."

Laura's mind whirled as she realized Markus had planted it in the radio pack so the seekers could find them. Kill them. Kill her! And she'd helped him! "It belongs to Markus," she blurted. "I've seen him with it."

Hooper looked confused. "Markus? Why would he …?"

"He wants the ship," Laura stammered. "If you call in an air strike, it's gone."

Hooper's expression grew dark. "That filthy son of a bitch!" He promised himself, if he got out of this alive, he'd ring Markus' neck. He went to hurl the transceiver into the woods, then caught himself. His eyes passed from the transceiver to the silver streak circling out in the forest, then he slid the tiny radio back into the pack's pocket.

"What are you doing?" Laura asked incredulously.

"Buying you time. Don't waste it." He threw Timer's radio detonator to her with a grim look. "Left button to arm, right button to detonate."

Laura stared at the detonator, knowing she now held her husband's life in her hands. She dropped the empty pistol and slid the detonator into her pocket, torn by the choice Hooper was forcing her to make.

The sergeant handed Conan to Liyakindirr, then said, "Point it like that, touch that mark to shoot. Got it?"

Liyakindirr shouldered the backpack and nodded, feeling the weapon's weight. "I shoot good."

Hooper gave Laura a final nod, "Good luck." He drew his pistol and pointed into the trees, away from the path. "That way." Liyakindirr started off in the new direction with Hooper close behind.

When they had almost passed from sight, the seeker sped through the trees close to Laura, pursuing Hooper, Liyakindirr and Markus' radio signal. It fired several bursts of brilliant white energy through the trees before vanishing from sight, then she heard the distinctive bang of Hooper's big .50 caliber pistol in reply.

Laura hid beneath the thick green ferns carpeting the forest floor for several minutes, listening to the receding sounds of battle. When she was certain she was alone, she ran crouched through the underbrush toward the east as the boom of a grenade rumbled through the forest. The seeker's cannons sounded distantly, telling her the grenade had missed. She knew they couldn't hold out long and when the seeker had finished off Hooper and Liyakindirr, it would come for her.

With Markus' treachery burning in her mind, she was determined to put as much distance between herself and the seeker as possible. Soon she reached the lip of a gully containing a shallow stream and gained her first glimpse of the rust colored cliffs of the summit a kilometer away. Breathing heavily, she scrambled down into the gully, her heart pounding from fear and exhaustion. When she reached the bottom, the boom of Hooper's gun carried to her from far away.

She did not hear it again.

* * * *

Beckman stepped into the domed chamber where Vamp, Dr. McInness and Timer were studying a three dimensional wireframe schematic of the mothership floating before them.

"I thought we'd lost you," Beckman said as the rest of the team entered and peeled off their packs, thankful for the rest.

"You almost did," Timer said.

"We just made it into the tunnel," Vamp explained,

"before the explosion."

Beckman turned his attention to the wireframe hologram. "What's this?"

"The ship's log," Dr. McInness replied. "It has technical specs on the ship all the way down to the molecular level."

Beckman glanced at the alien characters floating in the hologram, then at Virus. "Can you read that?"

Virus stared at the characters on the brink of understanding. "Sort of. Some of the symbols represent zones inside the ship. Territories. It's linked to their command structure. It's not organized the way we do it. It's like … clans or families." He winced, straining to remember. "They have ranks, but family relationships and gender are more important."

"Gender?" Xeno said surprised.

"There aren't many females, but they're in charge."

"I like the sound of that," Vamp said with a mischievous grin.

"This device records everything the ship sees," Dr. McInness continued, "everywhere it's been, and it's been to a lot of places."

Beckman's eyes narrowed. "Does it say why it's here?"

"In spectacular 3D," Dr. McInness replied soberly, then inserted his hand into the sphere of light to demonstrate.

The schematic vanished, replaced by the black velvet of space sprinkled with densely packed stars. To their left, a yellow-orange orb shone brightly, the only star larger than a point while floating all around them was a fleet of dark rectangular leviathans, barely discernible in the feeble light at the edge of the K Type star's system. The fleet moved as one, thirty great vessels spread across thousands of kilometers of space, each controlled by their own guiding intelligence, each Command Nexus seamlessly merged together to form one collective entity. Two columns of swirling characters appeared and began continuously morphing into new shapes as computations were rapidly updated.

"We are the ship," Dr. McInness explained. "We're seeing everything recorded from the ship's perspective, by its sensors."

"We're not going very fast," Markus observed.

"How can you tell?" Dr. McInness asked. "There's no point of reference. Those other ships are travelling as fast or as slow as we are, and the stars are far away, even the orange star."

Virus pointed to the swirling characters in a column on the left side. "That says the ship is slowing down."

"These ships appear to travel no faster than about ten percent the speed of light. Fast by our standards, but not fast enough to go very far."

Beckman motioned to the majestic sprawl of a barred spiral galaxy dominating the far wall. "Is that what I think it is?"

"Yes Major. No human has ever seen it from the outside before," Dr. McInness said, "but that is the Milky Way Galaxy."

"So how'd they get here from so far away, travelling so slowly?"

"Engines have stopped," Virus announced, pointing to a set of frozen symbols. "The ship is completely motionless."

The starry blackness of space blurred, then faded as the pinpoints of star light merged into a stretched ellipsoid surrounding them. The rest of the fleet was now obscured from sight, as was the universe beyond.

"Are we in hyperspace?" Timer asked.

"No," Dr. McInness said. "We're very much in normal space, what Einstein would call flat space. We're surrounded by a bubble of sharply curved spacetime. It pulls the ship forward by pushing spacetime behind us."

"How can you tell?" Beckman asked.

"It's a theory for us, a reality for them."

"But we stopped?"

"Yes. The ship is stationary in its own reference frame, only spacetime outside the bubble is moving. You can't see it, because nothing can get through the bubble, in or out."

Beckman looked incredulous. "They're flying blind?"

"Totally blind. It's completely dependent on the course it calculated before starting and on the quality of its navigational data."

"Isn't that kind of dangerous?"

"They don't have a choice. Providing they don't fly into a star or a planet, they're OK. It's not as risky as it sounds."

"Heat is rising," Virus translated. "I'm not sure of the numbers, but it's really freaking hot out there."

"It's Hawking radiation, from the quantum effects around the bubble wall." Dr. McInness said, speeding up the recording.

The bubble surrounding them collapsed and the walls once again turned black, only now, a thick band of stars snaked all the way around the chamber marking the plane of the Milky Way. The ship had followed its preplanned path blindly into the galaxy, skirting the dust clouds of the main spiral arms and avoiding the hidden gravitational shoals of black holes and dark matter, stopping only when it entered a small spur of stars branching off from a major spiral arm. Swirling characters identified a small yellow star glowing dimly off to one side, while other characters marked the locations of planets, moons and asteroids too small and dark for the naked eye to see.

"Welcome to our Solar System," Dr. McInness announced.

Markus looked worried. "From outside the galaxy? That was … fast!"

"It them took them several days to get here. Considering they came from a globular cluster outside the galactic spiral and those clusters are tens of thousands of light years away, this ship was travelling *millions* of times faster than the speed of light."

"Even though it wasn't moving," Beckman said, annoyed at the paradox.

"Exactly, not moving in local spacetime," Dr. McInness

said.

Xeno gazed apprehensively at the stars enveloping them. "It's bad for us that it's so easy for them to get here."

"It ain't good." Tucker said as he tried unsuccessfully to scratch the wall with his knife.

Bandaka put his hand to the wall covering a white star and watched the light refract between his fingers as he discovered the image was not on the wall, but floated in front of it.

"What do you think, Bandy?" Nuke asked, expecting the hunter to be overawed by the technology. "Is it magic?"

"No magic. TV."

Nuke looked at the wall and nodded. "You're right man. I wonder if they can get cable on this thing?"

Dr. McInness looked thoughtful. "Considering they can't see through the bubble, they'd need good navigational information to make that kind of trip." He gave Beckman a meaningful look. "You know what that means?"

"They need good maps."

"Yes, but no one civilization could possibly map the entire galaxy by itself. They must share navigational information to make travel safe and trade possible, which means every interstellar civilization in the entire galaxy knows where we are. All of them! They trade maps and those maps will have Earth's location as a footnote saying 'Warning! Primitive anthropoids with nuclear weapons live here'. Some people think we should hide, not send out signals or probes in case we let the wrong kind of aliens know we exist, but they've missed the point. There is no hiding. Everyone, thousands of civilizations across the galaxy, already know we're here."

"Now that," Nuke said, "is a scary thought."

"And notice, they didn't come alone." Dr. McInness pointed to several dark masses blotting out the stars in the distance. One by one, the other ships appeared until the entire Intruder Fleet had arrived, then the scientist fast forwarded again showing the great ships accelerating into the Solar System.

"Where's Earth?" Beckman asked.

"It's that tiny blue dot over there," the scientist replied, motioning to the left, well away from the fleet's flight path.

"They're not going to Earth?"

"No, they're not." He pointed to a white pinpoint accompanied by a swirling character above the plane of the ecliptic. "Pluto's up there." It passed above them as the fleet moved inside the dwarf planet's orbit. "And that's Jupiter, dead ahead. The rest of the outer planets are scattered around the walls. Neptune is on the far side of the Sun."

Beckman realized the fleet was accelerating through the ecliptic plane toward open space. "They're crossing the Solar System?"

Dr. McInness nodded. "We were never their destination, just a course correction."

Beckman looked confused. "So what's this ship doing on Earth?"

"It shouldn't be here," Dr. McInness said, as Jupiter's orange and yellow bands and swirling clouds grew before them. He pointed at the largest planet in the Solar System. "It's here because of them."

Emerging from the great planet's upper atmosphere were thousands of ships of many designs and widely differing technologies representing many civilizations, all rising as one to meet the Intruder threat.

* * * *

The Intruder Fleet accelerated through the Solar System in a disk formation that allowed its weapons to bear without one ship blocking another's firing arcs. The entire formation could wheel and pivot as one, fighting as a single entity, able to focus on any target within tens of millions of kilometers. It was a convergence of technology, discipline and tactics that had been proven in battle long before the emergence of *Homo sapiens* on Earth.

Minutes before the fleet's arrival, Intruder stealth ships had eliminated five research vessels studying the third planet's pre-stellar inhabitants. The system's restricted access, imposed to protect its primitive inhabitants, and its proximity to Tau Ceti made it the ideal location for the fleet's final course correction. The lack of adequate defenses in such a vital location merely confirmed what the Intruders had long suspected, that their enemy – while technologically advanced – was weak willed and indecisive.

They knew the galaxy had not known war for eons, because its most ancient and powerful civilizations did not permit such disturbances. The disparity in technology between old and new societies meant the issue was never in doubt. There simply was no alternative to peaceful coexistence for any who sought a place among the stars. It had been that way throughout the galaxy since time immemorial.

It was not so for the Intruder Civilization.

They arose in a remote globular cluster deep within the Galactic Halo, an immense expanse of highly ionized gas surrounding the Milky Way. Beyond the gaze of the great and peaceful societies of the spiral arms, their power grew unchecked. Each victory fed their predatory drive for territory, their maternal desire to safeguard the future of their species and their insatiable hunger for resources. Through careful diplomacy and selective aggression, they came to dominate their cluster, emerging as a mature civilization – a rare achievement for an intensely warlike species.

In time, they turned their attention to the riches of the great spiral of light spanning the sky. For thousands of millennia, they'd watched supernovas burst across the Milky Way giving birth to mineral riches beyond measure, all too aware that such cosmic explosions were rare in globular clusters. It was why their great civilization was so starved of resources, trapped amidst a sea of impoverished stars. For eons, the lure of the galactic treasure trove called to them, driving them to acquire the technology and power needed to grasp a dream they came to believe was theirs for the taking.

At first they approached cautiously, establishing small outposts in the Perseus Arm, then fortified strongholds, fleet bases and logistics centers. Like true predators, the Intruders stalked their prey, just as their ancestors had hunted the waterways of their homeworld. Once established, they began to expand with a speed and efficiency that stunned the inhabitants of the Perseus Rim. Densely populated worlds fell with frightening rapidity, primitive fleets were swept aside at a stroke, until an ancient Homeworld stood defiantly and enticingly before them, the greatest jewel in the Orion Arm. That magnificent world, orbiting Tau Ceti twelve light years from Earth, had known civilization for millions of years. Its name was legend throughout the galaxy, yet even though it stood on Earth's doorstep, mankind knew nothing of its existence.

Nor did the inhabitants of Earth know anything of the mighty fleet that glided across the plane of the ecliptic, for the Intruders had no interest in pre-stellar primitives. Their fleet searched for spacetime distortions that would warn of the enemy's approach, unaware that Jupiter's powerful magnetosphere concealed dozens of tiny sensors. Disguised as rock and ice fragments hidden within the gas giant's thin planetary ring, they listened for the distinctive emissions of massive ships under high acceleration. The sensors reported the invader's progress via tight directional beams that reached down into the gas giant's swirling clouds where a hidden armada lay in wait. The Alliance Fleet had gathered there because of intelligence given to them by one of the Intruder's subject species, information carried through enemy space by Kesarn agents from the conquered

Perseus Arm.

When the Intruder Fleet was almost within range, the Allied armada rose from Jupiter's depths on a tidal wave of expanding spacetime. The Inter-Command Nexus – the sum total of each ship's guiding intelligence integrated into one super consciousness – sensed the danger, wheeled the fleet toward Jupiter and powered weapons. Before the enemy ships had cleared the gas giant's outer moons, the Intruder Fleet's unified awareness had analyzed the attack, worked through dozens of tactical scenarios and devised its plans.

There was never any possibility of truly surprising the Intruder Fleet militarily, although the Inter-Command Nexus knew the Matriarchs would be surprised politically. Where one great galactic power had opposed their conquest of minor worlds in Perseus, now stood a grand alliance of major and minor civilizations from across the galaxy.

The most numerous ships were from the Orion Arm, led by the mighty Tau Cetins, whose spindle shaped attack cruisers were of the highest order, although their crews were inexperienced in battle from eons of peace. The other Orion ships were of substantially inferior quality. Some, like the Minkaran squadron were fast and well armored while the ships of Syrma and Merope were little more than transports hastily fitted with weapons. The most feeble ships were from Ascella, a civilization barely ten thousand years ahead of Earth. They lacked both effective shields and armor although, like many less advanced ships, were armed with Tau Cetin weapons making them a threat the Intruders could not ignore. For the minor powers, entering such a contest was tantamount to suicide, yet they joined willingly because they knew if the Tau Cetins fell, their defeat would quickly follow.

It took the Inter-Command Nexus only moments to scan every enemy ship and discover the mass transfer of technology that had taken place. Even surviving ships from the conquered Perseus worlds had been upgraded. The idea of an ancient civilization like Tau Ceti giving its knowledge freely to its juniors was completely alien to the Intruders who jealously guarded every secret they possessed. It told of their adversary's desperation and of their collective determination to resist.

Even more alarming to the Inter-Command Nexus was the discovery that the Alliance had spread far beyond the Perseus and Orion Arms. It detected small numbers of ships belonging to great and distant civilizations with whom the Intruders had had little contact. Leading one flank was a handful of Fenari ships from the neighboring Cygnus Arm, while commanding the other flank were nine D'kol ships from the Scutum-Crux Arm on the far side of the galaxy. Never before had the Intruders faced so many opponents, some of whom were their equals in technology, if not in military efficiency.

More than four hundred Alliance ships fanned out between Jupiter and the Intruder Fleet, advancing in a loose rectangular formation that revealed how unprepared they were for cooperative action. For a few moments, the fleets raced toward each other, then at over twenty million kilometers, the massive Intruder super dreadnoughts began a withering bombardment. The six heavily armored invasion ships they escorted held their fire, directing their energy into shield power and point defenses, knowing they were the enemy's prime target. The Inter-Command Nexus quickly discovered the weaker Alliance ships could not withstand direct hits from its energy weapons, so it focused upon them, rapidly degrading the enemy fleet's offensive power.

The smaller Alliance ships tried to evade the storm of energy pulses blasting at them from the Intruder behemoths, but they were too slow. When they were struck, their weak shields collapsed, their thin armor evaporated and massive explosions blew their hulls apart. Those ships that were not destroyed became glowing wrecks or tried to limp out of range. Each time an Alliance ship exploded, it hurled radioactive debris over the shields of its neighbors, creating an expanding graveyard of contaminated derelicts adrift in a sea of radiation. Weaving through the wreckage, emergency life pods tried to find a way out of the carnage, ignored by the Intruder ships, although many were destroyed by nearby explosions.

The minor Local Powers of Orion suffered tremendous punishment. The Ascellan flotilla was quickly annihilated, the ships of Syrma and Merope were destroyed almost as fast while the heavier Minkaran squadron was reduced to crippled hulks. Only the more modern cruisers from Gienah and Cor Caroli survived, although they were driven back before their weapons could degrade Intruder shields. The devastation of the Orion fleets was rapid, but they divided Intruder fire long enough to allow the Tau Cetins and their advanced allies from Cygnus and Scutum-Crux to race through the ferocious Intruder bombardment, bringing their weapons within range.

The Alliance heavy ships ignored the super dreadnoughts and focused on the massive assault transports housing the invasion force. The refugees from the Perseus Arm had warned the Tau Cetins that that was where the real threat lay. They'd told horror stories of heavily armored ships landing in remote regions, establishing fortified bridgeheads beneath impregnable shields and disgorging massive armies that overwhelmed their defenses. During each battle, Intruder invasion ships had used the planet's own resources to produce robotic armies faster than the defenders could destroy them, armies that fought alongside soldiers who showed no regard for casualties.

It was a way of war alien to civilized races who valued life and it was why the Intruders were so formidable.

The Tau Cetin commander ordered his ships to focus on two of the assault transports. They launched waves of relativistic torpedoes that swept toward the Intruder Fleet like a swarm of glowing insects. When they neared the

Intruder leviathans, tens of thousands of tiny beams licked out from the giant ships, slicing the torpedoes apart and filling the blackness of space with thousands of red and orange starbursts. Not one torpedo reached its target for the Intruders had done their homework. The Tau Cetins and the Fenari moved closer, focusing their directed energy weapons upon the two Intruder transports. They quickly overloaded their enemy's shields, but found they could not penetrate the invasion ships' triple neutronium armored hulls.

It was then the D'kol commander of the Scutum-Crux squadron, a stolid ursidaen more than two thousand years old, ordered his nine ships to attack. The D'kol vessels were white hulled spheres covered in spine-like emitters that generated incredibly resilient shields. Due to their main weapon's very short range and slow rate of fire, their ships were built to withstand the heaviest punishment. When the D'kol were in range, they fired simultaneously, launching relatively slow moving balls of brilliant red light that expanded into spheres hotter than the core of any star.

The Inter-Command Nexus came as close as it ever had to fleet-wide panic. The Intruder Civilization had theorized about nova weapons, but had been unable to solve the tremendous scientific challenges involved in controlling a novatic explosion. Never in their long history had an Intruder ship ever been fired upon by a weapon beyond their technological reach – until now.

The Intruder fleet focused their heavy weapons upon the nine glowing novas racing toward them, but their attacks only reduced each sphere's circumference by a few percent. The nova weapons punched through the assault transports' shields with a flash, drilled through their armor like it was butter, then melted through hundreds of decks before bursting out the other side. They flew on for several seconds until their cohesion collapsed and they exploded into expanding superheated fusion clouds heading out of the Solar System at one twentieth the speed of light.

The D'kol novaships kept up a slow, but steady barrage, striking the two assault transports again and again until the side of one exploded, sending huge slabs of armor spinning away into space. The second wrecked invasion ship tumbled out of formation with no power and fading life signs as explosive decompression vented atmosphere and equipment into space.

The Inter-Command Nexus, realizing it could not destroy the artificial novas, focused all its weapons upon the novaships themselves. The D'kol breeder shields had already endured terrible punishment and their capacity to convert a portion of incoming energy back into shield power was degrading. The third novaship in line exploded, then four others signaled they would soon suffer the same fate, so their commander reluctantly ordered them to withdraw. A second novaship exploded, then the seven survivors phase-shifted to the edge of the Solar System, shut down their overheated shields and prepared for emergency superluminal flight should the Intruders came after them.

Knowing they could do no more, the Tau Cetin fleet commander ordered a general retreat. The weaker Alliance ships fell back in disorder, leaving many glowing lifeless wrecks behind, while the Tau Cetins and the Fenari covered their retreat.

Twelve minutes after the Intruder Fleet had opened fire, the battle was over.

Following the fleeing Alliance ships were thousands of tiny life pods filled with survivors, many grievously wounded. The Inter-Command Nexus chose not to pursue its retreating enemy because it calculated that was what the Alliance wanted – to buy time. Instead, the Intruder Fleet resumed its course toward the edge of the Solar System from where it would launch its assault on Tau Ceti twelve light years away.

Thirty degrees from the Intruder Fleet's trajectory, the surviving Alliance ships limped toward the orbit of Pluto.

More than half their number had been lost, a heavy price for the destruction of only two Intruder invasion ships. To every member of the Alliance Fleet, the defeat meant disaster for the Tau Cetins whose ancient homeworld was now vulnerable to attack.

From their distant vantage point, the Alliance commanders watched thousands of maintenance drones crawling over the Intruder ships like ants, repairing battle damage and readying them for superluminal travel. They'd bought time for other allies to gather at Tau Ceti and for diplomats to reach the Virgo Cluster fifty-four million light years away where an immensely powerful First Civilization was rumored to have a presence, but the odds were against them. Even if the Firsts could be found, they might refuse to intervene, considering the Intruder War to be nothing more than an insignificant squabble among primitives.

Left behind by both fleets was a radioactive debris field drifting between the orbits of Jupiter and Neptune. Beyond the radiation zone, a lifeless Intruder assault transport drifted on a trickle of emergency power, spinning slowly toward the Sun. Thousands of robotic workers had been sucked into space, paralyzing its ability to self repair, while the six million troops in its sleep chamber had been incinerated by artificial novas, obliterating its offensive power. Worst of all, the ship's Command Nexus had been damaged leaving it disoriented and confused, and severing its connection with the fleet.

Yet to the Command Nexus, its mission remained clear, unleash its armies upon the enemy, no matter what the cost. While it survived, it would never cease striving to fulfill that goal.

It was the purpose of its existence.

* * * *

Three quarters of the log room surfaces hissed with white noise where hull sensors destroyed in battle no longer recorded imagery. The remaining surfaces were like windows into space, with stars drifting past as the mothership slowly tumbled end over end.

"They do get the engines working," Dr. McInness said as a sheet of white noise was replaced by a star field. "See, it's repairing itself."

Beckman paced alongside a wall of static to a functioning sensor view. He peered into space, forgetting for a moment he was looking at a flat surface, not through a window. "So where are those fleets going? Why did they leave this ship behind?"

"I don't know, but they're not at war with us."

"Then why do I get the feeling they are?"

"Paranoia?" Markus suggested, meeting Beckman's irritated glare.

"Fascinating, isn't it," Dr. McInness said absently, "that a war is taking place right above us, a war between immensely powerful civilizations and yet, the human race is blissfully unaware of it?"

"I'm more interested in who wins," Beckman declared.

"Let's hope it's the good guys," Markus said.

"Who are they?" Xeno asked.

"The bug-eyed guys with the white hats," Markus replied. "The same aliens who have left us alone for the last two hundred thousand years."

"I just want to get this over with," Nuke said. "I don't care who wins."

"You should," Markus snapped.

"Why? So another bunch of twisted freaks can turn us into lab rats?"

"They may have kidnapped a few of us to see how we tick," Markus said, "but they haven't conquered or exterminated us. If the political order out there is changing, everything down here changes too."

Virus remembered clouded memories. "He's right. The Intruders are conquerors, not diplomats."

"'The strong do what they will and the weak suffer what

they must'," Dr. McInness quoted. When Beckman gave him a curious look, he added, "Thucydides, a Greek general and historian, he said it twenty five hundred years ago. Looks like it's a universal principle."

"He also said, 'do not take lightly the perils of war'," Markus said. "That's why we want the status quo to remain. Whoever's been in charge has left us alone for a long time. We've been safe inside their borders. We don't want that to change."

"Hey man, I get it," Nuke said. "Earth is Yellowstone and we're the bears."

"Or Arnhem land," Xeno added, glancing at Bandaka, "and we're the aborigines."

Bandaka thought for a moment, remembering his people had lived in a protected environment since 1931, a stone age culture safe within the borders of a modern democratic nation. "It is better to be left alone."

Xeno gave Markus a thoughtful look, remembering their conversation in the forest. "You said there were no Nazi Germanys in space, but there are. There were a lot of different ships on the other side."

Markus nodded soberly. "I noticed."

"So?" Beckman said.

"So," Xeno explained, "lots of good guys ally against one bad guy – to survive."

"Well that sucks!" Nuke said, "The good guys just got their asses kicked."

"This ship shouldn't be here," Markus said. "It belongs to the side that might soon be in charge of our little corner of the universe. We can't destroy it. We need to study it, to work out a defense."

"Not to mention," Dr. McInness cautioned, "if we destroy this ship and its people win, Earth may suffer a reprisal."

"We have to destroy it!" Vamp declared, turning to Beckman. "This ship has factories capable of producing an army of robots. All it needs is minerals and it'll stomp us into the stone age." She turned to Dr. McInness. "You know I'm right. Tell him!"

Dr. McInness hesitated. "It's true. If this ship is hostile, even in its crippled state, there's no way we could defeat it."

"You don't know that," Markus said.

"You haven't seen their factories!" Timer snapped.

"All it needs is time," Vamp said. "It's weak now, but it's recovering. In a few weeks, a few months, it'll be unstoppable."

"If we blow the ship," Xeno said, "and the Alliance wins, they won't care. They might even thank us."

"And if the Alliance loses?" Markus asked. "Then what?"

"Not my problem," Beckman said. "Nuke, this is as good a place as any. Rig the package to explode, then you all get the hell out of here. I'll give you six hours to get clear, unless I have company, in which case, time's up."

"We can make minimum safe distance in that time, if we go back the way we came," Nuke said, slipping out of his backpack and pulling the flap back to reveal the recovered antimatter torpedo.

Markus casually let his hand rest on his submachine gun, determined not to let Beckman destroy their only hope of resistance. Certain he could sweep the room before they could get a shot away, he eased the selector to 'full auto', then hovered his finger over the trigger as Nuke began to connect the power pack to the torpedo.

"Wait," Dr. McInness said.

Beckman gave the scientist a frosty look. "This is no time to get cold feet, Doctor."

"It's not that. This ship's been hit many times by incredibly powerful weapons and it's still operational. Detonating your bomb here won't stop it."

"You know a better place?"

"I do." He activated the schematic again and zoomed to the center of the ship where a spherical chamber stood encased in armor. Thousands of connections fanned out from the chamber to every point in the ship. "That's where you have to set it off. It's the nerve center, the brain, the only part of the ship that survived a direct hit. You have to get inside its shielding to be sure."

Beckman studied the schematic. "It'll be guarded. I may not be able to give you six hours. I may not be able to give you six minutes."

There was a moment's silence as everyone took in his meaning.

"We know," Vamp said softly, voicing their collective decision.

Quietly, Markus removed his finger from the trigger and eased his MP5's safety back on.

* * * *

Both fleets had departed the Solar System by the time the crippled mothership brought one of its power plants back online. If any of the surviving ships had still been in the Solar System, they would have detected the mothership's return to life, but no one was listening. The interstellar war had moved on to more important systems and even more desperate battles.

The Command Nexus knew it would never again have the power to inflate spacetime and cross the interstellar expanse, but that no longer mattered. Its crippled sensors had detected more than four hundred radiation sources on the only habitable planet in the system, radiation blooms it assumed were the after effects of orbital bombardment rather than the cores of primitive fission reactors. It recognized the system bore no resemblance to Tau Ceti, but it attributed the differences to faulty readings from its damaged sensors and false signals generated by its enemies. What they could not hide was the vast radioactive cloud drifting among the orbits of the gas giants and littered with hundreds of wrecked ships. This the

Command Nexus took for proof of a terrible battle which it alone had survived.

Rather than scuttle itself as it should have done, it brought as many sensors, weapons and propulsion fields online as it could, preparing to repel an attack that never came. Its flawed analysis led it to conclude that the enemy's surface forces had been neutralized by the orbital bombardment and the opportunity to inflict a crushing blow lay within its grasp. All it had to do was land, establish a deployment zone and begin fabricating offensive forces.

It assigned its few surviving maintenance drones to repair enough propulsions fields to allow controlled flight and to restore those acceleration fields it needed to offset the inertial effects of a hard landing. With the cargo holds mostly emptied by explosive decompression, there was little equipment left, so the ship cannibalized its empty decks for raw materials to feed into its nanofabricators.

While the ship drifted inside the orbit of Mars, it surveyed its target, selecting a landing zone that was both remote from major population centers and tectonically stable enough to endure large scale mantle mining. With minimum propulsion, it maneuvered toward Earth, punching into the planet's upper atmosphere at a dangerously high velocity. Using a combination of atmosphere braking and propulsion field drag, it began to slow itself as it raced high above the Pacific Ocean.

The Command Nexus kept its few remaining hull weapons powered for an attack that did not come. It detected thousands of slow moving air vehicles far below, but none emitted high energy signatures or tried to climb toward it, so it held its fire, conserving its limited energy reserves for a genuine threat. The lack of planetary defenses led the Command Nexus to conclude the orbital bombardment had done its job and now it must strike fast while the enemy was still vulnerable.

When the mothership crossed the equator it nosed down toward the lower atmosphere. The propulsion fields gave the ship limited maneuvering and the pressure fields prevented the thickening atmosphere from blasting through the hull breaches, but there simply wasn't enough power to prevent atmospheric friction from heating the hull. By the time the target continent appeared on the horizon, the pressure wave of air surrounding the ship was glowing red hot and the ship's hull temperature soared, although it never reached the levels needed to ablate its armor. Even so, the mothership glowed like a brilliant red and orange light in the sky, but without the tail typical of a falling meteor.

The Command Nexus made a final assessment of its landing site. It had chosen a natural fortress buttressed by wide seas to the north and sprawling deserts to the south making approach by enemy forces difficult to conceal. Satisfied with its selection, propulsion fields altered course to a vertical descent, then automated collision warnings sounded throughout the ship.

Propulsion fields reduced its velocity to ensure the impact remained within the ship's structural tolerances, then acceleration field capacitors charged to maximum, preparing to offset the enormous inertial effect of a high velocity impact.

When the ship hurtled into the troposphere, its sensors scanned the surface in detail, detecting plants and animals in abundance, but no energy emissions, indicating the area lacked even a primitive civilization. Moments later, the mothership struck the ground at many times the speed of sound, conducting a kinetic energy assault landing that destroyed everything on the ground as surely as if an atomic bomb had exploded.

In that instant, the Goyder River Valley was transformed from a pristine wilderness into a hellish inferno.

CHAPTER 16

Nemza'ri slept for the first time since escaping imprisonment in the hull. She'd found the undamaged quarters of a senior officer, left the heavy lift suit in the corridor and locked the access portal to the passageway so the humans she'd encountered in the sleep chamber could not surprise her. She hadn't been asleep long when a thought entered her mind from her crew-net implant.

I have been monitoring your activities, Kaleezsha(Alashra-Warm)Nemza'ri.

She snapped instantly awake, startled by the mind link. It was the first time in all her years aboard that the ship's highest level command consciousness had spoken directly to her. That level access was reserved for senior officers only. More importantly, the Command Nexus had addressed her formally, using her spawn designation. 'Kaleezsha' was her clan, her bloodline. 'Alashra' was her crèche, where she was raised. Together they determined her low social status among the females. 'Warm' defined her spawn season, while Nemza'ri was her hatching designation, more a number than a name.

She wondered how, with so much damage, the ship had been able to observe her, then the response came instantly with perfect clarity.

Via the med drones.

The response startled her, because she'd not meant to ask a question, then she realized her implants gave the Command Nexus free access to her thoughts.

Your crew status has been restored.

She suppressed her surprise, then waited for her orders, but none came. After a while, she sensed the Command Nexus was waiting for her to speak.

'Do you have orders for me?' she thought.

I have a request, Commander.

Commander? She was a thruster technician, not a spawn leader. Her hopes fell as she believed the Command Nexus was still disoriented, then it hit her. It never made requests of crew, whom it outranked, it gave them orders, but with her crew status restored, she was the ranking officer.

Nemza'ri calmed herself. 'What request?'

I understand your intentions. They are tactically sound.

It was something a fully functioning Command Nexus might conclude. Undamaged, it was a master of strategy, capable of the most devious and complex calculations.

You are the only functioning female alive and you have transformed into a breeder.

Was the Command Nexus being obtuse? She wanted to demand what it wanted, but her training and respect for authority restrained her. 'Yes?'

I request you assume the mantle of First Matriarch of this world.

'What!'

The leap from lowly technician to brood mother for an entire world was unheard of. Her genetic class alone disqualified her from such a role, let alone her crèche and clan affiliations. And yet, as the only healthy female, it was a logical step that complied with the laws of maternal succession.

I have been boarded by hostile forces. My internal sensors are eighty nine percent inoperable, making it difficult to locate the enemy. I am cannibalizing myself to produce combat units, however, there are very few maintenance drones available for the work. I must, therefore, prepare for defeat.

Nemza'ri had explored much of the ship, and even though she wondered how clearly the Command Nexus was thinking, its assessment was correct. 'What do you propose?'

This world's oceans are adequate for your species while its dominant life forms are land dwelling mammals. They have craft able to sail beneath the surface, but they are limited to shallow depths. Therefore, the oceanic parts of this planet could provide you with a tactical advantage.

'You want me to leave the ship?' she asked, surprised.

I propose to relocate a power plant, med drones, clone tanks and nanofabricators to a deep ocean location where you can breed in safety. You could then release your eggs into the oceans in great quantities.

'And let the eggs mature on their own?' It was a shocking thought. How would they be implanted? Who would educate and train them?

Your species has superior intelligence to this planet's mammalians. In time, your spawn will pose an overwhelming challenge to them. With nanofabricators, you will be able to equip them with the technology necessary to overcome all opposition.

'Is there no other way?'

I will continue to repair myself, however, I have insufficient resources to restore my systems to operational levels within acceptable timeframes. Even if I continue to function at current efficiency, my simulations indicate I have a low probability of producing a force strong enough to protect myself before the enemy inflicts unsustainable damage upon the ship. With the enemy inside my hull, the probability of defeat is increasing rapidly.

She had explored enough of the ship to know the situation was desperate, and try as she might, she could not fault the Command Nexus' logic.

'If I accept, what should I do?'

You will need to relocate immediately. I will assign a battloid and two combat seekers to guard you, although the deep ocean and the secrecy of your location will be your main protection. After each spawning, you will use the vehicle to distribute your eggs to suitable oceanic zones around this world's equatorial regions.

The thought of spending her life in isolation at the bottom of what the humans called the Marianas Trench did not appeal to her, yet if they could not reach her, the plan might work. Even so, she wondered how her naked offspring could survive a hostile world without technology and training, and again the Command Nexus read her thoughts.

Many will die, but many more will survive. Eventually, your daughters will spawn. In time, this world's oceans will swarm with billions of your kind. They will become a greater force than any I could build.

She lay in silence, knowing the Command Nexus was only doing its duty, utilizing every resource at its disposal – and she was just another resource. While the ship had the potential to create a technological army, she carried within her the capacity to give birth to a biological army.

'I agree.'

Thank you, World Mother.

The Command Nexus addressed her as if she really was a Planetary Matriarch, implying it had already assumed a subservient role. In future, it would only suggest, for not even a Command Nexus would dare to direct the Spawn Mother of an entire world civilization.

I recommend you select the vehicle you require, the weapons it will have and whether it will be capable of interplanetary flight or not. There are also many different types of habitats I can construct, each of which will serve the strategy equally well, but may provide you with different levels of comfort.

'Can't you select what I need?'

It is your prerogative, Great Mother. You will be dependent upon both the vehicle and the habitat for the remainder of your life.

She was not used to such treatment, especially from an awareness that moments before had been her superior and an integral part of the ship's command structure.

'Very well. I will choose.'

The Command Nexus indicated where she could access the fabrication system and make her selections. After having encountered the humans in the sleep chamber, she'd equipped herself with a weapon and a photon field, the latter capable of warping light around her body making her invisible. With those two items, she would be safe enough to proceed without the bulky heavy lift suit.

Nemza'ri realized her life was going to be one of solitude and isolation, hidden beneath the oceans of a primitive world, but her life span was a long one. Perhaps in time, she would rejoin her kind after they had subjugated this planet. The years ahead would be lonely ones, but she would do her duty, without hesitation.

She was after all, this world's First Matriarch.

CHAPTER 17

Slab led the way down a narrow ladder inside a cramped maintenance shaft. They'd been descending for what seemed like hours, passing through many decks in search of a way out. A glimmer of light and a gently humming sound came from the next landing, so Slab swung off the ladder and waited for the others.

When they reached him, he glanced at the shaft that fell away into darkness with no sign of the bottom. "Still a long way to go."

"Not sure I can make it," Dan Mackay said wearily.

With silent agreement, they started along a short corridor toward the first brightly lit area they'd seen since escaping the bio lab. It led into a long room filled with rows of silver rectangular beds covered by transparent canopies. Slab froze when he realized seven of the beds were occupied.

"It's a morgue," Cracker whispered.

"If they're dead," Bill said, "why are you whispering?"

"Because he doesn't want to wake the dead," Wal said with a grin.

They relaxed, then started down the aisle between the humming beds, transfixed by the alien bodies floating just above them. Wispy white vapors swirled slowly around the bodies, not smoke or steam, but a substance that passed beneath the bodies as often as it passed above.

Cracker stopped at a bed, fascinated by its occupant's aqua dynamic features and elongated head. One side of its body was charred black and most of its left arm was missing, replaced by a translucent bubble filled with a dark green liquid.

"It's alive!" he exclaimed when he saw the chest move, revealing the alien was breathing shallowly.

The others gathered around, leaning closer as curiosity overcame their fear. Its bulging eyes and flat horizontal mouth were closed, while its vertical slit nostrils were open enough to breathe. The alien floated on an acceleration field that ensured its damaged skin did not touch the regeneration bed or its transparent canopy while the vaporous nanomachines worked tirelessly to repair its damaged cells. The translucent bubble over the alien's stump contained a dark mass that was slowly condensing into a new arm.

Wal scowled. "He's an ugly bugger."

Slab moved on to the next regeneration bed. Its occupant's burns were less severe, although it had lost both legs. Regrowth bubbles enclosing its stumps showed the first signs of new limbs while a cloud of nanomachines systematically removed charred tissue from its hips and chest. He stepped around the end of the bed, not taking his eyes off its occupant and slammed his knee into a low metal platform.

"Ugh!" Slab reached down to rub his knee, then saw a sleeping myrnod lying face down on the platform. "Jeez!" He jumped back startled, then realized the amphibious predator was unconscious. A thin tube filled with yellow fluid snaked from the creature's muscled shoulders to the base of the regen bed where nanomachines extracted the growth hormone.

When Cracker saw the unconscious myrnod, he whistled at the sight of its hook claws. "That bastard could rip your guts open with one swipe."

"Those teeth would give a great white a run for its money," Bill said.

Wal made a face. "No way, a great white would eat this thing for breakfast."

Bill examined the tube connecting the myrnod to the regen bed. "Looks like it's giving aquaman a transfusion."

"We better save the last bullet, in case we run into one of those things," Slab said.

"Suppose we run into two of them?" Wal asked.

"Then we'll throw you at the other one and run like hell," Slab replied as he headed for the next bed in line. Its occupant was burnt all over and a regrowth bubble enveloped its lower abdomen, attempting to regenerate failing internal organs before it died.

Cracker glanced around the hospital ward thoughtfully. "Someone put these things here and plugged old claw foot into that bed."

"The machines could have done it," Slab said.

Bill stopped at another regen bed, studying its patient. "I wonder if they have two sexes, like us? They all look the same to me."

Dan followed his gaze. The aliens were stripped naked, but showed no signs of reproductive organs. "They look a bit like fish. Maybe they fertilize eggs the same way."

Wal looked horrified. "You mean, no sex?"

Dan shrugged, "Maybe."

Slab grunted with disgust. "Bloody dickless aliens!"

"That's why they build such bloody big ships," Cracker declared. "Trying to compensate."

"Like Wal's V8!" Bill said with a smirk.

Wal gave up his search for alien manhood and headed to the last occupied regen bed. Its patient had lost a foot and was covered in a patchwork of burns. A second myrnod lay face down beside the bed being drained of growth hormone by a connecting tube. Wal leaned close to the transparent bubble and studied the alien's face curiously.

"It's got big eyes," he said. "I bet it sees good." The alien's eyes opened and stared straight at him, making him jump back in surprise.

Its eyes darted from one man to another, instantly assessing the situation. Crippled and outnumbered, an animal would have panicked, but the alien remained calm and focused. With its implants removed, it could not contact the ship directly so it pushed its left arm down through the weak acceleration field and touched a dark circle that instantly illuminated, then its lips began moving beneath the isolation canopy.

"It's calling for help," Wal warned.

A panel in the roof vanished and a spherical med drone floated down into the ward with a tranquilizer needle attached to one of its long, slender arms. It tried spearing Wal with the needle, but he jumped back, stumbling into the myrnod and tearing the tube from its shoulders as they both tumbled onto the deck. The animal snorted but didn't wake, its teeth close to Wal's face, then he scrambled away in fear.

Slab grabbed Bill's gun and slammed the butt into the side of the drone, sending it tumbling sideways through the air. It regained its balance, spun toward him and came flying back, trying to stab him with the needle. Slab dodged the attack and rammed the rifle butt into it again, sending it crashing into one of the beds, cracking the canopy. It wobbled and fell to the deck, then he hammered it several times with the rifle butt, remembering its twin had tried to cut his arm off. The drone's arms went limp as it shorted out, then he kicked it with the toe of his boot.

"Feel better?" Dan asked.

Slab scowled, then kicked the wrecked med drone again, sending it skidding across the deck. "Now I do."

Wal scrambled to his feet, eyes fixed on the med drone's long needle. "Man, look at that thing." He shuddered. "I hate needles."

Twenty-nine panels in the ceiling vanished and a needle armed med drone floated down through each opening.

"Oh crap," Slab said.

"Run!" Bill yelled, starting for the nearest archway.

They sprinted for the exit, ducking and dodging as the med drones stabbed down at them. Slab deflected one needle with his gun's barrel, then hammered it with the rifle's butt, knocking it back as Cracker caught the slender metal arm of another and drove the needle into a bed's transparent canopy, wedging it in place. A few paces away, Bill and Wal helped Dan to the exit as Cracker ran after them driving a detonator into one of his last two sticks of dynamite.

"Slab," Cracker yelled, "Get out of there!"

The ex-footy player backed toward the exit, parrying the stabbing arms of three med drones with his rifle. When he saw the dynamite in Cracker's hand, he swung the rifle once more and ran. Cracker tossed the dynamite into the hospital ward, then he and Slab raced into the corridor as med drones came surging after them.

The dynamite exploded in mid air, destroying the leading drones and knocking the others back. The nearer beds were blown sideways, hurling their patients onto the transparent canopies and bursting their fragile regrowth bubbles, splashing green liquid over them. After a moment, the remaining med drones regained their balance and surged toward the exit like a swarm of angry, oversized bees.

Outside the med lab, the men ran along a dark corridor toward a glimmer of light. They heard the distant hiss of cutting tools and the clang of metal in the distance as the spherical drones, silhouetted by the light of the hospital ward, came floating out of the shadows after them.

Cracker produced his last stick of dynamite and fitted the timer as he ran. He was about to throw it when Bill caught his hand.

"Save it," he said, remembering how they'd tried to dissect Slab, determined not to die that way himself, "for us."

Slab glanced back at the spherical robots gliding after them. "You won't get them all."

Cracker saw the grim looks on their faces. "OK, it's unanimous," he said, pocketing the stick.

"It's not bloody unanimous!" Wal said alarmed.

They reached an intersection of corridors. On one side, echoing to them from deep within the ship, came the sounds of feverish repair activity, while on the other, daylight flooded down the corridor.

Wal sniffed in surprise, eyes widening. "Fresh air."

They charged down the passageway toward daylight, through a jagged cavity gouged horizontally through the ship by a nova weapon. They hoped to see cliffs and trees as they neared the hull breach, but all they saw was sky blurred by the dome shield in the distance. They felt humid air against their faces as they ran through the triple layered hull, then caught themselves as they reached the edge of a precipice. Below was the sheer metal wall of the outer hull, dropping vertically like a cliff toward the ground hundreds of meters below. With no way down, they turned to the med drones which were swarming toward them, needles raised to spear them.

Slab sighed, caught Cracker's eye and nodded. "OK mate, light your cigar."

Wal's eyes widened in desperation. He glanced at the drones racing toward them, at the dynamite in Cracker's hand, then over the vertical wall of the ship's outer hull. "We need a rope."

Slab gave him a brutal look. "Brilliant Wal!"

Cracker set the timer for instant detonation then motioned for the others to gather around. He took hold of the detonator, about to trigger it.

"Wait!" Dan yelled, pointing at the hull breach behind them. "Look!"

A length of rope dropped down outside the mothership's hull, then a moment later, a second rope appeared.

Wal looked surprised and grinned. "Ask and you shall receive!"

* * * *

Beckman clipped his rappelling belt to one of two ropes secured to a massive energy cannon recessed into the ship's outer hull. Behind him, the gray armor plate dropped away like a sheer cliff to a charred ridge more than a kilometer below. On the other side of the big gun, Nuke and Xeno crouched in a cramped access tunnel that had opened after landing to ventilate the ship, while Tucker crawled forward with his machine gun.

Beckman pulled on the rope, testing it was securely lashed around the cannon's circular mount, then backed toward the edge. "You're sure about this?" Beckman asked over the radio, glancing apprehensively at the precipice behind him.

"Yes. The hull breach is about a hundred meters below you," Dr. McInness replied from the log room. The ship's schematic floated before him, zoomed in to a twenty deck section surrounding the ship's spherical nerve center. It showed the access points were either sealed or guarded, leaving the outside of the ship as the only way down.

Virus stood beside the scientist, nodding. He'd been able to translate enough of the alien language to confirm the scientist's conclusions. Beckman had ordered him to stay in the log room as an interpreter and because he was too weak to make the descent. Bandaka had also stayed behind because he lacked abseil training while Vamp and Timer were there to make sure Dr. McInness got out alive.

"OK," Beckman said, adjusting his harness as Markus crept past the big cannon, clipped onto the other rope and glanced over the edge.

"We're going to be sitting ducks out there."

"Just hope they don't fix the hull sensors when we're halfway down," Beckman said, checking his karabiner was securely attached as Tucker took up position between the two ropes with his machine gun. "Ready?"

Markus glanced over the edge and nodded, "Let's do it."

They backed over the edge together, kicked lightly out and slid down the rope, pushing gently off the wall of armor each time they swung in. As soon as they were gone, Nuke and Xeno moved up into position and clipped onto the ropes. Xeno looked anxiously over the edge.

"It's just a cliff," Tucker assured her. "Nothing you haven't done a hundred times before."

"It's not the descent that worries me. It's what's waiting for us down there."

Tucker watched Beckman and Markus rappel to the end of the first rope segment, stop to clip their second karabiners below the join and release the first, then continue on down.

"Go," he said, then Nuke and Xeno backed over onto the edge.

Now alone in the gun emplacement, Tucker watched them glide to the join, then he clipped himself onto the rope face-first, the reverse of how the others had rappelled. Going down face first, he could drop faster while covering them from above.

When Nuke and Xeno were past the join, he growled to himself, "Geronimo," and leapt off the edge.

* * * *

Wal grabbed the dynamite before Cracker could trigger the detonator, then the med drones swept over their heads, ignoring them as they streamed out through the hull breach and swarmed upwards. The men exchanged confused looks, then saw the spherical robots were rising to meet Beckman and Markus.

"There's a couple of maniacs abseiling down the side of the ship," Slab exclaimed.

"They're commandos," Cracker said.

"About bloody time," Bill declared.

The med drones rose alongside the ropes, aiming their tranquilizer needles skywards like silver spears. Beckman drew his M9 Berretta and, holding the rope one-handed, kicked sideways as he slid down so the drones were no longer directly beneath him. He fired slow, carefully aimed shots, striking the lead machine several times while Markus unclipped the MP5 from his chest harness and fired short bursts straight down, shattering the drone immediately beneath him. There was an electric flash, then the machine lost power and fell onto the drone below. Their arms became entangled as they bounced against the hull and spun off into the air, then the machine Beckman had struck exploded, showering those below with metal fragments.

Another drone rose toward Beckman, stabbing at his chest with its needle. He pushed off the hull, dodging away and firing, triggering a series of internal flashes inside the machine. Its arms froze as it tumbled away, striking other drones as it fell and forcing some to circle out from the hull to avoid being hit. Markus fired short bursts as he dropped through the swarm, kicking away a needle arm, then he was in clear air and dropping fast. Beside him, Beckman pushed lightly off the hull and stopped firing once the swarm was above him for fear of hitting Xeno and Nuke.

Several med drones dived after Beckman and Markus while the others continued climbing, then they reached the hull breach together and swung in. With their eyes fixed on the drones above, they were surprised when helping hands caught them as they landed. Beckman whipped his gun around in a reflex action, surprised to see five men standing there.

"Easy mate!" Cracker yelled, hands up, as he looked down the barrel of the major's M9 pistol.

"Sorry," Beckman said, angling his gun to the vertical, then he threw off the rope and began firing at the drones swooping toward them.

Markus released his karabiner and turned to unleash a series of well aimed bursts at the spherical robots. One flashed with sparks and crashed onto the deck at his feet while another struck the hull and exploded. A third flew in over their heads, turned sharply and came at Beckman from behind, aiming for his spine, then Slab slammed his rifle's butt into the drone, driving it into the tunnel wall.

High above the hull breach, Nuke and Xeno dropped into the swarm. One drone stabbed at Nuke, striking his backpack harmlessly while another lunged toward Xeno, plunging its needle into her neck. She blasted the med drone with her special, then gave Nuke a surprised look, closed her eyes and passed out. She dropped her special as Nuke tried to catch her, but she let go and fell. The rope whipped through her karabiner, spinning her from side to side, slowing her fall and slamming her helplessly against the hull.

Four machines now converged on Nuke, forcing him to jump sideways across the hull as needles stabbed after him, then the burp of Tucker's machine gun sounded and bullets from above raked the drones. The unarmored machines sparked and shattered as Tucker free falled past Nuke like he was performing a HALO jump, firing one handed. He dropped through the drones, shooting all the way, never slowing, then as the machine gun clicked empty, he threw it away and fixed his eyes upon Xeno's limp body below.

Holding the rope so it slid through his karabiner without snagging, he quickly closed the distance as her lifeless body twisted violently on the rope and her helmet slammed sickeningly against the hull. The rope dragged across her chest, shredding her jacket and exposing her Kevlar body armor, then Tucker caught her backpack's shoulder strap and dragged the rope hard against his belt. Wisps of smoke licked from his gloves as he used his leather belt to brake their fall.

They quickly slowed, but the end of the rope whipped through Xeno's karabiner, leaving Tucker's grip all that kept her from falling. He arched his back, muscles bulging, as he forced the rope harder against his belt, then the end of the rope slid through his hand and whipped against his karabiner. Tucker snatched at the rope above his head, slid a little more then came to a stop with the rope's end just below his hand.

Nuke abseiled into the hull breach on the other line, then helped Beckman and Markus blast the med drones swooping on them. One drone dived toward Tucker, its needle aimed at his straining neck muscles as he held the rope in one hand and Xeno's unconscious form in the other.

The med drone's arm retracted, preparing to plunge the needle into his neck, then a solitary crack rang out from above. The drone shuddered and rolled sideways, revealing a single large caliber hole in its side, then it fell away toward the ground far below. Tucker looked up to see Slab standing on the edge of the hull breach, sighting expertly along the Browning A-bolt's barrel, its last bullet expended.

The others grabbed the rope and hauled them up. When Tucker reached the lip of the hull breach, Slab grabbed Xeno's backpack straps and pulled her in, then Tucker rolled inside sweating and breathing hard. He glanced sideways at Xeno lying unconscious on the deck, a trickle of blood seeping from the tiny puncture mark in her neck. Her face was ghostly white but she was still breathing.

Tucker sat up, flexing aching shoulder muscles as his eyes settled on the rifle in Slab's hands. "Good shot."

Slab shrugged. "Dropping a 'roo doing seventy's harder."

Tucker nodded appreciatively.

"Where's the rest of the army, General?" Bill asked.

Beckman ran a quick eye over the five men. "We're it. What are you doing here?"

"Trying to get out," Dan said.

"They were going to dissect us," Wal said.

"But we dissected them instead," Cracker added with a wry grin.

Bill glanced meaningfully at the ground far below. "Get us a chopper and we'll be on our way."

Beckman shook his head. "There are no choppers."

"No choppers? What kind of a rescue is this?" Wal

demanded.

"It's no rescue. We're here to blow this thing." Beckman thumbed his mike. "We're in. Which way?"

Dr. McInness voice sounded in his earpiece, "Ahead to the first junction, then left, fifteen hundred meters."

"You're going to blow this thing up," Slab said, "with us inside?"

Beckman reloaded his pistol. "That's the idea."

"It's going to take more than a few kilos of C4," Cracker said.

"I know," Beckman replied. "You need to be five clicks from here when it goes up."

The four hunters exchanged stunned looks, then Bill said incredulously, "You've got a nuke?"

"Something like that."

"Holy crap," Slab said slowly. "How long have we got?"

"Thirty minutes. No promises."

Wal looked out at the ridge far below, scratching his head. "Anyone got a parachute?"

"If there are no choppers, how are you blokes getting out of here?" Bill asked.

Beckman turned to Tucker, motioning to Xeno. "Carry her."

Tucker climbed to his feet, stretched his aching shoulders and began removing Xeno's backpack.

"Hey mate," Slab said, "he asked you a question."

"We're not getting out."

It took Slab a moment to realize what he meant, then he said, "Well that bloody sucks. What frigging halfwit thought that plan up?"

"I did," Beckman said.

"Wait a minute," Wal said confused, glancing at Xeno's unconscious body. "You rescued her, so you could nuke her?"

Beckman nodded. "Nuts, ain't it."

Slab's eyes narrowed, deep in thought. "We must really

be in the shit?" Beckman said nothing, which Slab took as silent agreement, then he eased Tucker aside and lifted Xeno off the ground, slinging her over his shoulder. Beckman gave him a surprised look, to which Slab replied, "Well I'm not getting out of here in thirty bloody minutes, am I?"

Bill exchanged resigned looks with his mates, then said, "One in, all in," and retrieved Xeno's M16 from the top of her backpack.

Beckman watched Bill warily. "You know how to use that thing?"

Bill checked the ammo clip, sighted expertly along the barrel, then rested the weapon casually on his shoulder. "I'm a better shot than him," he said, nodding to Slab.

"Since when?" Slab demanded.

Cracker sighed. "Well, if we can't get out of this dog fight, we might as well have a bit of fun before you drop the big one." He waved for a weapon, "Give me something."

Beckman hesitated.

"This isn't a game," Markus said.

"Too bad," Slab said, "because we play to win."

Beckman saw the relaxed determination in their eyes, then turned to his team. "We'll use the specials, give them the guns."

They quickly passed M16s and pistols over to the four hunters and Dan, then Beckman pointed to Nuke. "He's carrying the package. Protect him at any cost."

Nuke casually saluted the civilians.

"Right, he's got the ball," Slab said, nodding at Nuke.

"Now what, General?" Bill asked.

Beckman drew his midget special. "We go kick some ass."

"You mean arse, mate. Arse." Cracker said emphatically. "That's what we call it down here."

Beckman allowed himself the barest of smiles. "Works

for me," he said, then started down the blast tunnel toward the Command Nexus.

* * * *

Laura stumbled between skinny, white limbed trees clustered beneath an eroded sandstone cliff. The trees provided cover from the air, but made finding a way to the summit frustratingly difficult. It had been a long time since she'd last heard gunfire, although several times she'd seen a distant black dot traversing the sky. From the way the striker quartered back and forth, she knew it was searching, but for who? She wiped sweat from her face as she paused to sip from her water bottle, knowing it would be empty soon.

An old survival mantra kept repeating involuntarily in her mind; three minutes without air, three days without water, three weeks without food. It was a recipe of death that underestimated the effects of tropical heat. She'd tried rationing her water, but her physical efforts were dehydrating her at an appalling rate. Thirst had always been the greatest enemy in this land, although now she knew something more lethal had arrived.

She screwed the cap tight on her water bottle and checked Timer's remote control was still in her pocket. It was a simple enough device, with 'arm' and 'fire' buttons and a telescoping antennae. She looked up, about to move again when she saw little Mapuruma standing close to the cliff face. Mapuruma raised a finger to her lips, indicating silence, then pointed at the trees. Laura glanced in the direction she'd indicated, but saw nothing.

Bandaka's daughter waved for Laura to follow. Deciding to trust the little girl's instincts ahead of her own, she hurried toward her. When she neared Mapuruma, the little girl vanished behind a fallen boulder at the foot of the cliff. Without hesitation, Laura followed, uncomfortably aware of the click of her boots on the rock compared to the soft patter of Mapuruma's bare feet. Once past the boulder, she saw the Mapuruma crawl under a low overhang, then she dropped to her hands and knees and scrambled after her, trying not to think of the poisonous creatures that made their homes in such shadowy recesses.

When they reached the rear of the cave, Mapuruma sat with her back to the rock wall, pulled her knees up under her chin and stared at the horizontal slit of light between the overhang and the rock floor. She made no attempt to speak or even look at Laura. If not for the whites of her eyes, her jet black skin would have made her invisible in the darkness. Laura hunched up in the confined space beside Mapuruma and followed her gaze to the sun bleached boulders outside. She burned to ask Mapuruma what had spooked her, but the intensity of the little girl's stare told her this was no time to speak.

Suddenly, Mapuruma tensed with fear.

Not knowing its cause, Laura froze, then she heard the rapid clatter of metallic feet on rock. The robotic footsteps grew louder, then a blur of silver metal swept past the white boulder outside. The footsteps faded into the distance, while Mapuruma listened intently. Laura forced herself to copy the child's silent intensity, determined not to speak until she said she could.

After an eternity, Mapuruma whispered. "It's gone."

"Where are the others?"

"Watching. They sent me to hide."

"Is Hooper still alive?"

"Not for long. He don't know how to hide."

Neither do I, Laura realized, certain if not for Mapuruma, she would now be dead.

"Liyakindirr with him," the little girl added sadly. "If he stays, he die too."

"Will he stay?"

She nodded. "He won't leave the soldier alone."

Laura sensed Mapuruma's fear that all she loved was being swept away, but Laura couldn't stay cowering in the cave. "Do you know how to get to the top of the ridge?"

"That way." The little girl pointed at the shadows to her right where a crevice carved through the rock by millions of years of wet season deluges lay hidden. It was a path Laura would never have found alone.

"Will you show me?"

"*Lili*," Mapuruma said in *Yolngu Matha*, 'this way', then she released her knees and crawled deeper into the cave.

Laura glanced back at the slit of sunlight, reassuring herself the seeker had gone, then followed Mapuruma into the darkness.

* * * *

The sizzle of cutting torches and the clang of metal grew louder as Beckman's team crept through the dark blast shaft created by a nova weapon, confident no internal sensors had survived the attack.

"Lucky this tunnel's heading our way," Nuke whispered.

"It's not luck," Beckman said. "They were shooting at the same thing we're after."

"Too bad they missed," Tucker said.

The circular shaft ended in a curved black metal wall with a ragged hole in its center where a nova core had smashed through the armored outer shell. Part of the damaged shell had been removed, creating a rectangular opening into a dimly lit, shiny walled spherical chamber. Maintenance drones flew twisted metal out through the opening and carried newly repaired replacements in, while more drones inside worked tirelessly restoring the damaged Nexus Chamber.

Beckman called a halt in the shadows, well back from the entrance, and studied the interior through binoculars. It was several hundred meters across with an inner black containment sphere at its center. The containment sphere was held in place by polished pylons arranged like spokes on a wheel set forty five degrees apart. Partially repaired walkways ran around the interior wall of the chamber, parallel to the decks outside. They gave access to the pylons which were indented with walkways and handholds for use in both positive and zero gravity. The pylons on the far side of the inner sphere were scarred, but intact, while those facing the puncture wound were either melted wrecks or shiny new replacements.

Beckman guessed a defense field surrounding the inner sphere had absorbed the worst of the nova core's primordial heat, although he had no way of knowing if it was still functioning. The defense field was many times stronger than the mothership's external energy shield. It alone had saved the Command Nexus from destruction, although the nova weapon's intense gamma ray emissions had, for a time, scrambled its logic patterns. An armor segment had been removed from the inner sphere through which beams of slowly rotating, electric blue light shone, illuminating the maintenance drones repairing the Nexus Chamber.

"Once they reseal that inner sphere," Beckman said, "our warhead will be useless."

Nuke look surprised. "Sir, this little bad ass turns matter into energy. There ain't nothing it can't kill."

"That we know of," Beckman said slowly, lowering his binoculars. "That chamber took a direct hit from something far more powerful and it survived."

"So we blow it here and now, before they fix it," Tucker said.

"Not here," Beckman said, nodding toward the inner sphere. "In there."

Markus furrowed his brow. "That's crazy. You'll have every robot in the ship after you, as soon as you show yourself."

"It's the only way to be sure."

"The inner door's open," Tucker said.

"And we have no line of sight to what's inside," Beckman said. "They might close the door or raise an energy shield as soon as they detect our warhead going off. We've only got one shot and I'm not going to waste it."

A heavily armored Mark III battloid with a third set of weapon arms, four antigravity sleds and thicker armor emerged from behind the central sphere, gliding slowly through the maintenance drones like a black shark through goldfish. It only deviated from its preprogrammed path to avoid a group of repair drones in the midst of removing a damaged segment from the inner sphere. The battloid slowly completed its circuit then passed behind the inner sphere, then as they watched in silence, it reemerged to begin another orbit.

When it passed out of sight a second time, Beckman said, "There's only one."

"One's enough," Markus said.

"As soon as they see us," Tucker said, "those little worker bees will call for mama."

Beckman calculated how long it would take to cross the nearest pylon, certain the battloid would be on them before they were halfway across.

* * * *

Dr. McInness' eyes were transfixed by a spherical blackness floating amidst a swirling disk of brilliant light. The featureless expanse masked a stellar beast millions of times denser than Earth's sun, a super massive black hole ringed by an accretion disk of hot glowing gas torn from hundreds of dying stars. Spiraling inexorably toward the glowing disk were more than a dozen stars that had lost all hope of escaping the graveyard of the galaxy. Slivers of hot gas snaked from the doomed stars into the whirlpool of light, warning that the star's own gravity was being overpowered by the colossus beneath them. Gone were the worlds that had once circled these condemned stars, long since wrenched from their orbits by the cosmic reaper's supergravity. Closer to the monster black hole's event horizon, differential gravity forces had destroyed all solids, reducing matter to its constituent atoms while frictional heating raised their temperature to extreme levels.

"We've got to get out of here," Vamp said from beside the entry. She had one ear tilted toward the passage outside, listening to the click of approaching metallic footsteps.

"Not now," Dr. McInness replied as he rotated his hand in the orb of light, fast forwarding imagery recorded by an Intruder probe. It dived past the doomed stars into the blinding glare of the accretion disk and then into impenetrable blackness. "We're inside the event horizon!"

"Incoming," Vamp declared urgently as the metallic footsteps grew louder.

"Do you know what this means?" he asked, completely absorbed.

Timer looked around at blackness on all sides. "A power failure?"

"They've explored the super massive black hole at the center of our galaxy. How could they overcome the gravity, the time dilation? How did they get a signal back?" He asked in amazement. "It's impossible! But they've done it!"

Vamp stepped toward the scientist. "Save it, Ian, we're out of here."

"Just a few more minutes." The blackness melted into a yet deeper blackness that funneled away to a distant radiance. "My god! It's an Einstein-Rosen Bridge!"

"I don't care if it's the Brooklyn Bridge, we're leaving!" She lifted him out of the chair, breaking his link to the log system and dissolving the view surfaces into static.

Dr. McInness tried to resist her grip. "You don't understand. That was a bridge to another universe. We have to see where it leads."

She dragged him onto her shoulder. "Virus, we need a way out of here."

Virus jumped into the chair, pulled up the ship schematic and drilled in to their location. "There's a gravity lift on this level, fifty meters away."

"Let's go," she said, starting for the opposite exit.

Bandaka darted through a newly opened archway, searching for any sign of movement ahead. Vamp followed with Dr. McInness slung over her shoulder, still protesting. When the seekers reached the log room entrance, Virus rolled a grenade toward the control chair, then he and Timer raced after the others. The grenade exploded as the seekers entered, knocking them off their feet.

Bandaka jogged past an alcove he didn't recognize, searching for the elevator.

"Bandi, back here," Virus called as Vamp and Dr. McInness stepped onto the acceleration plate and vanished.

Bandaka came back, looking the alcove up and down warily, then Timer gave him a gentle push as two weaponized seekers emerged from the log room. Timer fired his special, forcing them to raise shields, then Virus and Timer stepped into the alcove together as the seekers returned fired. An instant later, they stood in a long rectangular hall lined with alcoves, a meeting point for transit ways from all over the ship. They glimpsed Vamp and Bandaka run through a large archway, the only exit from the transport hub, as they stepped off.

"Wait!" Virus called, motioning to the other gravity lifts, but it was too late.

They followed the others into a circular room with walls lined with view screens and consoles, while in the center were two command stations placed side by side. The view screens were active with images of wedged shaped spacecraft of various designs and octagonal, multi-leveled structures with vertical slit windows. No one wondered why the screens and their terminals were active, or noticed an egg shaped blur pass in front of them as they entered.

Vamp turned, looking for an exit, realizing there wasn't one. "Oh-ho."

“You ran past a dozen elevators,” Timer said, turning to go back through the archway as an armored seeker appeared in the elevator lobby, “which, now we can’t use!”

Timer fired his special as he stepped behind a bulkhead for cover, striking one of the seeker’s shields, then Virus fired his recovered weapon, aiming low, shattering its knee joint. The seeker’s leg locked at an awkward angle as it staggered out of the alcove and fired both cannons, shaving Timer’s Kevlar helmet. He jumped back, ripping the helmet off, staring wide-eyed at its melted side, then felt the side of his head for burns.

“Close the door!” Vamp yelled, lowering Dr. McInness onto his good foot.

“How?” Timer asked, dropping his damaged helmet and firing blind into the elevator chamber.

Virus looked around the control room, straining to recall his implanted memories. There were no wall controls, he was certain of that. Through the fog of implanted memories he recalled they used low frequency sound waves to communicate with the ship, but lessers used command functions.

Vamp saw he was thinking, straining to remember. “Virus, do something.”

“Command functions,” he muttered, cautiously putting his free hand on the nearest console. It immediately dissolved and swallowed it, then his eyes glazed over as the terminal linked with him. Trance like, he dropped his special and plunged his other hand in. The console completed the mind link, assaulting his senses with nausea and a pounding in his head. He leaned forward, peering down into the terminal, focusing on the vaguely familiar symbols as he tried to remember which one he needed.

Behind him, the crippled seeker hobbled toward the entrance as others appeared in the lobby and rushed toward the control room. Timer fired at their legs, but they dodged sideways and kept coming.

“Virus!” Timer yelled as the seekers leapt toward the

open archway.

Virus broke into a cold sweat, unable to speak as he remembered how to declare an access emergency. He grabbed a curling yellow symbol deep in the console, causing the archway door to materialize and lock, then three thuds sounded as the seekers crashed into it. Sweat beaded on his face as the terminal told him over three hundred archways in that security zone had executed an emergency seal and lock out. He wanted to remove his hands, but in the recesses of his mind, he knew they could unseal the door if he didn't encrypt access. Virus wondered how to do that, then the console scanned his DNA and used that as the authentication code. Realizing the door lock was now encrypted, he pulled his hands out, blinking to clear his mind.

"How long have we got?" Vamp asked.

Virus turned to her, face pale, eyes blinking. He knew not even something called the Command Nexus could override the security encryption without a senior officer's parallel validation and the terminal had told him they were all dead.

"They … can't get in," he stammered, "and … we can't … get out."

"You cut that close," Timer said, then a blue bolt flashed across the room and blasted through his Kevlar body armor like paper. A fist sized hole appeared in his chest and a circular section of bulkhead behind him melted, then he crumpled, dead before he hit the floor.

Virus stood staring at Timer's body, too dazed from his mind link with the terminal to move, while Vamp drew her special and aimed at the source of the shot – inside the control room.

"Stealther!" she yelled as a faint distortion caught her eye.

She fired, blasting a wall screen as the blur darted across the room. Her fast charging Tom Thumb took a moment to recharge, then she fired again, grazing the alien's personal shield and triggering a ripple of electric blue force lines that lit up an egg-shaped photon field. Vamp fired again and the photon field collapsed, revealing an alien in a dark, skin tight body suit holding a bent, baton-shaped weapon.

Nemza'ri knew they could see her, but she was safe while her personal shield held. It had taken two hits from a plasma weapon, but couldn't survive many more, forcing her to kill the humans quickly. The wall screens told her the nanofabricators would have her sub-light transport and the deep sea habitat ready in less than twenty minutes. All she had to do was get to Flight Deck 286 where her equipment would be waiting and she could escape.

Her tactical implants fed her weapon's recharge status into her mind as she dodged away from the human with a plasma weapon. They told her the creature had no shield, so one shot would be enough, then her pistol announced it was ready to fire.

The alien aimed its baton at Vamp as Bandaka threw his boomerang. Its rhythmic beating of the air distracted the alien, who glanced toward the unfamiliar sound as it bounced harmlessly off its shield.

Virus dropped his hand to his holster, forgetting in his mind fogged state that he'd dropped the weapon, then he launched himself at the alien. When his chest and shoulders hit its force shield, it felt like steel, then his body sank into it. The alien lifted its hand to shoot, but he caught its wrist, pushing it away, forcing it to fire wildly into the ceiling.

Nemza'ri tried to twist free, but the human clung desperately to her. Its strength was surprising, even if its attack was absurdly physical. By nature, her kind were predators, yet they'd ceased practicing forms of combat based on physical strength long ago. With a shock, she realized her body, weakened by the sterilization antidote, might actually be overpowered by the semi intelligent lesser clinging to her shield.

Virus sensed the alien's movements were strangely awkward, as if it didn't know how to break his grip. With a spark of hope, he realized it wasn't trained in hand-to-hand combat, then he pushed its weapon away with one hand and grabbed its throat with the other. He found its suit, which looked like material, was stronger than steel.

She flashed a cry for help through her cerebral implants to the Command Nexus. The response was immediate. Every armed unit outside the Nexus Chamber instantly abandoned its current mission, and raced toward the control room. She twisted her weapon hand, trying to break free, but the human threw its greater weight against her, forcing her back.

Virus slid a foot behind the alien's ankle and pushed. It stumbled and fell against a console, triggering the panel's proximity sensor. A subliminal whisper instructed Virus to release the exalted being before him, making him hesitate, confused. He looked away in shame, about to let go, then saw Timer's bloodied body on the ground. Suddenly consumed with anger, he drove the alien's shoulders back. He slid his hand onto its face and pushed, trying to force its head down into the console.

Nemza'ri felt the command interface connect with neuron receptors in her shoulders, but only her hands were configured to communicate with the console. She began rerouting interface control to her shoulder implants so she could deactivate the console while the crazed human pressed its hand over her nose and mouth, pushing her head back.

She curled her lips back and bit its hand, tasting its bitter, unpalatable blood. The frenzy of survival suddenly stimulated ancient instincts that pumped a hormone many times stronger than adrenalin through her system. The primitiveness of it surprised her, but she felt her strength surge!

Virus felt pain explode through his hand as small, razor sharp teeth sliced through his palm. He ignored the pain, fighting desperately, telling himself they were dead if the alien got free. He'd thought for a moment he was the stronger, then its strength tripled in a heartbeat. It began to rise away from the console, straining to sink its teeth into his neck.

Bandaka jumped onto the console chair behind Virus and slid his spear into the alien's shield. The spear point pressed down on the amphibian's dome shaped sonar lobe between its bulging eyes, breaking its thick skin.

Instinctively, Nemza'ri recoiled, pulling her head back to protect her sensitive sonar lobe. The back of her head touched the console interface, allowing its quantum electric field to disrupt the implants in her cerebellum. Huge sections of her data net suddenly vanished as the console tried reprogramming the implants it encountered so it could link with her.

The sharpened stick pushed her head back into the console while implant fail safes began flashing warnings into her mind of impending, catastrophic failure. The Command Nexus, seeing it all through her eyes, started powering down the console, but the procedure was too slow. She had no choice but to trigger an emergency implant shut down.

A moment later, she was unconscious and every piece of technology sewn through her body died – but Nemza'ri lived.

The amphibian's hand relaxed, dropping its weapon as anger and confusion raged within Virus. He forced its oversized head deeper into the console's swirling colors and symbols long after it had ceased resisting, long after Bandaka had retracted his spear.

Vamp put a hand on his shoulder and tried pulling him off. "Virus, you've won."

"It's not dead!" His eyes were wild with vengeance as the alien lay helpless, its eyes closed, its small mouth limp and open.

Vamp pulled harder on his shoulder. "Virus, it's had enough."

"It killed Timer!" *It's in my head!*

"Yes and now it's our prisoner. Or do you want to start murdering prisoners?"

Virus hesitated as the rage consuming him faltered.

"It might be a useful hostage," Dr. McInness suggested. "Dead, it's just another corpse. I think there's enough of those in this ship already, don't you?"

Virus released his grip and stepped back, then Vamp lowered the unconscious alien to the deck, its defense shield still shimmering around it.

Virus' anger began to subside, replaced by a guilt and shame that shook him to the core, the result of implanted reverence, *What have I done?*

Dr. McInness hopped toward the unconscious alien for a closer look. He longed to speak with it, to examine it, but with no instruments all he could do was commit its appearance to memory.

"Take its weapon," Vamp commanded as she kept her special aimed at the alien's body. "It might come to."

"I was out for over a day," Virus said.

"Yes, but it's smarter than you," Dr. McInness explained. "No offence."

Virus grunted, then retrieved the alien's weapon.

Bandaka slipped his spear through the shield and angled its fire hardened point at the exposed flesh beneath the amphibian's angular chin. "When fishman wake up, he going to give us no trouble."

"Damn straight," Vamp said. "If it so much as twitches,

spear its ass."

"Throat easier," Bandaka said.

A squeal of tortured metal sounded from the locked archway door. They all turned to see the door bend slowly outwards. Timer's special slid across the floor and clanged against the door, then crawled slowly up to its center.

"What the hell?" Virus said confused.

"It's a magnetic field," Dr. McInness said as the metallic door groaned again, "a strong one."

A concave bubble slowly formed at its center while outside the control room, the Command Nexus gathered an army to rescue its only hope of victory.

* * * *

They watched, crouching in the shadows, as the lumbering Mark III battloid completed another preprogrammed orbit of the Nexus Chamber's inner sphere while coolie hat repair drones worked tirelessly to restore the Command Nexus to full functioning.

"It don't look so tough," Slab said, watching from the shadows.

Markus nodded to the borrowed M16 in Slab's hand. "Those weapons are useless against it." He was certain the untrained civilians would be quickly massacred by the battloid, which would then do the same to Beckman's team. He hoped that would prevent the destruction of the ship, but if not, he would ensure they never detonated the torpedo.

"Then we'll just make a lot of bloody noise," Cracker said with a grin.

"We'll get you a couple of minutes, General," Bill said to Beckman. "But don't stuff around. Whatever you're going to do, do it fast."

"We will," Beckman assured him. He'd initially planned to take the torpedo in alone, but it was clear that was now impossible. There'd been no vote, no discussion, just an unspoken agreement that they'd do it together.

Nuke held the torpedo in his hands. It was armed, requiring only his thumb on the control surface to detonate. Tucker knelt beside him, responsible for his protection, while Xeno lay unconscious in the corridor where they would have to leave her.

"They've got it free," Cracker whispered as maintenance drones removed a thick rectangular block from the inner sphere. Drones at each corner floated the damaged armor clear as flickering electric blue beams poured from the opening.

"You're up," Beckman said as the drones floated the block toward the outer shell, intent on carrying it to the nanofabricators for recycling. "Good luck."

"You don't need luck to get killed," Wal said miserably.

Slab stood and led them through the shadows to the opening in the Nexus Chamber. He took a moment to check the battloid's position, then jumped down onto the twisted walkway inside the chamber and ran to the right with his companions close behind. Their footsteps rang noisily on the metal walkway as they closed the distance to the battloid, which detected them immediately. It angled its shields at them and brought its weapons to bear as every repair drone with a cutting torch turned to face them.

"It's seen us!" Dan Mackay said, then the battloid fired, forcing them to dive for cover as blasts seared the wall behind them. They immediately jumped to their feet and ran along the walkway to where four drones floated with a replacement armor block. For a moment, it floated between them and the battloid, obstructing its line of fire.

"Ready," Cracker said, preparing to throw his last stick of dynamite at the battloid as soon as the segment moved away, knowing the explosion would do little more than distract the robotic warrior.

Slab fired a burst from his M16 at the maintenance drone holding the upper left corner of the armor block. The unarmored drone sparked, lost its grip and fell.

"It works on them," Slab said as the block's upward movement slowed, its weight now supported by only three coolie hats.

Bill shot the drone holding the top right corner with Tucker's pistol, then the massive armored block overbalanced and began to sink under its own immense weight. Other drones, sensing the danger, dived to assist, catching it before it fell.

Cracker depressed the detonator. "Get down!"

The others looked at him confused as the battloid was still hidden beyond the armor segment.

"What are you doing?" Slab demanded.

"Improvising!" Cracker declared as he threw the dynamite at the top of the armored block where repair drones were gathering. The dynamite struck the upper edge, bounced and exploded. The feeble chemical blast had no effect on the armor, but it shattered the repair drones along the top edge and caused the block to pivot over the two lower drones like hinges. Before they could stop it, the block pancaked onto the battloid below, sinking through its shields and driving its emitter and weapon arms down. The battloid toppled off its antigravity sleds and fell like a stone. The Nexus Chamber rang loudly as it struck the outer shell, then the armored block crashed onto the battloid, pinning it down.

"Good one, mate," Slab said approvingly, then shot one of the maintenance drones as it swooped down to lift the neutronium block off the battloid. The others joined in, shooting at the drones swarming around the battloid, intent on keeping it trapped.

In the shadows outside the Nexus Chamber, Beckman jumped to his feet. "Let's go," he said, then ran to the opening, jumped onto the walkway and started across the nearest horizontal pylon toward the inner sphere. The square sided pylon was a meter wide with no guard rails and although it was polished to a mirror sheen, it was not slippery.

In single file, the others followed Beckman across as maintenance drones dived toward them, bombing them with pieces of twisted metal. Beckman ducked as a melted panel flew over his head, then dodged part of a blackened support beam that bounced off the walkway behind him.

Tucker fired Thor at a diving drone, blowing it apart, while Markus sighted his MP5, but held fire, hoping one would knock Nuke off the walkway. Only when a drone dived directly at him did he let off a burst, then stepped aside as it crashed at his feet, bounced off the pylon and fell. He tracked another drone as it flew past, using it to disguise lowering his aim to Nuke's throat.

Have to sever his spine, Markus thought, so there was no possibility of a nervous twitch triggering the warhead.

Markus' finger tightened on the submachine gun's trigger, then a drone dived over his shoulder as he fired, taking the burst. The drone flashed with electrical short circuits and spun wildly away. Nuke looked up, thinking Markus had saved him.

"Thanks man," Nuke said, then Tucker vaporized another drone.

"Keep moving," Tucker barked, forcing Markus to turn and follow Beckman.

Once the maintenance drones had dropped their burdens, some dived down to help lift the armored block off the battloid, while others began using their cutting torches as weapons. Tucker blasted a drone with a burning torch as it dived at Nuke, while Beckman fired his special left and right repeatedly.

Over on the rim walkway, Slab and his mates raked drones trying to lift the armored segment off the flailing battloid. Each time the repair drones exploded and shorted out, the block crashed back down. The battloid wasn't damaged, but its arms lacked the strength to lift the super dense armor.

When Beckman reached the walkway encircling the inner containment sphere, he ran to the rectangular opening left by the removed block, firing his midget at the increasingly desperate drones diving after him. Behind Beckman, Markus reached the inner sphere, firing only to defend himself as repair drones with glowing torches circled and lunged rapidly. One torch wielding drone crashed into the containment sphere and exploded. Another smashed through the inner walkway, leaving a small gap they had to jump over.

A drone lunged at Nuke, forcing him to dodge and overbalance. He fell off the walkway, clutching the torpedo as Tucker stuck out a hand and caught his arm. For a moment, Nuke hung in the air, looking down at the long drop to the bottom.

"Don't drop me, man!" he yelled.

Tucker scowled. "Don't tempt me," he said, lifting him back onto the walkway. He turned and destroyed a drone diving at his back then followed Nuke to the containment sphere walkway. When a drone dived, he blasted it at close range, sending a wave of heat washing over Nuke's skin.

"Hey man," Nuke said, leaning away, "not so close with that thing."

"Quit complaining, Lieutenant, you're alive aren't you?"

The silver blur of a seeker at speed caught Tucker's eye as it leapt through the opening in the outer shell toward the inner containment sphere. He fired, catching it in mid air, cutting it in half, then its separated leg and arm sections skittered down the side of the sphere, its cannons firing wildly into the air.

"Runners incoming!" Tucker yelled.

Beckman jumped into the opening in the containment sphere to face a flood of sparkling blue light pouring from its interior. At the end of the short passageway, thousands of scintillating surfaces slid across the opening. It took Beckman a moment to realize he was seeing part of a multifaceted, crystalline orb turning slowly on its axis. The blue light pouring from the tiny diamond-like facets covering its surface carried orders from the Command Nexus to every component, weapon, robot and system aboard. It was how it controlled every aspect of ship functioning, while the beams radiating from the inner wall provided it with constant sensor and system updates.

Facing the Command Nexus for the first time, Beckman raised his special and fired a single blast of super heated plasma that flashed down the short passage and burst harmlessly against an inner defense field.

Beckman shrugged to himself. “Worth a try.”

Markus jumped down into the entrance, quickly replaced his magazine and fired at a drone diving straight for him. The machine plunged against the containment sphere’s outer wall, then slid away in flames as Nuke jumped down into the passageway. He set the warhead down and quickly checked it had suffered no damage.

“It’s good to go,” he said quickly.

Beckman thumbed his radio. “We’re in.”

Tucker fired once more, then jumped into the entrance. He rolled, coming to rest with his back against the wall as an armored seeker leapt into the passageway. Markus fired, but the seeker’s shields deflected his bullets. It took a step toward them as Thor completed its recharge cycle, then Tucker blew the runner out of the entry.

“It’s going to get crowded in here, real fast,” he said.

* * * *

Vamp and Virus backed up to the consoles lining the control room wall, fighting against the magnetic field tearing at the metallic items they carried. Dr. McInness gripped the sides of the command chair in the center of the room watching the bubble form in the door while Bandaka kept the tip of his spear pressed firmly against the unconscious alien’s throat. The bubble ballooned out, slowly encompassing the surrounding walls and filling the control room with the squeal of tortured metal.

"Ideas anyone?" Vamp asked.

Virus started moving from console to console, searching for a way to buy them time. The screens above the consoles came to life with technical diagrams and data displays, then one filled with a three-dimensional image of the Solar System. Virus glanced at it and moved on, but Dr. McInness' eyes did not.

"What's that?" the scientist asked, pointing to a tiny speck close to Earth.

Virus glanced at the console and shrugged. "It's nothing, just a navigational feed. It's useless, we're not moving."

"Zoom in on Earth."

Virus sighed, certain it was a waste of time, but he plunged his hands in and zoomed toward Earth, resolving the tiny speck into six silver dots floating beside a pictogram. "Hmm."

"What is it?"

Virus winced, straining to remember. "That symbol. I've seen it before. It means …" He furrowed his brow in frustration as he groped for an answer just beyond his reach. He zoomed toward the silver dots floating close to Earth, then six silver cylinders with rounded ends and sprinkled with thousands of tiny lights appeared. They floated above northern Australia in two rows of three, holding a precisely equidistant formation.

Dr. McInness fumbled for his radio, all thumbs, as he pressed the transmit button. "Major!" He yelled. "Can you hear me?"

Through a sea of static, Beckman's voice sounded. "What is it, Doc? I'm kind of busy down here."

"There are six ships in orbit! Right above us!"

"Friend or foe?"

Dr. McInness hesitated. "I can't tell."

"Give me your best guess!"

Dr. McInness stared at the screen, watching the six highly reflective ships floating serenely against black velvet. With no point of reference, he couldn't gauge their size or technology. He glanced at Vamp. "I don't know."

"Call it, Ian," Vamp said urgently. "Your best guess."

His eyes returned to the screen, unable to decide. "I … I've never seen this design before."

The magnetic field engulfing the door pulsed, opening a hairline fracture and wrenching the radio from his hand. Behind him, the metallic gear carried by Vamp and Virus was caught in an iron grip. Both of them grabbed the console chairs to prevent being pulled to the door, frantically shrugging off ammo belts and straps with buckles as their weapons and radios were sucked away. Gear that had been firmly sealed in pockets shredded their clothes as it shot toward the super magnetic field.

"McInness, are they friend or foe?" Beckman's voice sounded hollowly from the radio stuck to the center of the door.

Dr. McInness stared at the six shapes, unable to decide, then the radio sparked and crumpled as it was crushed under its own weight.

Virus gave the scientist an angry look. "He needed an answer. That's what you're here for. You should have guessed."

"Hey," Vamp snapped, "he didn't know!"

"I'm sorry," Dr. McInness said miserably.

Virus turned back to the screen, drawn irresistibly to the symbol floating beside the six ships, its meaning almost within reach. The magnetic field pulsed again, more strongly, then the door squealed and folded out like rubber, creating a vertical tear through the bubble that revealed glimpses of the armored seekers outside.

The fog hiding the meaning of the symbol cleared from Virus' tortured mind. He turned to Vamp with a shocked look on his face. "The symbol! It means … 'Unknown'."

* * * *

Cracker fired down at the maintenance drones working to free the battloid, then his pistol clicked empty. "I'm out."

Slab slammed a fresh magazine into his weapon. "This is my last one."

Metal footsteps approached rapidly, then a weaponized seeker landed on the walkway with a metallic clang. Slab sprayed it with bullets, but its shields deflected the attack as its twin cannons rotated toward them.

"Uh-ho," Wal said, backing away.

A brilliant orange blob flashed out from the containment sphere, smashed through the seeker's shields, shattering its torso and slamming it against the wall. Slab turned to the containment sphere in surprise to see Tucker standing in the entry with Thor still aimed at the crippled seeker. Tucker lowered the weapon, gave Slab a nod, then looked for a new target.

"Not bad," Slab said with grudging approval.

The echo of more metallic footsteps charging toward the Nexus Chamber sounded from the corridor as a second weaponized seeker appeared near the smoking ruin of the first. Slab fired at its legs which buckled beneath it.

Seeing Beckman's team were now inside the central sphere, Bill said, "They're in."

"Let's get the hell out of here," Cracker said.

"The big bastard's almost free," Slab said, glancing toward the battloid. He destroyed a repair drone with a single burst, then his M16 clicked empty.

"Now can we go?" Wal asked.

Slab nodded, then they started along the walkway as the crippled seeker pushed itself upright and began firing its cannons at them. Energy blasts peppered the wall beside them as they ran to a small opening in the outer shell.

At the entrance to the containment sphere, Tucker aimed at the crippled seeker, waiting for Thor to recharge. "Come on, damn you," he muttered, then a drone swooped down and scooped it up and flew after Slab and his companions. The hunters ducked through a small doorway, then the drone flew in after them just as Thor finished charging, too late for a shot.

Beckman thumbed his radio, trying to hear through a hiss of static. "McInness, call it!" he yelled, but the radio remained silent. *Six more ships?* he thought desperately, then turned to Markus and Tucker. "Cover the entrance. Nuke, you're with me."

"You can't go through with it," Markus said as he and Tucker backed away from the entrance. "Not now. You heard what he said, there are more ships in orbit!"

"Yeah, but who's side are they on?" Beckman asked as he led Nuke toward the Command Nexus.

Their skin prickled as they approached the defense field and got their first glimpse of the inner chamber. It was almost twenty meters across with five meters on each side separating the crystalline orb from the inner wall, which itself was lined with millions of tiny diamond-like points creating a smooth, scintillating surface. Blue beams flowed in both directions between the orb and the wall, transferring data and orders at the speed of light. As the orb rotated, a soft white light glowed at its core, pulsing with life as it shared its thoughts with its artificial minions.

"That's the biggest damn diamond I've ever seen," Nuke exclaimed.

"Every woman's dream," Beckman agreed. "Now blow it to hell. One minute."

Nuke set the torpedo down, fixed his eyes on his watch and hovered a finger over the detonator button. "In sixty seconds, mark."

Beckman thumbed his mike for anyone who could still hear him. "Listen up, people. If you need to make your peace, now's the time. We go in one minute," he said grimly, then added less formally, "see you on the other side."

At the passageway's outer entrance, the battloid floated up into view, finally free of the neutronium block. Markus backed away, as if distancing himself from it, intent on getting closer to Nuke and the torpedo.

Tucker fired, but Thor's massive blast evaporated harmlessly against the Mark III's upgraded shields. Its weapon arms took aim, but didn't fire. Tucker wondered why, then glanced at the antimatter warhead, seeing it was ready to detonate.

"Too late, asshole," he muttered, guessing the battloid's energy cannons would punch through the field surrounding the crystalline orb, destroying the Command Nexus.

That was something it could not do.

CHAPTER 18

After a treacherous climb through the cave, Laura and Mapuruma scrambled out into the shade of a low overhang. Laura moved to step out into the narrow, sun baked crevice when Mapuruma grabbed her hand and pulled her back. Drifting across the rock floor only meters away was the striker's winged shadow.

They held hands, barely breathing as it passed above the rock they hid beneath. It stopped and turned as its thermal sensor struggled vainly to filter out the tropical heat radiating off the rocks, heat that obscured their weak thermal signatures. A marbled velvet gecko, sunning itself in the open, watched the black winged shape drift toward it with instinctual fear, then sensing it had been seen, the tiny lizard darted for the safety of a cleft in the rock. The striker's motion detectors immediately spotted the movement and both its wingtip cannons swiveled and fired.

Below the overhang, Laura and Mapuruma tensed as the striker's cannons vaporized the gecko and several meters of rock. Laura tried to edge back into the cave, but Mapuruma tightened her grip, eyes wide with fear, pleading for her to remain still. She relaxed, trusting the young girl's instincts as the wedge shaped shadow floated up the weathered cliff face and moved off over the ridge. They remained motionless a long time, listening and watching for the winged hunter, scarcely breathing. When Laura believed it was gone, she released Mapuruma's hand and drew Timer's radio detonator from her pocket.

"Wait here," she whispered, then crept out from under

the overhang.

She looked up past shriveled trees and baked rock to the shield dome shimmering high in the sky. There was no sign of the striker, so she hurried along the crevice floor to the edge of a cliff overlooking the Walker River, a snaking, tranquil waterway surrounded by sandstone canyons and lush forest. Far across the valley, the shield dome rose out of the forest like a translucent curtain and curved to its apex above the mothership.

The perimeter towers were obscured by trees and by the inside of the shield itself, leaving her to wonder if she was even facing the right way. She pulled the telescoping aerial out to its full length and pressed 'arm', then her finger hovered over the detonate button uncertainly. Her mind filled with memories of her husband, of happy times and shared love. She knew if she pressed that button, that would be gone forever.

While she stared at the detonator, Mapuruma emerged from the overhang and came up beside her. "What's the matter?"

Laura looked down, trapped by Mapuruma's innocent brown eyes. She realized if she didn't do it, she was putting every child at risk. *Dan, I'm sorry!*

She held the radio detonator out at arm's length and pressed the red button. At that distance, she couldn't hear the sound of Timer's demolition charges exploding, shattering the emitter array at the top of the perimeter tower while the trees hid the explosion south of where she was looking. Laura stared at the shield dome, seeing no change, then she pressed the fire button again, several times.

"Is it broken?" Mapuruma asked.

Before she could answer, a vertical tear appeared to the south east, above the shattered emitter array. It ripped up the side of the curtain like a zipper, forming a narrow slit revealing blue sky beyond. When the tear reached the apex, a flash filled the sky as the instability triggered a cascade failure, forming a tiny hole that expanded slowly at first, then rapidly rolled down the dome, dropping the shield with perfect symmetry.

"It is now," Laura said solemnly.

Mapuruma pulled on her sleeve. The little girl was staring back along the crevice, terror on her face. Laura turned to see the black striker gliding toward them, its menacing black hull stark against the clear sky. It slowed to a hover and nosed down, angling its cannons at them.

Laura glanced over her shoulder, searching for an escape, but their backs were to the cliff face. Mapuruma put her arm around Laura's waist, hugging her tight, while she cradled the girl's head, pulling her face toward her.

"I'm sorry, Mapu," Laura said, knowing they were about to die, knowing it was her fault, unable to take her eyes off the deadly machine.

She saw the tips of its cannons glow as its weapons charged, then a brilliant white streak of light flashed down out of the sky and slammed the striker into the crevice floor like a pile driver. There was no explosion, only the thud of impact and a white cloud wafting above a steaming black pool of molten metal. For a moment Laura couldn't believe her eyes, then she looked up astonished.

There was nothing above them but empty blue sky.

* * * *

Beckman watched the seconds hand on Nuke's watch tick down to detonation while the battloid floated helplessly at the end of the corridor awaiting instructions from its master. The Command Nexus analyzed the object sitting at the threshold of its inner sanctum and knew from the radically unstable elements that it was an antimatter weapon utilizing a technology far beyond the reach of the planet's indigenous civilization. The Command Nexus assumed the weapon was proof these primitives had been armed by its enemies and were part of a deception plan whose existence it had long suspected. Now it faced a quandary, for the battloid could destroy the warhead with a single blast, but in so doing would release enough antimatter to destroy the Command Nexus as surely as if the warhead itself had detonated.

Beckman glanced at the crystalline orb, unaware the entirety of its great intellect was focused upon him and the warhead now poised to annihilate it. He resigned himself to his fate, tormented by the knowledge his family would be told he died innocuously, in a car crash or a training accident rather than in the line of duty.

Tucker thought of Steamer. This was payback for him. He wished Steamer could have been there at the end, so they could have gone out together.

Nuke tensed, surprised he was going to die this way. He wanted to take one last look around, but knew his duty was to keep his eyes on his watch. When the seconds hand reached twelve, he said, "That's it."

Beckman gave him a final confirming nod. "Do it."

Nuke reached forward to press the detonator when three heavy blows struck him between his shoulders. He fell forward, never hearing the burp from Markus' submachine gun.

Beckman saw Nuke cough blood, then he turned to see Markus aiming his MP5 at him.

"Get away from the bomb!" Markus ordered.

Beckman froze. "What are you doing?"

"I'm not going to let you destroy this ship. Now back away." He nodded to Tucker who was waiting for Thor to recharge. "Drop it or Beckman's dead."

Tucker hesitated, then removed one hand from the firing surface and lowered Thor to the deck with the other.

"Now kick it away."

Reluctantly, Tucker pushed the big special across the floor with his boot just as it finished recharging.

"You can't get out of here alive," Beckman said.

"I'm not going anywhere. None of us are, but this ship's staying right where it is, in one piece, for those who'll come after us."

Outside the containment sphere, the battloid didn't understand why one human had shot another or a third had abandoned its plasma cannon, but it saw the antimatter weapon operator was wounded and incapable of detonating the torpedo. Recognizing the tactical opportunity and knowing it could not fire its own weapons without damaging the Command Nexus, it drew back one of its cannon arms and hurled it forward, releasing the mount when its arm was fully extended. The pyramidal weapon shot through the air like an oversized dart and speared Markus in the back with tremendous force. The impact hurled him forward, over Nuke's body and onto the torpedo, then together they skidded toward the crystalline orb, coming to rest exactly where the battloid had computed – out of Beckman's reach.

Markus looked down in confusion at the triangular black metal point protruding from his chest, then he slumped forward. His face struck the torpedo's activation surface, followed instantly by a flash of light as the antimatter warhead detonated, then before the shock wave had moved a micron beyond the torpedo casing, a spherical black emptiness engulfed it. A hemisphere of the neutronium armored floor caught inside the black void vanished as Markus' corpse was sucked into it, leaving a bloody smear on the deck.

"What the hell?" Beckman said, confused. He knew every cell in his body should have been converted to pure energy as a huge crater formed beneath him. He'd seen the Lunar images of an antimatter explosion and knew what to expect. Instead he stared at a black void, absent of texture and depth.

Tucker furrowed his brow. "I thought it'd be bigger."

Beckman fired his Berretta into the black void, but instead of the bullet striking the warhead's metal casing or emerging from the other side, it was simply swallowed into the blackness as if it had never existed.

"Son of a bitch!" Nuke wheezed, spitting blood, crawling away from it. "I lugged that mother all the way through the stinking jungle … and it's broken!"

He had no way of knowing the antimatter explosion was trapped inside a supergravity sphere. If Dr. McInness had seen it, he might have recognized it had the properties of a black hole, although he would have thought it impossible to stand so close to its event horizon and not be torn apart by gravitational force. He would have known nothing could escape its grip, not a bullet, not a plasma blast, not even the shockwave of an antimatter explosion in full annihilation. What he would not have guessed was that an antigravity bubble could enclose a black hole, perfectly offsetting and containing its super gravitational force. Such a notion would have confounded him as he would never have believed such an effect could be artificially created, let alone projected from orbit.

To Beckman, it was simply incomprehensible. A weapon far more powerful than a fusion bomb had detonated in his face and yet its massive destructive force had been completely neutralized. He didn't know how. He didn't care. Instead, an old lesson screamed at him from memory, a lesson that told him why they'd never really had a chance. It was a lesson he'd been taught over and over again, about how infinitely advanced technology would look like magic to primitives, yet it had never really sunk in until now. And it was wrong.

It's not like magic, he thought bitterly. *It is magic!*

Throughout the great ship, sirens sounded as a high pitched computer generated voice announced something unintelligible in an alien language. Beckman and Tucker exchanged confused looks, then the mothership shuddered as if struck by a series of giant hammer blows.

An orbital bombardment had commenced.

* * * *

Hooper slumped to the ground with just one round left in his .50 caliber pistol. Liyakindirr crouched beside him, aiming Conan back the way they'd come, searching for the metal beast that hunted them.

"I don't see it," Liyakindirr said.

"It's close," Hooper wheezed, exhausted and deathly pale, the burn on his right side now a hideous mass of blood, sweat and dirt.

Liyakindirr had never seen such a wound, but he knew what the tropics did to injured men and was certain Hooper did not have long to live. "Can you walk?"

"No," he croaked, looking up at the sky, seeing clear blue firmament for the first time. It took him a moment to realize the shield dome was gone. "She did it! … Give me … the radio."

Liyakindirr slipped off the backpack and placed it close to Hooper. The sergeant dropped his pistol and with feeble fingers, pulled the short wave from the pack. Off to the right, they heard the familiar sound of metal whipping against leaves as the seeker circled around for another attack. Liyakindirr turned toward the sound, his finger hovering over Conan's firing surface. He'd learned quickly that when the seeker circled, it was too fast for the bulky weapon to fire, but Hooper had told him, if it came straight in, the weapon would work.

Hooper holstered his pistol and pulled the radio's aerial to full length, set the frequency and spoke into the mike. "This is Charlie Tango Alpha. Enact citadel, repeat, enact citadel. Acknowledge." As he listened for a reply, a flash of energy struck the radio, hurling it into the trees and tearing the mike from his hand.

Liyakindirr sighted back along the shot's flight path and touched Conan's firing surface. The alien plasma rifle pushed his hand to the left, but refused to fire as the seeker swerved away at high speed. "Did they hear?" he asked.

"Don't know," Hooper said, glancing at the smoking wreckage of the radio. Not a sound had come from it, not even static, as if no radio waves were getting through, which should have been impossible now that the shield was down.

The armored seeker swept out of the forest at an oblique angle. It circled in toward Liyakindirr at tremendous speed while he pressed down hard on the special's firing surface. The alien weapon stubbornly refused to fire because the seeker had precisely computed the angles and velocity needed to confuse its inertial targeter. Liyakindirr saw the seeker's twin cannons target him, then he leapt away as it fired. The two blasts flashed past Hooper and felled a tree with a crack, sending branches and birds flying.

Liyakindirr rolled to his feet as the seeker darted toward him like a silver blur through the underbrush. Frustrated the weapon wouldn't fire, he swung it like a club, but the seeker deflected the blow with one shield arm and sent him crashing against a tree with the other. It then swerved toward Hooper who reached for his pistol, but the seeker was on him in a flash, planting its metallic foot on his forearm, crushing bone and pinning his hand to the ground.

He groaned with pain as the robot magnetized one of its circular shield emitters to its torso, freeing its hand, then pulled the gun from Hooper's fingers. The seeker held the pistol in front of its sensor disk for analysis, curious at the effectiveness of such a crude weapon. As Hooper watched the seeker, unable to pull his crushed arm free, he glimpsed a storm of fiery meteors streaking to earth in the distance, then he heard thunder rolling over the land and felt the earth tremble with each impact.

Something's attacking the ship, he realized, certain the meteors weren't human weapons.

The seeker dropped the .50 caliber pistol and aimed an energy cannon at his head.

"Screw you," he growled, lifting his face defiantly, then three white blasts flashed through the trees from the left, tearing the armored seeker apart and sending its twisted remains flying. Hooper blinked, confused, then turned toward the source of the attack. Floating ten meters away were three bulky bipedal forms, each slightly shorter than a man. They floated effortlessly through the trees toward him in white deep diving suits. Plants in their way swayed aside, never coming in contact with their suits, yet no branches were broken, ensuring they left no trace of their passing.

More robots? he wondered apprehensively, his fear tempered by the knowledge that they'd just destroyed the seeker. He looked up at the meteor storm pounding the mothership to the west, then realized the three forms were coming from the east.

They were waiting outside the shield? he thought, *waiting for it to go down!*

The three forms had arms, but no hands. Where the left hand should have been was a short barreled energy weapon, while the right hand held a spherical bulge fitted with highly miniaturized support devices. When they floated past, one turned and aimed its utility arm toward him, analyzing his physical condition and equipment. The data was immediately sent to the orbiting fleet, which relayed it to a command center six thousand light years away. It was just one of trillions of pieces of information the Alliance headquarters received every second from forces scattered across thousands of systems covering a third of the galaxy. By the time Hooper's heart had beaten ten times, the information had been integrated into the theater of operations tactical view, translated into dozens of languages and dispersed to Allied civilizations up to thirty five thousand light years away.

To Hooper, it had been no more than a vague gesture.

The second figure scanned the destroyed seeker while the third drifted a short distance to the west, aiming its utility arm at the mothership, gathering ground based intel on the progress of the bombardment. Hooper noticed how they turned toward each other as if talking. It was not a machine-like movement, but communication between living beings in personal contact.

They're wearing helmets! he realized, oversized by human standards, but definitely helmets rather than the flat sensor disks used by the Intruder robots.

The alien floating in front of Hooper drifted closer, then a narrow, horizontal slice of its helmet dissolved from white to clear, revealing dark green, almond shaped eyes and dappled skin. Its eyes seemed to bore into Hooper, then a blue cone of light transmitted from its utility arm enveloped him. He felt a cold shock drive away the pain of his wounds and eradicate the tropical fever that had started to take hold.

The Tau Cetin blinked once, then the helmet window faded back to white armor and it turned to follow its companions. They were on a strict timetable and had to be in position when the bombardment ended. The three aliens floated off through the trees toward the mothership as their white suits dissolved into the colors and textures of their surroundings, more camouflage than invisibility.

Hooper watched them go with the eye of a professional soldier. He didn't know they were Earth's closest neighbors or that he stood millions of years behind them, but he knew with complete certainty what they were.

Infantry!

* * * *

Flaming meteorites appeared to rained down over the ship, only they weren't meteors.

The Command Nexus quickly determined they were a previously unknown type of energy weapon that ionized the atmosphere on contact. They struck gun emplacements, shield emitters and sensor nodes, vaporizing everything they touched. There was no heat, radiation or antimatter after effects, only a mysterious spacetime shockwave felt throughout the ship that warned the Command Nexus that it now faced a technology completely unknown in theory, possessing a precision and speed far exceeding the clumsy nova weapons that had crippled it out near the orbit of Jupiter.

It tried firing its defensive armament, raising shields, jamming and deceiving the incoming fire, but no defense system would activate. When it ordered maintenance drones to manually fire point defense weapons, the drones acknowledged the instruction then inexplicably shut themselves down.

While the ship shuddered from multiple impacts, every combat drone outside the hull was annihilated before they even knew they were under attack. When more battloids and seekers emerged to defend the ship, the incoming energy blasts changed course on the way down, pursuing and destroying them before they could offer any resistance.

When the Command Nexus saw the energy blasts maneuver, it created an entirely new weapon classification – an energy vector – to describe it. Everything the Intruders knew of directed energy weapons told them that once released, they could not change course in flight, but these energy vectors – though formless – maneuvered as if under intelligent control.

With that one discovery, the Command Nexus knew the war was lost.

The bombardment rendered it blind and defenseless, while noncombat systems and maintenance drones simply ceased to obey instructions. Following behind the vector storm, twenty silver elliptical transports streaked down toward the mothership, protected by more energy vectors that orbited them, ready to destroy any Intruder attack.

While the Tau Cetins were among the most technologically sophisticated civilizations in the galaxy, the Command Nexus realized it had been disarmed by a far more advanced adversary, one it had never encountered before who possessed weapons it had not imagined possible.

The shining Tau Cetin transports decelerated rapidly

until they hovered above the mothership and over the surrounding ridges. Armored infantry then emerged, some flying down through the hull breaches into the mothership, others fanning out through the surrounding valleys, securing a perimeter and searching for inhabitants who had come in contact with Intruder forces.

Special operations infantry, having flown overland toward the ship when the shield dome went down were already inside the wreck, providing real time tactical intelligence to the assault teams. Assault force elements raced to their objectives, conscious of the limited time they had to achieve their goal. The Tau Cetins knew their great partner was containing an antimatter explosion with a technology unknown even to them and that such massive energies could not be held in check for long. Once the matter annihilation wave passed the artificial black hole's event horizon, its destructive powers would be released in full.

If that happened, a great opportunity would be lost.

* * * *

Vamp watched helplessly as the control room door ballooned out into the corridor and the walls buckled to the wail of rending metal. The bubble tore away, flew back several meters and struck a rectangular field generator with a clang, then was crushed flat against the emitter.

"They'll have to shut down the magnetic field for the runners to get in here," Dr. McInness warned.

"Do I kill fishman now?" Bandaka asked, pressing his spear tip against the alien's throat.

Vamp glanced at the unconscious alien. "No." She wasn't about to murder a helpless life form, even if it had killed Timer.

The white flash of a pulse grenade burst outside the control room followed by a chorus of sonic booms and flashes from energy weapons. The magnetic field generator was hit and shorted out in a shower of sparks, letting the flattened door bubble clatter to the deck. An explosion sounded, then an armless seeker torso skidded through the doorway and came to rest in front of Virus.

They stared at the smoking wreckage in surprise, then a floating, translucent blur floated past the magnetic field generator. When it entered the control room, its camouflage field dropped revealing a suit of bulky white battle armor. The Tau Cetin assault trooper scanned them with its utility arm, then satisfied they were no threat, turned its attention to the unconscious amphibian on the floor.

The Intruder's personal defense shield still distorted the air as Bandaka resolutely held his spear to its throat. The armored soldier turned to Bandaka, who listened briefly then stepped back, absently wondering what had possessed him to move.

A tiny golden sliver emerged from the warrior's utility arm and floated toward the unconscious alien. There was a hint of electrical distortion as it passed through its shield, then the sliver entered the amphibian's forehead, leaving no puncture wound. The golden sliver took control of the Intruder's implants and ended its self-induced coma.

Nemza'ri awoke, relaxed and unafraid. An irresistible thought appeared in her mind, compelling her to deactivate her personal shield. She immediately complied, then stood with an overwhelming sense of well being and a desire to obey any request. Absently, she knew she was under the control of a capture technology, but it made no difference. Nothing mattered, but the intoxicating joy of obedience.

Vamp watched the amphibian stand trance-like before the armored warrior, its arms limp by its side, eyes staring blankly ahead. It seemed to be listening to a voice only it heard, then it walked out of the control room unescorted.

"What just happened?" Vamp asked, careful to make no sudden movements.

"It appears our amphibian friend was just taken prisoner," Dr. McInness replied.

"Fishface didn't put up much of a fight," Virus said, surprised at how submissive his former adversary had become.

Dr. McInness raised his hand, trying to attract the warrior's attention. "Excuse me, could you tell us what's going on?"

The Tau Cetin seemed not hear, but floated along the line of consoles until it reached Vamp and Virus. They suddenly felt inexplicably compelled to step aside, which they did without question.

When Vamp regained her self control, she said, "What was that?"

"Hypnosis?" Virus suggested, then he brightened. "Hey, the pounding in my head is gone."

The battle armor clad alien continued gliding alongside the consoles until it found what it was looking for, then aimed its utility arm at the control panel. Data began appearing on the screen above the console, scrolling so fast that the symbols blurred into each other, while the armored warrior fed instructions into the console using its utility arms.

"They're ship status reports," Virus said. Now that the headaches had vanished, he found the forced memories were easily within reach. "I can read it." He glanced from one screen to the next, eyes wide with astonishment. "I can read them all!"

Dr. McInness watched the interaction between machine and alien mind, impressed by the speed. "That's how it's supposed to work."

Vamp shook off her artificial sense of well being and stepped up to the armored warrior. "Hey, space monkey, what the hell is going on here?"

The Tau Cetin continued assessing the damage suffered by the ship, seemingly unaware of her existence, so Vamp rapped on his armor with her knuckles like she was knocking on a door. "Hey, Michelin man! I'm talking to you."

Before she could get another word out, she fell into a deep and peaceful slumber, floating gently to the floor. Moments later, they were all fast asleep.

* * * *

The battloid glided into the passageway, holding its fire as Tucker scooped Thor up off the floor and fired at its antigravity sleds. One of the battloid's shield arms absorbed the blast while another slammed him into the wall, knocking the big special from his hands and sending it skidding over the side. Tucker groaned and crumpled to the deck with broken ribs and fractured vertebrae, unable to move.

It doesn't want to risk hitting the crystal! Beckman realized as he fired his special, lacing the battloid's shields with ineffective pencil-thin plasma bursts.

Nuke crawled toward the wall, trying to get out of its way as he fired his Tom Thumb, but his weapon was even less effective than Beckman's.

"Busted ass alien crap!" Nuke rasped through bloody lips, then the battloid swatted him with one of its shield emitters, hurling his tiny weapon across the deck toward the black void. When the Tom Thumb's barrel poked through the antigravity bubble containing the void, it stretched like liquid plastic as supergravity tore it apart and sucked up the weapon like water.

When Beckman saw what the void did to Nuke's weapon, he turned toward the crystalline orb, placing the void between himself and the battloid. He pushed against the protective field guarding the Command Nexus, feeling his hair stand on end as it slowly gave way.

The lumbering Mark III, fearing Beckman would get his weapon through the field, lashed out with the arm that had thrown its cannon at Markus. It coiled around Beckman's chest like a snake, pulling him back, then the outstretched tentacle touched the antigravity field enclosing the void and stuck fast. A rivulet of metal trickled from its arm into the blackness which quickly became a stream then a flood, pulling Beckman and the battloid with it.

Unable to determine what the blackness was, the battloid tried to protect itself by angling its shields toward it, but they became caught in the crushing grip of collapsing spacetime. Electric blue force lines flashed as the shields collapsed and the disk shaped emitters were sucked in, drawing the battloid toward the voracious blackness.

Beckman felt himself being dragged out of the Command Nexus' defense field, unable to break free of the robotic arm wrapped around his chest. He realized the metallic tentacle was no longer under the control of the battloid, but was dragging him with it into the void. He twisted, aimed his plasma pistol at the coiled tentacle and fired. Searing pain erupted across his chest as a swath of skin was incinerated and the robotic arm was severed. Pieces of it fell from his chest onto the deck while the remainder was sucked into the blackness.

On the other side of the supergravity sphere, the battloid's torso passed inside the counteracting field. It toppled over, its armor turned to water and its body poured into the blackness.

Nuke coughed blood. "Ouch."

Beckman backed away, ignoring the pain across his chest, distancing himself from the featureless menace floating above the deck. He turned toward the Command Nexus, realizing the blue light streaming from its faceted sides was dimming and its spin rate rapidly decreasing. In moments, the crystalline orb came to a complete stop and the white glow at its center began to fade away.

Nuke saw it too. "What does it mean?"

"We won," Beckman said.

"How?" Nuke asked.

"I don't know."

"Major!" Tucker yelled through clenched teeth.

At the end of the passageway, armored warriors appeared, their camouflage fields shimmering in the fading blue light of the Command Nexus. One aimed their utility arm at Tucker, another did the same to Nuke, assessing their injuries. The warrior examining Nuke emitted a soft yellow light from its support arm, temporarily sealing his gunshot wounds, preventing him from bleeding out.

Seeing this, Beckman lowered his special as other battle armor clad soldiers flew past the black void, ignoring him and heading for the Command Nexus. They were briefly surrounded by sparkling auras as they passed through its protective field, then they slipped into the space between the orb and the inner containment wall, taking up positions around the Command Nexus.

It's not us they want! Beckman realized.

The warrior's camouflage fields glistened like thousands of reflected diamonds in the dim blue glow of the dying Command Nexus. Beckman didn't know the ship's guiding intelligence was self terminating, but the Tau Cetins did. They deactivated their camouflage fields, revealing their white battle armor that, in spite of their bulk, seemed as flexible as silk. Each had bulges over the shoulders, oversized helmets and a small triangular insignia at the left breast.

Tiny disks emerged from their utility arms that sank into the crystalline orb and dissolved at its center. When all of the disks had melded with the orb, rewriting its quantum level programming, the central white glow ceased fading, signaling the Command Nexus had fallen into a hypnotic state.

Two more aliens floated into the passageway, one was shorter than the Tau Cetin soldiers, the other much taller and thinner than a man. The shorter alien wore an unarmored one piece space suit with a patchwork of control surfaces along each arm, an equipment belt, a weapon at its hip and a close fitting helmet with a transparent face plate. The tall alien wore a skin tight, light brown body suit that showed no signs of equipment or weapons, and its long face was obscured by an opaque field rather than a helmet. It had a spindly, fragile look and was surrounded by a glowing white aura that hugged its body and made it virtually invulnerable.

The tall alien ignored the humans and went straight to the supergravity void, while the shorter alien waited. Beckman sensed the tall alien was in charge and its diminutive companion was merely its assistant. While the tall alien determined how long they had before the antimatter blast would break containment, the short alien approached Beckman, studying him with black sloping eyes that had no iris or pupil. It tilted its head, glancing at the plasma pistol in his hand, then the Zeta retrieved a silver weapon attached to its hip and held it close to Beckman's midget for comparison. They were identical.

"We have a match," Beckman said, then the alien held out its other hand, palm up.

"He wants his toy back," Nuke wheezed.

Beckman sighed and placed the plasma pistol in its hand. "Indian giver."

The Zeta recognized it was a model they hadn't used in half a century, then attached his weapon to his hip and magnetized Beckman's weapon to his thigh.

A few meters away, the tall alien floated back as a hole opened in the neutronium armor above the supergravity void. There was no blast of heat or energy, simply a slight hiss as tightly compacted neutrons lost atomic cohesion. The Zeta turned to watch, as confused as Beckman as to how neutronium armor could be made to evaporate in such a way. A shaft appeared above the supergravity void, rising vertically up through the mothership to daylight. A moment later, the miniature black hole floated up into the shaft and climbed toward one of the great ships in orbit.

"What are you going to do with that?" Beckman asked,

finding the diminutive alien's lifeless black eyes unnerving. He'd seen classified photographs of dead Zetas, but they hadn't prepared him to meet one face to face. When it made no attempt to answer his question, he said, "I guess you guys really screwed the pooch this time, letting those fish heads down here."

The Zeta heard a perfect translation, but rather than respond, it transmitted an irresistible wave form sending Beckman and his companions into a dreamless sleep. Earth's gravity was counter balanced before they fell, letting them float comfortably, while Nuke began to snore.

Not far from the sleeping humans, the white glow at the heart of the crystalline orb brightened, marking its forced return to life, its encyclopedic knowledge of Intruder secrets, plans and tactics captured intact. Slowly, the orb began to spin again as the Command Nexus became the first Intruder guiding intelligence ever to become a prisoner of war.

* * * *

Laura climbed to the top of the rock cleft overlooking the steaming metallic pool marking the remains of the striker. She was alone now that Mapuruma had gone in search of her parents. Laura dreaded the prospect of reaching the summit where she expected to see a massive crater in the distance. She'd mistaken the pealing thunder of the orbital bombardment for the detonation of the torpedo and had given up hope of ever seeing her husband again.

When she could see over the trees to the Goyder Valley she found to her astonishment that the scarred hull of the mothership lay intact. Fear overwhelmed her anguish as she assumed Beckman had failed and wondered what the tiny silver dots floating above the mothership were. The dots drifted out away from the massive wreck, then a column of faint yellow light reached down from orbit and enveloped the mothership. The silver dots moved in close to the wreck, locked tow beams onto it and began rising in unison, lifting the stricken ship with them. Laura mistakenly believed it was flying under its own power, unaware one of the ancient ships from the Virgo Supercluster had isolated it from Earth's gravity.

While the massive bulk of the mothership rose into the sky, a shadow passed over her. She turned fearfully, thinking it was another striker, but found an elliptical craft floated above her, its mirrored silver surface reflecting the forest and sky. Laura saw her reflection on its pristine hull, then a brilliant light blinded her. She felt dizzy and glimpsed the ground drop away, then she was floating in a large circular room, dark except for a feeble light in the ceiling. Nearby was a group of men she didn't recognize, Slab and his companions. They were awake and surprisingly comfortable within their weightless confinement. She realized her fears had vanished, replaced by a blanketing calm.

"Look," Wal exclaimed, nodding toward Laura, "another one."

"G'day luv," Slab said amicably. "Welcome to the mad house." He glanced meaningfully down at his feet floating a meter above the metal floor.

"Don't mind us," Wal said cheerfully, "we're just hanging around."

Slab tried whacking him with the back of his hand, but the smaller man leaned back, easily dodging the blow with a mischievous grin. The action sent Slab turning slowly for a few moments until he came to rest facing in the opposite direction.

"Laura!" Dan called, craning past Bill.

She hadn't seen him, masked by the other men. "Dan! You're alive!"

The others looked at Dan curiously, who explained with a beaming smile, "That's my wife."

Laura reached out a hand toward him, but he was too far away. "I thought I'd never see you again."

Bill caught Dan's hand and pulled him in, then once they were close, he pushed Dan toward her. Dan drifted a short distance through the inertial dampening field, then slowly came to rest while Cracker pushed her gently toward her husband, sending himself tumbling backwards and finishing upside down.

"Uh-oh!" Cracker said as he flailed his arms uselessly trying to right himself, much to his companions' amusement.

Floating in the center of the chamber, Dan and Laura reached out to each other until their finger tips met, allowing them to pull themselves together through the treacle-like dampening field. Laura threw her arms around her husband as tears welled in her eyes while Dan stroked her hair, unable to speak, then they kissed.

The darkened room flashed, then Djapilawuy appeared on the far side of the chamber. Her face was a mask of terror until the neuroelectric waves bathing the compartment dissolved her fears.

"Hey," Wal declared with a grin, motioning toward Djapilawuy, "there's another one!"

* * * *

A wave form ended the sleep programming in Beckman's hominid brain. He opened his eyes and squinted against a bright white light. Instinctively, he raised his hand to shield his eyes, but the intensity of the light diminished to a tolerable level before his hand was in place.

We prefer more light than you, the Biologist explained with a thought that was warm and soothing, yet strangely detached.

Beckman sensed someone standing to his left. He turned toward the being, expecting a diminutive Zeta, but found instead a slender, fragile looking humanoid three meters tall, the same race as the tall alien he'd seen in the mothership. The alien's eyes were large and circular, luminescent indigo in color with no whites and a triangular iris set in a long face. His long vertical nose protruded very little, while his mouth seemed too small for his head and his lengthy ears folded forward, cupping the ear drum.

Beckman remembered one of his orientation courses: if their mouths are small, they'd see our mouths as too large. If their eyes are large, ours will seem too small. He made a mental note to try to keep his eyes as wide as possible and his mouth small while speaking.

Unnecessary, a single perfect thought assured him. The Biologist knew of millions of species across the universe, all physically different from each other. He could not be offended or repulsed by any physical appearance, such was his complete acceptance of difference.

"Where am I?" Beckman asked, glancing around the room. There were no doors or windows, only a long curved chair in one corner facing into the room. Several small machines floated near the Biologist, waiting to respond to any need, while a marble sized object hovered behind Beckman, seemingly watching him and moving out of sight each time he turned to look at it. It was then he noticed he was floating with his feet just off the floor.

The Biologist, sensing his unease, issued a telepathic command that gradually returned gravity to the three dimensional area Beckman occupied. He settled like a feather to the floor as his weight slowly returned to normal.

Move slowly, the Biologist informed him. *If you leave your personal gravity field, your weight will increase eighty three percent.*

"Personal gravity field?" Beckman asked curiously, sticking his arm out, contravening his instructions. For a moment, his arm felt heavy and started to sink, then the gravity field refocused around him, returning his weight to normal.

They told us your species would disregard guidance.

"Yeah, we're disobedient sons of bitches," he replied, then looked up curiously. "Who told you?"

Your neighbors.

"Is that what they think of us, disobedient? After how many years of spying on us?"

Studying, observing, not spying.

"So, you're not from around here?"

No, I am not.

"Where are you from?"

This ship is my home.

"I meant what planet. How far away?"

Our origin system ceased to exist before your star had formed. The supernova remnant that remains of it is in a distant galaxy.

It took Beckman a moment to realize what the tall alien was telling him. "I guess that makes you the top dog around here."

We are one of the First.

"The first what?"

The first to know, to think, to create.

Beckman studied the slender alien, noting his pale, hairless skin and long, vaguely ellipsoid head. He wore white gloves, a simple maroon jumpsuit covering long spindly arms and legs, yet Beckman guessed he must have been a good deal stronger than a man, considering the higher gravity he preferred.

"So, did we win the war?"

The Intruders have been returned to their proper place.

"But you're going to go kick their butts, right? Teach them a lesson?"

That would be unnecessarily aggressive.

"They kicked ass out there. All those ships destroyed. I saw the movie. You can't let them get away with that."

There shall be no punitive retaliation. We have no desire to damage their civilization. They are young. In time, they will develop. The penalty for not doing so would be severe.

Beckman looked surprised. "Wait a minute. They're young? I thought we were young and they were old?"

They are old, from your perspective, young by ours.

"So what are we? Amoeba?"

You are younger.

Beckman was irritated at the thought of being younger than young, but that was fate and he'd been taught over and over again, no matter who you meet, there'll always be someone older, more powerful. He put it out of his mind. "Suppose they attack again? Suppose they attack Earth?"

They have no interest in your world.

"We've got their ship. They're going to want it back."

The Biologist stepped toward a wall. It vanished, replaced by an image of space. Hundreds of kilometers away, a shining cylinder with round ends floated above the exquisite blue and white globe of Earth. It was unlike any ship in the battle he'd seen from the mothership's log room. Beyond the cylinder were two more ships of similar design.

"Nice window."

It is a view. The Biologist pointed toward the lead ship closest to them. *You see, you need not be concerned, they will not come looking for their ship.*

Beckman leaned forward, studying the massive cylinder. Floating beneath the central section was a tiny gray splinter ringed by silver specks.

"Wait a minute!" Beckman said in disbelief. "That ship was huge."

Size is relative. For now, your perspective is small. In time, that will change.

The Biologist issued a thought and the view zoomed toward the splinter, revealing the wrecked Intruder mothership surrounded by silver Tau Cetin transports. Beckman swallowed, his mind spinning as he realized each cylindrical ship was hundreds of times larger than the Intruder ship.

"That ship was a wreck. How'd you get it off the ground?"

We isolated it from your world's gravitational field.

The derelict mothership drifted toward the cylinder. Beckman thought they were going to collide, then the intruder ship slid through the cylinder's hull and vanished. A moment later, the tiny Tau Cetin ships streaked away and the view returned to the wide angle perspective.

"What are you going to do with their ship? Study it?"

Their primitive technology is of no interest to us.

"But you captured that sphere thingy?"

We assisted your neighbors in capturing it, so they may study it and come to understand the Intruders as we do. It is the first Command Nexus to be taken with its consciousness intact. It will help involved civilizations contain future aggression.

"Involved? In the war?"

Involved in relations between developing societies.

"Developing? Like us?"

You are not involved. Neither are we. Your time of involvement is yet to come. Ours has long since passed.

"Right," Beckman said thoughtfully, "but you're here now, so you are involved."

We have reset the balance, nothing more. This is not our responsibility and we shall not return again for a very long time.

"But you set the rules?"

No, not now, not for eons. Only those active in relations between life forms who see dissimilarities determine law. For those without difference, law is unnecessary.

"So when we get out here, they'll be setting the rules for us?"

You will not have to concern yourselves with that for many centuries.

Beckman gave the Biologist a surprised look. "We'll be out here one day, soon."

Not soon. You greatly underestimate the difficulties.

Beckman furrowed his brow. "What do we have to do to get out here with you guys?"

Evolve. Your species will become an interstellar

civilization within a thousand of your Earth years – if you do not destroy yourselves first – but you will need to advance your understanding of your place in the universe and learn to embrace those who are unlike yourselves. If you cannot live in peace with other humans, how can you coexist with those not of your world? It is something every species must learn. In time, when you are ready, your neighbors will help you.

"Help us? How?"

The resources you need no longer exist in this system. They were mined out long before your species came into existence.

"Damn! So someone stole our stuff?"

There was no sentient life on your world at that time.

"So even if we figure everything out, we're still stuck here?"

Your neighbors will give you the resources you need, when you are ready.

"Hey, we're ready!"

They will decide that, not you. It is why they study you so intensively. They know your time is coming and are preparing for you.

Beckman scratched the back of his neck. "But they don't understand us, right? Our emotions, how we work. So how can they judge?"

It is a vanity of your species that you believe you are not understood.

"But they're aliens. You're an alien, no offence. No one is supposed to understand anyone. Isn't that how it goes?"

Everything you are, they once were. They know more about you than you know about yourselves. We are the ones your neighbors do not understand.

Beckman looked surprised. "Why is that?"

The greater encompasses the lesser. The lesser cannot encompass the greater.

"Right," Beckman said slowly. "So what's going to happen now? Everyone down there is going to know you guys are out here."

Nothing will change for your world.

"I don't mean to be telling you your business, but satellites were destroyed, planes were shot down, nukes exploded. People tend to notice stuff like that."

There will be no proof.

"There's alien crap everywhere."

All Intruder technology will be removed from your southern continent. All mineral extraction shafts will be collapsed. Nothing will remain.

"We nuked them. Something must have happened to make us do that."

The view adjusted. The northern tip of Australia appeared below a pair of silver ellipses, each towing a large rock. The two craft released the small asteroids and pulled away, leaving their burdens to tumble toward Earth. The small asteroids began flaking tongues of fire as they punched into the atmosphere, following precisely computed trajectories.

"What are you doing?" Beckman asked anxiously.

The first asteroid will land on the military base the Intruders destroyed, the second on the crash site itself.

"Are you nuts!"

The asteroids will not seriously affect your climate. Global temperatures will fall slightly for less than a decade, but your world will recover.

Beckman's mind swam. "You can't hit us with asteroids? Whose side are you on?"

It is for your own good.

The two small asteroids became engulfed in flames as they tore down into the thicker atmosphere, side by side.

"Suppose you miss."

There is no possibility of that.

"They'll detect the shockwaves. They'll know they hit days after the ship crashed."

The only seismic impact your world will have record of is that of the Intruder ship itself. When these two asteroids land, all of your world's seismic sensors will be inoperable.

"You know where every sensor is?"

No, your world's energy supply will be disabled before the impacts.

Beckman's eyes widened in surprise as he looked down at Earth, seeing the lights of Asia burning bright on the night side of the terminator. "How are you going to do that?"

Your technology is fragile. It is easily neutralized.

Beckman knew there wasn't long until the asteroids hit. "Aren't you cutting it a bit close?"

You are looking the wrong way.

"Huh?" Beckman said, turning to look in the opposite direction, toward the sun. To his surprise, a brilliant orange cloud was racing toward them. It swept over the six great ships, momentarily illuminating invisible eggs surrounding each one, then the plasma cloud engulfed the Earth. The upper atmosphere glowed brightly as the lights of Asia suddenly winked out. For several seconds, glowing orange fire filled space, enveloping the Earth, then it continued on toward the Moon.

"What that hell was that?" Beckman asked, shocked.

You call it a coronal mass ejection.

"It came from the sun?"

Yes.

"You caused it?"

We did. Your planet was at the center of the effect, the most severe such event in your recorded history. At this moment, there is no electrical power anywhere on your world. No seismic sensors, no satellites, no radars are functioning. Your world has suffered no permanent harm, although the inner planet you call Mercury sustained slight damage.

"Tough break for Mercury."

It is a lifeless world. The damage will not prevent you utilizing its resources when your civilization is more advanced.

Beckman studied the Earth, taking in the full magnitude of what it meant for all electricity to suddenly fail. "There would have been thousands of aircraft flying when that hit."

All have crashed. I am sorry. It was necessary.

"This will start a war. We have thousands of nuclear weapons down there."

None are functioning.

"Oh." Beckman said, shocked by how easily the world's militaries had been disarmed.

We do this to protect you. Your world is not ready to know its place.

"No one's going to believe two asteroids hit the Earth at the same time."

They will believe it was one asteroid that broke apart as it entered your atmosphere. Analysis of the asteroid debris will prove that beyond doubt.

"What about the satellites and aircraft those aliens shot down?"

The early losses will be attributed to the beginning of the solar eruption. Whatever else your military know, they will not reveal. They fear your people discovering how vulnerable your world is more than they fear us.

"You got that right," Beckman said, certain there would be a massive cover up.

The twin asteroids become brilliant white stars as they dived toward the vast tropical forest of northern Australia. They struck seconds apart, the first one precisely on the ruins of Tindal Air Force base, the second in the center of the Goyder River Valley. Two brilliant white flashes bloomed like enormous fusion explosions, sending shockwaves expanding in circular patterns around both impact sites and launching millions of tons of debris into the atmosphere. Beckman watched stunned, chilled at the prospect that they could easily do the same to Earth's cities. Slowly, the two brilliant points of light in northern

Australia turned to brown clouds billowing up through the stratosphere.

"You're forgetting one thing. I know. The people with me know what really happened." Beckman glanced down at the Earth with a sinking feeling. "That's why I'm up here, isn't it? You're not letting us go back?" After the loss of life caused by the global electricity failure, he assumed his team was equally expendable.

You have been brought here for cleansing. No trace of contact will remain within your cellular structures. That is all.

"You're sending us back?"

Your military leaders will use your expedition to explain what happened. You must return.

For the first time, Beckman remembered the plasma blast that had burned his chest. He looked down, finding no trace of the wound. He rubbed the perfectly healthy hair and skin on his chest, wondering if the self inflicted wound had been a bad dream, then he stared out at the technological leviathans floating above a beautiful and ignorant world.

"But I'll still know."

The Biologist's response was a long time in coming.

No, you won't.

* * * *

Dr. McInness peered at the dust cloud ten kilometers away. It filled the western sky, obscuring the last rays of sunset as it was carried away to the north by the prevailing winds. In spite of the long hot hike from the coast, he felt remarkably refreshed, surprised his fitness had held up so well. He had no idea that only hours before, the bones in his ankle had been crushed.

Standing beside the scientist, Beckman aimed his binoculars at the base of the nearest asteroid impact. The debris cloud was still too thick to see the impact area, but it was clearing. "We'll be able get in there tomorrow."

"We should wait another day," Dr. McInness said. "The air is like soup down there."

"No, I want to get this over with. I have letters to write," Beckman said grimly, glancing uncomfortably at the four freshly dug graves laid out under a white limbed gum tree. Burying Markus, Steamer, Cougar and Timer had been grisly work. He wasn't even sure they'd put the correct body parts in the right graves, but they'd done their best. At least, that's what the implanted memories told him. He didn't know why Steamer's special had exploded, killing all four, but the sight of his men being torn apart was something he'd never forget. No autopsy would ever discover that the body parts in the graves had been synthesized from DNA samples and irradiated as if exposed to a plasma overload. He kept telling himself it was an accident, but even so, he was going to kick some egghead's butt when they got back to Groom Lake. They should have known the damn things were unstable.

We should stick to weapons we understand. This alien crap is too unpredictable.

Beckman would fight hard until the day he died to make that policy. It was an implanted drive programmed by a quantum electrical device buried deep within the cellular structure of his brain. It isolated some memories from his conscious mind, but otherwise did not interfere with his functioning. The quantum implants that he and his companions now carried would function only while they were alive. Once their core body temperatures cooled, the implants would dissolve into the surrounding tissue, leaving no trace of their existence.

"We'll hike in tomorrow," he said, then started down the slope to the camp.

Virus had his headphones on and was channel surfing the short wave. It was an exact, indistinguishable copy of the radio that the seeker had blown out of Hooper's hands. Care had been taken to ensure that even the impurities in the metals were copied, to prevent any indication that the radio had been fabricated by a vastly superior civilization.

"Have you established contact yet?" Beckman asked.

Virus shook his head, motioning toward the southern sky. "It's a total shut out."

"Keep trying. I want those choppers here in forty-eight hours."

Beckman walked over to the Australian zoologist standing near the campfire with her husband. The aboriginal trackers and a group of local hunters sat around the fire watching a big kangaroo roasting in the flames. Laura was gazing up at the colored lights winding across the darkening sky with a puzzled expression. Beckman glanced up at the waves of color streaking the heavens, impressed. He'd heard they were similar to the northern lights but now that he saw them, he realized they were much bigger and brighter.

"They're beautiful."

Laura looked confused. "They are, but I've never seen them this far north."

"What do you call them?"

"Aurora Australis," Dan said. "You normally have to be way down south to see them. And they're never this spectacular."

"It's the unusual solar activity," Xeno said. "It's a once in a lifetime event."

Slab glanced at the sky with little interest, then pushed the kangaroo into the flames with a stick, more interested in dinner than the glowing sky. He was still silently cursing Bill's lousy navigation for them hitting a submerged rock and losing the boat. He should have been downing his favorite beer now, not drinking tasteless water full of purification tablets.

Guess it's better than dying of thirst, he thought miserably.

Sergeant Hooper looked at the roasting kangaroo dubiously. His left arm showed no sign of having been broken, although his right side felt strangely stiff, a side effect of the accelerated cell regeneration that had healed his burns. In a day, the stiffness would be gone and forgotten, although it would not be until he returned to base that he would discover the inverted dagger and triangle tattoo on his right shoulder had inexplicably vanished. "What's it taste like?"

"Chicken," Wal declared with a grin.

Bill smacked his lips together in anticipation. "Lean beef."

"I don't care what it tastes like," Nuke said eagerly, "I'm starving." Like Hooper, he felt stiff, although it would take almost a week for his cloned lungs to fully meld into his system. Even though his chest had been opened by alien surgeons, there were no scars, while the synthetic blood flowing through his veins would significantly increase his life span.

"You don't mind eating your national symbol?" Hooper asked.

"Meat's meat, mate," Cracker said indifferently.

"You should try tiger shark," Dan said. "Now that's boot leather."

"I'd eat fried eagle, if I was hungry," Tucker said, fingering his knife impatiently.

Hooper sniffed the aroma rising from the roasting meat, deciding it smelt like beef. He was hungry enough to eat half a dozen steaks, but then increased appetite was a common side effect of the treatment he'd undergone.

Bandaka pointed to the western sky. "Look."

Beckman and the others turned in the direction the hunter indicated. Approaching barely a hundred meters above the ground were three brilliant lights. Two were spheres of glowing white light, dazzling against the darkening sky and the debris cloud in the distance, while darting back and forth between them was a much smaller, brilliant red light. The red light zigzagged erratically, making acute angle high speed turns, while the two glowing white orbs floated in formation as they glided toward the east. The leading white light was slightly higher and ahead of its trailing companion. When they were almost due south of the camp, the two white balls of light hovered motionless, while the small red light came up into formation between its two larger companions. For a moment the three lights floated in the sky, then in perfect unison, they streaked away to the south, curving vertically as they shot straight up out of the atmosphere.

"Did you see that?" Laura asked with amazement.

Beckman looked around, feigning ignorance. "See what?"

"I suppose they were weather balloons?" she asked, glancing meaningfully at the midget strapped to his hip.

"Or Venus," Beckman said, then he shrugged. "Or maybe someone else finds this asteroid impact as interesting as we do."

He didn't know it yet, but his tiny alien weapon would never again fire. It had been returned to him with its power source depleted. In time, they would discover all of the recovered weapons had inexplicably ceased functioning. A panel of experts would eventually conclude the mass malfunction was caused by the same extraordinary electromagnetic effects that had temporarily knocked out the planet's power supply.

While Laura gave Beckman a reproachful look, a small form emerged from the shadows at the edge of camp. It was Mapuruma, anxious and uncertain, confused by the adults' relaxed natures.

"There she is!" Bandaka exclaimed with relief, rushing over and scooping his daughter into his arms. "Mapu, I was worried about you."

Mapuruma hugged her mother and father with wide, flitting eyes that darted anxiously toward the darkening forest.

"Where have you been?" Djapilawuy asked.

"Hiding," she replied in a tiny voice.

Bandaka looked surprised. “From what?”

Mapu stared into her father’s eyes, unsettled by his calmness, then she gazed up in amazement at the colored lights rippling across the firmament while her father pressed her for an answer. Finally, she replied, telling a bizarre tale of demons in the forest and evil spirits in the sky. She told it with a sense of awe, for in her eyes it was a tale of magic and monsters. When she finished, she swore every word was true, and that a spell had stolen the truth from their minds.

Though she pleaded for them to believe her, no one ever did.

EPILOGUE

During her captivity, no one spoke to Nemza'ri. She knew her implants had been repaired and reactivated, but they were no longer under her control. Her captors used them to drain her mind of her most personal experiences and gather all she knew of her own kind. While she sat in isolation in a white walled room with nothing but a small bed to sleep on, the information extracted painlessly from her mind was spread to more than a thousand civilizations who were now intimately aware of the true nature of the Intruder species. Formal alliances multiplied across the Milky Way to ensure the security of all peaceful societies would never again be threatened, while the Galactic Forum planned their containment strategy. Those unfortunate worlds that had fallen under Intruder control had been liberated in the blink of an eye by the Firsts and were now being restored by the Alliance to the levels of development they had achieved before their conquest.

Nemza'ri knew none of this. She'd expected, when her interrogation was over, to be executed. She was of a military clan and deserved nothing less, for she had failed. She wondered if her homeworld had been destroyed and her race exterminated. She even pondered the possibility that she was the last survivor of her race, so brutal did she expect the reprisal to be.

When her interrogation ended, one of her implants induced her to sleep. What followed was a dreamless state more akin to stasis than slumber. When she awoke, she was surrounded by med drones of a familiar design. To her surprise, her implants were again under her control.

Nemza'ri sat up, confused. Medical officers of her own race told her she was in perfect health, and that high clan officers were waiting to speak to her. They wanted a full account of her experiences and especially her contacts, for she was the last to return.

She'd thought she was the only survivor of the attack on the Tau Cetin homeworld, but they corrected her misunderstanding. Only two ships had been lost, both in the system where her ship had crashed. The rest of the fleet had appeared at their objective, only to discover their technology did not function. Weapons and sensors had been instantly destroyed by the mysterious energy vectors and every ship's propulsion system, along with tens of thousands of drones, had simply ceased functioning. Even the fleet's Inter-Command Nexus had fallen asleep, only to awaken later with no memory of the disaster, of what they now called the Inexplicable Defeat.

Out of all the thousands of technologies within the fleet, only life support had continued to function. A short time later, the entire fleet appeared above their homeworld, with only maneuvering propulsion restored to maintain orbit. In the hours that followed, hundreds of other Intruder ships appeared in the same condition, removed from the conquered regions of their far flung empire, although the many Intruder colony worlds within their globular cluster were untouched.

After their crippled fleets had appeared, communication devices on every channel across thousands of light years of Intruder space received the same message:

HOSTILITY AGAINST OTHER SPECIES WILL NEVER BE TOLERATED.

Every scientist began working feverishly to understand how their ships could have been disarmed, how their technology neutralized so easily and how their communications compromised on such a massive scale, but for all their efforts, they could explain none of it.

Nemza'ri stood up, feeling a strange sensation. Without speaking to the doctors, she checked her biostatus implants, discovering she was sterile again. She felt no disappointment, only understanding. It had never been intended that she would breed. Once the doctors discovered her condition, they simply reversed the process, returning her to her appropriate biological status.

Nemza'ri walked to a view port through which familiar yellow-orange sunlight shone. She discovered she was in an orbital city, surrounded by thousands of other cities and ships floating above a beautiful blue world with steel capped mountains and quilted oceans. It was a strangely comforting sight.

Kaleezsha(Alashra-Warm)Nemza'ri was home.

* * * *

Fifty thousand microscopic eggs drifted down the Goyder River. They'd been poured into the river's ashen waters by two med drones, emptying the mothership's last surviving gestation tank. Once the Command Nexus had given the order, it deleted all record of their existence from its memory. The med drones and the reproduction tanks Nemza'ri had assembled were all demolecularized by the nanofabricators, wiping out all trace of their creation. When the fleet in orbit discovered from Nemza'ri memories that she had tried to spawn, they found no trace of her eggs in the mothership and concluded they had been destroyed during the bombardment. Even Nemza'ri herself was unaware of their escape, as the Command Nexus had not informed her of its plan.

With no tell tale technology implanted, the microscopic eggs were missed by orbital sensors during the cleanup operation. Their presence on this unusually fertile world was hidden by a mass of complex life forms so dense, it had few equals anywhere in the galaxy. Some eggs attached themselves to submerged rocks and fallen trees.

Others reached the sea and were carried along the coast to mangrove lined estuaries or out to teeming coral reefs. Everywhere they went, they found warm tropic waters offering a near idyllic habitat.

Imbued with the myrnod hormone, their cellular structures would experience accelerated growth. After hatching, their battle for survival in a world of predators would be strangely similar to the life their distant ancestors had led millions of years ago. Sharks and crocodiles proliferated throughout the region and would quickly acquire a taste for them. Some hatchlings would perish in the harsh environment, but many more would survive.

Without technology or education, they would start life with nothing but their prodigious intellects and predatory instincts to rely upon. As was their natural inclination, they would form family groups and evolve strictly hierarchical structures around matriarchal concepts. They would not understand from where they came, or why the humans were intent upon their extermination, but they would quickly come to understand which species was the superior.

In time, they would thrive.

More books from the
Mapped Space Universe

The Mothersea
The Antaran Codex
In Earth's Service

Visit the author's webpage at:
http://www.stephenrenneberg.com

The Mothersea

by

Stephen Renneberg

"Everything a great sci-fi novel should be: visionary, immersive, and thematically profound."

- *Kirkus Reviews*

Ten years after *The Mothership* crashed on Earth, an alien probe from 65,000 light years away splashes down in the Pacific, seeking to solve a cosmic riddle.

A trawler inexplicably vanishes at sea and a body washes up on a deserted beach with a single extra-terrestrial clue that reaches all the way to Area 51.

Colonel Beckman and two of his team are dispatched to unravel the mystery. They board an oceanographic vessel which carries them to one of the most remote places on Earth, where an elusive alien presence is preparing to challenge the dominance of the human race.

It is there, in the baking tropical heat of *The Mothersea*, they learn a terrible truth – that one world cannot have two masters.

ISBN: 978-0-9941840-3-0

The Antaran Codex

by

Stephen Renneberg

"This high-octane sci-fi novel is powered by grand-scale action and adventure, larger-than-life characters, a richly described backdrop and, above all else, relentless pacing."

- *Kirkus Reviews*

Two and half millennia after *The Mothersea*, mankind nears its goal of Galactic Citizenship.

Sirius Kade, trader and Earth Intelligence Service deep cover agent, learns that wealthy and powerful leaders from across Mapped Space are vying for control of an alien relic they believe is the key to untold riches – unaware they are being deceived.

Sirius soon finds
himself entangled in an interstellar plot to make humanity a cosmic outcast, denying it its place as the newest member of the vast and ancient community that has governed the galaxy for eons.

With mankind's fate in the balance, Sirius must overcome ruthless alien adversaries and deadly human rivals as he seeks to discover the secret of *The Antaran Codex* and safeguard man's future among the stars.

Paperback Length 335 pages
ISBN: 978-0-9874347-9-1

In Earth's Service

by
Stephen Renneberg

Utterly Satisfying. A sci-fi novel that offers a relentlessly paced, action-packed, and undeniably epic in scope adventure.

- *Kirkus Reviews*

An alien colony world, a routine deep cover mission gone wrong, a chance encounter with a mercenary hit squad and the murder of an Earth Intelligence Service agent combine to launch Sirius Kade on a desperate mission to the distant reaches of Mapped Space.

He finds himself embroiled in a complex web of alien technologies, pirates, gun running and stellar intrigue, where ancient galactic enemies and new ambitions vie for supremacy.

While Sirius seeks to unravel a conspiracy threatening to shatter Human Civilization, he discovers Mankind may soon find itself caught in a gathering whirlwind building far beyond the limits of Mapped Space.

As an interstellar minnow among galactic giants, it is a cosmic storm Humanity – the youngest space faring civilization in the galaxy – may struggle to survive.

Paperback Length 400 pages
ISBN: 978-0-9941840-0-9

38607789R00213

Made in the USA
Middletown, DE
21 December 2016